"Great run."

The Texas drawl startled Montana. She recognized the cowboy she'd seen watching her from the stock pen.

"Thanks."

He grinned from beneath his straw Stetson, gray-blue eyes studying her with interest. "I'm Luke Holden, a friend of Clint and Lacy's."

"Montana Brown." His handshake was strong, and he was about as cute as they came.

"Clint said you're here to compete in the upcoming rodeo."

He'd been asking about her. The idea sent an unwanted thrill through Montana. "I plan to."

He grinned. "You'll win if that's the case."

Her stomach did a little electric slide at the way his face lit up. "So, Luke Holden, what do you do in the rodeo?"

"I'm supplying   need to get back to it.   wn." He tipped his hat   exit.

Many women   husband, but Montana had no room for comp

And Luke Holden was one cowboy who had complications written all over him.

A sixth-generation Texan, award-winning author **Debra Clopton** and her husband, Chuck, live on a ranch in Texas. She loves to travel and spend time with her family and watch NASCAR whenever time allows. She is surrounded by cows, dogs and even renegade donkey herds that keep her writing authentic and often find their way into her stories. She loves helping people smile with her fun, fast-paced stories.

Arlene James has been publishing steadily for nearly four decades and is a charter member of RWA. She is married to an acclaimed artist, and together they have traveled extensively. After growing up in Oklahoma, Arlene lived thirty-four years in Texas and now abides in beautiful northwest Arkansas, near two of the world's three loveliest, smartest, most talented granddaughters. She is heavily involved in her family, church and community.

Her Rodeo Cowboy

Debra Clopton

&

The Rancher's Answered Prayer

Arlene James

LOVE INSPIRED
INSPIRATIONAL ROMANCE

LOVE INSPIRED®

INSPIRATIONAL ROMANCE

ISBN-13: 978-1-335-20194-2

Her Rodeo Cowboy & The Rancher's Answered Prayer

Copyright © 2020 by Harlequin Books S.A.

Her Rodeo Cowboy
First published in 2011. This edition published in 2020.
Copyright © 2011 by Debra Clopton

The Rancher's Answered Prayer
First published in 2018. This edition published in 2020.
Copyright © 2018 by Deborah Rather

This edition published by arrangement with Harlequin Books S.A.

For questions and comments about the quality of this book, please contact us at CustomerService@Harlequin.com.

Love Inspired
22 Adelaide St. West, 40th Floor
Toronto, Ontario M5H 4E3, Canada
www.Harlequin.com

Printed in U.S.A.

CONTENTS

HER RODEO COWBOY   7
Debra Clopton

THE RANCHER'S ANSWERED PRAYER   215
Arlene James

HER RODEO COWBOY

Debra Clopton

To Chuck with all my love. God is *so* good.

I know that I have not yet reached that goal, but there is one thing I always do. Forgetting the past and straining toward what is ahead, I keep trying to reach the goal and get the prize for which God called me through Christ to the life above.

—*Philippians* 3:13–14

Chapter One

Her timing was going to stink. Montana Brown wasn't one bit happy about it as she and her horse, Murdock, rounded the last barrel in the arena. They were too far away from the barrel, and it was all her fault. Poor Murdock was giving it his all and she wasn't. Her mind—her focus simply wasn't where it was supposed to be....

It wasn't on the barrels they were running, despite the awesome opportunity she'd been given to train here in this beautiful huge covered arena that belonged to her cousin Lacy Brown Matlock and her husband, Clint Matlock. It was a wonderful place on the outskirts of Mule Hollow—which just happened to be the cutest little Texas town Montana had ever seen. Honestly, she couldn't ask for anything more perfect. But even with all these perfect conditions, instead of concentrating on barrel racing, her mind kept going where she did not want it to go...her dad.

"Focus, Montana," she muttered, feeling her horse's muscles bunch and gather beneath her as the powerful animal cleared the barrel. Digging her heels, knowing they needed all the speed they could gain, she urged Murdock to give it one last shot of speed as they raced toward the timer.

Forgiveness. The word snapped into her thoughts like the pounding of Murdock's hooves. She'd been thinking about this place since she'd gotten up that morning, and her riding showed it. *How do I forgive him—*

"Stop," she commanded through clenched teeth. *"Focus!"* Shoving all thoughts away, she tried to concentrate on moving with Murdock. No doubt about it, yes, sir, her timing was going to be as rank as a skunk on a windy day!

Crossing the time line, she pulled on the reins and leaned back with Murdock as the gray dug his hooves into the dirt and slowed. Cringing, she forced herself to look at the digital reading and her heart sank at the number, despite already knowing it wasn't going to be good.

Some might be satisfied with the time; she wasn't some. If she wanted to win, her time had to be better than good.

And Montana Brown was here to win.

This was her shot, and she didn't plan on wasting it. She just had to get her head back in the game.

These last few weeks, so much of her life had been turned inside out.

When Montana quit her job and walked out of her dad's accounting firm, she hadn't known what she was going to do.

Uncertain and confused, she'd called her cousin, Lacy Matlock. Lacy had insisted Montana come stay with her and her husband Clint. The small town of Mule Hollow where she lived was holding a huge homecoming rodeo in a month, and Lacy wanted Montana competing in it. She'd even insisted Montana could help take care of their new baby boy, Tate, if she was worried about a job.

Montana had needed a job, but she'd been so angry when she'd quit that she hadn't really given it much thought and taking care of a sweet baby would be wonderful while she took a chance on reviving her old dream of becoming a professional barrel racer. Believing this was the answer to prayer, Montana'd packed her bags, stored her things and headed to Mule Hollow.

She was glad to be here. Glad to have family who cared. She could practice all she wanted, and by the time the rodeo started up in three weeks she knew she could be in the running for the win. She needed that. Montana knew as well as Lacy did, that her parents' breakup had affected her deeply.

"Stop thinking about it," she muttered. Leaning forward, she patted Murdock's neck. "Don't you worry, fella, we're going to practice hard so you won't be embarrassed."

As if relieved, he nodded his head and pranced a few feet. Despite their bad score, Montana chuckled. "You are the vainest horse I know and I love you."

And she did. Poor horse had been put out to pasture the last few years as she'd gotten sidetracked with her career. Sidetracked with pleasing her dad and doing what was expected of her. But that was done now. It wasn't an issue anymore.

Forgiveness was.

"Okay, this is ridiculous. Let's go again, Murdock. And this time I'll give it my all, just like you are giving it yours."

Looking up at the huge, covered arena, she closed her eyes and imagined the stands full of spectators here to watch a competitive rodeo. There was no way she was going to come out here and embarrass herself *or* Murdock by doing a poor job. No way! Breathing in the quietness of the place, she tried to settle her thoughts and focus. "Please, God, help me do this," she whispered. Closing her eyes once more, she let the silence of the huge space fill her senses.

Opening her eyes, she set her lips in a firm line and her sights on the barrels.

She was going around those barrels again; but this time she was going at them like the cowgirl she used to be.

The cowgirl that she'd come back to Mule Hollow to find.

And to do that, she'd better get her head on straight, concentrate and stop letting this forgiveness issue wage war on her.

Because forgiveness just wasn't in her heart right now.

"The cowgirl can ride." Luke Holden propped a boot on the bottom rung of the arena fence, as he watched the horse and rider practically fly at the speed of light from one barrel to the next. The horse and rider seemed to move as one. The woman, who looked to be in her mid-twenties, was pretty in a girl-next-door sort of way. She had dark hair the color of a bay horse's mane that glistened in the overhead lights of the arena, and it hung in a short braid from beneath her straw cowboy hat. She was focused and intent as she urged her horse on.

"Yes, she can. That's Lacy's cousin, Montana Brown," Clint Matlock said without looking up from the clipboard. He was studying the list of livestock Luke would be providing for the upcoming Mule Hollow Rodeo. "She's staying with us for a while and plans on competing in the barrels at the rodeo. Lacy says she hasn't been riding for a few years, but ever since she got here a week ago, she's spent hours on her horse."

"It shows. She's good."

"Evidently, she was well on her way to the national level when she quit to concentrate on college a few years back. She could still be great."

Watching her as she crossed the time line, Luke saw her frown at the digital reading—which he couldn't see from his vantage, but knew had to be good. "No doubt about that. I'd never have known she hasn't been riding." He shot a grin at Clint. "The other competitors better be on their game."

"No kidding," Clint agreed, glancing up, then back to the list.

Luke decided it'd be a good thing to get his mind back on business and not the cowgirl. "Do you think that'll do it?"

"It looks great." Clint handed the clipboard back to him. "You have first-rate stock. These rodeos are going to be a big draw to everyone around. Including bringing back some hometown folks. It'll be good for everyone, including helping you build a solid reputation with your rodeo stock."

It was true. Mule Hollow was sponsoring three different rodeos over the summer to promote the town, calling them the homecoming rodeos, and he was supplying the stock for them. "I appreciate you putting in a good word for me, so I could get the contracts on all three events. I owe you."

Clint shot him a frank look. "You don't owe me anything. I'm glad to do it. Even after all the years you worked on the ranch with me, I'm doing this because you deserve it."

"I learned from the best."

Clint nodded, looking thoughtful. "Yeah, my dad knew his stuff."

Luke had learned much from Mac Matlock, but he'd learned a lot from Clint, too. Though Clint was only a few years older than Luke, the guy had been working beside his dad since he was barely old enough to ride. He had a relationship with his dad that Luke envied. "Don't sell yourself short. You know a few things yourself. That's why this ranch is what it is today. Mac taught you well."

The Matlock Ranch was one of the biggest, most successful ranches in the region. It was his legacy, something he would pass on to his son someday. Luke was aiming at building something similar, if all went as planned. These rodeos were going to help his finances and his reputation grow.

"It's going to be a busy summer, with all of the town involved in these homecoming rodeos."

Clint gave him a don't-I-know-it look. "The gals are gonna drive us all crazy."

"No doubt about that. I saw Esther Mae yesterday,

and she was buzzing at a hummingbird's pace with her plans." Esther Mae was in her sixties and fairly excitable when it came to…well, pretty much everything.

"Lacy's pretty excited, too. But you know her, she loves to plan all these festivals. And I have never been able to keep up with the woman."

Luke agreed. Mule Hollow had been hosting all manner of festivals, dinner theaters—you name it, they had it. The place had been alive with activity ever since Esther Mae and her two friends came up with a plan to save their beloved town from dying. A few years ago, they'd advertised for ladies to come to town and marry all the lonesome cowboys. Lacy had arrived and supercharged their idea with her own kind of energy—falling in love with Clint in the process. To the men's surprise, the ladies' idea had worked above and beyond what any of them had anticipated, totally astounding all the men in town.

These rodeos were their latest idea. But this was a little different. These three rodeos, one a month stretching out across the summer, were geared to bringing home "the runaways" as Clint called them. The good folks of Mule Hollow wanted family and friends who had moved away to come home and see how much the town had changed. They wanted some familiar faces to move back to town and, like Esther Mae, everyone seemed extra excited about the summer events. Esther Mae, Norma Sue and Adela, known as the matchmaking posse, had zeroed in on anybody they could "help out" where love was concerned. They'd tinkered with him a time or two, but probably decided he was a lost cause. Luke just wasn't ready to look for love, and no one could change his mind about that until he was good and ready.

He wondered if Montana Brown was here looking for love. Looking to find a lonesome cowboy and make the posse's matchmaking dreams come true. If she wasn't, she'd sure better watch out.

"Speaking of all of this, Luke, you've been around from the beginning and you're still single. What's up with that?" Clint asked.

"Determination, that's what." Luke laughed.

"Maybe so," Clint said, grinning. "Hey, I've got to get to Ranger and a bull show at the stock barn. Thanks for coming by with this. We'll talk more, but in the meantime, you set up in here however you think is right. And…" He'd started to head out but paused, grinning again. "I'm wondering how much longer that determination of yours is going to hold out. The way I see it, you and those brothers of yours have been holdouts way too long. Your time is running out, my friend. Love's a beautiful thing, you might want to try it someday."

Luke looked over to watch Montana make another run. He had to admit that just driving into town did tend to lift his spirits. But make him want to jump on the bandwagon and find a wife?

No way.

He had a new ranch to build and grow, and a new livestock business to get up and running. He was driven to make something out of himself, and wasn't slowing down until he did it. He'd scrimped and saved like many of his friends, and on a cowboy's pay, that wasn't easy. A wife and family…maybe later. And maybe not.

Right now, he had a good life. He dated some when he felt like it, but it was never ever serious.

He was focused, happy and determined to be better than his dad expected him to be. And nobody, not even the matchmaking posse, could change that.

Watching Montana round the last barrel again, he saw grit and determination in her expression. He found himself curious about what motivated her. What put that fire in her eyes that flashed as she leaned in low and thundered toward her mark?

"Great run."

The Texas drawl startled Montana as she walked around the corner of the arena's fence, heading toward the stall with Murdock in tow. She recognized the cowboy as one she'd seen watching her from the stock pen. She'd ignored him up till now. He'd been talking with Clint earlier, but hadn't left when Clint did. Too bad. She'd been determined not to let him break her concentration. She'd had a horrible morning run, but then she'd found her focus and made some decent runs.

"Thanks," she said, slowing so she wouldn't be rude. He grinned from beneath his straw Stetson, a flash of white teeth standing out against his darkly tanned skin. He had a lean face, prominent cheekbones and a jawline that seemed chiseled from stone. He looked like a man who knew his own mind. The laugh lines around his eyes told her he knew how to smile, even if he looked like a fairly serious dude.

"You're welcome. You sure can fly on that horse." He tipped the brim of his hat, as intriguing brown eyes studied her with interest. "I'm Luke. Luke Holden. I'm a friend of Clint and Lacy's."

He held out his hand and Montana shook it briefly. "I'm Montana Brown. It's nice to meet you." His handshake was strong and his hand callused. From the look of him, she figured he did some kind of cowboy work. Not that she was interested. Even if he was about as cute as they came. Even if she had to admit that God hadn't held back when he'd put Luke Holden together. The solid-as-a-redwood cowboy was impressive.

"Clint said you were Lacy's cousin, and you're here to compete in the upcoming rodeo."

He had been asking about her. The idea sent an unwanted thrill through Montana. She frowned at the feeling. "I plan to. I've got a long way to go, though."

He grinned. "You'll win, if that's the case."

Her stomach did a little electric slide at the way his smile lit his face up. "I'll give it my best shot," she said, trying hard to ignore the attraction sparking between them. She patted Murdock's neck. "I can't let Murdock down," she said with a wink, that just sort of slipped out on its own. "He's working way too hard for that. Isn't that right, ole boy?" As if understanding exactly what she was saying, the big gray nodded his head and snorted.

Luke's smile spread slow and easy across his face, lifting his cheekbones higher and causing his eyes to spark with unmistakable teasing interest. *And why not? You winked at the man.*

"He's a competitor, that's for sure," Luke said. "But you've obviously got some fight in you, too."

Why had she winked at the man? Crazy was what

she was. Just looking at him made her cheeks flush. But there was no stopping her curiosity about the cowboy.

"So, Luke Holden, what do you do in the rodeo?" There was nothing wrong with asking that, right? The guy was cute and his grin was unhinging—but the buck stopped there.

"I'm supplying the stock. I've never competed myself. I was always too busy working. Speaking of which, I need to get back to it. Nice to meet you, Montana Brown." He tipped his hat and returned her earlier wink with his own. "Ride hard and hang tight. You're gonna blow them out of the water." That said, he turned and strode toward the exit.

Montana watched Luke as he left, his stride strong, no hesitation and no looking back over his shoulder at her…unlike herself who stood there gawking when she should be taking care of business.

"Come on, Murdock, time to rest. Tomorrow we're going twice as hard so we can at least make a decent showing."

Despite her determination not to, she looked over her shoulder once more, but Luke Holden was gone.

Something about him lingered, and Montana found her thoughts continually turning back to him as she brushed Murdock down.

And that just would *not* do. Many women came to Mule Hollow to find a husband. But Montana had come to find herself. To do that, there was no room for complications.

And Luke Holden was one cowboy who had *complication* written all over him.

Chapter Two

"How's my little Tater-poo?" Montana cooed, taking Tate from Lacy. The six-month-old was all cuddly and warm. "He's getting to be a hunk."

"Tell me about it." Lacy handed over the bottle that she'd been feeding him. "He eats like his daddy, don't cha, little man?"

"Hey, he's a growing boy."

"So true! You finish feeding my sugar pie while I get the rest of my grocery list made out. Guess I should tell you that we're having a barbecue this weekend."

"We are?" Montana settled into the rocker as Tate attacked the bottle with gusto. "Why? What's the occasion?"

"For you, silly. I want everyone to come meet you, that's why."

Montana was startled by this information. "Do you have time for that? I mean, I thought you had a lot of planning to do for the rodeo?"

"Oh, we've got that handled," Lacy said, brushing the thought away with the wave of her pink-tipped fingers. "The matchmaking posse's got that under control. Things are rolling right along with the rodeo and the festival we're going to have in conjunction that same weekend. Yep, we've got food vendors coming, and Cort and Lilly Wells always head up a petting zoo with their adorable donkey, Samantha. All kinds of fun stuff is getting ready to happen this summer. It's going to be great," she said with gusto. "But first we're having *your* barbecue."

A lump formed in Montana's throat. She loved her cousin. That was all there was to it. She fought to steady her voice. "You know, you've really helped me when I needed it the most."

Lacy's brilliant blue eyes twinkled as they looked to Montana's and held. "I was concerned for you. You know God loves you more than I do—though I love you like a sister, and wouldn't give you up for anything in the world. But it's true, He does. And I was concerned that you were forgetting that, with all this drama you're going through. I needed to help you know that."

That was Lacy, so strong in her faith. "I'm not going through it anymore. If my mother and my dad want to get divorced, that's their business." If she said it out loud, then maybe it would be true. The anger she felt over everything that had happened welled up inside of her once more. When would it end?

"You know, Montana, people let you down sometimes. That's just the way it is. But God never does," Lacy said, as if reading her thoughts.

Montana knew how strong Lacy's faith was, but right now she didn't want to hear about how wonderful God was. She was angry at everyone—including

God. "I really don't want to get into this right now. Is that okay?"

"Sure thing. That's fine. You're here to relax and to love my precious baby boy all you want. And to win that rodeo."

She was ready to talk about something else and grabbed hold. "Poor Murdock is so ramped up. He can feel that we're getting ready for something. Poor horse has missed the barrels. But he's doing so well, it's like he was out in the pasture practicing while I was off at school."

Montana rubbed her face against Tate's neck and he grabbed her hair, making her laugh as she disentangled herself from him. One day she was going to have a baby like Tate, and she wasn't going to make him feel guilty for having dreams different from her own. She was going to love him and help him as he went after those dreams.

"This is 'the good stuff,' Lacy."

"Yes, it is," Lacy chirped. "I'm so happy, I really, really am. I wish you'd find someone like my Clint." She grinned mischievously. "But all in God's timing."

Montana was happy for her cousin. She and Lacy had always been a lot alike. Neither of them really needed a man to make them happy, and yet, there was no denying that Lacy seemed more content now. "Lacy, honestly, I'm so mad at my dad right now, and his lying, that I don't even want to think about letting a man in my life."

"I know, and you have every right to be upset. But I'm praying you'll get over that. All men don't lie. Some men happen to pride themselves on being honest, and that's the kind of man God's going to send your way."

Montana gave Lacy a scowl. "He better not send him anytime soon, or it won't matter. I'm not interested in any man but this little man *right* here." She cuddled Tate, burying her face in his chubby neck.

"You, my dear cuz, have good taste. By the way, I saw Luke Holden was here earlier. Did you meet him?"

The cowboy's image whipped into her mind like a red flag. "Yes," she said warily.

"Well, what did you think of him? I happen to think he's a real cutie pie and a real fine man, too."

Surely she wasn't thinking… "Lacy, I told you I'm not interested. I'm here to win a rodeo, not a man."

Lacy stuffed a fist to her hip, her eyes dancing. "Yep, yep, yep," she sang. "You thought he was cute. I *knew* it!"

Montana gasped. "I didn't say that."

"Didn't have to. Your refusal to answer my question said it all."

"Okay, he isn't hard on the eyes. But don't go getting any ideas." The fact that Lacy might be having ideas about her and Luke had Montana's nerves rattling a bit.

"Oh, I'm not promising anything. I was just checking your pulse." Lacy smiled mischievously.

Montana lifted Tate into the air and looked up at his cherub face. "Tell your momma that my pulse is just fine, and you're the only man I'm gonna be interested in for a good long while." She shot Lacy a teasing but serious glare. "And I mean that. Got it, *cuz?*"

"You seen her?"

Luke was sitting at the counter in Sam's diner, waiting on his breakfast. It was 6:00 a.m. and the crowd hadn't bombarded the tiny diner yet—but they'd be in at any moment. Applegate Thornton and his buddy Stanley Orr were already glued to the chairs at the window table. It was their usual morning spot to spit sunflower seeds at their spittoon, play checkers and get in on the happenings and business of everyone in town. Today they were starting with him.

Applegate spit two sunflower seed shells into the old brass spittoon then repeated his question again loudly, as if Luke was the one who was hard of hearing instead of he and Stanley.

"Did you see her yet? Montana Brown. Lacy's cousin."

Oh, he'd seen her all right. And he'd been thinking about her since. "Yes, sir, I saw her yesterday. She was practicing the barrels out in the arena when I was there going over the stock list. Why?"

App shrugged nonchalantly, looking about as convincing as a little kid trying to sneak a cookie. "I was jest wonderin'. She's a cute little thang. And a real good rider. We saw her the other day, too. She knows her way around a horse."

"That's fer shor." Stanley paused, coughing as he studied the checkerboard. Not as chipper as usual, he scratched his balding head. The two men were in their seventies and about as hard of hearing as a tree stump. Though it was questionable whether they just had selective hearing, because they kept tabs on everyone's business.

"Yup," he continued. "She rode that horse of hers out into that arena like greased lighting. I ain't never seen a gal ride—" He suddenly paused and jumped his red checker over App's. "Gotcha, ya old coot."

App's frown deepened, making his thin face droop into a ripple of expanding wrinkles. "I was wonderin' when you was gonna make that move. I wasn't payin' attention when I made that thar mistake."

"Ha, you're jest gettin' whupped. As usual."

App snorted, "I don't always lose, and you know it." Ignoring his turn to move, he kept his attention on Luke. "I heard Lacy was throwing a barbecue this weekend in honor of her cousin. You goin'?"

Lacy had called him last night and invited him and any of his brothers who might happen to be in town. She'd sounded excited about the party. He had to admit that he was looking forward to it himself. "Yeah, I'm going. It'll be nice to help her get to know all of us."

"You oughtta ask her out," App continued. "You know, make her feel welcomed and all."

"That'd shor be nice of ya." Stanley coughed again, glaring at App. "Times a wastin', I'm gonna be dead before you start playin' this here game."

Taking that as his clue to close the conversation, Luke spun his stool back toward the counter. Sam came out of the back in that moment. His short bowlegs were moving as he hustled through the swinging café doors from the kitchen. He slapped Luke's plate in front of him. "Eat up, Luke. Yor gonna need yor strength."

"Why's that?" he asked, hoping App and Stanley had decided to play checkers instead of delve further into his love life. He'd already been thinking about asking Montana out, but he didn't need anybody's help where that was concerned.

Sam gave him a weathered grin. "'Cause my Adela and the gals are countin' on them animals of yours to be in tip-top shape. They want them bull riders comin' in droves fer all the rodeos." It went unsaid that bull riders and bull riding drew women. That was what "the gals" wanted. The gals being the matchmakers of Mule Hollow, Esther Mae Wilcox, Norma Sue Jenkins and Sam's wife, Adela Ledbetter Green.

There was no need for them to worry. "I've got Thunderclap entered, and his reputation attracts riders. They always do wherever he happens to be."

"That's good. Norma Sue and Esther Mae are about ta drive me pure crazy with their planning and carrying on. Adela's even having trouble keepin' them corralled. Why, they're strategizin' about every kin folk they can think of who might be comin' fer the rodeos. I'm telling y'all, that little gal Montana Brown's got a number on her back—and it ain't her barrel racin' number, either. So, jest a word of warnin', in case you ain't figured that out already. If you ask that one out, you might have a big ole bull's-eye show up on yor back, too."

The back of Luke's neck began to itch. "They've tried that a time or two with me, and realized I'm not interested in anything long-term.… You know I'm honest with everyone I go out with about that."

Not saying anything, Sam poured him another cup of coffee and started to go tend to his other customers. Mornings were busy, and he usually worked them alone, till his help came in around eight. But as busy as he was, he held his position, his eyes narrowing as he looked at Luke.

"It's true. Ever'body knows you're a straight shooter

on that topic. But—" he grimaced "—from what I hear, that ain't makin' at least one person too all-fired happy."

Luke had a bad feeling he knew where Sam was heading. "What do you mean?"

Sam leaned in close. "I heard tell that thar artist you went out with a time or two ain't happy at all."

Erica. He'd been honest with her from the beginning, and had only gone out with her twice. On their second date, she'd started talking about looking for Mr. Right. He shook his head. "Sam, I broke it off with her the instant I realized she was looking for Mr. Right. I don't do forever. I'd told her I wasn't looking to be anybody's Mr. Right. She got all upset anyway, and I didn't know what to do." The woman had actually thrown dishes at him for "dropping her," as she put it. He'd tried to keep his mouth shut, but that hadn't stopped her from giving him the stink eye whenever she saw him. To keep peace, he'd been trying to steer clear of her, and hoped that soon her anger would blow over. One thing was certain, they weren't compatible, and he was more than glad of it. He didn't like all the drama that came with a woman like that. He'd just missed the signs.

"If you were honest, then you ain't got nothin' ta hold yor head down about. Some women are jest plain high-strung. Now, women like my Adela, well, that's a prize. You jest keep bein' honest. It'd be a shame fer you ta miss out on love. The posse might jest have ta fix that fer you."

"Sorry, Sam. Like I said, I know my own mind and if I decide to ask Montana out, everything will be just fine. Don't you worry about me. Or her. She'll know right off the bat that I'm not looking for anything serious."

Sam's eyes crinkled at the edges. "One of these days, one of them dates is going ta wrap her finger around yor heart, and then you won't be so cocky about how good you are at walkin' away."

Luke took a bite of biscuits and gravy. He wasn't being cocky. He was being honest. He had plans. Goals. Nothing was getting in his way.

Sam hiked a busy brow. "Yup, that cockiness is gonna be yor downfall. Mark my words, son. Yor time's a comin'."

Chapter Three

"Well, well, hello, Luke Holden. How's life treatin' ya?"

Luke grinned at Montana's perky, playful greeting. They were standing near a fragrant rose bush at Lacy's. The shadows from the oil lantern cast a soft glow on Montana's skin—she looked beautiful. "I'm fine, Montana. Life's fine. I can't complain. How about you? Enjoying the party?" He'd arrived at the barbecue at the Matlocks' a little while earlier, and mingled while Montana made the rounds talking with groups of people Lacy had introduced her to. He'd caught her looking at him a few times across the crowd. Something about her drew him, and he got the feeling she was just as curious about him.

She took a sip of sweet tea, watching him with steady blue-green eyes. "The party—it's good."

"I agree." He caught that she didn't say anything about how life was treating her and he wondered about that. "How's your riding going?"

"Okay. Murdock's a little happier with me today. He wants to win, and he knows the problem is me."

"You always this hard on yourself?"

"Always."

Thoughtful eyes held his. He smiled at her. "Seriously, you need to relax." Man, did she ever. "I saw you laughing a few minutes ago, so I know you can do it."

She laughed then. "Hey, I do laugh now and then, but I'm dead serious when I say I'm always hard on myself. I expect a lot of me." She paused and her eyes drilled into him. "I bet you expect a lot of yourself, too."

"And what gives you that idea?" He liked the way she seemed sure of herself. Sure of her impression of him. He wondered if she was that sure of everything in her life.

"Well, you just do. From what I understand, you have a ranch and cattle and livestock. Plus, you have Thunderclap, your prized rodeo bull. You, Mr. Holden, are a busy man who reeks of expectations."

Had she been asking about him? "I like to keep busy and yes, you're right, I expect a lot of myself. If I don't, then who will?"

"Right. Then again, if your dad was anything like mine, he expected plenty from you."

He gave a derisive grunt. "I can tell you our dads were nothing alike. Mine expected little of me."

Her eyes widened. "What do you mean?"

Luke didn't talk about his dad much, and he wasn't sure why he'd done so now. He'd given her a glimpse into his past that he didn't like thinking about, much less discussing. "Little, as in nothing. My dad didn't push me to be anything but a failure."

"I'm so sorry," she said sympathetically.

"Hey, low expectations drive some harder than high expectations." He gave her a teasing smile to throw off the seriousness of his words. "So, what about you? Your dad expect you to be the best barrel racer in the country?"

"Hardly. He expected me to be valuable to the human race, and that had nothing to do with racing around barrels on a horse."

He grimaced. "Rough. From watching you ride, all I can say is you must have been one rebellious child."

That made her choke on her tea. He moved toward her and patted her on the back. "Didn't mean to choke you up."

"I'm fine," she said after a second. "But let's just say neither one of us is doing very well on reading each other's background."

"So you weren't rebellious? I'm shocked."

That made her eyes twinkle. "I wish. Hardheaded, but not rebellious." She frowned, crinkling her eyebrows in a cute way. "I can't say there haven't been many days that I have deeply regretted my lack of rebelliousness."

He wasn't sure if she was teasing or serious.

She winked at him. "But I'm making up for it now."

That had him even more curious than ever about what was going on behind her pretty eyes. Before he could dig a little deeper, Esther Mae came walking over. The redhead wore a bright green shirt and matching pants that ended just above her ankles.

"Yoo-hoo! I'm so glad y'all are getting to visit. I told Norma Sue and Adela y'all looked so cute standing over here together that I hated to disturb y'all, but one of the kids said the horses in the stall barn were making all kinds of noise. I thought you might want to go check on your horse, Montana."

Montana was instantly alert. "I appreciate the heads-up." She dropped her paper cup in a trash can and was walking down the steps before Luke had time to react.

"Well, don't just stand there, Luke. Go help her."

Luke's eyes narrowed, and he caught the flash of mischief in Esther Mae's spunky green eyes. Instantly, he shot her friends a glance where they were all huddled up on the lawn. Oh, brother, they were all watching, Lacy included. She grinned and waved, then laughed in delight. So much for subtlety.

He gave Esther Mae a look that said he knew exactly what she was up to, then hurried after Montana. She was already halfway across the yard that separated the main house from the arena and horse stalls. Clint didn't keep all of his horses in the arena; instead, he kept them in the barn that was on the back side.

The cowgirl obviously didn't have a clue that she'd just been hoodwinked. Her boots scraped on the gravel as she quickstepped toward the barn. He wondered what her reaction would be to know she'd just been set up. He'd already decided, before the matchmaking effort, that he was going to see if she'd like to go to dinner. Now would be a good time to ask.

The barn was quiet. No sounds of restless horses or anything else for that matter. The arena was a huge covered building with stadium seating on both sides, and a concession stand area and an announcer's box at the front. There were stock pens both front and back, and an area on the outside connecting them. Murdock was stabled at the front, behind the stock pens and announcer's box. The huge building was quiet and lonesome in the late evening. Ahead of him, Montana reached Murdock, put her hand to her hip, looking left then right. Murdock gave her a contented snort as she slowly turned on her heel and stared at Luke. Her eyes flashed like glass in the muted overhead lighting. Her eyes narrowed.

"First of all, this area is way too off the beaten path for the kids to have heard any ruckus—unless they'd been back here causing it. Second, I don't see any signs that Murdock's been the least bit distressed recently."

He couldn't help the grin that tugged at his mouth. "I'd—"

"*I'd* say," she broke in before he could begin, "that there's something fishy in the air."

"And I'd say you catch on slow," he drawled, teasing, "but at least you catch on."

"Oh, so you've had it figured out all along, have you?"

"Pretty much. Of course, you were already halfway across the lawn before Esther Mae stopped talking. I got the benefit of spotting Lacy, Adela and Norma Sue along with the little crowd gathered around them, watching us like we were the drive-in movie of the week."

"That is so not good. I'm going to get my cousin! I love her, but I'm gonna get her good."

He got the feeling she wouldn't like it, but the woman was cute, all hot as a firecracker. Looking near to blowing up, she turned in her frustration and began petting the star between Murdock's eyes—as if the action would calm her nerves.

"Actually, I'd planned on seeing if you'd like to go to dinner Saturday night." The moment the words were out of his mouth, it hit him that it might not be the best time to ask her out.

Montana's hand stilled and her gaze shot to his. "No, thanks. It's nothing personal, but I'm not dating right now."

She was turning him down. So his timing hadn't been good, but he knew when a woman was interested. He'd felt the chemistry between them. "It's not *dating*. It's just *one date*—dinner."

Montana studied him with unsympathetic eyes. "I'll tell it to you straight. You and I both know that one date will stir up those ladies out there. I'm not up for that. I'm here to get my head on straight, win a rodeo and help with the baby. Nothing more. I don't need a bunch of sweet, matchmaking ladies fixing me up with a cowboy…who just happens to be you. Sorry. But no."

He felt slightly insulted. "They know I'm not looking for anything long-term. I've made that clear to them. And every woman I go out with," he clarified, thinking she'd like that better.

Her eyebrows rose slightly. "Lots of them, huh?"

That eyebrow didn't bode well. "What?" he asked warily. "Oh, lots of dates?"

"Lots of women."

"Um, a few."

She crossed her arms and tilted her head slightly, silently assessing him. He felt like a science project.

"I'm sure that knowledge helps you get lots of dates."

He was confused with where she was going with this conversation. "It doesn't hurt. I mean, for someone like you I'm not a risk. I'm just a date. Conversation, company. You know, no strings attached." That didn't sound good, even to him. What was wrong with him? He scrubbed his jaw, thinking suddenly that crawling under a hay bale might be in order, judging from the appalled expression on her face.

"And it works out well for you? All these different women who don't want any strings attached."

Was she teasing him—or was she really irritated by the whole idea? He wasn't sure anymore. "Yeah, it works out great."

She grinned sarcastically. "Good for you," she gushed. "I'll stick to *not* jumping into that." She gave him a pat on the arm, rolled her eyes and headed toward the exit.

He stood there, not sure about what had just happened. "Hey, whoa. Wait up."

She rounded the corner out of sight, her voice rang out singsong, "I don't think so."

The sound echoed in the hall, drawing him. He chuckled and jogged to catch up to her. She was already out in the open and heading up the hill toward the house. Laughter could be heard drifting on the barbecue-scented night air. As if in a hurry to get away from him, she strode with purpose, her boots crunching the gravel as she went, her braid swinging in time to the fast pace.

"What's your hurry?" he asked, skidding on the gravel, coming up beside her.

She slid him a glance. "I don't want to give anyone the idea that you and I lingered in the barn for romantic reasons. That wouldn't be good."

He grinned. The woman tickled him. She was so blunt about things. "No, I guess that wouldn't be good. Might get rumors started, and boy, we wouldn't want that, now, would we?"

"No way." She didn't smile, but he thought she was teasing. "I certainly wouldn't want anyone thinking I was joining your string of random dates."

What did women expect from a guy these days? Just because he wasn't interested in marriage didn't mean he wasn't interested in women. "There's nothing wrong with not settling down. Not being ready for forever." He shifted from one boot to the other.

She hiked a brow. "It's random and cheap."

Her attitude irritated him suddenly. He wasn't doing anything wrong. Hadn't done anything wrong, he reiterated to himself strongly, as she started walking off again.

He followed her, not real happy about the situation but not certain what he wanted to do about it.

The party was in full swing when they reached the backyard. Montana clomped up the deck steps. Distracted by his irritation, he was intent on following her just as he caught movement out of the corner of his eye.

"Luke," Erica said, nothing nice dripping from her words.

"Erica. Um, hi." She didn't look happy. Nope, matter of fact, she looked really unhappy—throw things unhappy. He hadn't expected to see her. But he should have known Lacy wouldn't have left her out of the party.

Montana turned back toward him and met his gaze before connecting with Erica's.

"What are you looking at?" Erica snapped at Montana, right before throwing her soda at him!

Yup, throw things unhappy was about right. One minute he was standing there irritated and confused by Montana's attitude. Now, he was drenched with the contents from Erica's tall glass of Texas *sweet* tea!

"What?" he gasped, blinking through the tea dripping from his eyelashes.

"You two-timing jerk!" Erica huffed, then strode past him, shooting a glare over her shoulder—as if he hadn't already gotten the message.

"Two-timing…" he stuttered. He was well aware that everyone within earshot had heard and witnessed the scene. "We just went on two dates. *Just dates,*" he said, looking at Montana.

A twitch of her lips told him she was fighting off laughter. "Yeah," she managed. "Looks like all that dating is working out well for you, huh?" She winked at him, then strode into the house, leaving him dripping on the deck.

"Everybody's a comedian," he muttered. It was time to have a serious—and he meant serious—talk with Erica. He was not the marrying type. Never was and most likely never would be.

Chapter Four

Norma Sue Jenkins efficiently blocked Luke's way when he headed toward Erica. A robust ranch woman, Norma Sue was hard to avoid when she wanted your attention. She handed him a dishtowel. "I tried telling Erica you and her wouldn't match up." She looked worried. "This isn't good, Luke."

He glanced past Norma Sue and saw Erica tear out in her small compact car. Wiping the sticky tea from his face he shook his head. "No, Norma Sue, it isn't. I wasn't trying to hurt anyone. I told her straight up that I was just dating. I wasn't looking for forever, and she seemed okay with that. Until the second date, and then she started in on all that Mr. Right stuff."

She patted him on the back. "I know. I know. I told her you weren't looking for love, just companionship. I knew she had her sights set on forever, and I told her you weren't the one to count on for that—"

"I think I'm supposed to say thanks to that."

"It doesn't sound good to me, either, but we both know, up till now, that's where you stand. Erica thought she could change your mind and lied to you about her intentions." Norma Sue frowned, her pink cheeks drooping. "All I've got to say is, you may be in for it. I don't know if you noticed, but Erica is a bit high-strung. She doesn't take rejection too kindly."

The woman had just tossed tea on him. He was standing there drenched. "Yeah, Norma Sue, I get the picture loud and clear."

"I figured you did. Why don't you give her some time to cool off, then I suggest you go see her and try real hard to smooth this out. We aren't used to this kind of trouble going on in Mule Hollow."

"Tell me about it. I'm not used to this kind of trouble, either."

He spent the next hour getting ribbed and teased about the incident. Cowboys loved teasing and giving each other a hard time, so, thanks to Erica, he was probably going to be the brunt of jokes for the rest of the year. The talk at the diner alone was going to drive him crazy. And if Erica thought her actions were going to help her find "Mr. Right" anytime soon in Mule Hollow, she was about to be up a creek without a paddle. Getting a date might have just gotten a whole lot harder for her.

Then he thought about Montana—getting a date might have just gotten harder for him, too. The idea didn't sit well. As he drove home, he figured he had some digging out to do. He didn't like having Erica so angry at him, so he was going to have to smooth that out somehow. Didn't change his feelings though. Norma Sue had been right on the money about them not being compatible—there were just some things that couldn't be changed. He didn't figure you could fall in love with someone you weren't attracted to, but he'd seen plenty of times when people who were in love fell out of love. Or one of the two killed the love that had been shared. Luke had seen that plenty. He'd seen it up close and personal where his parents were concerned—yeah, love could be killed. But there was no way it could be forced. Erica was barking up the wrong tree if she figured he was the one for her. He'd get that straight and he'd get it soon. Surely she would understand where he was coming from.

He wasn't going to feel bad about the situation. He had done nothing but be honest in all of this. Montana might hold it all against him, especially after witnessing the sweet tea scene, but in all honesty, he couldn't figure out why.

Then again, maybe he was missing something....

It was a beautiful day, the morning after the infamous barbecue.

"Come on in," Esther Mae called out as Montana walked into Lacy's Heavenly Inspirations hair salon carrying Tate. Instantly, she was bombarded by the spunky redhead. "Oh, there's our baby boy!" Esther Mae cooed, reaching to take Tate.

"We're glad you came," Norma Sue said, moving to give Tate a hug.

Lacy had Adela in the chair and was snipping away at the dainty lady's short, white hair. "He looks so happy!" Lacy said, smiling in his direction. "You are so good with him, Montana. Thank you so much. He's always in such a good mood with you."

"Ha! It's not me. The little fella likes everyone. Although, we did have a great morning. He loves the playpen we fixed up next to the office." The building that housed Lacy and Clint's arena was one of the nicest she'd been in. She was blessed to have it for her own use. "He played happily all morning while I practiced." Montana could still get her barrel racing practice in while watching Tate in the playpen.

"He's content around you." Adela smiled, her electric-blue eyes warm. "Babies know good people when they're around them."

Esther Mae looked up from where she had sat with Tate in the dryer chair. "Little darling bellows every time Hank comes around. It hurts Hank's feelings something fierce."

"Roy Don was the same way." Norma Sue chuckled. "He started to get a complex about it, until one day Tate took to him—" she snapped her fingers "—like the snap of a finger."

"Men, they get their feelings hurt too doggone easy," Esther Mae said while rubbing noses with Tate. "You aren't gonna do that, are you, my sweet potato pie man?"

Norma Sue grunted. "That Luke should have gotten his feelings hurt last night." She looked at Montana. "He needs a woman in his life, and he has no clue how many women want to be 'that' woman. Why, most every woman who goes out with him is secretly hoping he'll notice them, despite knowing he's not planning to get married. They all find out he's more interested in work and building up that ranch than in building a relationship, and they move on. Who knows, maybe

Erica's little hissy fit might have been just what he needed to make him think about taking a woman seriously. About taking his life seriously."

"That's right," Esther Mae interrupted. "Life's too short to only think about building things here on earth. He needs a family to leave that ranch to."

Montana started getting uncomfortable with the conversation.

"It's going to take the right woman to help him see that God has more out there for him than work," she chimed in.

"And how about you?" Norma Sue suddenly turned her attention to Montana. "Don't you think he's one handsome cowboy?"

"I've already had this conversation with Lacy." She met her cousin's mischievous eyes in the mirror. "Yes, he's handsome. But I'm not interested."

"What about living in Mule Hollow?" Norma Sue probed. "Are you interested in maybe making this your home?"

"It's a great place," Lacy said, pausing her cutting the wispy hair around Adela's face. "I'm trying to convince her of that, too. Y'all help me."

Adela smiled understandingly. "That would be lovely, dear. If you moved here, you would have all the time you need to sort out whatever it is that's bothering you."

"And then you could appreciate Luke for the man that he is." Norma Sue looked as if she'd just come up with the best idea of the century.

"Aren't y'all supposed to be having a meeting about the fair on the opening day of the rodeo?" Montana reminded them of the reason she'd come to town. She wanted the conversation to move away from her. And Luke.

Lacy took the cape off of Adela, shaking the loose hair from it. "You're a free woman, Adela," she said, smiling. "We're heading over to the diner now. I just needed to finish Adela's cut first."

"By the way, how's Sheri doing?" Esther Mae called from the dryer chair. "Is she and Pace having fun in Australia, training horses?"

"Yes, they are." Sheri was the nail tech and Lacy's partner in the salon. She'd come to Mule Hollow with Lacy when she'd loaded up her 1958 pink Caddy and drove from Dallas to open her new business. "She said that she was thinking of moving there full-time."

"What?" All the matchmakers gasped.

"Whoa!" Lacy waved her hands to hold off any more outbursts. "I was only teasing. She said she's enjoying Australia but will be back home in Mule Hollow in time for the rodeos. Pace is going to ride broncs."

"Whew, that's a relief," Esther Mae said. "Plus, I need a manicure something terrible."

Adela agreed. "It certainly is. We'd miss her and her frank honesty and dry sense of humor."

"Boy, are you right about that." Norma Sue wagged her kinky gray head. "Talk about a hard one to match up. We didn't think the right cowboy was ever going to come along for that little gal."

"But God always sends the right cowboy for the right woman. In the right time." Adela hugged Lacy. "Thanks for making my hair look so wonderful! We are so glad God also sends hairdressers to the right towns, too."

Lacy looked pleased. "Oh, He did that." She held her hands out for little Tate. He immediately lifted his arms for his momma. Taking him into her arms, Lacy snuggled his neck with her nose and held him close. "God knew this hairdresser needed to be right here in Mule Hollow, so I could meet Clint. So this sweet baby boy could be born."

Montana's heart tugged with emotion watching them.

"Okay, let's go, gals," Norma Sue said, moving to the door and holding it open. "Let's get over to Sam's. I'm sure we have a big group waiting for us over there."

Montana followed the chattering, excited group, but she couldn't stop thinking about them matching her up with Luke. Montana knew they all meant well. After all, it was easy to see that all their hard work was producing lots of happy couples. And families to fill up the town.

Still, she wasn't buying in.

That's right. It was going to take more than the goodwill of the matchmaking posse to make her see things differently. She knew she would feel that way for a long time.

If they thought Sheri Gentry had been a tough cookie to match up, they were in for a surprise because they hadn't seen nothin' yet.

Luke almost turned around and went back to his truck when he walked into Sam's and saw the crowd. The place was packed! Spotting Montana—and no

Erica—he decided to stay. He'd dropped by Erica's apartment that morning to see if he could talk to her, but she hadn't been home. He still couldn't get over the fact that she was so angry with him.

He hadn't made it to the counter to grab a seat on a cowhide stool before Esther Mae called out his name.

"Don't sit over there," she called. "We're discussing the rodeo and festival. We need your input."

Sam grinned from behind the counter. "You came in at the wrong time. Even App and Stanley hightailed it outta here the minute they all came marching in."

Luke looked around the room and realized it was all ladies sitting in the booths on one side of the diner, and the other side was empty. "Looks like I missed the memo."

"Yup. You did that. But yor here now, so you might as well dig in and bear it. I'll brang you a nice, *tall* glass of sweet tea. You want a burger ta go with that?"

"Funny, Sam. Real funny. A burger's fine." He crossed to the table next to the one Montana was sitting at. She didn't look too thrilled to see him.

"Hey, Montana, how are you?" he asked. She might not have a high opinion of him, but that wasn't stopping him. After all, he wasn't a bad guy, and maybe if she'd go out with him she'd see that. At least, maybe she'd see that he hadn't deserved a glass of tea in the face.

"Hi, how's it going," she said, looking uncomfortable.

"Good." He tipped his hat. "Hello, ladies." He pulled a chair from a table, and was very aware of all their eyes on him. As they acknowledged him with hellos, he spoke to most of them individually. Many of them were around his age, and moved here in the last two years and married his friends.

Montana took all the interaction in, and he wondered what she was thinking. These ladies knew he wasn't a horrible person. Maybe this was a good thing.

"How's your morning going?" he asked her, leaning across the space toward her. "Did you get your riding done this morning?"

"I did. Tate watched me from the play area while I took a few runs. He likes watching me and Murdock round the barrels."

Lacy held the little fella, who was standing up in his mother's lap, looking pleased with himself.

He started to ask how old Tate was, when Norma Sue began talking about all the things that were going on the opening day of the rodeo. He settled in, gave a sideways glance at Montana, who was particularly intent on everything Lacy and Norma Sue were saying. Luke hadn't known they were having so many vendors coming in. The dunking booth, pie throwing, cow chip toss, three legged race; the list went on and on. He also didn't know a small carnival was coming to town and setting up in one of the pastures.

"A carnival is coming?" Montana asked, perking up in her seat.

"Yes! Isn't it exciting?" Lacy said. "I wanted to tell everyone today as a surprise. I just found out this morning. It's not a big outfit. Just a few rides."

"I hope there's a Ferris wheel," Esther Mae said. "I just love those things."

"Yes, that's one of the rides, and then there's one of those octopus rides."

Esther Mae gasped. "I love that, too. This is going to be sooo much fun."

Montana nodded and he caught her lips twitch. He decided then and there that he was riding the rides with her. That might be a bigger challenge than getting her to go out to dinner with him.

Meanwhile, Montana kept ignoring him, no matter that he sat just two feet away from her.

Frustrated more than he liked to admit, he got up, made his goodbyes to all the ladies and headed down to pick up some supplies at Pete's Feed and Seed. He was walking back to his truck a little while later when Montana drove past him in one of the Matlock Ranch trucks. She didn't even glance his way.

He almost followed her. After all, he needed to stop by Clint's, and it might as well be now. He finally talked sense into himself and turned his truck toward his place instead. What was wrong with him?

Montana didn't think very highly of him. Following her around certainly wouldn't help matters. Her opinion of him wasn't looking any brighter than Erica's. But truth be told, Montana's opinion had him lying awake long after he'd fed his horses and Rover, his lab.

Yup, Montana Brown had him stumped, and he wasn't at all sure what he was going to do about it.

Chapter Five

On Sunday, Montana let her hair hang loose, put on a red dress and went to church with Lacy. It was quite an experience as she entered the quaint, white wooden church with the tall steeple.

Chance Turner was the pastor of the Mule Hollow Church of Faith, and she'd met him briefly at the barbecue. He was around thirty, handsome and a total cowboy. Instead of a suit, he wore starched jeans, Western belt, starched shirt and cowboy boots. When he greeted her outside, he had on a cream-colored Stetson that he wore low over his eyes. It looked completely at home on his head, as did the rest of the Western attire he wore. She wondered what he would say if she told him about the anger that was rolling around in her gut. The anger toward her father that she couldn't seem to shake. He seemed like he would offer some good advice. As she was leaving the service, the need to talk to someone tugged at her.

She hesitated as she shook hands with him. "It was a great sermon," was all she could bring herself to say.

"Yes, it was," Lacy agreed. "Chance always has a way of looking into hearts and touching on things we need to hear. I'm going to run and get Tate from the nursery. I'll be right back."

She saw a flicker in the pastor's eyes when he looked back at her, as if he knew something was going on in her head—or her heart. Did he realize that she was fighting a war inside?

"I'm glad you enjoyed the service," he said, his smile fading to a more serious one. "Is there anything I can do for you, Montana?"

Her stomach went bottomless. "N…no. I'm fine." *Liar, liar pants on fire*—the childhood chant rang in her ears.

His eyes narrowed slightly, digging, as if he'd heard through her denial. He smiled encouragingly. "I'm sure you are. But if you change your mind, I'm easy to find and I'm always ready to listen."

"Thank you, Pastor Turner."

"We're pretty laid-back here. Call me Chance. Did you get to meet my wife, Lynn?"

"I did, and your boys, too."

He smiled. "You have to watch out for those two."

"They're boys. It was nice to meet you." She turned to leave.

"Remember, if you need to talk, the door is always open. Lynn helps out up here, too, and she's here if you wanted to talk to her."

"I'll remember that. Bye." She couldn't get away quick enough. Her heart was reeling with the heaviness and confusion she was carrying inside of it. What to do?

She was almost running to find Lacy as she rounded the corner, getting away from Chance's knowing gaze. She very nearly ran over Luke in the process.

"Whoa! You running barrels without your horse?" he asked, dodging her, jumping off the sidewalk.

"Um, yes. I mean no." There was nowhere for her to go, though she would have liked to avoid the cowboy. Small towns made avoiding a person hard. But it really didn't matter, she told herself. After all, she'd made her position on dating clear. She hadn't seen him during the service, though she'd been looking around for him—there was no denying that she'd been looking for his handsome face in the crowd.

"You look like you're in a hurry. Is everything all right?"

"Yes. I was going to look for Lacy and then head out. I'm planning on riding this afternoon." Why was she explaining herself? What was it about the man that made her so defensive. Then again, maybe it was the entire morning that made her defensive. Attending church when she'd rather have stayed home and ridden Murdock around endless barrels.

"You have a good day, then," he said, and headed for the parking lot.

She watched him go, startled that he hadn't tried to talk longer.

Startled more because she wished he had….

Luke went straight home after church. His younger brother, Jess, was arriving with a new load of cattle from Fort Worth. It was a good excuse to keep him from thinking about how pretty Montana had looked that morning. She'd had on a red dress that looked great on her—but he thought she'd look fantastic in anything. What was it about the woman that had his head spinning?

Jess pulled into the lot about the time it took Luke to change clothes and get to the stock pens. He watched his brother back the big bull wagon cattle trailer up to the chute—bumping the chute in one try. Luke smiled every time he watched Jess do it, remembering the first time his little brother had made it without having to pull forward and back the big trailer up to the chute a second or third time.

Taller and leaner than Luke, Jess stood at about six-four. Luke and Colt had always called him "the little big brother," because he surpassed them in height before they'd reached high school. Colt was smaller, more compact at five-ten, and built like the bull rider he was. All three brothers were close because they'd banded together in defense of their drunken father's treatment. Watching Jess climb down from the truck, Luke felt a sense of brotherly pride. He was proud to call both Colt and Jess brother.

"Hey, honey, I'm home," Jess teased, walking up and clapping him on the back. It was a joke they all passed between themselves since all three had issues with settling down.

Luke chuckled. "I missed you, too."

"Yeah, that's a lie. From what I hear through the grapevine you've been fairly busy juggling women to have missed your ole brother."

"I should have known you would hear about the

tea. You probably almost had a wreck laughing about that one."

Jess gave him a sly sideways glance and nodded. "That I did."

They walked to the back of the hauler. No telling who Jess had heard the story from, but he was sure he'd learn the answer eventually, so he didn't bother to ask.

"You should have known that woman wouldn't take kindly to being dumped."

"I didn't dump anyone. I took her to dinner twice. That's it."

"I saw *marriage-hunter* written all over her the moment I saw her. Why do you think *I* didn't ask her out?"

Luke shook his head and grunted. "She seemed nice, and she told me she wasn't looking for anything but a date."

Jess hiked a brow. "And I'm ready to settle down yesterday."

"I know that's a lie."

Jess chuckled as he slid back the trailer latch and they pulled the gate open.

"Erica's just aggravated her plans didn't work out. She tossed that tea on you because she thought she'd have you wrapped around her finger by the second date, and y'all would be on your way to the altar by the third date."

Surely she hadn't thought that.

"You gotta watch out for some of these gals. They can be conniving when it comes to getting what they want. At first they can put on a show, but down the line they start showing you who they really are. I'm just sayin' you need to watch a little closer, bro, or you might wake up married to—"

"Okay, okay, I get the picture, Jess."

Jess propped a boot on the corral and gave him a skeptical glance.

There was one thing the Holden brothers under-stood loud and clear—marriage didn't always mean happy or better. Luke was beginning to worry if Jess had backed off completely from the idea of marriage.

"They look good," Luke said, changing the subject back to the yearling heifers moving from the trailer.

"They should, for the price we paid." Jess grinned. "But they're worth it."

"How was Okeechobee?"

"Still deep in the heart of Florida, and one long drive home."

Luke laughed. "You're the one who likes to drive."

"Uh-huh. That I do. Gives a man breathing room. So tell me about this Montana Brown I've heard about."

"Are you sure you've been gone? Not hiding out in the back of my truck?"

Jess cocked a brow and gave a dog-faced grin. "Hey, man, I've got my sources. Sooo? You like her?"

"She's interesting," Luke said.

"I hear you've drawn the attention of the posse." Jess stopped smiling. "You might be in trouble if you aren't careful."

Luke closed the trailer and slapped the lock lever down with a clank. "I'm not worried about those three."

"Maybe you should be. Maybe you need to back off before they latch on tighter."

"They have this rodeo and festival to occupy their

time. They won't be concentrating on me for about two weeks. There'll be so much going on then that they'll forget all about me."

Jess laughed as he strode to the freight liner and climbed up into the seat. "Yeah, you go on and keep that lazy attitude. I figure you'll be married by fall."

"Hardly." Luke scowled as he headed toward his own truck. Montana intrigued him, it was true. But being pushed into marriage by the loveable matchmakers wasn't happening, and his brother good-and-well knew it.

Chapter Six

Luke dropped off some extra panels they'd need to hold the excess stock. Montana was in the barn racing like lightning when Luke went by the arena. Her braid slapped against her back as she and Murdock raced by. She wore a blue-green T-shirt that matched her eyes. Eyes that were completely focused on the barrels. It was not something that had to be done immediately, but it was a good excuse to stop.

She'd gotten her time up even better than it was and she looked more at ease in the saddle than she had the last time he'd watched her. She was concentrating so hard as she came around the last barrel, he figured she probably didn't see him sitting on the top rung of the arena fence. Which was a good thing. She had her mind on her barrels today. On the other hand, he hadn't been concentrating like he needed to. He'd had Montana on his mind much more than he'd wanted, but there didn't seem to be anything he could do about it. Luke liked a challenge. And he wasn't used to being told no. So what was this all about?

He watched as she dismounted from Murdock before he'd fully stopped his gallop. She landed with boot heels planted in the soft dirt and ran a little with him.

"Are you thinking of competing in goat tying?" he drawled, startling her, because she hadn't known he was there. Seeing him, her chin whipped upward.

"Where did you come from? I didn't see you come in." She was breathing a little hard from running alongside her horse.

"I think that's because you were obviously concentrating. That's a good thing, right?"

"Right. But I thought I was alone."

"Sorry. You looked like you were going after a goat."

She shook her head, her eyes flashing with irritation. "Can't do that after college."

"You still looked like that's what you were doing."

She bit the inside of her lip and looked embarrassed. "I used to do that, too. I was, well, I was seeing if I could still dismount like I used to." She rubbed her palm down the front of her faded jeans.

He grinned. "And you didn't want anybody to see you."

Her brows wrinkled above eyes that would have pinned him to the barn door if they'd gotten any sharper. "I *thought* I was alone."

She was embarrassed—and mad. Her eyes flashed blue-green fire as she looked away from him.

He wondered about that suddenly. It hit him, slammed into him with a force that knocked him back. What was she so mad about?

He stepped forward, drawn to her. Lifting his hand, he touched her cheek. She was breathing hard but didn't move. "What's digging at you?" he asked gently, his thumb tracing her cheek.

Something was there, under the surface eating at her. He sensed it with all of his heart. And he wanted to help. "Tell me what you're so mad about, Montana."

Her heart had stopped beating at the look in Luke's eyes. At the tender touch of his hand and the concern in his voice. "Nothing," she denied, when the turmoil raging inside of her pleaded to be heard. She'd been struggling all morning, having had a phone call from her dad earlier. She hadn't taken the call, but just seeing his name on the ID had upset her.

All the guilt and confused feelings she'd felt Sunday had resurged with a vengeance, and the anger at her dad for causing it all had sent her into a tailspin. Now the uncertainty clung to her once more. The uncertainty of whether she had any forgiveness in her heart. Was it her dad who needed to ask her forgiveness? Then why did she have such guilt hanging over her head about it? After all, wasn't it her dad who'd pretended to be the perfect father, provider, husband?

It was her father who was in the wrong. It was her father who'd made her respect him enough to give up her barrel racing dreams, dreams she'd wanted with all her heart…and it was her father whose lies about who he really was and his betrayal that cut so deep that when she thought about it, the anger tore her up inside.

She didn't think anyone could understand what she was feeling, not even the pastor, not even Lacy—but Luke's questioning gaze blasted through the dark emotions swirling around inside her. It was as if he could see into the deepest corners of her heart, straight to the pain. The very idea set her into action. No, she didn't want him or anyone else seeing that deeply.

She didn't want him knowing how torn up she was. How weak it made her feel. It wasn't his business, and she didn't want to share.

Sharing meant letting him in and she wasn't ready to do that. It was dangerous.

"Nothing is wrong," she repeated, her voice stronger. She stepped back, away from the touch of his hand.

The touch of his dark eyes remained, holding her. His shoulders seemed wide enough to hold her troubles. "I don't believe you," he said. "Something tells me you need a friend. Someone to talk to. Talk to me, Montana."

As if he knew he was onto something. The man was as solid as a redwood, and she wondered how it would feel to be sheltered in his arms. Able to trust again.

"No. It's none of your business," she said. "Leave it be."

"Why? So you can be eaten up by whatever is bothering you. So you can let it get between you and this dream?" He waved toward Murdock.

"Mind your own business," she snapped at him, feeling suddenly ugly inside.

A sudden and devastating smile cracked across his tanned, handsome face. "Sorry, Montana. I've got a feeling that's one request I'm not going to be able to keep."

Montana's heart practically swooned, dipping and tumbling. Shaken by the sincerity in his eyes she did the only thing she could—she spun around and stormed across the arena toward Murdock.

How dare the man try to penetrate the wall she'd built up to protect herself? How weak of her to be tempted to let her defenses down.

Grabbing Murdock's saddle horn, she swung easily onto his back. Feeling like an Indian warrior hitting the warpath, she grabbed the reins, wheeled the poor, startled horse around and galloped him back into the alley. If it hadn't been for the closed gate, she'd have been tempted to keep on riding out of the building.

The worst part about it was Luke knew she was hiding something.

How could a near-total stranger seem to see through her? How?

He'd hit a nerve. Luke watched the ticked-off cowgirl race out of the alley as though a pack of hungry coyotes were chasing her. She was most definitely stewing about something. Something that cut deep. Something still very raw.

As he watched, she and Murdock flew toward the first barrel. Montana's eyes were zeroed-in on the barrel, but she wasn't in rhythm. They were too fast and she was too close as Murdock started around the barrel.

The sound of her knee connecting with the barrel rang out. The hard impact toppled her from the horse like she'd been shot, and she hit the ground with a thud. Dust flew up around her as she rolled and landed face-first in the soft dirt.

Luke started running the moment she fell. Skidding to a halt, he gently rolled her over. She blinked, gasped for air, then struggled to sit up. Pain etched her pretty, dirt-streaked face as she grabbed her knee.

"Are you all right?" He could barely hear his stupid question over the pounding of his heart. Of course she wasn't all right. What was he thinking? he wondered as she hugged her knee in pain.

She nodded, but didn't look up at him.

Hurting for her, Luke scooped her into his arms. "Let's get you over here and look at that."

"Put me down," she said, but the tremble in her voice gave away her pain.

"No," he said, holding tight when she struggled against him. "Not till I make sure you're all right." He had a feeling he should do as she demanded—for his own well-being, he should put her down and walk away.

That would be the smart thing to do on his part, but something about Montana Brown brought out the need to dig deeper and find out what had hurt her. Because there was no doubt in his mind that she'd been hurt. And he wanted to help.

Jess would tell him to hit the road and not look back. But he couldn't. For the first time ever, he couldn't walk away.

Montana's knee was still stinging from the direct hit, but it was easing. Being in Luke's arms had sent her reeling. "Not till I make sure you're all right," he'd drawled like John Wayne. Truth be told, if she hadn't been so distracted by being in his arms, she might have thought he was charming!

His arms tightened around her as she struggled to

get free of his hold. It was useless, because the man was carrying her firmly toward the benches outside the arena. There was no getting free of him.

"I'm fine." She crossed her arms and tried not to notice how strong he was. *Or* how nice he smelled, a combination of pine and something citrus that drew her to inhale a little deeper. *What was she doing?* A few seconds ago, she was trying to get away from him. Now, she was in his arms…and liking it!

"My knee doesn't hurt anymore." She squirmed for good measure.

"Good. I'm still going to check it out. Be still," he told her, almost harshly as he halted at the bench.

"Why are you here anyway?" she asked, relieved as he lowered her to the first row of the metal grandstand benches.

Sweeping his hat from his head, exposing his dark hair, he went down on one knee and looked her straight in the eyes. Goodness—she was speechless. His dark eyes seemed to burn through her. "Because I wanted to come see what you were doing."

Her pulse skittered at the straightforwardness of his answer. She gulped. "Why would you do that?"

"Because, despite everything, I like you. Does this hurt?" He looked at her knee and gently probed around on it.

Was he kidding? She was feeling no pain at the moment! "It's tender but fine. It won't do you any good to like me. I've told you that." She meant it, too—even if she *had* been tempted to spill her guts to the man only a few minutes ago.

He gave a disbelieving laugh. "Get over yourself,

Montana. I thought you and I could be friends. That's all. Whatever it is that's eating at you, you might feel better if you talked about it. *Just* talk."

She studied him, mad at herself because she was tempted. "Why are you so interested in what's eating me?"

"I was right. Something *is* eating at you."

"I didn't say that—"

"Oh, yes, you did."

"Did *not*."

He dipped his chin, giving her a look that was just plain cute, even if it was a look of disbelief.

He was almost eye level with her, since he was still kneeling and his hand rested on her knee. Her knee that had long since stopped hurting, but was now very aware of his touch.

"Believe me, I know that some things can't be changed." His tone vibrated with sincerity. "But I can tell you that talking does help soften the sting."

That did it, time to move away from the man! Standing abruptly, she took a step away from him, tested her knee and was thankful it felt halfway okay. If she stayed that close to him much longer, she would be in deep trouble.

He stood, too. "It's a wonder your knee didn't swell to the size of a watermelon. And how's your back? I'd give you a score of ten for the dive-and-roll you did when you got tossed."

She laughed, easing the tension. "Amazingly, I'm feeling fine there, too. Of course, that might not be the story when I wake up tomorrow."

"True." He continued watching her as she worked

her knee, pacing a little. "Now, do you want to talk about it?"

The man was impossible, she thought, as they stared at each other. She didn't want to tell him her life story. Lacy knew the ridiculous details of her parents' divorce, but she certainly wasn't sharing it with Luke.

Even if he had a way of looking at her as if he understood who she really, really was.

Chapter Seven

"You look like you're moving slow today," Sam said the next morning when Montana limped into the diner. The scent of Sam's mouthwatering breakfast lingered in the air of the rustic diner.

"Yeah," Applegate grunted from the jukebox in the corner. "What happened to you? Get thrown from yor horse?" He grinned and stabbed the music selection he wanted with his boney finger.

"Has somebody been in here talking?" she asked suspiciously.

"Nope," Sam denied. "We didn't need anyone to tell us anything. With you riding like you are and limping like that, too, it ain't rocket science."

"Yup, it shor ain't." App walked to his table and sat down.

"Where's Stanley?" Montana asked. The vacant chair at App's table looked odd.

"He's got the bazooties, ain't nothing more than a bad cold, but he decided he'd better hole up in his house and let it run its course."

"I'm sorry about that." She liked Stanley. Applegate and he might be nosey, but they'd always been sweet to her.

"Me, too. Leaves me without a playin' partner."

Montana held back a chuckle at his sour-faced frown.

"How are you at checkers?" he asked, brightening like a lightbulb at his idea.

"I thought you'd never ask," she grinned, unable to resist plopping down across from him. "Pass me some sunflower seeds, please."

"Really?" His jaw dropped.

She held her hand out. "Oh, yeah, I'm sure. I've been wanting to do this ever since I got to town."

A huge smile lit up across App's face. He handed her the five-pound bag of sunflower seeds and she dug out a small handful. "Is this enough?"

"Might be a few too many. You'll look like a chipmunk if you put too many in."

"I'd watch out if I was you," Sam warned, from the table near the back where a booth full of cowboys were chomping down on breakfast like it was their last meal.

"I'm not afraid of Applegate," she huffed, and tossed the sunflower seeds into her mouth.

He hiked a bushy brow. "You shor about that?"

She rubbed her hands together in anticipation. "Oh, I'm *shor,* all right," she warned. "Show me what you got, dude." This was going to be fun.

She and App studied the board.

"You go first." He squinted at her from across the table, like a gunfighter gauging his opponent. He looked to Montana like he had an itchy trigger finger.

Holding her in his sights, he leaned out then one, two, three—he fired several sunflower shells at the spittoon on the floor next to the table.

Feeling like the shells were growing in her mouth she leaned forward and took aim then fired away. Sadly, her shells spurted out kind of sickly like, missing their mark and hitting the floor in silence. Laid there with no glory. It was embarrassing, really.

App hitched a caterpillar eyebrow. "I hope ya play checkers better'n ya spit."

She pushed the shells still in her mouth to the side so she could speak. "I'm going to try. It's been a while, but it's probably like riding a horse."

"Ya think?"

"I think." She winked at the older man, then made the first move. "Game on," she said. It had been a long time since she'd played checkers. Chess had been more her dad's speed. "More of a thinking-man's game," he'd been fond of saying, and had challenged her often. She'd been bored with the game, but she was glad to play it with him. Getting close to her dad had never been easy. Some kids played catch with their dad. She played chess. Not that she'd been very good at it, but she'd tried. She'd always wished they could have gone horseback riding together. The fact that he'd gotten her a horse when she was twelve had been a total surprise. Thinking back on it now, it was also about the time he'd begun to spend more time at the office.

"You gonna move that checker or jest stare it ta death?"

"Oh," she gasped, nearly choking on a shell. She'd zoned out for a minute. "Hold your horses, I'm jumping." She took a jump, and he immediately jumped two of hers.

"You ain't too smart at this here game, are ya?"

Sam shook his head across the room. "I warned ya not ta get involved with ole App thar. He ain't too good of a sport."

The door opened and she glanced over her shoulder. Instantly, she froze. Luke strode inside and his gaze locked onto hers like a missile onto a target. His eyes flicked from her to the room, then back to her.

"Hey thar, Luke," App bellowed. "Get on over here and help a poor old fellow out."

"Whoa, no outside help," Montana growled, staring at the checkerboard, then making her move. She could feel Luke standing there, looking over her shoulder.

"Looks like he's not the one who needs help," he drawled.

She twisted her head and scowled up into his cocoa-colored eyes. He blinked innocently and smiled.

"Don't look at me like that. I'm only sayin' that was a lousy move you just made."

"Well, don't be sayin' then. I'll make my own moves and suffer or celebrate on my own." She spat a sunflower seed at the spittoon, and it hit the edge before landing on his boot. Perfect shot.

The look on his face was priceless. She grinned at him.

"Cute. Real cute." He slid across the floor to stand beside App. "I think I'll watch you suffer from over here."

She wasn't planning on losing, but App made his jump, and after she made her next move, the sly man

wiped her out! Talk about feeling foolish…it was piti-
ful. After that, the game was short and not so sweet. It
was humiliating. Chess was more complicated, and yet
she'd lost to App like a schoolgirl who'd never played
a game of chess or checkers.

Eyeing her, App chucked a handful of sunflower
seeds into his mouth and grinned, showing teeth all the
way back to his molars. "That was like taking candy
from a baby."

Luke chuckled. "Those very well could be fighting
words, App. Montana doesn't take losing very well."

Sam had stopped by to watch the last play, and now
he snorted. "App don't, either. Stanley usually whups
him good."

"He does not," App grumbled.

Sam hooted with laughter. "You can deny it all you
want, Applegate Thornton, but you know it's the truth."

"It's all right, App." Montana grinned, feeling at
peace with the loss. She'd enjoyed her game despite
Luke's presence. Why was it, when she didn't want a
man in her life, God sent one along who totally made
her crazy?

"Fellas, it's been fun, but I've gotta go," she said.

"But you ain't ate nothin'," Sam said.

"I just came in to say hi. I was picking up a few supplies down at Pete's and thought I'd pop in."

App grinned. "You didn't know you was gonna get
yourself talked into a rowdy game of checkers, did ya?"

"No, App. I had no idea I was going to be a stand-
in for Stanley. You tell him he better feel better soon,
because I'm not doing his empty chair justice."

"I'll tell him. I'm goin' over thar in a few minutes

ta take him some chicken noodle soup ole Sam cooked up special fer him."

"You better be careful and not catch his bug."

"I can't catch it. I ain't goin' past the porch. He's on his own from thar on out."

Montana could understand App's attitude. He really didn't need to catch what his buddy had. But what if Stanley needed someone to check on him more closely? Her immune system was excellent; she hadn't been ill in ages. "What would he say if I took the soup by to him?"

All three men stared at her as if she was the last person on earth they expected to offer such an act of kindness. "Why are y'all looking at me like I just said the last thing any of you expected me to say?"

Sam slapped his white dishrag over his shoulder. "Fer starters, you don't hardly know Stanley."

"I know Stanley. I've been in here several times since I came to town, and he's been nothing but nice to me."

"That is true," App said. "Stanley's loud, but he liked you from the moment you stomped in here with Lacy. 'Sides that, any friend of Lacy's is a friend of ours…and better than that, yor her family."

"That's awful sweet of you to say. I liked the three of you from the first time I met y'all, too." She included Sam in the three. She did not look at Luke on that one.

Sam gave her a frank look. "I kin tell you fer shor that Stanley would prefer gettin' his chicken soup delivered by a purdy gal like you a whole lot more than from a shriveled up old geezer like App. I'll go fix it up right now."

Luke crossed his arms, watching her with an expression that was part amused, part amazed. Did he really not think she could be nice and take a sick man a bowl of soup?

"Do you know where Stanley lives?" Luke asked finally.

"No. But App can give me directions."

"It's kinda off the beaten path," App said. "Stanley lives off a dirt road, off of another dirt road, way down past my house."

"You can tell me. I can follow directions pretty good." Did they really didn't think she couldn't take directions? How hard could it be to find a dirt road?

Sam came out of the kitchen with a large carryout bag. "You jest take this to him and tell him it should last him a couple of days. But if I was you, I'd get ol' Luke here ta drive ya out thar. Ain't no tellin' what in the world you might run into out thar in the boonies."

"Guys, I can take care of myself."

Sam wagged his head. "It ain't got a thang in the world ta do with that. My Adela called me while I was back thar gettin' this ready and I told her you was takin' it out to Stanley and she said I was not to let you go alone. Under no circumstances were you to head out thar without Luke here drivin' you." He dropped his chin. "And if my Adela tells me that, then that's what I aim ta tell you."

Montana would have protested and done exactly what she wanted. However, she glanced over at Luke, who gave her a what-are-you-afraid-of look. What *was* she afraid of? Nothing. She wasn't scared of him. She could let him drive her out there and it made no difference to her.

"Load up then. What are we waiting on?" Taking the soup, she headed toward the door. When she got there, she turned and gave App and Sam warning looks. "But you two better not make anything out of this little trip, other than me letting Luke take me out to Stanley's."

Two sets of bushy brows rose to meet thinning hairlines despite both men trying their hardest to look innocent. She almost laughed, but one glance up at Luke and she scowled instead. The man was simply tóo good-looking for his own good. Okay, the man was too good-looking for *her* good. As he held the door open for her and she squeezed past him with the bag of soup, she reminded herself that she wasn't supposed to be thinking about how good he smelled, how good he looked or how nice he was going along with two old men with matchmaking on their minds.

"It's nice of you to take this out to Stanley." Luke held the door of his truck open for Montana, and just naturally took her elbow to help her up into the seat.

"It's the right thing to do."

He liked that, he thought, as he closed the door and headed around to his side. He glanced toward the diner's big window and there stood Sam beside App's table. Both men were grinning like two kids thinking they were pulling a good one. He chuckled as he got behind the wheel.

"They think they're so sneaky. Do you believe the story about Miss Adela calling?" Montana asked.

Luke started the truck and backed out before he answered. He wanted to get away from prying eyes. He had seen a few other eyes staring out windows, too. From over at the candy store. And he thought he'd seen Esther Mae looking out of Ashby's Treasures—the ladies' clothing store that was directly across the street from Sam's diner. Everyone in town would know about this little trip before they even made it out to Stanley's.

"It sounded like something she might say, so it could be true. If not, Sam's getting pretty creative, isn't he?"

She laughed at that. "Oh, yes, he is. So, is Stanley's place really that hard to find?"

"Oh, yeah. The man lives down by the river, and you have to drive halfway across Texas as the crow flies to get there." He grinned at her. "You'll see. And you'll be glad you decided not to be scared of me and let me drive you."

"I wasn't scared of you."

"Yeah, you were. Are."

She shot him a glare that would have stopped a raging bull in its tracks. He challenged her with his expression before turning back to the road. Even ornery, she interested him. He wondered what it was that had her so mad and tense half the time. He aimed to find out, just like he aimed to get her to go out with him. He liked a challenge, and if there was one thing about Montana Brown that was as clear as the blue sky in front of them, it was that she was a challenge.

He sometimes wondered how his life would be if God hadn't created him to be as stubborn as he was, and as determined to meet a challenge head-on. Jess and Colt always called him bullheaded, but it was his bullheadedness that had helped them all cope whenever their parents were yelling and screaming at each other back when they were younger. He'd only been ten when the worst fights were going on. When his poor mother was at her wit's end and just barely coping with the struggles of being married to his alcoholic dad. He'd been old enough to know he needed to get his brothers out of the house. They'd end up out in the neighbor's big barn, down the dirt road where they lived. Or they'd go fishing in the pond around the corner.

He'd been fourteen when his parents had finally split. And his mom left him to be in charge of his dad—and his brothers. She'd left him there. Nothing had ever been, or would be, harder than that day. He still had a hard time thinking about it. His brothers did, too, especially Jess.

"So, how's it going out at Lacy's?" he asked a few miles down the road, after the silence had stretched about as long and tight as it could go.

"Great."

He turned onto the first dirt road of many connecting ones, then he gave her a long stare. "That's it? That's the extent of our conversation?" She looked at him and her lips lifted into a half grin that did funny things to his insides.

"I guess ignoring you isn't going to work, is it?"

"Or be very nice."

She laughed. "No, I guess it wouldn't be that, either."

"It does tend to take a lot of effort to be rude," he said. She turned slightly in her seat, so that she was facing him. He kept his eyes on the road.

"This is very true. It can be exhausting when the man can't take a hint."

It was his turn to chuckle. "I'm stubborn that way."

"I've figured that out. But so am I. I'm just giving in because I need all my energy to compete with Murdock. Poor horse is giving me two hundred percent, so I have to try to give him at least a measly little one hundred. I have enough things stealing energy from my concentration without being rude to you, too."

"You're honest, I'll give you that."

"I'm *very* honest. Riding the fence hasn't ever been one of my strong points. At least not usually."

"I have you figured to ride it when you don't have options." He wasn't sure where this conversation had come from, but he knew they were hitting close to home on something. Her sudden thoughtfulness made him certain of it. She looked straight ahead, chewing her lip. Something was going on inside that head of hers, and for some reason he was eaten up with wanting to know what it was. He shouldn't want to, but there was no way of denying the truth. He wanted to know what made Montana Brown tick.

"You have a lot on your mind?" It was as much a statement as a question. He'd let her take it whichever way she wanted to.

She blinked and her troubled eyes cleared. "Yes. Doesn't everyone?"

"Yes, frankly. But sometimes, it helps to talk about it. Do you need an objective point of view?"

"Are you always so nosy, Mr. Holden? If so, this may be why you can't hold a date."

"Hey, I hold a date as long as I want."

"Yes, you keep reminding me of that unflattering fact about yourself."

"I'm not always this nosy," he growled, choosing to ignore her comments. There was obviously no changing her view on his personal life. They'd reached a fork in the road, with a third dirt road feeding off of one of the forks. It was the third road that he took. From here on, the road would get more rutted. Stanley really needed to get the county to come out and grade the thing. If the river was to suddenly rise, he'd be cut off. That wasn't good.

"Why me? Why do you want to poke around in my business?"

Man, the woman had a way of putting things. "I want to know why you're always this angry. I want to help. Believe it or not, I know what it's like to walk around eaten up with anger."

"I'm not always like this. And you don't know how much I wish I wasn't. But there are just some things in this world a person can't change. Some folks are just going to disappoint us."

"Now, *that* I know something about." He wished he didn't. "Sometimes you just have to learn not to expect too much out of people. Sad but true."

Anger crossed her expression, her eyes flashed as she crossed her arms and shook her head. "That's just a sorry excuse. I want people to expect a lot out of me. I want people to know that I'm who I say I am. Others should, too."

He could feel her pain. What had caused it? Stanley's house came into view up ahead, and Luke wished he lived about ten more miles down the road. He gave the only advice he believed in. "Then be that person, but don't expect it from others. You only control your standards."

"Is that what you do? How you live your life?"

He pulled to a stop in Stanley's yard. "To a point. I mean, I know that here in Mule Hollow, there are plenty of folks who'd come through for me in a heartbeat. But still, let's just say, when you're raised to expect the worst from those who're supposed to care for you—there is always a part of you that expects the worst from everyone."

Looking straight at each other, neither one of them moved. The ebb and flow of a pulsing tension connected them. He felt the connection and knew she did, too.

She finally gave a nod.

"I guess that's one reason I wanted to bring Stanley his soup."

The tension eased. "And I guess that's one reason I wanted to come along. Like you said, it's the right thing to do."

Some of the trouble in her eyes wasted away, replaced with a little sparkle. "You are just full of surprises."

He wanted to press for more, but the teasing banter was a good thing. He liked it. "It's about time I got a little love."

She laughed and opened her door. "Oh, don't get a big head now. I wouldn't go that far. Not by a long shot."

Chapter Eight

Poor Stanley! When he opened the door, his plump face was pale, his cheeks extra pink and his nose was a bright, rosy red. "I hate to say it, but you look terrible, Stanley."

That got Montana a smile despite his ill looks. "I feel tur-rable, too," he said. "What are y'all doin' here?"

She held up the bag of soup. "Didn't you hear? Sam has hired us out as his new delivery crew. You're our first client. Between you and me, this character they have drivin' me is a bit shady. I think I was hired on to keep him from scaring old ladies."

Stanley coughed, long and hard, but grinned and nodded as he put a tissue up to his red nose. "He sure looks like a character, all right," he managed.

"Cut it out, you two or I'm about to get insulted. I drove all the way out here to rescue you with soup, Stanley. *And* to keep *you* from getting lost in the boonies and causing half of the county to come out and search for you, Montana. The phrase is 'thank you very much.'"

His drawl was cute, Montana thought as she rolled
her eyes and looked at Stanley in the doorway. He was
leaning against the door, looking weak. "He's a big
baby, if you didn't already know that. Just what I don't
like about a man. Always whining." She was enjoying
this, and Luke was being so nice playing along, helping to lift Stanley's spirits.

Stanley battled another fit of coughing. "Need ta
watch out fer the likes of him. I'd invite y'all in, but
you might catch whatever I've got that's kicking my
rump." He frowned, held on to the door frame and
wheezed, "And that wouldn't be good." He held his
hand out for the soup.

Montana held tightly on to the bag. "Nope, not leaving," she said breezily, and scooted past him into the
house. "I'm going to sit you down somewhere comfortable before you fall down. Then I'm going to warm
this up for you."

Luke followed her in, despite the look of dismay on
Stanley's lovable face. Set on getting her way on this,
she saw the edge of the counter through a doorway
and headed that way.

"But you might get sick," Stanley protested, pad-
ding along behind her in his stocking feet.

"And we might not." She stopped in her tracks at the
kitchen door—oh, what a mess! The poor man probably hadn't washed a dish since he started feeling bad.
It was apparent. He'd probably barely felt like figuring
out *what* to eat. Turning around, she pointed at Luke.
"Could you take him into the den and help him get
comfortable? I'll have this heated up in a jiffy. Then
I'm going to clean this kitchen while you keep him

company as he eats. A little conversation might make you feel better, Stanley."

"Aw, y'all don't have ta go ta all that trouble."

"Are you kidding?" Montana grimaced. "I had to play checkers with App this morning. It was horrible. You've got to get better so you can go back in there and defend me. He tore me up."

"No way," Stanley grunted.

"Oh, it's true," Luke joined in. "I witnessed it. Montana can ride a horse like greased lightning, but at checkers, believe me, she stinks."

"That's turr-able." *Cough.* "Jest turr-able."

"Not as terrible as it's going to be when you play him again and whup him in my defense. Soup and a clean kitchen in trade for a little good ol'-fashioned payback. How's that sound?"

"I kin do that," Stanley agreed, already walking into the den. She could see his recliner and quilt waiting for him. "Sounds like I get the easy end of this deal." He paused to cough, his shoulders shaking before he trudged forward and made it to the chair.

Setting the package of soup on the counter, Montana went in search of a clean bowl. This had certainly not been the morning she'd envisioned when she'd headed into town for feed for Murdock. As she waited for the soup to heat in the microwave, she began scrubbing dishes to go in the dishwasher. It was a really good feeling, to know she was doing something good. If she did get sick, it was going to be well worth it.

She thought of Luke's teasing and the smile he'd given her just now. Getting sick could definitely have its positives if he brought *her* some soup. One thing she was realizing about Luke was that he was a giving person. He had work to do, but he'd taken time out and come along with her. It was sweet.

He was sweet. She paused scrubbing the dish in her hands—Luke had his good side, it was a fact. She sighed…whupped, on that count.

There was simply no way to deny it.

Even if she wanted to!

By the expression on her face, Montana gauged Norma Sue's mood to be jolly. More like ecstatic. Her smile was practically stretched from ear to ear as she strode into the arena the day after Montana and Luke had gone to see Stanley. Word was out just like she knew it would be.

People were talking. The matchmakers, that is, and Montana had set herself up for it like a crazy fool. Trailing behind the grinning cattlewoman was Esther Mae. She was beaming brighter than her red hair, and her eyes were twinkling so brightly, with the sheer pleasure of the hunt, that Montana knew she was in trouble. Behind both of them trailed Adela, looking for all the world like a woman who knew a secret.

She might have messed up. Really. She'd gotten so caught up in trying not to let Luke bother her, she'd taken up the challenge and let Luke drive her out to Stanley's place. Now she was going to have to pay the consequences.

Even if there was no truth to what they thought was a blossoming romance, the seed was planted. "Romance, ha!" she muttered to Murdock as she leaned down to pat his neck. "Me and that man would drive each other crazy." *But you didn't yesterday. You enjoyed helping Stanley with him.*

"What are y'all ladies doing out here?" she asked, ignoring the voice in her head as she loped Murdock over to the fence.

Esther Mae fanned herself with her hand. "We've come to make sure the concession stand is in order for the crowds in two weeks."

"We wouldn't want everyone to get here and not be able to buy a soda and some popcorn." Norma Sue stuck her hand through the fence and scratched Murdock's chin.

"How are you today, dear?" Adela asked, her smile warming Montana, despite knowing she was about to get the third degree.

"I'm great. We're coming along better every day. Murdock's not quite so upset with me lately."

"Well, that's wonderful," Esther Mae gushed. She wore a pair of bright pink pants and a white shirt with a huge, sparkly pink rose on it. She looked as cheerful and happy as any woman Montana had ever met. "That was such a nice thing you did yesterday, taking soup out to poor Stanley. And Luke was such a gentleman to drive you. That Stanley, he lives too far out in the sticks for a young woman like you to travel there all by herself. I'm glad the fellas were smart enough to send along Luke."

"I thought Adela suggested Luke drive me?" Montana watched Adela's blue eyes widen in surprise.

"Me?" Adela placed a delicate hand to her cheek. "Well, um, those men must have thought you might listen to my advice. I'll have to say something to Sam about that."

"It's fine." Montana chuckled. "He said you'd called—"

"I did call. And he did tell me what you were doing. I did say that it would be nice if Luke drove you, but that was after Sam said he was going to get Luke to take you."

"I didn't mind," Montana said. "And Stanley's place was way out in the boondocks. Oh, my word—if I'd have taken a wrong turn, there's no telling where I'd be right now."

"Ain't that the truth," Norma Sue grunted.

"What about that Luke?" Esther Mae beamed, stepping closer, her eyes wide with enthusiasm. "Y'all had a good time didn't y'all? He's such a cutie-patootie!"

Montana almost choked. "Does he know you call him that?"

"Why don't you call him up and tell him? I don't mind. You could call him a few names yourself while you're on the phone...sugar pie, honeybunches, sweetheart."

"That's okay, we'll let it slide this time."

"You could go out with the poor ol' cowboy—"

"Norma Sue, I am *not* interested. Honestly, how many women has he been out with this year?" Did they not get that the man took nothing serious about a relationship? A relationship—when she did decide to have one—would be a very serious commitment. A man had to take it seriously, too, and be loyal—obviously something her dad knew nothing about.

"He's been out with a few," Norma Sue said apologetically. "He just needs the right one to come along and make him want to get to know you a little better."

"But I don't *want* to get to know him better."

Esther Mae frowned. "You are young and pretty, and need to be doing more than holing up with a horse and a baby. I love baby Tate with all my heart, but Lacy and Clint don't want you spending all your time babysitting. Everyone needs a night out. And I know you've got dreams and goals and all, but this horse is not going to keep you warm at night, and hold your hand when you get old and gray like us. Not that I'm gray-headed like Norma Sue here, but you know what I'm talking about."

Norma Sue was looking at Esther Mae like she'd lost her marbles. "You know good and well that beneath that red dye your natural red has disappeared. For all you know, you might be as white-headed as Adela!"

"No offense, Adela, but I am not that white-headed. Thank you very much," she huffed and fussily patted her flaming red hair.

Montana enjoyed the three ladies' teasing for a few more moments. She wondered if they would leave without checking the concession stand, which had been their ruse for coming to hound her about Luke. It would be funny if they did. Oddly, as much as she didn't want to be set up by the posse, it was fun to see them in action.

"I love babysitting Tate," she said in the baby's defense. "As a matter of fact, I'm watching him tonight so Lacy and Clint can go to the movies and out to eat in Ranger. This is the anniversary of the day she first came to town and met him."

"Oh, what a day that was!" Esther Mae exclaimed.

"It was a true blessing," Adela added.

Norma Sue pulled her hand away from Murdock and stuffed it into her overalls pocket. "And they are a perfect match. We did good, helping out with that, if I may say so myself."

Lacy and Clint were perfect for each other and Montana was so happy for them both. But she was content to not join the married mix. If only the ladies could understand that. She didn't let herself consider that she might be unfair to Luke. The niggling thought hovered at the edge of her conscience, though.

She was relieved a good while later when the posse left. After they had, in fact, made a trip inside the concession stand. She wasn't sure if they got what they were after, but she was relieved to see them go.

The rest of the afternoon as she and Murdock practiced, men tramped in and out of the arena area, working on various areas of the building. She wondered if Luke might show up, and found herself watching for him. After all, it was his animals going into the pens that were being worked on.

She spent the rest of the afternoon looking toward the entrance more times than she wanted to count.

Luke did not show up.

When she finally took Murdock to his stall and brushed him down before turning him out to relax in the outside lot, she berated herself for letting her thoughts dwell on Luke the entire time. True, she wasn't interested in the man. But still, she felt a hum of expectation when he was around. In addition to a *very* loud hum of irritation.

She watched Murdock nibble grass and lazily enjoy his freedom.

For the first time in her life, she, too, was experiencing her freedom. Freedom from her father's and mother's expectations. Freedom from worrying about pleasing them. And freedom from the guilt they'd made her feel when she wanted to do things her way. When did a girl become a woman who could make her own choices? When was a woman able to go her own way and decide her life on her own terms?

These had been the questions plaguing her while growing up and longing to hone her talent and see if she could make it as a professional barrel racer. She'd felt she'd had the talent to make it into the money, to gain sponsorships and to provide for herself with a lifestyle she'd dreamed of. But she'd honored her father's and mother's wishes. She'd set her dreams aside and become an accountant, then entered the family firm. There was nothing wrong with being an accountant—but she hadn't chosen it for herself. Her father had said it was a respectable, well-paying career for a woman. And so she'd become one. She'd put on her business suit and stowed her boots and jeans, along with her dreams. As she'd picked up her calculator she left Murdock to while away in a pasture, his unbelievable talent wasted.

Freedom. She had it now, but oddly, it came at a high price. Her father's betrayal and her mother's betrayal by living the lie and not telling Montana what was going on had done the thing she'd longed for all her life. It had given her the freedom to feel no guilt over choosing her own way. And here she was, living life on her terms and loving it.

Despite the heartache that brought her here, she did love it. The idea struck Montana as gently as the breeze that whispered across her skin.

She loved her life right now.

And if there was a niggling feeling of guilt over not being able to forgive her dad for lying to her. For betraying her mother. And being such a hypocrite about being so respectable, when in fact, he was so *not* respectable in his behavior. If there was any guilt at all over any of that, then she was learning to live with it.

Turning to head to the house and her date with a darling boy named Tate, she breathed deeply of the fresh, pine-laced air and let the joy of her freedom take hold. She was happy.

Yes, she was still angry, and she had her moments where the anger snuck up and ate her up, but it was getting easier each day to ignore it.

She opened the back door to the house and walked inside, choosing to acknowledge the denial.

Denial meant freedom. And that denial didn't need a man complicating it and messing it up.

Chapter Nine

"So you're sure that you're going to be all right with us going out?"

Montana bounced Tate on her hip, making him giggle. "Are you kidding? Me and Tater can't wait to have the house to ourselves. We plan on having a party. He's got all his buddies hiding in the bushes, waiting to see y'all's taillights disappearing down the drive. Isn't that right, little buddy?"

Clint wrapped his arms around Lacy from behind and grinned at Montana. "You and the kiddo have fun, then. I'm taking my wife out on the town. If the party gets too rowdy, call the cops. Brady or Zane will come to the rescue."

"Or you could call Luke," Lacy added innocently. "Word has it that it's only a matter of time before the matchmakers have you two tied up tighter than a—"

Montana threw Tate's stuffed puppy at her, hitting Lacy in the chin. "You are really pushing it, cuz."

Lacy laughed, walking over to kiss her baby goodbye. "You know I love you. But seriously, they *have* targeted you."

"And you haven't?"

"Well, no. Now, why would I do that when I know you aren't interested?"

Clint rolled his eyes and cleared his throat loudly.

"Don't worry, Clint, I'm not buying her innocent act, either."

"Then fine. You know that I want you to relax and get on with your life. But I also want you to think about what God has in store for you, and we both know that there is something going on between you and that handsome cowboy."

"Maybe it has nothing whatsoever to do with God."

"*Maybe* not," Lacy said. "But maybe it does."

"Luke's a good guy, Montana," Clint said, serious now. "He had a rough upbringing. Not your typical happy family. Not even your *almost* happy family. He worked here on the ranch beside me after they moved here growing up, and he idolized my dad. He's a quick learner and as reliable as they come. But he's never, ever talked about marriage. So, in that respect, you two match up. As a guy, I'll tell you he might be one who never marries. Though I know he's building a ranch he can pass on. He's setting down roots that will last and become a legacy." He hunched his shoulders and tilted his head. "The matchmakers may be wrong about him—and his brothers Jess and Colt. Some men aren't married because they just aren't ready and haven't met the right woman. And then there are some who got such a bad taste growing up that it's not a place they want to return. That said, I for one can tell him that, when

God puts the right woman in his path, there is nothing on earth that can compare to the fullness life takes on from there. That goes for you, too."

Montana was shocked by such a long speech from Clint, as much as the words he spoke about Luke. "Thanks, both of you. I'm touched by your concern. I know you both mean well, and it means a lot to me. You will never, ever know how much. Luke and I will be just fine. For starters, we do understand each other, so it's good. Now go, have a good time." She waved them toward the door. "Tater's little buddies are probably sucking their thumbs fast asleep under the mesquite bushes by now."

Montana was watching Tate show off his new crawling skills when a truck pulled up in front of the house. She wasn't expecting anyone, she realized as she headed toward the door. Through the big windows, she saw Luke step out of the truck, hesitate, then slam the door and stride her way. The rush of pleasure at his appearance surprised her. All afternoon, she'd looked forward to his showing up in the barn, and the disappointment hadn't been something she wanted to think about. Now a glimpse of him in a chocolate-brown button-up shirt that matched his eyes had her pulse bouncing off the charts.

She pulled the door open before he knocked, startling him. "A little late to be checking on the arena setup, isn't it?"

"I didn't come for that." He looked past her into the house.

Following his gaze, she glanced over her shoulder to

see Tate rise up on wobbly knees and reach toward the coffee table. "Oh, no, you don't." She laughed, hurrying back to the tot. "Come on in," she called, catching Tate just in time to keep him from bumping his tiny chin. Swinging him into her arms, she kissed his cheek as she turned back toward her unexpected guest. "Clint's not here. He and Lacy went on a date."

He looked puzzled as he scanned the room. "A date? But—where's everyone else?"

"Who?" Now it was her turn to look puzzled.

"I saw Norma Sue at the feed store and she asked me to come to a rodeo committee meeting here at seven."

Montana laughed. She couldn't help it. The sneaky Norma Sue. "You've been had. You know that, don't you?"

"I should have known." He gave a short laugh, snugged his hat tighter to his head, in a movement that spoke of embarrassment. "I've watched those women in action over and over again, and they *still* got one over on me."

"They knew I was going to be watching Tate tonight. They came poking around earlier, when I was riding." She tried to figure out what to do next. Did she ask him to stay? Did she want him to go? It was one weird situation she found herself in. Shifting Tate in her arms, she used him as a sort of emotional shield between the two of them. Something to keep her from thinking about hugging the man or kissing him.

She held Tate tighter as Luke walked toward the kitchen. "So, do you have anything to eat?"

"I might, but I don't remember inviting you to stay." He shrugged one muscled shoulder and hooked a thumb in his pocket as he studied her. He looked as if he could care less whether he stayed or not. It had her insides feeling queasy. Was that romance in the air, or just butterflies in her stomach at the thought of wondering such a thing? She didn't want romance. She didn't want the hint of it. Did she?

"There's roast beef in the fridge, and potatoes," she heard herself say.

"You sit and I'll fix it."

Her mouth dropped. "I didn't invite you to stay for dinner."

"So?"

She looked at Tate. "Did you hear that, Tate? This is not the way to act. He—" she nodded her head toward the unbelievably good-looking man in her kitchen "—has a lot to learn in the romance department."

"Who said anything about romance? I'm just having dinner. The way I figure it, if you won't go out with me for dinner, then I come to you. I owe the posse for this one."

"But I haven't told you that you could stay yet."

He opened the door to the fridge and studied the contents in silence. Acting like he didn't need her invitation, he pulled the pot from the shelf and set it on the counter. "This looks good."

Yes, it did. The cowboy had skills, she thought, as he began opening drawers and finding the items he needed: forks, knives, glasses. She cuddled Tate and watched in silence while Luke made himself at home in Lacy's kitchen. It amused her that he didn't ask. That he just did it.

He was taking charge…and oddly enough she liked

it. It was flattering that he wanted to have dinner with her this much. She admired his never-give-up mentality.

"Lacy and Clint seem really happy," he said at last while he was ladling roast and gravy onto plates and nuking them in the microwave.

"Romance is alive and well at the Matlock house."

Luke leaned against the counter, hooked his thumb in his jeans pocket and held her gaze. "Do you ever wish that for yourself?"

"You've come into the house, invited yourself to dinner and now you're asking some *very* personal questions. I'm not too sure I want to play this game."

He hiked a shoulder. "I'm just curious. I ask everyone the same question—well, sort of."

"Ah, yes, the no-strings-attached question. And here I thought you were about to ask me to marry you."

"Not today. So *do* you?"

"Persistent little badger, aren't you?"

"Yes. And I'd rather be called something a little more masculine than a badger. You sure know how to knock a man's ego down a notch."

She laughed full and hard at that. Tate grinned and clapped his hands. Luke laughed at them, sending a ripple of awareness through Montana. His smile faded suddenly, as something passed between them. Same as she'd felt that day in the arena when he'd tried to get her to talk to him, she felt drawn to Luke. It was unmistakable.

She admitted it. Admitted to herself that she liked him. She liked his blunt manner and his frank openness about what he wanted out of life. The man was truthful when it came to his expectations. At least it appeared so. When a woman went out with the guy, it was with eyes wide-open, because he'd made himself clear. Honesty was a good thing. Montana had felt bad for tea-tossing Erica that night at Lacy's barbecue. Now that she really understood Luke, she realized that tea tosser had to have understood the reality—Luke wasn't looking for marriage, and just the mention of it had him throwing on the brakes.

"I think I owe you an apology," Montana said.

"You talkin' to me?" he asked, spinning from where he'd just closed the door to the microwave, a look of mock disbelief on his face, his hand to his heart. "Say it ain't so, Sally. What in the world for?"

"The man is crazy," she said to Tate. "My name isn't Sally. Is yours?" Tate grinned at her and tried to pull her hair. "Maybe you didn't deserve to have tea poured all over you the other night."

"Now that is interesting. Very interesting. How did you come up with that deduction, Sherlock?"

She cocked her head to the side. "You make yourself very clear about you not being a marrying man. Tea tosser had to have known that, or you slipped up."

"I didn't slip up."

"Didn't think so. Anyway, I'm sorry I was so hard on you. But I still don't want to date you."

"And yet, here we are having dinner at Lacy's. Together. No date intended."

"Well, there you go. That fixes both our dilemmas." Not exactly, since it was a setup by the matchmakers, but she'd go along with it.

"If that's settled, then let's eat. I'm starving."

She'd have fixed Tate something, but he'd already had his bottle. Instead, she walked across the large living room and set him down in his playpen. Handing him his favorite teething ring and plush toy, she then headed back to the kitchen. Her pulse skipped like a dozen pebbles skimming over water as she watched Luke. They were having dinner. Sucking in a deep breath, she tried to relax. Luke had set the plates, napkins and flatware out, and was filling glasses with tea as she sat down.

"I figured you wouldn't toss this on me."

"I'll behave. I promise."

He placed the glasses on the counter next to their plates, then sat down beside her on a stool. Montana wondered if, by sitting at the kitchen island instead of the table, he thought she'd feel more inclined to believe this wasn't a date.

It *wasn't* a date, but the posse would never believe it.

"Earlier, I was teasing Lacy and Clint that Tate's little buddies were hiding outside in the bushes waiting for them to leave so they could come inside and play with Tate. But it's actually the posse who's probably out there. I can see them in the bushes wearing camouflaged outfits with mud swiped under their eyes, believing that we're on a date."

His eyes danced. "Right. I can almost hear the sound of their chatter."

He picked up a glass of tea and held it up in salute. "Let them have their fun. We understand each other. Agreed?"

Smiling, she picked her glass up and touched it to his. "Agreed."

Chapter Ten

They made small talk over dinner. Montana knew, from the day in the arena, that Luke was curious about her and she was curious about him and his past. But he didn't ask her and she didn't ask him. She was fighting through her issues on her own, and knew that, though he'd tempted her a couple of times with his strong shoulder to cry on, she was *not* going to go there.

It didn't matter how many times those deep, dark eyes of his called out to her to spill her guts to him.

Instead, they filled the blank space with small talk that led to stories about Luke's friends who had been targeted by the matchmaking posse and lost. His smile was warm and teasing when he said *lost*. They both understood what that meant.

There had been rumors of emptied gas tanks, wild hog encounters, help from a matchmaking donkey, which he promised to introduce her to at the festival. Samantha would be the main attraction of the petting zoo.

"It's never totally clear how much of a hand the gals have in all the matches," he said halfway through the roast beef. "But no matter what, we all know they're in the background, pushing love buttons to get whoever they've decided to match up together."

She had a feeling there were several women wishing the matchmakers' button-pushing had included them and Luke. Erica was at the front of the line. "Lacy says they get a lot of help from above."

"I suspect she's right. The matches seem to be good ones. Tate looks like proof to me."

Montana laid her fork down and glanced over at Tate, who'd conked out. He looked so peaceful. "Sadly, kids don't always prove a couple's happiness. Don't get me wrong, I believe Lacy and Clint were a match made in heaven. They didn't have to have Tate to prove it, but I know what you mean." Why, oh, why, had she just done that—opened her big mouth?

Her words had instantly drawn that look back into his eyes, and they were seeking as they settled on her. "I understand that more than you can know. Children don't always mean all is well on the homefront. Wasn't anywhere near right when it came to my home. But then I guess nothing on earth is perfect."

Silence stretched between them for a few moments. Montana held back voicing all the thoughts in her head, because it was just so personal. Still, she wondered about Luke's childhood. The way her thoughts kept swinging over to such a topic was a far cry from the distance she claimed she wanted to keep.

How could it be that she was so put off about the idea of a man in her life, and yet she couldn't seem to stop thinking about Luke and being interested in his past?

He leaned back in his chair. "My thought is that if God isn't in it, then marriage shouldn't be an option."

She was wading into the deep end, and she knew it. "Again, something we agree on."

"What's got you so adamant about that?"

She considered changing the subject, staring into his dark eyes. But the words wanted out too much and she couldn't hold them back. She felt too compelled to say something. "Growing up, I thought my parents had the perfect marriage. They never fought—they didn't really spend time together, but I never thought much about that. In my mind, they'd be together for all time. It's a major blow when you find out your parents are getting divorced. Or that your dad was having an affair." She shook her head. "It's just crazy. Disappointing...pointless, really..." Her voice trailed off and she didn't finish, as she felt the hard nudge of anger try to surface.

He gave her a gentle smile. "Is that what has you so angry?" he asked cautiously, as if afraid she was going to run out of the house and throw herself against a barrel again.

The very idea almost made her chuckle, and in a weird way lifted her up. She sighed. "You know...I can't—" She shook her head slightly, realizing she didn't want to mess up the evening by talking about her troubled past.

"I guess it can go both ways when it comes looking from the inside out," Luke began. "My parents were loud and fought over everything. They made no pretense about not enjoying each other's company. I've never been able to figure out why they were together in the first place. But they were. At least until my mom left when I was about twelve—not sure I blamed her. My dad was a drunk who couldn't hold a job. Worse, he didn't want to hold a job. He wanted everyone else to do the work."

"Your mom left?"

He nodded.

Surely she misunderstood. "Left you with your dad?" Did he mean his mother had left her three small sons with a man who drank and didn't work? He nodded again, and she felt ill. "How did y'all survive?"

"We worked. Me and my brothers."

Though he said the words in a matter-of-fact tone, Montana got a sharp image of Luke and his brothers working at young ages doing any jobs they could find to help support their family. She'd heard the edge to his words, and she studied him. He'd done what he'd had to do to survive. Luke had started overcoming challenges early. He'd learned to accept life as a challenge and to want to overcome it.

She was amazed by him. And she admired him. Talk about a complete turnabout on her part.

"How old were you when you started working?" she asked.

"About ten—if you count small odd jobs I did for people. It was good for me. There's nothing wrong with working. We—my brothers and me, are good at that."

"I bet you were. Are."

He gave a small grunt of a laugh. "Yeah, Jess and Colt say we were due for retirement by the time we were in high school."

She chuckled. "I guess that's one way to look at it."

He gave that shrug that she'd come to learn was

his. No big deal, it said. "You do what you have to do. We're the men we are today because of the kind of man my dad was. He was the worst role model around, and frankly, I could be bitter about it. And I've had my moments, believe me. But—" he gave an assuring look "—we've made peace with our childhoods. All three of us, in our own way. We each know what we don't want to be—my dad drank himself into an early grave. I couldn't do anything about that. Mac Matlock opened the Bible and showed me Galatians 6:4. It says. 'Each one should test his own actions. Then he can take pride in himself, without comparing himself to somebody else.'"

He rubbed his thumb along the edge of the granite counter and studied it as he did it. "That's what I'm trying to do."

Montana didn't have the words. She was trying to process all he'd said when he reached for the plates and stood up, as if needing to move.

"Those are strong words," she said. "You are doing great."

"I'm trying. My mother married a couple more times, then decided to give it up. She lives in Fredericksburg and manages a small restaurant. She loves her life now, and that's important to us. We tried to talk her into moving out here, when we bought the ranch last year, but she wouldn't hear of it. She has her church family there that she's involved in. She wouldn't budge."

Placing her elbow on the counter and her chin in her hand, Montana marveled at his attitude. His mother had left him in charge of his two younger brothers *and* a drunk dad, and yet he was acting as though nothing out of the ordinary had happened. Wasn't he angry at her?

She was angry for him.

What kind of woman did that? She'd left her boys to fend for themselves, and now Luke was talking as if they were best friends.

It was hard to swallow, especially in light of what was happening with her dad. She reached for the collar of her shirt, feeling hot suddenly. Galatians 6:4 played in her head. It said test her own actions...

Her hand trembled slightly as she thought about that. She had to change the subject before she said something she would regret. He had moved on with no anger—she was moving on, too, but she couldn't lose the anger. Not yet, anyway.

"Can I ask you something?" She got up and went to help clear the dishes away, hoping it would help her calm down.

"Sure," he said, opening the dishwasher.

"If you and your brothers have a need to own this ranch so you'll have a legacy for your families, why aren't any of you married?"

He placed a glass in the dishwasher.

"I figure Jess and Colt just haven't met their matches yet. Sure, I want to leave a legacy, but for me that includes helping Colt and Jess build theirs for their family. I'm not getting sidetracked until I do that. My brothers will fall in love, and I'm determined that this ranch will be something they can be proud of when that happens. That's my legacy."

It suddenly made sense. He was the protector. His mother had left him in charge of Colt and Jess, and he was doing that. It didn't matter that they were strong, capable men; this was a challenge he'd accepted, and he was seeing it through. He was taking pride in himself, like the verse said.

Focused. That's what he was, just like she was focusing on her riding. But he was also thinking about God's direction in his life, too. She was more amazed by him with every moment that passed. "We're a lot alike, it seems, Luke Holden." Not exactly, but sort of— what was she saying? She'd handed him the emptied glasses. He took them and his fingers brushed hers. His touch sent her pulse skittering. They were standing close enough for her to see the light flicker in the depths of his eyes.

"How's that?" he asked, his voice smooth as he held her gaze.

Thoughts of his arms around her slammed into her. "We…we're alike—" Her mind went totally blank and she had no clue what she'd been about to say.

He cocked a brow ever so slightly, and one corner of his lips turned up. "We're both focused," he prompted. "And we know what we want."

Yes, that was true. She leaned against the counter and he did the same, his arm touching hers as he watched her, amusement lighting his eyes. Her heart suddenly was pounding inside her chest, and there was a flutter of butterflies in her stomach. "Yes, that's right," she managed. Did she truly know what she wanted? Looking at Luke, she seemed to forget for a minute.

"Are you all right?" he asked, leaning closer, her heart thumping like a rabbit's foot.

In the other room, Tate stirred and whimpered. The sound was like an ice chest of cold water being dumped on her head. She snapped to attention and immediately put distance between them.

"Gotta check on Tater Man!" As if on cue, he started crying. Scooping him up she hugged him to her—unceremoniously, using him as a shield again as she turned back to Luke. He had stopped at the edge of the large area rug. He looked about as uncomfortable as she was—she had a feeling he'd felt exactly what she'd been feeling. There was no way to kid themselves that they weren't attracted to each other. But that was all it was. Attraction. Nothing more…well, admiration. And that was dangerous to her.

"I need to change his diaper," she said, glad to have an excuse to bring this impromptu dinner to a close.

He yanked a thumb toward the door behind him. "I need to head out. I've stayed longer than I should have."

She wasn't about to suggest that he stick around—oh, no, that was not a good idea. She held Tate closer. "Okay, see you later. Sorry there was no meeting."

"You mean sorry we were set up?" He gave a light smile.

Was she sorry? Not exactly. "That's right. Watch out for the posse in the bushes."

He laughed as he strode toward the door. "I'll let myself out. You tend to that little guy."

She trailed him to the front door but held back a few feet. "See you."

"Yeah." He opened the door and grabbed his hat from the hat rack next to the door. Snugging it onto his head, holding her gaze the whole time. "Good night, Montana. You aren't half-bad."

She laughed. "You, either."

Grinning, he strode out, closing the door behind him. Through the bank of glass windows she watched him stride off toward his truck. His stride long and sure, his shoulders straight—she liked the proud, strong look of him. Especially after hearing about his childhood. "Not half-bad at all," she said to Tate. "Not half-bad at all."

Luke couldn't get the picture of Montana holding Tate in her arms out of his mind. Her bright eyes, her soft skin, and the gentle look of a loving mother touched him. He thought about that all the way home. She was focused, perceptive and interesting. He was drawn to that. As a rule, he didn't talk about his personal life on his dates. At least not like he and Montana had done. He didn't care to rehash a past that he hadn't enjoyed nor been able to control. He didn't like thinking about his dad. What kind of man would destroy his own life and then almost destroy his own sons? It was something he'd never understood. And nothing he'd ever talked about. Though there had been a moment there when he'd been tempted to tell Montana everything. He'd been tempted to see what her take on his dad would be. How she'd analyze Leland Holden. She'd pegged his mom's motivations dead-on. Like hitting the nail with a hammer in one strong strike she'd done so with his mom. It was almost as if she understood because of insight. Deep insight that only came from a true understanding.

Pulling into his carport, he turned off the ignition and sat staring out at the darkness. What in Montana Brown's background gave her that kind of insight into his life?

Chapter Eleven

"Luke! Watch it—the calf," Jess yelled from where he was separating the calves from the herd. The air was thick with the sound and scent of dusty cattle.

"Sorry," Luke said. "My fault." He was supposed to be opening the gate.

"Where's your head, man? That's the fourth calf I've had to cut out again."

"It's on Montana," Colt called from where he was giving shots at the chute. "I heard he got set up last night."

"Oh, really now," Jess rested his arm on his saddle horn. "Why haven't I heard about this? I'm in town way more than Colt."

"I thought we were working cattle. Not talking about my private life."

That got hoots of laughter from both his brothers.

Colt gave the calf its shot, looking up as he released it from the steel chute. "Private. What's private about it? All they're talking about between conversations about the rodeo and festival is you and Montana. What

I heard at the diner first thing this morning was the posse got you out there to a false committee meeting. App said you had dinner with Montana."

"How did App know?" Luke asked.

"He said Hank came in around six. Esther Mae had been out at Norma Sue's—at the real committee meeting—and came home all excited about you and Montana having dinner together."

Luke scowled. "How did they know we had dinner?"

"So you *did* have dinner." Jess was all ears now.

"I'm not denying it. I went out there thinking I was going to a committee meeting and it was just Montana watching Tate while Lacy and Clint went on a date. We ended up having dinner and talking."

"So, what did you think of her?" Colt stared at him through the bars of the squeeze chute. "I figured she might have sent you packing. Did she know it was a setup?"

"She realized what was going on before I did. And I like her. She's…" He paused, thinking about the evening. "She's observant and funny and interesting."

He saw the wide-eyed look that passed between his brothers. "What's wrong with that?"

Jess straightened in the saddle. "Nothin'. We didn't say anything. You, on the other hand, said plenty."

"I had dinner with her at her cousin's house with a sleeping baby. What's the big deal?" He wasn't sure why he was being so testy, but he was. He'd had dinner with other women, no big deal.

"Colt, you ever seen him get defensive over a woman?"

"Nope. Never. What's up with that, bro?"

"I'm defensive because we're supposed to be working."

"Not buying that." Jess shook his head. "You're the one letting the cows run free because your mind's on some cute cowgirl."

True, but Luke wasn't going to give them the satisfaction of an answer just so they could hound him endlessly. He could give as good as he got, though, and if roles were reversed, he'd more than likely be the one digging and teasing. He looked nonplussed. "Colt, don't you need to be done here and hit the road? I thought you had a string of bull-riding events lined up starting tonight?"

He grinned, pulled the lever and let the vaccinated calf free. "I've got time. Don't worry about me. I've got *plenty* of time to hear all about you and Montana."

Luke figured, sometimes it didn't pay to have brothers. There was just no pity there at all.

"Seriously, Luke, let's talk about this. You're thirty-four. We're out here working to build this business into something that we can pass on to our children. Something lasting. You know you aren't getting any younger."

Colt chuckled from behind the protection of the squeeze chute. "That's right, big brother. You might want to start thinking about starting that family, so you won't be too old to play with your children."

"Jess, you're thirty, that's not far behind me. And Colt, you're twenty-eight. One of you is going to have to step up before I do."

"You like this girl?" Jess asked, all kidding aside.

Luke could have shrugged it off, made a joke, gone

back to work. But his brothers understood him like no one else. It was a bond forged by years of taking care of each other. Teasing aside, he knew he could shoot straight with them. "Yeah, I do. There's something about her drive and determination that attracts me. I honestly haven't figured out what makes her different."

"That's easy," Colt called, as if Luke had just missed the obvious. "You like her because, unlike the ones who are looking to change you when they tell you they aren't—" Luke shot him a sharp look that had Colt throwing up his hands. "Hey, I'm telling it like I heard it. As I was saying—this gal thinks like you do."

Jess tapped his hand on his thigh. "Maybe you need to not think so much about how you aren't planning on getting serious, and let things just happen. Let yourself see where this leads."

"Yeah, what could it hurt?" Colt added.

"I know y'all mean well. But do I seem unhappy to y'all? What's the deal here?"

"Nothing," Jess said. "We just thought—"

Luke interrupted him. "I'm good, okay. Or I was, up until matchmakers started zeroing in on me, setting me up. And now y'all are ganging up on me. I'm fine, and whatever I do or don't do will be at my own time and pace."

Colt grinned, teasing, "Okay, okay, no need to get all in a huff. Right, Jess?"

"Yeah," Jess said, his own grin wide across his face. "Huffy isn't good on a cowboy such as yourself. Rest easy, we're not fixin' to tie you down and haul you to the altar."

"Jerks." Luke laughed, knowing they'd pushed his

buttons and enjoyed watching him sweat bullets. "Get to work. We're burning daylight."

"What's the hurry? You got a date tonight?" Jess called, his chuckle moving wickedly over the breeze to blend with Colt's.

Luke hid his grin. *Brothers.*

The days after her "set-up dinner" with Luke flew by for Montana. She practiced her riding during the day, and helped out with Tate when she was needed. The baby spent some days with her and some with his mom and dad. The plans for the rodeo seemed to be falling in place and the excitement was building. Everywhere she went, they were talking about all the different people who'd been past residents of the tiny town who were coming back. The list included Adela's granddaughter Gabi. And Adela was very excited about that. Everyone knew that it was a long shot that any of the people would be able to actually move home. But like Norma Sue said, "Letting them come home to see the changes was a positive, and the attention they were drawing was always a good thing. Who knows, maybe some would find a way. And maybe some would fall in love."

Of course, she'd been looking right at Montana when she made that last statement. Montana'd been getting a lot of that over the last two weeks.

Ever since Luke had shown up at her house, it had been on lots of minds. She wasn't saying much, just shrugging it off with a snappy retort, finding that teasing about it was about as easy a way out as anything. And besides, she and Luke had an understanding. They both knew they weren't looking for love, and that was all that mattered.

The fact that she now found the cowboy very likable and extremely attractive was no big deal—really. It was as if knowing they were on the same page helped her relax around him. Not that they were going on any more dates, but when she saw him she was able to not be on the defensive.

There was, however, the problem of Erica. The woman had issues. Montana had run into her a couple of times, and both times had been awkward, since Erica had ignored her when Montana had spoken. One of those times had been at church—which seemed a very odd place for someone to act that way. What Montana wanted to know was what she had done to the woman. Montana noticed that she had behaved the same way to Luke when he'd given her a casual hello. If only Erica would just move on. However, Montana didn't let it bother her.

She wasn't in the wrong. Luke and Erica were not an item and never had been. He'd made it clear from the beginning that he wasn't in the market. But Erica had ignored his warning. She was out of line—she needed to accept responsibility for her mistake and move on.

Speaking of out of line, Montana was straightening up a barrel that was way off base from where it should be. One of the cowboys who worked for Clint had driven the tractor around, spreading and refreshing the dirt during lunch. He hadn't been exactly worried about where he placed her three barrels when he was done. They were way out of line—but if she could handle Erica's bad attitude, she could handle fixing a few barrels.

"Hey, cowgirl, they making you move your own barrels around these days?"

At the sound of Luke's voice, she spun around to find him watching her from the other side of the pen. Her heart did the wacky little jangle it had started doing when he was around; she promptly ignored it. Giving him a cocky grin, she walked toward where he was standing. "Yup, I can't prove it, but I think Clint's trying to get me in better shape for the event, so he told Bill to move them way out of line, so I'd have to wrestle 'em into place. It's a workout but it's all good." She flexed her muscle. "These babies are growing by the day."

He squinted at her arm. "You sure you call that a muscle?"

The beeper he wore on his belt suddenly went off. He snatched it up and stared at the message. "Fire at Esther Mae Wilcox's place," he said, his words clipped. "I'm on the volunteer fire department. I've got to go."

"But wait," she called, already having climbed to the top of the fence and thrown a leg over. She was about to jump to the ground when he turned, reached up and lifted her down.

"Sorry, gotta go," he said, then headed at a trot toward the exit.

Obviously, the cowboy had misunderstood, thinking her call to wait was a call for help off the fence. She jogged after him, her mind on Esther Mae's fire. She hoped it wasn't bad. "I'm going with you," she said, rounding the truck as he was yanking open his driver's side door.

He had the truck cranked by the time she had her door opened and had slung herself into the seat beside him.

"You sure?" he asked, already backing out to turn the truck in the right direction.

"Sure I'm sure. You might need help, so hit the gas, buddy!"

He nodded and punched the gas. They peeled out of the drive, and from across the pasture she could see Clint's black truck spraying gravel as he tore up one of the roads snaking deeper into the ranch. Clint and several of his ranch hands were on the volunteer fire department, too.

The sun beamed down hot as they sped past the area designated for the festival. Starting tomorrow, which was Wednesday, the vendors would start turning up, and by Friday the festivities would begin. But none of that mattered as she thought of Esther Mae and Hank. And the fire. She prayed they were all right. Prayed for their safety.

Luke snatched up a radio handset and shot questions at the dispatcher. It was a grease fire. Esther Mae had called it in. Hank was home, but out in the pasture somewhere. She was trying to put it out herself.

"That's not good," Luke said, his expression growing grimmer. "Esther Mae is so excitable, she might get burned if she tries to deal with burning grease."

"The house isn't worth her getting hurt." Montana started praying harder for God to protect Esther Mae, and that the fire would be easily contained.

The radio crackled, alive with communication, as men all across the community reacted. "You don't have to go to town for your gear?" she asked when she realized they weren't heading toward town.

"It's in my tack box in the truck bed. Clint will go to town and get the truck."

"There isn't any smoke," Montana observed a few minutes later as the house came into view. "Oh, look there they are! On the front porch." Relief swamped her.

"They look okay. That's a blessing."

"Oh, my gracious!" Esther Mae exclaimed, flying off the porch to greet them with excited hugs. "Y'all got here so fast! Thank the good Lord."

Her yellow shirt was smeared with something white, and her flaming red hair and face looked like they had been rained on with flour. Her long, yellow shorts were streaked and the bottoms of them were dripping wet. Her right side was splotchy with water, too. Hank sat on the porch looking glum, totally drenched from head to toe. He held an ice pack to his forehead, and beneath it was a large purple knot.

"What happened to you?" Montana and Luke almost said in unison. Other trucks were pulling in behind them, and there was small crowd of firefighting cowboys gathering, asking questions, too. Hank frowned and didn't look at all enthused to speak.

"Oh, Hank came to my rescue…" Esther Mae gushed, ever so happy to share. "At least he tried. See, I was frying up some catfish for lunch. And Norma Sue called on the phone—" She paused, shooting Luke and Montana a pink-tinged glance. "We were, um, talk-

ing—and I walked into the other room for a few minutes and forgot about the grease. When I came back in,
it had started flaming. I screamed and called 911—I
still had the phone in my hand. Then I ran to the door
and shouted, 'Fire!' Hank was working in the barn and
I was sure hoping he could hear me."

Hank rolled his eyes and shook his head, looking
more and more like he had a bigger headache coming
on than the goose egg growing on his forehead.

"Did you get that bump when you were putting the
fire out?" Montana asked.

Hank grunted, turned a deep shade of magenta.
"Not exactly."

"See, I shouted for Hank to bring water. I meant the
water hose, but I guess the first thing that hit him was
the cow pond. He grabbed up a bucket and bolted toward that pond as fast as a man his age can go. I don't
know what I was more shocked at, him running or the
fire! Well, I turned back to the kitchen and the flames
were shooting up toward the ceiling, I gasped and let go
of the door, and you aren't going to believe this, but the
wind suddenly came up out of nowhere, slammed that
door back, ramming it up against the wall so hard that
it shook the shelves on the wall above the fire flaming
on the stove. The giant can of baking soda sitting up
there fell off the shelf, knocking the lid off, and showered down on the fire and me like rain from the good
Lord! It was a plum beautiful sight—and a miracle for
certain." Esther Mae blinked back tears and beamed
happily at them all.

Everyone was silent, glad the fire was out, amazed

how it had happened, but still puzzled. What about Hank?

It was suddenly apparent that whatever had happened to Hank must have been embarrassing, and no one was asking questions. Montana had to know, though.

"So, what about Hank?" she asked. Everyone leaned in a little closer.

Esther Mae's head tilted. "I hurried to holler at Hank that it was okay. He'd just reached the pier and was breathing hard, but when I yelled he looked at me and he tripped."

"Yep, I tripped."

Esther Mae placed her hand on his shoulder and looked down at him. "Tripped on the edge of the water, and it's shallow and muddy there. He skidded across that muddy water and slammed his head right into the pier. I had to run down there and fish him out."

Hank raised his head up, ice pack and all, and met Montana's eyes first. And the most amazing thing happened…his lip twitched at the edge. His eyes twinkled, like the first glow of a star at night. When his lip twitched more, so did Montana's. And then Hank chuckled.

Montana chuckled with him, and then like popcorn beginning to pop, chuckles erupted one by one through the group.

"Oh, Hank," Esther Mae cooed, plopping down beside him and hugging him. "That's my man. And you really did stop the fire. You're the one who put that monster can of baking soda up there, just in case there ever was a fire."

Hank patted his wife's hand and beamed when she leaned in and gave him a kiss on the cheek. And suddenly all in the world was right.

Chapter Twelve

"That was the sweetest thing I've ever seen," Montana said. She and Luke were driving back toward the ranch. "Hank was so embarrassed, but then it hit him that it could have been so much worse."

"Esther Mae cracks me up," Luke added. "I didn't think she was ever going to get the story told. And there sat poor Hank, dripping wet, with the lump on his forehead growing by the second."

Montana laughed at Luke's humor. "Here I thought you were feeling sympathetic toward Hank's situation."

"I was. Poor guy. I knew something was up when he wasn't saying anything. But I couldn't figure out how he got so wet."

"I'm just glad they were all right. And their house looked pretty good, considering what it could have been. I'm sure it will smell like burned grease for a few days, but for there not to be much flame damage shocked me."

"They were lucky. And what little damage that was

done, Cole Turner can have changed out in a day. Fixing disasters is what he does."

She sighed, feeling good. "I'm really glad it turned out like that."

He glanced at her and slowed at a dirt road that split off the main road. "Thanks for coming along. You were great in there, helping clean up like you did."

"I didn't do much. Not after Norma Sue and Adela arrived."

"You got it started until you got booted out."

Montana hooted. "Ha. It was so obvious that they wanted us to leave and go get this trailer full of calves you said you needed to move."

"Are you sure you're okay with this?"

"I guess so. I know this is just your way of trying to get another date, but really, Luke, getting Esther Mae to almost burn her house down is taking it a bit too far."

"Yeah, that's even too extreme for the matchmakers."

"True, but how about you?"

His eyes twinkled when he looked at her. "I'm thinking right now that it's all working out real fine."

Montana felt a warm glow fill her at his words and the look in his eyes. She hadn't expected flattery. "You surprise me," she said quietly.

"Yeah? How's that?"

"You're sweet. I mean, I thought Hank and Esther Mae were sweet but I wasn't expecting you to be sweet."

"And you say that with such conviction."

She laughed at his dry tone. "Thanks, I really try

hard," she said drily, mocking his tone and making them both smile at the teasing banter between them.

His ranch was neat, the wood fence around the small ranch house was old but had a fresh coat of black on it and the house looked as if it had just been painted, too. The white exterior gleamed in the clear May sunshine, making the black shutters and front door stand out. She liked the way it looked. The barn was a faded red that had withstood many years, but looked sturdy and very neat. She could tell just looking around that Luke and his brothers hadn't bought the newest place in town, but it had good bones, and the land surrounding it was flat and full of cattle. Like most places it looked like the lack of rain was affecting it. But it was still pretty land.

"I like your place."

He surveyed the land through the truck's windows. "Thanks. We're proud of it." They drove past the house and down the lane to a stockyard where a trailer was backed up to the loading pen. They got out and he opened the gate. A truck whipped in as they were getting out and a man hopped from it.

"You must be the one and only Montana Brown." Striding up and holding out his hand, he grinned. "I'm Jess, Luke's brother."

"Hi, Jess. I'm almost afraid to ask what you've heard about me."

He gave a cocky grin, his amber eyes lit with humor. "Oh, it's all good, I guess, if you don't mind being the talk of the town and all."

"The matchmakers?"

He chuckled. "And App and Stanley. And Sam.

Stanley was singing your praises again this morning when I went in for coffee and eggs. Seems you've made a friend for life, rescuing him with warm soup and your big, bright smile."

Montana felt warm inside, knowing she'd done the right thing taking that soup to him. "Luke helped, too."

Jess gave his brother an appraising glance. "He drove, no big deal. It's the smile and warm heart of a pretty woman that Stanley remembers. That's what helped him heal up 'lickety-split,' as he put it this morning."

"I didn't do anything but be the delivery girl."

"So be it, but you'll have a fan rootin' for you loud and long come Friday night when you're out there blasting around those barrels."

"After the fire today, she'll have a couple of others doing the same where Esther Mae and Hank Wilcox are concerned."

"Fire? What fire? Did I miss something?"

Luke filled him in on what had just transpired out at Esther Mae's. When he was done, Jess flashed his pearly whites at her again. She had a feeling he was a heartbreaker like his brother. Like his brother, she wondered if he walked around grinning and smiling and leaving a trail of women behind with broken hearts and dashed dreams of happily-ever-after.

"Y'all keep it up and you'll both be up for the Mule Hollow Good Samaritan Award." Jess gave them a thumbs-up.

Luke grunted and turned to the pen full of calves. "I'm fixin' ta move 'em in if you'll work this end."

"Sure thing." Jess winked at her and then went to man the gate.

Luke was taking the teasing fairly good-naturedly. She wondered, when she wasn't around, if it was better or worse. "I'll help," she said, and followed Luke into the pen.

"You don't need—"

"Hey, I came to help, remember? And I do know a little about livestock."

"As you wish. Just stay clear of them. I don't want you getting slammed up against the rails or anything."

"You got it, pardner."

They made quick work of herding the load onto the trailer, and then left the grinning Jess standing in the drive as they took off once more.

"You must get teased all the time." Her observation drew one of his nonchalant shrugs.

"It comes with baby brothers."

"Is your other brother as bad?" she asked.

"He has his moments. He's a bull rider and stays out on the road more than Jess. We don't see him as often as we like, but he's going after his dreams. He's down in Mesquite this week, riding in a PBR event. Then he'll be here late Friday night, in time to catch the bull event here in town before heading to another event on Saturday night. Like you, he has a shot at the big time if he holds out and doesn't make a mistake."

She scowled at him. "You saying I'm going to make a mistake?"

He wasn't smiling when he looked at her. "Nope. I'm saying you're good, Montana. Real good. And if you keep putting in the time and start hauling to rodeos and making the points…" He paused, gave a small, serious little smile that evoked a feeling of encouragement that shot straight to her heart. "You do that, and you know as well as I do that you can go all the way to the finals and take it."

Montana's heart clutched in her chest, looking at the sincerity in his eyes and hearing it in his words. It was her cowgirl dream, and suddenly she felt energized and lifted up.

A lump lodged in her throat. When she managed to get past it, she grinned and teased him. "You're just sayin' that because you're still trying to get a date with me?"

"That'd be an affirmative on the still-trying-to-get-a-date front. And you did just say I was sweet." He batted his chocolate eyes at her, and her insides quivered like gelatin.

"Funny man." Pretending this wasn't getting to her was hard work!

"Hey, gotta try. And what I said is the truth, too. God gives us all talent in different areas. I don't know you well enough to know what all kinds of talents He gave you, but I've known from day one of seeing you ride that when it comes to barrel racing, you've got it. He loaded you up with that talent, and with drive and heart, too. It's an unbeatable combination. You don't need to waste it."

There was a lot the handsome cowboy could have said. A lot she would have expected only a few weeks earlier from her first impressions of him. This wasn't any of it.

This touched her deeper than he could know. "Thank you," she said, unable to find the right words. His smile warmed her heart. Suddenly feeling like the inside of the truck was too small, she studied the countryside as they rode. They were quiet the rest of the way back to the ranch. When he pulled up to the barn, she was relieved. She needed some space. She might have been quiet on the ride, but her thoughts had been full of Luke and what he'd said. *He believed in her.*

She found that extremely appealing.

That she could handle, but it wasn't that she was thinking about. Nope. She was thinking about a kiss.

She'd been curious about his past, curious about his thoughts and what made the cowboy tick. And now he'd gone and had her wondering what it would be like to be held in the arms of a man who believed in her. Mostly, she wondered what it would feel like to have his lips meet hers.

Yep, her feet had just lost touch with the bottom of the pond and she was dog-paddling in murky waters. She wasn't supposed to be wanting to kiss anybody! She wasn't supposed to be thinking about falling in love!

But sometimes a gal couldn't control her thoughts, especially when a man said all the right things—meant them.

That was exactly why, the minute they got to the ranch, she made her excuses and headed back to the house with a closed door between them.

She needed time to get her head on straight.

On Thursday, the ranch was buzzing with activity. Lacy had taken off work for the next three days and it was a good thing. It was chaos. Vendors were pulling into the ranch lane with their snow cone trailers, dog-on-a-stick shacks, kettle-corn setups and so much more. Montana was able to hole up in the arena and practice during the morning, but it was impossible soon after that. Livestock was arriving by the trailer loads, too. And the bulls! Hulking bulls that looked as mean as the reputations that preceded them, began being delivered from various sources.

Luke was in and out, moving animals and helping make certain all manner of things were taken care of for the rodeo. Montana had been thinking about him more than was good, and tried to avoid him as much as possible. Since there was so much going on with the rodeo, avoiding him wasn't all that difficult.

She was with Lacy when Lilly and Cort Wells came into the barn. They were in charge of the petting zoo on both Friday and Saturday, but also helped with the rodeos at night. Samantha, their mischief-making donkey, was always the star attraction at the zoo, and she was going to be housed in a stall in the barn on Friday night.

They were a great couple, and were in the process of adopting a set of twins. Montana laughed when they told her how they met and how Samantha had had a part in their matchmaking. From what they said, she was an escape artist that liked to roam instead of stay in her stall. Because of this, Lilly was a little worried about her getting loose and interrupting the rodeo, so they'd come to look at her stall to see what precautions needed to be made to ensure she didn't escape.

Montana went with them to check things out, and

had to agree that it would need a little something to hold it shut better. All a smart animal would have to do was nudge the latch up with its nose and be free. Not a good thing.

The matchmaking posse drove up just as they were exiting the barn. Cort went to find Clint. Lilly, Lacy and Montana went to help the posse set up the concession stand.

"Hold your horses," Norma Sue said when Esther Mae started toward the grill. "You are not getting near the grill."

"I'm not, but I wouldn't have caught anything on fire if you hadn't called me," Esther Mae shot back with a chuckle, looking happy. "I tell you girls, there is nothing like a near miss to make a body realize how blessed they are. I very nearly lost my house. Of course, a house is just a house, and my Hank banged his head on the pier and nearly drowned. If I hadn't been there— now that would have been a loss I couldn't have stood. I'm a very blessed woman."

As she was speaking, everyone had jumped in and started organizing different areas. Lacy was putting cups up on a shelf and paused.

"I know what you mean, Esther Mae. When I finally got pregnant with Tate, I was just so overjoyed. I really, really was. I mean, I'd finally come to grips with the fact that God might have a different plan for me and Clint. Like he did with you and Cort, Lilly. But then, when I conceived…I felt so very blessed. It's amazing the way we can take things for granted, isn't it?"

"It really is," Lilly joined in. "Me and Cort understood, even before we were married, that he couldn't have children. We felt blessed that we had Joshua." She smiled, showing off her dimples. "My grannies might not have ever had any luck with men, but I tell you, I got such a treasure in Cort. He might not be Joshua's biological daddy but he *is* his daddy. And he is going to be the most wonderful daddy to our new boys."

"Yes, he is," Adela said, opening napkins and placing them in a holder. "Psalms 107:21 tells us to give thanks to the Lord for his unfailing love and his wonderful deeds for men." She smiled sweetly. "I love when I hear young people like you two giving Him the glory He so deserves. He likes it, too."

Montana was filling the ice chest with sodas and was glad she was off to the side, away from everyone. Her thoughts were filled suddenly with how disgruntled she'd been feeling about her parents' divorce and the way her life had been before coming here to Mule Hollow. She didn't look up as she took soda after soda and placed it in the insulated container. She felt so deeply ashamed. In thinking about the things in her life that she was *dis*satisfied with, had she lost sight of the blessings God had bestowed on her? The thought settled on her like a mudslide.

Chapter Thirteen

"This has been a long one," Jess said at the end of the day. "See you in the morning, bro," he called, looking at Luke out the open window of his truck.

"I'm not far behind you," Luke said. "It's going to be a long day tomorrow, too." After watching Jess leave, he headed toward his truck but found himself detouring into the barn, heading toward Murdock's stall. Montana had disappeared in that direction earlier. With the festival there on the premises, it was a fairly congested area, and he'd been lucky to see her at all.

He found her in the far corner, sitting alone on a five-gallon bucket. "What's up? You look like you lost your best friend. Are you worn out?"

She looked up at him with serious eyes, more blue than green in the shadows. "Have you ever realized you were a jerk?"

This didn't sound good. "What did I do now?"

Her eyes widened and she huffed a short laugh. "No, not *you*. *I'm* the jerk."

Her gaze shifted from him to some far-off place in

her thoughts. He spied another feed bucket, snagged it up, flipped it over and sat down in her line of vision. "You aren't a jerk. Talk to me."

"I was listening to everyone working in the concession stand talk about all their blessings. Everyone was looking at all the good things God's done in their lives. Despite the fact that there were lots of bad things happening. It made me think about where my head has been since I came here. I honestly can't remember the last time I actually thanked God for all the good things He's done for me. And He has given me tons of things to be thankful for—like coming here, for instance. It's been wonderful to have Lacy and Clint's home to come to, and to have a place to ride Murdock. It's been great to spend time with Tate, Lacy and Clint."

"And me?" he teased.

"Yes, it's been a real blessing getting to know you. And that's a big shock to me."

He dipped his brows into a mocking scowl. "Hey, you were on a roll till that."

She gave a light huff, and seemed to relax doing so. "I'm just being honest. I did think you were a bit of a jerk when I first met you. But then I changed my mind."

"I'm glad about that. And even if you hadn't changed it, you still aren't a jerk. Lots of people lose sight of the good things in their lives when they've got junk from their past filling up their days. It's not always easy to let things go. Believe me, I know that from experience." He felt as if something about her parents' divorce was bothering her, but he wouldn't ask. She'd tell him if she wanted. He wasn't sure how exactly she viewed him. Sure, they'd become friends in a way. It was a little hard to explain *what* they'd become. He knew that he enjoyed being around her, his world did tricks when he was around her…he was more relaxed when he was near her, but at the same time he was tense. He couldn't concentrate when she was around because he kept getting distracted lately with the idea of kissing her. If he kissed her, she'd probably slap him and call him a jerk for sure. Which wouldn't be a good thing. Wait! What was he doing? Here he was sitting here, trying to figure out what was wrong with Montana and suddenly he was thinking about kissing?

Yup, not good.

"I'm not sure what's bothering you, but if I can help, I'm here." She could choose to talk or not. He realized he wished she would feel comfortable enough to talk to him. He wanted to get closer to her. The idea startled him a bit. It was different than when he'd dated other women. Different than just feeling attracted to a woman. He was trying to wrap his emotions around it and understand.

"I've come here to try and fulfill my dream of being a cowgirl. That's what I'm doing. But I gave it up years ago to become the career woman that my dad wanted me to be. You're supposed to do what your parents want—right?"

Not exactly. He thought of his dad. If he'd done what his dad had wanted, he'd be wallowing in self-pity, spending his days looking for the next bottle.

But that was not what Montana needed to hear. "To an extent," he said, quietly finding his way. The anger that he'd sensed in her from day one had crept back into her voice. Her attitude was locked up with it.

"I knew what I wanted to do with my life. I could have been a champion. I may still be able to be one—but I've been filled with a lot of resentment lately, and it's overshadowed everything in my life these last few months. I turned everything upside down on a whim, and came out here to stay with Lacy."

"My first question is, why all of a sudden are you having these feelings? Didn't you resent it all when you gave up your dream?"

"My dad." Her words were full of anger. She took a breath, visibly calming herself as she started over. "My dad pushed me to be what he felt was of greater status. He was very aware of how and what others thought of us as a family. He thought riding was a great thing for me to do during my school years, but that should stop there. I was expected to go to college and get the accounting degree he felt would be appropriate. *Pro rodeo cowgirl* just didn't have the right ring to it."

Montana had been the good girl and done as her dad wanted. "But why are you suddenly rebelling and doing what you want? Why all the resentment now? The divorce?"

She stood and walked a few paces away before she turned, and he saw the flash of fire in her eyes. "Partly. But mostly because of his affair. When I found out about that, I hit the road."

"You can't let this eat you up. Believe me, I know."

He went to her, wanting to brush the strands of hair from her face that had escaped her braid. "I can remember the first time I understood that my dad had a drinking problem. Like I told you before, I was young. I don't even remember how old I was, but I remember the fights my parents had. There was nothing physical, only bitter blowouts. This particular day, my mom was crying in the bathroom and I asked my dad why he always made my momma cry. He told me she'd known he drank when she married him, and so she had no reason to always be harping on him. And then I watched him lift the bottle up and drink the whole thing without stopping. It made me sick watching. He looked at me and told me for the first time—of many—that I would be just like him." He paused, remembering. It still made him sick thinking about it. "I never will forget that. I was young but I knew then that I didn't want to be like him. I wasn't sure if what he said was a fact—being young I didn't understand exactly. I just knew I didn't want it. I grew up quick after that."

"I'm so sorry." She laid her hand on his arm and the warmth seeped into his skin.

"It happened a very long time ago. And like I told you the other night, God helped me move on."

"Still, you don't get angry?"

"Yeah, actually, I did. I didn't have the feeling of betrayal that's shadowing you, but I resented that he was my dad. Unlike you, there were no expectations for me. You're resentful because you were pinned to your dad's hopes and dreams because you were doing what you knew was right." He could tell that hit a mark. "You were honoring God's plan by honoring your dad, doing what he expected of you."

"And he let me down."

"Yes, he did. My dad let me down, too, but it was out in the open. No surprises. That was just the way it was. Whereas you were blindsided by it. And now, the way I see it, you're still staggering from being thrown off the bull and mowed down. You're entitled to some resentment."

She stiffened, pulling her shoulders back. "I've got that. No doubt about it."

"Look. We don't get to pick our parents. But we get to pick who we'll become. That's what I'm doing. I don't know if you know about Clint's mom, but in a way, she did what your dad did. She left, and it was real hard on Clint and his dad. But Mac remained hardworking, honest and someone I could look up to. I started working for him the day we moved to town when I was fifteen. He was a great influence in my life."

"I've heard Clint talk about his dad. He built this ranch on hard work and honesty. Clint has carried that out and expanded every aspect. Lacy is so proud of him and the man that he is."

She sighed, looking lost. "I used to be proud of my dad. I believed he was an honorable man. I believed he loved my mother. I've been torn up over this—mad, furious, and torn by the idea that I'm somehow supposed to forgive him for making me feel this way. *Enough* of this." She waved her hand, as if shooing the thoughts away. "Anyway—it hit me today that this stuff is all I've been focusing on. It's horrible how I've forgotten what good things God has done for me. I'm going to try to be more positive."

He put his hands on her shoulders. Couldn't help it. "Good. That's what you need to do for now. You can deal with these feelings later, but you need to clear your head tonight and get ready for tomorrow. You need to put this all out of your head and get in the zone. Murdock is counting on you." He grinned, knowing she wanted to make her horse proud. "You've got this in the bag if you just get your focus on the ride tomorrow night. Maybe it's nerves shaking you up right now."

"Maybe. Some of it."

"Focus, Montana Brown—cowgirl extraordinaire." That got a tiny smile from her and he touched his forehead against hers. When she didn't draw away, that got a big smile from him. "Ride like the wind tomorrow night and make yourself proud." Pulling back, he looked sternly into her eyes. "Don't ride with anger. Don't ride to prove anything to anyone but yourself. And God. He's the one who gave you this talent, and you've been working hard to polish it up. That's all you can do, is give it your all. This other stuff…it'll work itself out in time."

She leaned her head on his chest and nodded. He pulled her into his arms and hugged her. Just held her close, giving her the comfort and support that he knew she needed. He liked being able to be there for her in this moment. Again, she drew him, just as she'd been doing from the first day he saw her.

And he wasn't exactly sure what to do about it.

Chapter Fourteen

It was a gorgeous, sunny day for the festival.

"Isn't that just the cutest thing," Esther Mae cooed, waving at Tate. He was dressed in a baby cowboy outfit, complete with chaps and was sitting on the top of the fattest little donkey Montana had ever seen.

Samantha the donkey was adorable. She was gray with white whiskers, and so fat that she had rolls rippling from her shoulders to her hips. She had big, brown, mischievous eyes, and when she batted her eyelashes it made Montana wonder what the little gal was thinking about. Tate was loving his time spent being held on her back. There was no doubt that, with all the cowboys in his life, Tate would be a cowboy himself someday.

"He loves it," Lacy said, beaming at him as she held him. He stuffed his fist in his mouth, grinning at his mom, then everyone else, when they oohed at him. He was enjoying being the center of attention. At six months old, he was already a big flirt with his big blue eyes.

"Yoo-hoo, Luke," Esther Mae hollered suddenly, startling everyone including Samantha, who popped her head up, looking past Montana to see what the fuss was. Everyone, including Montana, turned to see Luke striding toward them.

"I thought you were fixin' to walk past us," Esther Mae said, looking more mischievous than Samantha ever thought about.

Luke's gaze met Montana's and she saw his own glint of mischief. "I thought about it, Esther Mae, but with all you pretty women standing over here, I wouldn't have been able to pass y'all by."

Montana almost laughed at the twinkle in Luke's eyes. The instant she'd heard Esther Mae yell his name, her pulse had jumped into overdrive. He'd been so supportive last night, and she was still mesmerized by how safe and comforted she'd felt, wrapped in his arms. She'd had a hard time pulling back and watching him leave. Her heart had sighed as he'd driven away, leaving her standing on the front porch. She was glad the house was silent as she'd entered because she was sure Lacy would have seen her float up the stairs.

Montana Brown, cowgirl wannabe, was in danger of falling in love.

"What are you doing right now?" Norma Sue asked, walking over to stand near him. Hooking her thumbs in the straps of her overalls, she studied him intently. "You don't look like you got much sleep last night."

Montana looked closer at him, and didn't see what Norma Sue was talking about. The man looked absolutely perfect. His coffee-colored eyes looked bright and alert to her. They widened at the ranch woman's comment.

"I slept like a baby."

"Good!" Esther Mae exclaimed. "Then you can take this one—" she shocked Montana by placing her hands on Montana's back and pushing her toward him "—over to the competitions and join in. I hear they're going to have a three-legged race any minute, and that's always a good one to—"

Adela stepped up and broke Esther Mae off. "It's a good one to get the heart pumping and the laughter flowing."

Esther Mae crossed her arms over her peacock-blue blouse and harrumphed. "It's also good to get to know your partner. And don't forget about the octopus ride!"

"I wasn't planning on joining in any games," Montana said.

Lacy chuckled, looking at Tate. She rubbed noses with him, and he grabbed at her hair. "Oh, no, you don't. Hey." She continued looking at Montana. "I'm going to go feed him and then I'm coming back to defend my championship title in the cow chip throwing competition. I'm officially challenging you. Every cowgirl needs to know how to toss one of those bad boys."

"I wasn't—" Montana was feeling a bit trapped. The light in Luke's eyes told her he knew how she felt, but he was also very amused by the situation. He had no clue how trapped she was feeling, how seriously her feelings were changing where he was concerned. She'd known it the moment she opened her eyes that morning. Looking at Lacy, she couldn't say no. "Okay," she agreed. "I'll be there, and you better come prepared. Because, believe it or not, I can toss a chip a very long way."

And so, she found herself walking through the crowd beside Luke, and feeling as if she was heading down a wrong-way street with her hands tied behind her back. Luke, on the other hand, looked like he was on the same road but totally enjoying the crazy ride, judging by the twitch of his lips when he looked at her.

"So you actually throw cow patties?"

"Haven't done it in a while—probably a decade—but I can."

As they wove through the crowd, he gave her a disbelieving glance. "You touched them?"

"That'd be a *nooo.* I wore gloves. Those things are—well, you know what they are. I'm not touching it. But I can sure give my cousin a run for the money."

"I have no doubt about that. How about tonight? Are you ready for the barrel racing?"

"Yes, I am. But I think the three-legged race is going to be a great warm-up for me. The posse was right. This is a good thing, you and me."

"Stuck like glue," he said.

Montana chuckled. "That's right. You and me, babe."

Luke laughed. The low, husky sound made Montana's pulse dance.

They walked past booth after booth of handmade crafts, tons of jewelry and half a dozen food trailers. Luke stopped in front of a burger booth. "I've got to eat something before we race."

"That's good thinking. I wouldn't want to lose because you were slacking."

"Oh, you don't have to worry about that. I can handle myself."

She put her hands on her hips and made herself not laugh. "A little competitive, are we?"

He tapped her nose with his index finger. "And don't you forget it."

"Then we're a great match." The words were out of her mouth before she realized what she was saying. Looking at him, his eyes twinkling, she decided maybe now would be a good time to stop speaking. The look in his eyes told her he might be wondering the same thing. Suddenly she was wondering, *were* they a great match? She flashed back to being in his arms, and it struck her like lightning that they were.

She took a step back. Her arm had been lightly touching his, standing in line. Suddenly, feeling a little faint, she wanted to sit down or pass out. She didn't have time to be getting crazy. She didn't have time to be thinking things she hadn't been thinking in a very long time.

She didn't trust men. Right?

She didn't want a man in her life. Right?

She didn't want to fall in love. Right?

But he was great. He was unbelievably sincere. He was funny. He was…easy to fall in love with.

Oh, my goodness—she was in trouble.

His eyebrows crinkled as he looked at her strangely. "Are you okay?"

She slapped a hand to her stomach. "Nerves," she squeaked, gasping a little.

"Really? You're white. Come on." Taking her arm, he led her out of the line and toward a spot behind all the booths, away from the traffic. They'd used square bales of hay in some areas to give seating to weary festival goers, and Luke spotted a pile of extra hay. Leading her to it immediately, he gently pushed her down to sit.

"I'm fine," she said. "Really I am." She was seeing black spots.

He knelt down in front of her and his concerned brown eyes seemed to melt into her as he searched hers. He touched her forehead with his fingers. She gasped at his touch and then stuck her head between her knees and gasped for air.

"Breathe, Montana, breathe." Luke rubbed Montana's back. He wasn't sure what was going on. One minute she'd been fine—teasing and rattling on and making him laugh. Then all of a sudden, she'd turned as white as a sheet and was threatening to pass out.

"I'm fine," she groaned after a minute, and sat up, looking more stunned than anything.

She was staring at him like he had two heads. "Did I do something wrong? Are you sure this is about your ride tonight?" He'd been thinking about her all night long. He'd never had a woman on his mind like he had Montana. He'd done his best to steer clear of her all morning because he wanted to see her so bad. Maybe she'd wanted him to show up this morning. Maybe she was mad at him. Maybe that was a good thing— he wasn't certain.

"No, you didn't do anything wrong."

He leaned forward. She sucked in a breath and leaned back, keeping him at a distance. "Okay, then what's up?"

She shook her head as if trying to clear it, and then shot up from the hay, glaring at him. "I don't want this."

"Want what?" he asked, maintaining his calm in the midst of a growing gale.

"This." She waved a hand toward him, then back toward herself. "This, this *thing* that's happening between us. And don't try and deny it, because I know you feel it, too. Or maybe you don't."

He shouldn't think she was cute. But he did. That made him smile inside. He honestly liked everything about Montana Brown, including her odd tendency to get mad at herself when she was feeling things she didn't like...or felt threatened by. He grinned at her, despite the fact that it was thoughts of him that were making her so mad.

"I do know I enjoy being around you. But right now, I'm also looking forward to you and me smoking a bunch of three-legged couples in a few minutes. You know what I think?" He scratched his jaw, then crossed his arms and studied her.

"What?" She glared at him but paused her pacing.

"I think you need to relax. You're making more out of this than it is." He needed her to calm down. "The fact is that I like you and you like me. No big deal. We're still in control of what we do with that. Right?" He nodded, slowly urging her to agree.

She looked a bit puzzled, but nodded in response to his. "Yes."

"Good, then relax and let's go win a race. And don't forget, I want to see you chuck a cow chip farther than anyone else."

Chapter Fifteen

"You ready for this?" Luke asked Montana as they tugged the feed sack over their legs. They'd tied her left leg to his right leg with the twine that Stanley handed them.

"I'm always ready for a little competition," she said, narrowing her eyes, teasingly preparing for battle. She let her gaze swing slowly around the gathering group, sizing up the competitors.

"You're looking serious. I need to warn you that I've never done this before, so I hope you don't get too disappointed."

"Hey, you need to focus, Luke Holden. Focus and get a little can-do spirit. Look at me." She took his face between her hands and turned his face toward her. "Now read my lips and repeat after me. 'I can do this.'"

He chuckled. "I can do this."

"See, it's all better now. We're going to do this, aren't we, fellas?"

Stanley and App were standing in front of them.

Each man had his arms crossed over his chest as he studied them with critical eyes.

"You might better tighten up that thar string," App grunted.

"That's right. Too much slack can lead to tripping," Stanley said, looking like he wanted to jump in and take over the tying.

Luke grinned as he reached down and studied the string once more. "I've got it handled, Stanley. Don't worry." He shook the string, noting that it was loose but comfortable.

"I don't know about that. It still looks a little loose. A loose string kin trip you up and throw off yor hop-'n'-run move."

"Hop-'n'-run move? What's that?" Montana asked, getting a kick out of Stanley's serious attitude.

"It's the way you get the job done," he said.

"Yup," App butted in. "You hop together—like this. Then you run one step together with the outside legs—like this."

Everyone around enjoyed the demonstration from Applegate. The skinny stick of a man was dressed in his starched jeans and shirt, topped off with his pristine, go-to-town straw Stetson—he'd explained to her the difference earlier, when she'd told him she liked his new hat. He'd beamed and told her it wasn't new, it was just the one he wore to church on Sunday. His everyday hat had gotten eaten by an ornery old goat at the petting zoo. "I had to go home and get my church hat—stinking goat. I couldn't be up here at the rodeo without wearing a hat." Montana smiled as she watched his demonstration carefully.

"We can do that," she said to Luke.

He nodded seriously, and showed her some of his new can-do spirit. "Sure we can. Would you mind doing that again, App? Just in case we didn't get it the first time."

App frowned. "It ain't that easy ta do. Yor tryin' ta be funny, Luke Holden, but I'm tellin' ya, this is the move ta win...." His voice trailed off when Erica walked up with a cowboy in tow. She glared at Montana and then at Luke, before she snatched the string and burlap sack from Stanley, who'd shut his mouth the instant he saw her walk up and held out the armload of bags he had to hand out.

She sat on the hay bale across from Montana and gave her the evil eye. Montana thought it was a little ridiculous that she was continuing to act the way she was. Montana looked away, while Luke was concentrating on tightening the string around their ankles. "If you tighten that any more, we aren't going to be able to feel our feet," she said in a hushed tone.

"Sorry, but I don't know how to make this better."

She knew he meant the thing between him and Erica, and not the string cutting the circulation of her foot off. Montana tried not to look at Erica, but she couldn't help herself. Erica caught her looking and glowered at her. Montana tried to let it slide by focusing on her group again, but there had to be a way to make this better. She caught App's eagle eye.

"You two 'bout ready to do this?" He hiked a bushy brow. "Ain't no call to get intimidated by a little unpleasantness."

He, of course, was talking loud enough to wake the

dead. "App, behave," Luke muttered, looking perplexed by the entire issue.

"I am. The way I see it, we're all adults here, and we can act like it." He looked sternly at Erica, reminding Montana of a schoolteacher giving a child a warning in class for misbehavior.

Erica crossed her arms in a huff and glared at the cowboy sitting beside her. He was watching the mini-drama unfolding in front of him with all the enthusiasm of a man about to get a healthy tooth pulled.

"Are you going to just sit there and let him talk to me that way?" she huffed.

The cowboy looked at her with a hint of humor in his eyes. "Hey, you're the one who threw tea all over Luke. Grow up, Erica." Without another word he dropped the string he was holding, tipped his hat and strode off. Fury destroyed Erica's face and she turned the color of an eggplant. She threw the sack down and stormed after the man who'd just humiliated her in front of everyone.

Luke had behaved like a perfect gentleman.

Montana was impressed. As hard as Erica had pushed, he'd barely even voiced his frustration. It was far better than the way she'd have handled it. Yet she knew that was the Christian way to handle it. Though he didn't talk about his faith much, in small ways she saw how he lived it. It wasn't put on to impress others. It was a true faith, a quiet faith lived through character, honesty and trying to do the right thing.

Talk about getting the wrong impression of a person right from the get-go. Boy, had she done it.

The three-legged teams got downright rough when

it came to winning. Montana soon learned that, before the next festival, she was going to have to practice if she wanted to make any kind of mark in the world of three-legged racing.

"I still can't believe we got whupped," Luke said, laughing as he and Montana made their way over to the cow chip throwing contest thirty minutes later.

"Well, the hop-'n'-run didn't work for us."

"But that wasn't all our fault. It was partly due to that other couple who tried out the maneuver, got tangled up and took us out."

"They did kind of resemble a bowling ball."

"And we were the pins."

"More like sitting ducks," Luke grumbled. "I still should have been able to get us up and make it across the finish line before we did. We got 'plum whupped' as App and Stanley would say. They were not too impressed with us." He chuckled so hard his shoulders shook. Looking at him she found herself smiling, too. It had turned into a great day.

Hooking her arm in his, she felt closer to him than she wanted to, but she wasn't worrying about it at the moment. Like he'd said earlier, she needed to relax where they were concerned.

"We did just fine," she said, then halted dead in her tracks at the cow chip competition. "Whoa, Nelly!"

The last thing she expected to see after they'd gotten whupped in the three-legged race was a line of women raring to throw cow chips! But there they were, lined up, studying the pile of chips, trying to figure out which one would fly the farthest. It was serious business.

"Looks like I have a little more competition here than just Lacy." She spotted Lacy and headed toward her. She was grinning and waving them over.

"Hey, just remember to be positive. A little can-do spirit and you've got this."

She rolled her eyes. "I think I've created a monster."

"Nope, I was like this before I met you."

"Oh, that's so good to know."

He threw an arm around her shoulder and pulled her close. Montana's stomach erupted in butterflies. She wasn't sure how much longer she could stop herself from falling for Luke.

The stands were full, and that put huge smiles on the matchmaking posse, as they worked the welcome station next to the entrance of the arena building. App and Stanley, along with Sam, were helping out at the booth, while Norma Sue's husband, Roy Don, was the announcer, and Hank, Esther Mae's husband, was helping work one of the gates. No doubt about it, they were all having a good time seeing familiar faces and reconnecting. It was part of the fun for all the older people of town, and Lacy was thrilled to be meeting them, too. She and Tate were acting as greeters. Last time Montana had glimpsed them, they'd been busy. This was why Montana was shocked when she saw Lacy come around the corner of the barn, where she and her horse were warming up before their barrel race. Lacy was clipping along just short of a run as she halted in front of Murdock.

"Looking good, Miss Queen of the Cow Chip Toss,"

she cooed, rubbing Murdock's forehead and grinning up at Montana.

"Thanks, Mrs. Barely Runner-Up." It had been big fun, and she'd only beaten Lacy by a nose. "I feel good. I'm hoping our good fortune in the cow-chip toss will continue on." Lacy's smile beamed up at her. "You can do it. You and Murdock are ready, and I know God's going to smile at your efforts."

"Thanks, Lacy, really. What are you doing out here? Don't they need your smiling face at the welcome table?"

She waved a dismissive hand. "Naw, I left little man Tate in charge for a few minutes. It's all good." She chuckled, then placed her hands on her hips and tilted her head. "I wanted to come out here and see you before your ride. Can you dismount and let's say a prayer?"

"Sure, I'd love to." The instant Montana's feet touched the ground, Lacy threw her arms around her.

"I love you, Montana! I just want you to know that. And I know, whatever happens out there, God's going to be with you. Win or lose, you've trained hard and given it your all, and you'll give God the glory. I feel it in my heart of hearts that you're going to do great. Yep, yep, yep, I do," she sang, grinning widely. Just the joyful sound of it made Montana feel positive and happy. "Now, let's talk to God, girlfriend."

Montana's heart was pounding as Lacy said a quick, heartfelt prayer for everyone's safety that night, and for victory for Montana, if it be God's will. After she finished, Montana hugged her tightly, holding on for a long moment. "Lacy, you don't know what coming here has meant to me. Thank you so much." She let go, but kept talking. "I was floundering in anger and bitterness when you reached out to me. You've helped me start finding myself again."

Lacy's brilliant blue eyes glowed with warmth as she smiled deep into Montana's. "I love you and I know you've still got a lot going on inside your heart. I know you're hurt and betrayed and all kinds of mixed-up things going on in there. I'm praying you give it all to God. Just give it to Him and let Him show you the freedom that comes from giving all your troubles over to Him. But right now, you have to focus. Let God help you do that, too. Now, get in the zone," Lacy grabbed her by the arms and turned her toward Murdock. "Get on this horse and then go out there and fly, baby, fly!"

Luke had a death grip on the rail as he watched for Montana and Murdock to step into position for the next run. Standing on an elevated walk beside the arena's chutes gave him the perfect vantage point to see both the arena floor and the alley where Montana would begin and end her run. He watched another rider as she and her horse made the last barrel and charged back toward the alley and the finish.

The times had been good tonight, and yet he knew if Montana was on her game she'd take it. But that required her focus, and he wasn't sure she was there. Not after their incident behind the popcorn stand earlier that afternoon. He was nervous as he waited for her turn to come up. Nervous knowing that if she didn't win, it could very well be his fault. He hadn't meant to cause a problem.

Roy Don called her name out over the loudspeaker,

and Luke watched Montana move into position. He almost hunkered down so that she couldn't see him. He didn't want to distract her in any way. Then he realized how ridiculous that was. There was no way she could see him amid all that was around her. Thankfully, from the intense look on her face, she wasn't thinking about anything but the barrels. This was good. This was what she needed.

Murdock snorted, ready, his body quivered with the excitement and energy, waiting to explode out of the gate the instant he got the go-ahead.

"Settle down," Luke murmured, despite the fact that Montana couldn't hear him. "You've got this, Babe. You've got this." He said a silent prayer and his fingers tightened on the cold steel bar, felt it biting into his palms.

"Not nervous, are you, bro?" Jess asked, walking up to stand beside him. "Any tighter and you're going to bend that rail."

Luke acknowledged him but didn't spare him a glance, not wanting to miss the moment Montana charged the gate. "I want her to win."

Come on, girl, give your all. Focus. She was riding hard. Murdock was blazing. They kept their pattern close, Murdock dug in as tight as he could rounding the first barrel. He was so low as he made the turn that Montana was on the level with the barrel, her knee just missing it by a breath of air as they headed toward the second barrel.

"She's doing great," Jess said.

She was, and from somewhere in the stands he heard her name being yelled above the rising roar, as others realized they were seeing an extraordinary run. He knew Stanley was one of them, and Esther Mae, too. And others she'd touched in some way. As she rounded the last barrel, as clean and close as was possible, Luke's spine tingled. His fingers had welded themselves to the rail for life or he'd have jumped over the chute into the arena. Man, he was proud of her.

Her expression was totally intense, as she and Murdock moved as one at the speed of light toward the timing point. Relief hit him the instant she passed the mark and her unbelievable time clicked onto the reading.

"She did it!" he exclaimed, grinning like a kid with a new pony.

Jess grinned back. "Yeah, bro, she did it all right. Now, do you want to fess up and admit that there's a *little* more going on between the two of you than friendship?"

Montana's adrenaline was flowing like Niagara Falls when she hopped from her horse. She'd known, coming around the last barrel, that they'd done well. Her determined sweetheart of a horse had plunged forward with all the power he possessed, and laid it all out there as he raced for the time.

The instant she was out of the alley and clear of the other riders, she leaned forward and hugged Murdock's neck. "You did great!" If they lost tonight, it would be because someone else rode exceptionally well and deserved to win. Several other riders congratulated her on a good ride. She locked her arms around Murdock's neck and buried her face in his mane. Fighting to control her emotions, she said a prayer and praised God.

They hadn't announced it yet, but she knew this had been the ride of a lifetime.

And all because of God and this amazing animal. "Thank you for not giving up on me," she whispered, talking to Murdock and God at the same time.

"Hey, cowgirl, good ride."

The sound of Luke's voice sent a thrill racing through Montana. She turned to find him smiling down at her. "Thanks! Did you see him?" she exclaimed, beaming from the inside out, so proud of Murdock she could burst. "What a champion. Murdock came through with flying colors." She patted him again and felt so proud, she knew she was glowing.

Luke laughed, stepped in and completely took her by surprise when he swung her into his arms, lifting her feet off the ground for a second. "You did okay yourself," he said, their mouths only inches away from each other as he looked into her eyes. "But I knew you would. I had every confidence in you."

Breathless, her arms around his neck, she tried to focus on what he was saying and not on how nice it felt to be wrapped in his arms, or that he was still holding her. She was beaming with joy and wishing he would kiss her. He believed in her! He had confidence in her. The idea was intoxicating. She remembered their first meeting and how he said she could ride. It felt good that he would be so sure of her.

"Th-thanks, Luke," she managed, knowing she should move out of his arms, but was unable to make her feet move. Everything around her seemed to fade into the background. They just stood there looking at each other, smiling.

The loudspeaker crackled to life. "It's official. Montana Brown is our top score in the women's barrel racing!"

The words rang out, reverberating through the building. Montana's heart jumped in her chest. "Yes!" she exclaimed, unable to believe that she'd won her first rodeo in years. She'd hoped for it, dreamed of it—and God had blessed her hard work. Her excitement was so great that she reacted without thought—okay, maybe there was a little thought. She engulfed Luke and kissed him.

Luke was kissing Montana. He'd wanted to kiss her the second he'd scooped her up, but he'd made himself behave. He'd been thinking about it though, and then he'd made himself let her go.

When she'd thrown her arms around him and kissed him, he'd responded automatically to the feel of her lips on his. Her arms held him tightly and their hearts were beating together. Tenderness surged inside him and he felt as if he'd found something he'd lost. He'd been tense the entire time she'd been riding, and Jess had been right when he said there was more here between them. He hadn't realized how much he was rooting for Montana. How much he cared whether she still had what it took to pursue her dream.

He knew that she was kissing him purely out of excitement and celebration. A quick peck on the lips and a hurrah she'd won. But the instant her lips met his, Luke pulled her close and kissed her with feeling.

They heard the oohing and ahhing at the same moment.

"It's about time," Esther Mae cooed, as they broke

apart to find the matchmakers grinning from ear to ear. Beside them stood App, Stanley, Sam and Lacy. They looked like they were watching the ending of a romantic chick flick.

And he and Montana were the stars!

Chapter Sixteen

"I think it's a blessing," Adela said, smiling gently at Montana. She was standing at the entrance of Murdock's stall with Esther Mae and Norma Sue.

"Your first rodeo in forever, and you win!" Esther Mae gushed, her green eyes flashing with excitement. "*And* you get the cowboy!"

Montana felt queasy. She really, really did.

"And at our first hometown rodeo. I'd call that a success," Norma Sue clapped her hand on Montana's back.

After being discovered kissing in the alley, Luke had quickly disengaged himself—he'd been polite, even joked a smidge—then disappeared. She'd done the same using Murdock as an excuse to head back to the stall.

She was brushing him down when the posse showed up blocking the stall entrance. There was no way out. There was no escape. She was stuck while they discussed her as if she was part of the conversation. She wasn't, though; she hadn't said a word.

"Y'all," she said, pausing her brushing. "I hope y'all

don't get your hopes up too high. Me and Luke are just friends."

Three sets of eyes looked at her like she was crazy.

"Friends?" Norma Sue grunted. Her white cowboy hat was pushed back on her head. Her kinky gray hair surrounded her head like a halo, as she looked skeptical. "That wasn't a friendly kiss."

"You can admit it," Esther Mae urged. "Love is a wonderful thing. You make such a sweet couple. My goodness, y'all took my breath away. It was just plumb beautiful."

Adela laid a gentle hand on Esther Mae's arm. "It's okay, Esther Mae. Maybe Montana needs a little time to adjust to the idea."

Esther Mae's eyes flashed wide-open. "Ohhh! That's right. It could have just snuck up on you. Swept you right off your feet in surprise. I mean, you did just win and all. Love blossoms in the midst of exciting moments."

Montana wasn't so sure about anything at the moment. She didn't really want to think about it, standing here with all these eyes and hopes and wishes pinned on her like this. She wanted to go off and try to make some sense of all of this. She was overwhelmed. There was no doubt about that.

But she wasn't in love.

"Y'all, I just won my first rodeo. I'm planning on winning a whole lot more. And nothing is going to get in my way this time."

"That was uncomfortable."

Luke was standing at the back of the building. He

could hear Roy Don's voice announcing the next event. He wasn't expecting company when his brother stepped around the corner. "You saw that, did you?"

Jess's forehead crinkled up. "Who didn't? You two were in sight of almost the entire arena. Or at least those who were behind the scenes."

"That's right," Colt said, poking his head around the corner. "I saw it from clean across the bull pens."

"When did you get in?" Luke asked. Colt looked tired. His eyes were weary, and he knew he'd been driving a long haul in order to make it in for this ride. Rodeo life wasn't easy. When you were going for the national level and the big money and fame, paying your dues was a strain on the best of them.

He jabbed his hands in his pockets and looked at the ground before bringing his gaze up to meet Luke's. "I just rolled in. I was checking out my ride when I heard them announce Montana's name. I just happened to glance in the direction of the alley when I saw you two have your little moment. Big brother, if you aren't into having your love life open and on the lunch plate special, I'd say cool it when you're in the public."

"Didn't do it on purpose. It just happened. And by the way, I wasn't the one who initiated that. Montana did and honestly, it was purely out of excitement of winning. Believe me, I know."

Jess let out a low whistle. "What news station you been watching? The broadcast I just got a few minutes ago said loud and clear that the woman was every bit as interested in that kiss as you were."

"I'm watching the same station you are, Jess. Maybe

you need to tune your TV a little, Luke," Colt advised with a weary grin.

Luke knew they didn't mean anything by their teasing, but he wasn't feeling it at the moment. His thoughts were locked on Montana. What was she thinking right now?

She'd kissed him out of excitement. He knew it. Yes, there was that "thing" going on between them that she was so adamant about not wanting. And he understood why. She'd had her dreams put on hold for long enough. He'd seen her expression as she rode. He'd been watching her dedication for weeks now. There was no way she was letting anything get in the way of her dreams ever again. And this win…it cemented the deal. Nope, she didn't have to tell him that she wasn't interested in falling in love if it meant she couldn't devote all of her time to fulfilling that dream. "It doesn't matter what y'all saw. What matters is Montana won tonight. And that's just the beginning of the journey. She's about to hit the road just like you, Colt."

"If you want it bad enough, there's a way to make it all work." Jess was studying him with steady eyes.

"Yeah," Colt agreed. "I see fellas making it work out on the road. Sure, it's tough, but they tell me where there's love, there's a way."

"There you go. That 'bout sums it up right there. Montana Brown isn't going to let a little thing like love get in her way. Because she loved her dad, she put Murdock out to pasture and got a degree in accounting."

"Accounting? Montana?" Colt asked while Jess whistled. "That's the craziest thing I ever heard. No way she's an accountant."

"Not exactly a fit, is it?"

"Well, no. Nothing against accounting—but Montana looks like someone who'd have a career that involved something outdoors. Accounting's an office job. It just doesn't fit."

"No, it doesn't fit. Montana is an outdoors kind of gal. This is what she's meant to do. Just like you were meant to ride bulls, Colt."

Colt's eyes narrowed, and he rubbed the five o'clock shadow on his chin. "If you're right about that, then you might be in trouble, Luke."

Luke stared out across the darkness to where the Ferris wheel lit up the night. "Boy, don't I know it."

"You didn't make the posse too happy," Lacy said when Montana climbed into the stands to watch the bull riding event. It was late, but the stands were still packed. The bull riding was the main attraction. She hadn't seen Luke since their kiss, and she wondered where he'd gone to. Her stomach was a little queasy, thinking about the entire thing.

"I don't know what to say, Lacy." Tate was sleeping in his carrier, looking peaceful despite the ruckus going on around him. She studied him instead of looking at Lacy.

"I'm sorry all of this is getting in the way of your celebrating your win tonight."

Not exactly what she was expecting Lacy to say. "It's all right. I'm happy about the win. But I'm confused about everything else. Please don't tell anyone else though."

"I promise. I really am sorry. I want you to be happy,

Montana. I'm so happy with Clint and Tate that I get a little pushy sometimes." She smiled. "You know me."

Montana laughed. "If you weren't jumping into things with both feet, then we'd all think something was wrong with you. I know your heart's in the right place. And I know that about the posse, too."

The arena was busy as the bull fighters got in place. A clown, not to be mistaken for the bull fighters, came out and started acting silly, running around and doing tricks and talking to the crowd. He'd been entertaining the crowd all night, but he was doing one last stint before the fighters took over.

"You'd probably make a great bull fighter if you wanted," she said, looking at Lacy. "You'd be good at rescuing people. I mean, that's what you did to me."

Lacy ran a hand through her tousled blond hair. "I don't know about that. I know I get folks into trouble sometimes. I hope I help them, though. You'd have been okay with or without me. You know that, don't you?"

"I'm finding my way, I think."

The bull riding had begun, and the first bull exploded from the gate with a wild twist that immediately had the rider flying to the ground. The bull fighters moved in, one dodging between the fallen rider and the bull, drawing the bull's attention as the other fighter moved in and helped the cowboy up and got him headed toward the fence. A bull fighter's job was one of the most dangerous jobs out there. These guys tonight were good and Montana hoped nothing bad happened. She was always worried during this event, always dreading the worst. She was relieved that it was starting out with the promise of a good night.

Lacy had stopped talking to watch also. Now that the danger was over, she looked at Montana and asked, "Has that finding your way got a little to do with Luke?"

She couldn't deny it. She knew that somehow, spending time with him had helped her. "Yes, it does. Just getting to know him has helped me. The man has been through some tough times. And yet, he's mostly positive."

"He seemed that way to me. I don't know everything he's been through, but like Clint told you the other day, I know he's been working and saving since he was young. And I know his dad was a pretty bad alcoholic."

"I admire him. He's helped me think about things. Like not letting this anger at my dad eat me up. And when I'm really down on myself, he's been there to pick me up and tell me not to let it get to me." She thought about all the times that he'd helped her focus on her goals. She smiled, thinking about him.

"He sounds like a great guy." Lacy was watching her closely.

"He is," Montana admitted quietly.

"And what about that kiss?" Lacy asked, biting back a grin, her brows lifting expectantly.

Montana laughed, remembering. "You just couldn't help yourself, could you?"

"Nope. I couldn't. It was too good. You should have seen the look on your face when you threw your arms around him."

"I was excited, Lacy. I'd just won my first rodeo,"

she said, defending her actions. "He was there, and I kissed him out of excitement."

Lacy smiled. "Whatever you say, it's your business. But something tells me you wouldn't have thrown your arms around just anyone and kissed him like you did Luke."

"You've got me there," Montana said, with a sheepish smile. There was no way around that one. "Lacy, to tell you the truth, I don't know what's going on. I think about him all the time. But I didn't come here to get involved with anyone. And I don't want to get involved with anyone. But that doesn't stop the fact that, when he's around—or even when he isn't—I think about him. The man just does something to me, and I don't seem to be able to stop it. And I just don't know what in the world I'm going to do about it."

Lacy was beaming at her. "Relax, girlfriend. You're in love."

Montana shook her head in vigorous denial. "No, I'm not."

"You can deny it all you want, but I'm telling you it's true."

"Then I'll just get right out of love. I've got plans. I've got things I need to do—barrel races I have to win and points I have to gain in order to make it to the finals. I do not have time to fall in love."

She was not in love.

She wasn't. No way. No how.

Just as she was in the middle of her internal argument, she saw Luke walk out onto the elevated metal walkway that connected the chutes where the bull riders climbed down and settled onto the backs of their rides. Luke was walking beside a bull rider. The man was not as tall as Luke, but he had the same swagger that Luke had. Though she couldn't see his face because of the protective facemask that he wore, she knew without doubt that this must be the younger brother, Colt.

"Is that Colt that Luke just came out with?"

"Yes, that's him. You haven't met him, have you?"

"No." As of yet, she hadn't met Colt. Luke spoke to the cowboy, placed his hand on his back and bowed his head briefly. They looked like they were saying a prayer. When it was done, the cowboy, Colt, climbed over the side of the chute. Looking at Luke, he then eased himself down onto the restless bull's back. Montana held her breath. Luke and Clint were gripping Colt's protective vest—the vest was to protect his chest from the bull's horns, and Clint and Luke were there to help the rider get out of the chute in case the bull went wild in the close confines of the chute. The rider could be harmed easily if he was trapped or slipped between the bull and the gates. Montana held her breath.

"This always makes me nervous," she said.

"Me, too," Lacy agreed, tapping her fingers on the metal bench. "I don't want to see someone get hurt. But from what I understand, Colt is really good."

The gate was pulled open and the bull blasted from the chute, twisting and turning and kicking like he was the meanest, orneriest bad boy around. And Colt held on! It was a wild ride. But Colt held his seat on its back. He was on at the end of a great eight-second ride! "Wow, that was awesome." Montana admired his style and smiled when he jumped from the bull's back, waved to the crowd, dodged the angry bull and jogged to the fence, scaling it like he was out for a Sunday afternoon stroll.

Lacy laughed. "He's a little cocky, wouldn't you say?"

"Just a little. But I guess if you're that good, you can be," Montana said, thinking about all the time he spent working in order to qualify for the nationals. It was something she and Murdock were about to begin.

"Fans enjoy seeing some personality from the riders," Lacy said.

Luke met Colt coming over the fence and gave him a high-five and a back slap. He was all smiles as they stood there. Looking at him, her heart had begun thundering louder than if she'd been the one riding the bull. Luke Holden was a threat to her dream. The idea sent a chill racing down her spine. She didn't want to be in love. She didn't want to worry about trusting a man.

No, what she needed was to focus. And stay focused, if she wanted to have any chance of making her dream a reality.

"Lacy," she said, taking action. "I'm going for it."

Serious blue eyes met hers. "It's time."

Luke's words of encouragement came to mind. He'd told her God had given her a special talent. He'd been so confident in her all along.

"Yes. It's something I have to do." She thought about it for a moment, then decided to say it. "I believe God gave me this talent and He has a purpose for me in doing it." Luke's words echoed again. "I can't let it go to waste another day."

"You know you can help out with Tate as long as you want."

"I know, and I love it. But I think I'm going to need something else on the side to help with all the expenses. Unless I start out winning money, I won't be able to last long."

"The old saying, 'where there's a will, there's a way,' comes to mind. You've got the will, and if it's in God's plan, He'll make the way."

Montana knew in order for her to reach the National Final Rodeo Championship, it would take a miracle and thousands of miles hauling and racing time. It would take money and commitment and it would be harder for her than most because she would be doing it on her own.

Montana wondered if she was biting off more than she could handle. She sighed as her gaze settled on Luke, leaning on the fence, talking with a group of cowboys and watching the bull riding. Her heart clutched inside her chest and again his words encouraged her. She knew he'd tell her she could do this, and even more, she knew he'd tell her to go for it.

Chapter Seventeen

Montana couldn't sleep. She finally got out of bed around five, after staring at the ceiling for hours. She took a shower, got dressed, then quietly padded through the house with her boots in her hand. Outside, she sat down on the deck steps and tugged her boots on. The sun was just coming up and she wanted to be riding before others were stirring.

She needed space. Time to think and be totally alone.

Time to pray. She closed her eyes and let the calm of the early morning seep in around her. The air had the scent of fresh hay. She inhaled and asked God to guide her because she needed him desperately.

She needed help getting her life figured out. She needed some peace in her heart and in her head, and she wasn't getting it. Even the rodeo win hadn't helped. The satisfaction that she'd hoped to find with the win wasn't coming. Yes, she'd been excited—she'd shown that when she threw her arms around Luke—but peace? Nope, there had only been more confusion.

She'd thought when she talked to Lacy about starting her quest by hitting the rodeo trail that she'd feel some kind of satisfaction, but she didn't. All she felt was a heavy heart. All her life she'd wanted to be a cowgirl, and now here was her shot. Why couldn't she be happy?

Across the pasture she could see the shadow of where the festival trailers and booths were set up. But other than the soft bark of a dog in the distance, all was quiet. It was different from the way it had been last night, or would be later that day. One thing was certain, the first night of the rodeo had been a big success.

She was walking toward the arena when she heard Samantha let out a lonesome *hee-haw,* as if the little donkey had heard her approaching and was begging for some company. Instead of going to the arena where Murdock's stall was, she walked across the gravel to the barn. The smell of fresh hay filled the air as she entered. Immediately, Samantha hee-hawed again.

"Hold your horses," Montana said, striding toward the back of the stalls. The low lights illuminated the area well and Montana had no trouble seeing that the little donkey had been busy. The wooden bar they'd used to secure the gate better had been worked halfway out of its slot. Batting her big brown eyes at Montana, Samantha curled her plump lips back and gave a grin.

Montana was tickled at the sight. "Are you proud of yourself?" she asked through her chuckles. "If I'd have been out here a little later, you would have been free, and then where would we be?"

"From what I hear, she'd have let all the livestock out and enjoyed it," Luke said from behind her.

Montana whirled around. "What are you doing here?"

He shrugged. "I couldn't sleep. And I've been a little bit worried about Samantha getting loose and causing problems. So I decided to head over here and make sure things were secure."

Montana stuffed her hands in her pockets. "This donkey must really be good to have y'all so worried."

"I had visions of driving up and seeing my livestock running free while everyone was asleep."

Montana grimaced. "That wouldn't be good." She was so glad to see him. It was all she could do not to go over and hug him...but that wasn't what she needed to do. She didn't want to get involved. *You* are *involved*.

She knew she was on the verge of falling hard for the cowboy if she didn't watch herself extremely carefully. That meant not throwing herself at him.

Instead, she glanced down at the donkey who still had her head stuck through the bars of the gate. She batted her eyes and curled her lips back, exposing her big-toothed grin again. "Is this donkey human or what? She smiles like she knows what I'm thinking."

Luke chuckled and moved to stand beside her. "Maybe she does. A donkey is a very perceptive animal."

Luke stood close to her, his arm almost touching hers. It was like torture. Why did he have to stand right there? Didn't he know she was having trouble controlling herself? Probably not.

"I'm going to say that she was probably thinking you have a lot on your mind," he said quietly as he reached out and rubbed Samantha's nose. The little burro closed her eyes and breathed heavily—like a sigh.

Montana was almost jealous.

"How would she know this?" she asked, realizing what he'd said.

"She could tell, because you came to the barn so early. She would also think you're thinking about all the things you're going to have to do to get ready to hit the road for qualifying."

So the man had her figured out. "Think you're pretty smart, don't you?" she asked, sliding a look his way.

"Me? Nah, I'm just saying what Samantha is thinking. But if I was the one who was perceptive, I'd say you had a certain cowboy on your mind, too. And you were probably beating yourself up about kissing him last night."

Her heart was thumping like a rabbit running for its life. In a way that's how Montana felt, too. Looking at Luke, she saw how easily she could forgo her dreams and settle for a life right here with him. Be content like Lacy was with her home and family. She could love Luke.

"You have a high opinion of yourself, don't you?" she teased, but it wasn't easy to do.

He leaned against the gate so that he was looking at her. "You know me and Samantha are right about everything about you."

She laughed. "And just how are y'all so sure?"

"For starters, it is five in the morning. That's awful early for you to be out. I'd say that spells sleeplessness."

"What about the kiss?"

"Ahh, the kiss," he drawled, giving her a slow, toe-curling smile. "That was actually wishful thinking on my part." He lifted a hand to touch a strand of hair that was hanging over her shoulder. He slowly wound it around his finger, staring at it before lifting his beautiful brown eyes to hers. "I've been thinking about that kiss ever since it happened. I tried to distract myself from it all night, during the rest of the rodeo, but it didn't help. You—and that kiss—were on my mind the whole time. And then I couldn't sleep. I guess a tiny part of me was hoping you hadn't just kissed me because of the win."

She was toast!

Done. Stick a fork in her.

The sigh came out, despite all efforts to keep her head.

The guy was just plain irresistible. She took a step toward him. He opened his arms, and the next thing she knew, his arms were around her and they were kissing. The feel of his lips was firm yet tender as he kissed her. Pulling away slightly, he searched her stunned and confused eyes before lowering his lips to hers again. It was as if she'd been waiting all of her life for this moment. For the feel of this man's lips to connect with hers, for his heart to connect with hers.

He broke the kiss and laid his forehead against hers. Everything faded away in that instant. Her head was quiet. Her heart was calm.

Montana could have stayed like that forever.

"I can't get you off of my mind, Montana. I'm sorry." He sighed. "I know I've been trying to keep this simple. But it's complicated."

"Boy, don't I know it," she said, nodding her head

against his. His arms tightened around her and at some point hers had wrapped around his neck.

He looked about as serious as a man in a face-off with a rattlesnake. "Montana, I came here to ask you to go to dinner with me. It's time for you to go out with me. Yes, I know it will cause rumors—but with that kiss last night getting full coverage by one and all, everyone knows there's a little something going on between the two of us."

"Yes, I think you're right."

"I know I am. You can just—wait, you said yes, I was right? Does that mean you're saying yes to dinner?"

Her lip twitched with a smile she couldn't contain. It was adorable. He was flustered. "I meant yes on both counts. Dinner would be wonderful. And long overdue."

"Did you hear that, Samantha? You're my witness," Luke said, looking at the little burro. She laid her bulbous nose against Luke's hip and snorted.

Montana and Luke laughed, and as if knowing she'd done something good, Samantha snorted again, pulled her head from between the rails and let out a long *hee-haw*.

"Tell me about it, Samantha. We should have come to you a long time ago so you could set us straight." Luke gave Montana a nod and tugged her close again. "Yup. We might all be getting on the same page, finally."

Samantha pranced around her stall, her tail lifted out and her head held high. She looked as if she was about to bust out in dance as she batted her eyes at them.

"That is one funny donkey." Montana chuckled.

Luke looked down at her and cocked a brow. "That is one smart little gal, is what she is."

"I wonder." Montana sighed, leaning her head against Luke's shoulder. "What her advice would be on something else I have going on in my life?"

"I don't know, darlin', but you hang with me and I promise you we'll get whatever's bothering you all figured out." He kissed her forehead and rubbed her shoulder. "I promise, I'll help you, and so will God."

Montana breathed in slowly. There was a mixture of excitement and comfort in his arms. Of anticipation for the step they were taking. And worry of what it could bring.

Worry and joy, too, but for now, there was comfort and peace.

And the gentle touch of a very special man's hand.

Chapter Eighteen

"Yoo-hoo! Montana." Esther Mae waved from her position at the top of the Ferris wheel.

"Stop waving, Esther Mae," Norma Sue barked. From where Montana and Luke stood, waiting in line to get on the ride, it was clear that Norma Sue was white as a sheet. Her hands were glued to the protective bar. "Can't you see this thing is moving every time you do that?"

"Norma Sue, are you afraid of heights?" Luke called, tipping his Stetson back so he could see her better.

"Yes, she is," Esther Mae called for all to hear. "I practically had to drag her on here with me. Look, Norma Sue, it rocks." The redhead moved side to side, living dangerously when Norma Sue elbowed her in the ribs.

"You just wait till I get my boots back on the ground. I'm going to get you."

"She better have her running shoes on," Montana said.

"I wouldn't want to tangle with Norma Sue when she's out for payback," Luke said.

"Esther!" Norma Sue squealed, and Esther Mae hooted with laughter.

Luke laughed. "You sure you want to get on this thing? It does wobble a lot!"

"Are you afraid of heights, too?"

"Even if I am, I'd risk it to get to ride it with you. I was just worried about your safety."

She patted his arm. "I'll be fine. And don't you worry, big guy, I'll take good care of you up there."

He hugged her and she slipped her arm around his waist. Standing arm in arm with him, they watched the buggy with Esther Mae and Norma Sue lower a little more, as each car between them and the ground emptied out. Montana was living dangerously, knowing they'd spotted Luke's arm across her shoulders. But she didn't care.

"Glad that's over with," Norma Sue said, relief surging in her voice. "Y'all sure you want to go up in that bag of nuts and bolts?"

"We're going," Luke assured her.

"That's a good place for y'all to go. Have a good time," Esther Mae said. "And just don't pay Norma Sue no mind. She had fun. She's just too stubborn to admit it."

Luke leaned close and whispered in her ear as they were leaving. "Did you catch how sly they were being about my arm being around you?"

"Yes, they don't want to mess up a good thing."

He helped her into the buggy and then sat down beside her, immediately placing his arm across the seat behind her. "I don't want to mess anything up, either."

Montana breathed the cotton candy-scented air and

let herself enjoy the ride. "It would be wonderful if life could be as carefree as this feels," she said, as they reached the top of the wheel and were looking down on all the people milling around below.

"Yeah, from up here it feels removed from all that down there."

She smiled, her thoughts traveling to all that she'd pressed to the back of her mind. "The problem is, it's an illusion. All my problems are still waiting for me when I get back down." Why was she going there, when everything had been so perfect? She was with the perfect guy, on a perfect day, and she was opening her big mouth.

"True, but I can tell you, anything can be overcome."

She looked at him as the wheel swept them under before sending them back up to the top again. Anything can be overcome. Montana wasn't so sure.

The first of three Mule Hollow Homecoming Rodeos was a success. On both nights, they'd introduced all former residents who'd come home for the event. There had been several families who'd moved away, children all grown-up, some single and some with families of their own, coming back to show their kids where they'd once lived.

They all enjoyed remembering the town when it was a thriving oil town. They'd been sad when their parents had moved away to find work after the oil boom busted and all the work had dried up in Mule Hollow.

Sunday morning, the church lawn was filled with talk of the weekend. It was a roaring success.

Esther Mae and Norma Sue looked like they could

fly they were so happy. Esther Mae especially, since the summer hat that she wore was covered in feathers. Feathers that fluttered with every bob her head made as she talked nonstop about the festival.

Everyone was in an exceptionally good mood. Montana listened and took all the congratulations on her win. Everyone wanted to know what she was going to do next, and she told them she was going to hit the road for more rodeos the following week.

It seemed strange to her that she would actually be starting her lifelong dream. She was going to find another part-time job in addition to her helping out with Tate, and then she would just pray that she'd start winning. The money would help pay her way, or she wouldn't be able to make it. There was a lot of wear and tear that went along with hauling. There would be travel expenses, and then upkeep expenses on the truck and trailer, which Clint was lending her, and of course vet bills and entry fees. The list went on and on. It wasn't cheap shooting for the National Rodeo Finals in Las Vegas. Being one of the top fifteen in money and points was no easy feat. It was one thing to dream about it and another to take it on.

But that was exactly what Montana planned to do.

And if she was committing, she was committing one hundred percent.

She and Luke had talked a little about it the day before. After they'd gotten off the Ferris wheel, they'd hung out together some and talked about her riding. She'd told him of her decision to find another part-time job, and he'd told her he thought that was a good idea— until she started winning the big money and went full-time. She still smiled at the conviction in his voice. He hadn't been saying that to make her feel better; he'd been saying it because he really did think she would do well. The very idea had her waiting anxiously to see his smiling face come striding across the parking lot.

He didn't make it until the last song was being sung, just before Chance got up to preach. When the door opened, Montana glanced over her shoulder and her heart did the now familiar happy thump. As if their eyes were connected by a beacon, he zeroed in on her instantly, and strode straight up the aisle and scooted into the seat beside her.

Adela's piano playing seemed to pick up the pace, drawing Montana's gaze to find the delicate lady's blue eyes beaming from around the corner of the music sheet. And up in the choir loft, Esther Mae's and Norma Sue's smiles seemed to merge together, they were so huge.

Whether she wanted it or not, there was no denying that they had a successful match on the mind. Montana tried not to think about it. She tried to think only of enjoying his company. No strings attached. There had been nothing said, no indication that things were any different with her than with any of the other women he'd dated.

And she was fine with it. They were going out to dinner that evening and she'd teased him. Funny, she wondered if these butterflies and sick stomach were what all the others had felt.

As they sat beside each other, he closed the hymnal and placed it in the holder on the back of the pew in front of them. "You doing good this morning?" he asked as he leaned back beside her.

"Good," she said, listening to Pastor Chance's opening statement about the rodeo and festival. "How about you?"

He grinned. "I'm great. I've got a date tonight with a beautiful woman. What's not to be happy about?" His smile was as dazzling as his words, and it felt crazy wonderful, knowing he was talking about her.

Looking at him, Montana was very aware that Luke made her feel like a woman…and she loved it. It caused her to long for things she hadn't thought about in a long time.

Whistling a happy tune, Luke jogged down the steps and over to his truck. Tossing the keys into the air, he caught them on a flip and grinned. He was feeling good. He had a date with Montana Brown.

He had a surprise for her tonight, and he hoped she'd take him up on it. He had thought all afternoon about it, and felt like this was the perfect solution to her problem. Dinner was the perfect place to tell her, but he was a little worried about how she'd handle it.

He couldn't get to her house quick enough. He felt like a schoolboy on his first date. He'd been smiling all afternoon and was still smiling when he knocked on her door.

"Come in, come in," Lacy said, opening the door wide when she saw him. She was holding Tate as she beckoned him in. "I've been pacing the floors, waiting for the clock to hit six and for you to drive up. Yep, it's true, I think I may be more excited about you two going out than y'all."

"I hope not. I was kind of hoping Montana was excited. I know I am."

Lacy chuckled. "That's exactly the answer I wanted to hear. If you weren't excited, I'd think something was wrong with you. Clint had a call from one of his ranch hands that a cow was down so he had to go check on it, or he'd be here to see y'all off."

"Hey," Montana said, coming into the room. Her glistening dark hair was down around her shoulders tempting him to touch it. She wore a frilly white blouse with dressy jeans, and with the sparkle in her eye, she took his breath away. "Has Lacy given you the third degree? Has she made sure you understand that my curfew is ten sharp, and I must be home then or I'll be grounded for life, and never ever get to go out with you again?"

"Ha!" Lacy said. "I was just about to."

Luke chuckled. "I'm game for whatever Lacy throws at me. Whatever it takes to get this dinner date, I'll do."

Montana smiled. Her big eyes were bright with what he hoped was excitement about him being there. His heart was pounding in his chest, looking at her. And it was like nothing he'd ever experienced before. Everything had faded away and all he saw was her.

"I don't have any questions. You two crazy kids need to just get on out of here." Lacy's teasing words broke the moment, reminding Luke that he'd spoken to her before he'd gotten caught up in the unchartered feelings Montana evoked inside of him.

He'd had his hat in his hand ever since he'd rung the

doorbell, and now tapped it lightly to his hip. "Then are you ready?" he asked.

"Yes she is," Lacy said, giving Montana a little nudge.

A few minutes later they were trucking down the road toward Ranger. He couldn't explain how happy he was as they drove the seventy miles to the closest large town near Mule Hollow. On the way they talked about various aspects of the festival and rodeo. He'd made reservations at a restaurant that overlooked a lake. He'd never been there before, but had heard it was nice, and he'd decided that he wanted to take Montana somewhere he'd never been before. He thought Montana was special, and he wanted this date to be special, too. He wanted Montana not to feel like just one of many women he took to dinner.

"This is beautiful," she said as the hostess led them to a table on the deck beside the water. A swan was floating in the water as Luke held Montana's chair out for her. She looked over her shoulder at him and smiled. Luke froze. He could live forever with that smile directed at him.

The idea was a sobering one.

"Luke, are you all right?" she asked, when he didn't scoot the chair up for her to sit in.

"Yeah," he said, jolted by the thoughts racing through his mind and the sudden longing tugging at his heart. What was happening with him? "Yeah, I'm good. Just thinking—Montana, you have the most beautiful smile I've ever seen."

She laughed as she sat down. "I'm sure you say that to all the girls."

He shook his head. "No, Montana, I don't. I'm telling you that your smile is the most beautiful I've ever seen." It was important for her to understand he was serious, and not just saying the words.

Her smile was genuine as he sat down across from her. "Thank you. I like that," she said quietly. "Whew, I'm a little nervous."

He reached across the table and laid his hand over hers, where she was picking at the edge of her napkin. "I'm nervous too." He held her unconvinced gaze. "Why don't we both take a breath and relax."

She nodded and breathed in. "Sounds like a good idea. I wasn't expecting to feel like a girl on her first date."

"I like the idea of that. I feel like a boy on his first date."

Their confessions made them laugh as the waitress came. By the time she left to fill their order, they'd both relaxed somewhat. Luke knew in his heart that this was a life-changing experience. Looking across the candlelit table at her, he knew he was feeling happy. And he liked it. Three weeks ago he wouldn't have believed it was possible. But that was before Montana Brown had ridden into his life.

Chapter Nineteen

The meal had been the most romantic meal Montana had ever had. The gentle lapping of the water against the deck, the soft moonlight that seemed to hover over the lake just for them. The swan gliding about on the water beside them added to the romance, along with the music that drifted lightly on the breeze to them. There was so much that made the night special, but it was the look in Luke's eyes that had her heart fluttering from moment to moment. The light touch of his hand when he'd grasped hers. And his words left her feeling like she was floating on cloud nine.

This was what falling in love was like...would be like, if it was happening to her.

When they were leaving the restaurant, Luke took her hand in his. "Would you like to walk along the lake path for a little while?"

The warmth of his hand felt so nice. She nodded. "I'd like that."

They headed to the side of the restaurant and down to the pier. There was a sidewalk that led along the edge for a distance, past benches that had been placed along the way, and they followed it. Ahead of them, several yards away, an older couple strolled hand in hand, enjoying the night. They paused in a shadow and the woman placed her hand on the man's cheek. He bent and kissed her. A tug of emotions washed through Montana as she watched them. How many years had they been together? They could easily be newlyweds, or they could have been married for fifty years. Either way, just the sweetness of the gesture inspired her.

Looking up, she found Luke watching her. "I love that," she said, waving toward the couple as they disappeared.

His expression was thoughtful. "Makes you wonder what their story is, doesn't it?" He pulled her toward him.

Still holding his hand, Montana went willingly, her heart stopping, then it started racing. She felt off-balance. Luke Holden did that, set her world tilting.

"Yes, it does." She forced her voice to work as her gaze rested on his lips.

He lowered his head slightly, looking into her eyes as he paused mere inches from her. "You shake my world up, Montana," he murmured, and then kissed her.

The night was still, peaceful, easy. The instant his lips met hers, everything stopped, and she knew she was in danger. So many emotions she'd never experienced came into play in his arms. Her heart sighed and she felt as if she could stay there forever. As if God were smiling down on her.

Was this love?

There were so many reasons why she didn't want to fall in love. But she had.

How had this happened? In his arms, the walls she'd built around her heart seemed to crumble. She pushed gently on his chest and he pulled away, looking as stunned as she felt. Letting go of her, he walked a few feet, studying the moonlit water.

"Montana, I..."

Neither of them had been looking for anything serious, and yet they seemed on a collision course toward it. Was he feeling the same? Was that what had him turning his back on her?

"Montana, I've fallen in love with you."

His words took her breath away, even though she'd been wondering if it was possible that he could be feeling what she was feeling.

"No," she said, saying the first thing that came to her. "No, Luke." She paced to the water's edge, and it was her turn to stare out across it, with everything inside of her clashing. "I don't want to fall in love and neither do you. Remember, this was all just an infatuation and a friendship. It's not love. You don't want that. You want to get your ranch up and successful before you think about a marriage and a family. And I—" She slapped a hand to her chest. "I'm going on the rodeo circuit. I don't have time to think about being in love—"

That slow smile of his spread with maddening beauty across his face, lighting his eyes with humor. "Montana, it's true I wasn't looking for this. But it's also true that it's happened. Are you telling me that what I'm feeling from you isn't true?"

She glared at him. "You…you've taken a perfectly good evening and ruined it."

His eyes were twinkling with mirth. "Montana, it's going to be okay. I wasn't expecting this any more than you were, but I love you, and there isn't anything I can do about it but tell you."

"Well, don't sound so enthusiastic." She tried to think. Tried to figure this out.

He laughed. "Hey, I'm just being honest." He pulled her into his arms again.

"Montana, I've been feeling something inside myself, since knowing you, that I've never felt before. I feel joy every time I see you. And it runs deep and strong. I'm praying you'll see it, too."

"We haven't even finished our first date," she protested.

His grin widened. "I know a good thing when I see it, and you're the best thing I've ever seen. Montana, the first time I saw you racing around that barrel at Lacy's, I felt drawn to you. I wasn't expecting it to be more than a passing attraction, but there was no shaking it. One date, two, fifty. It doesn't matter, I'm in love with you."

She backed away from him. "I'm going on the rodeo circuit, Luke."

He stepped toward her and cupped her face. "Yes, you are. Nothing I'm saying is changing that. I'm just telling you that I love you, and I want a life with you. I want to raise babies with you and watch them grow up on the ranch."

Montana felt dazed. He was trying to sweep her

off her feet. There couldn't be any sweeping going on right now. She had to focus. And she had to focus *now*.

And not on Luke. *No*. The only male she needed in her life right now was Murdock.… "I need to go home," she said. "I need to go home now."

Heart pounding, she ran back to Luke's truck.

Monday came bright and early. Montana woke up and saw Lacy and Tate sitting on the bed looking at her.

"So, how was it?" Lacy asked, grinning like a sly cat.

Montana rolled away from her and covered her head with her pillow. She hadn't slept at all, or at least she hadn't felt like she did until Lacy woke her. The last time she'd remembered staring at the clock, it had been 4:30 a.m. "What time is it?" she asked from beneath the pillow.

"Six. Me and Tate couldn't wait for you to get up. The little fella is just a Curious George when it comes to knowing what's going on in his aunt Monty's love life."

Montana groaned. "It was a disaster."

"What happened?"

Montana yanked the pillow from her head and sat up, staring at Lacy in disbelief. "He told me he loved me! That's what."

"Woo-hoo!" Lacy exclaimed, clapping Tate's hands between hers and bouncing him on her lap. "We knew it! We knew it, didn't we, Tater!" Tate was grinning, his little mouth wide-open and his eyes bright. "Hold it." Lacy stopped midexclamation point. "What did you tell him?"

Montana was still reeling. "I told him we hadn't even finished our first date."

Lacy gasped while making an are-you-crazy face. "Montana, y'all have too been on dates. Maybe not technically, but you've had dinner here. And then there was the barbecue. And all that time at the arena. Oh, and going to put the fire out. Y'all have spent lots of time getting to know each other—"

"None of those were dates."

"You're being technical again. You've spent time with him. Don't forget all the time in the arena and the festival. You know there is something special there. I see those blue-green eyes of yours go dreamy when he enters the room."

Montana's stomach did somersaults. She'd thought about her feelings all night. It had been a quiet trip home, both of them tangled up in their own thoughts. She'd wondered what he was thinking of her reactions. There was no denying that she was crazy about him and that she had never felt with anyone the way she felt when she was around him.

Love. Yes, the emotion had actually entered her thoughts last night, too. But she couldn't believe it. It was irresponsible—she actually heard her father saying the words in her head, as she'd gone over and over her feelings toward Luke.

"How could he love me so soon?"

Lacy's expression was still stuck in a smile. "God has a way of letting hearts speak to each other. Don't get me wrong, I believe in knowing what you're doing. Yep, there is nothing worse than a woman letting a man sweet-talk her into making a bad mistake. But I do believe that some love happens quickly and some love grows slowly. To each his own love journey. You aren't denying your feelings because of your dad, are you?"

"Maybe in a way," Montana said. "I loved my daddy. Trusted him. Lacy, have you ever found out that the one person in all the world who you thought was most honorable and upright was a liar? That's what I did. And worse, I gave up my dreams for him." Her stomach lurched.

Lacy patted her knee. "I can't imagine how that must feel."

Montana hugged her pillow, watching Tate as he played with his momma's necklace. "I feel like such a whiner. I'm an adult. I am a CPA—whether I like it or not. I'm a strong, independent woman and I'm acting like a baby. I hate this."

Lacy was studying her with thoughtful eyes. "Do you love Luke?"

Montana buried her face in her pillow. "I think I do," she said, her voice muffled in the pillow. "But I can't," she said, sighing.

"The romantic in me is thrilled and happy and wants you to go throw yourself into his arms and let's have a wedding." Lacy laid her hand on hers. "But this is what I'm going to do. I'm going to continue to pray. I know God has a plan. He always does." She nodded her head enthusiastically when Montana frowned. "I think y'all go together like pie and ice cream."

"Only you would think that way," Montana said, her lip twitching despite her misery.

"There's no rush on this. Take it one day at a time. Just do me a favor and don't close your heart to this wonderful man God has put in your path, simply because your dad messed up. God can mend all fences and bring good from all things bad. Life is full of bad things. Wrongdoings and devastating blows. But God is always, always, always steady as the rock that He is. He will never leave you or forsake you, and He will not give you more than you can handle." Lacy rattled off promises from God like she was really expecting them to come true. "And I'm telling you that, in the process, He's making you stronger than you ever thought you could be."

Montana thought of Luke and all he'd been through as a kid growing up, and the man he'd become. She admired him so very much. Talk about strong. He was amazing. There was so much he could have held against God, and his mother and his dad. But he didn't seem to. It was something she longed to understand.

Montana took a deep breath. There were so many things going on in her life. So many conflicts swirling around in her head and heart that she felt dizzy. "I'm not going to think about any of that today. Today, I'm going to make a plan before I hit the road hard."

"I told Clint yesterday to get the trailer and truck ready because you were about to shoot for the stars. You deserve it."

Did she? Montana knew the anger that was still bolted inside her heart. Luke had somehow dealt with issues of his own, and she wanted to know how he'd done it. Her heart hadn't softened, and it wasn't because she hadn't prayed about it. She had.

She wondered what Luke would think of her if he

knew exactly how angry she was inside? He was the honorable one, she wasn't so honorable.

How could she feel so angry and then feel so guilty for not being able to forgive her dad?

She was just one goofed-up cookie, was all there was to it. God was probably looking down, wagging His head and wondering if she was ever going to get things figured out.

Montana wondered that, too.

"Luke, we came to talk."

It was practically the break of dawn, and the matchmaking posse was standing on Luke's front porch a couple of days after he and Montana had gone out. He pulled the door open, and there they stood with the rising sun at their backs. The roosters had barely stopped crowing it was so early.

"Okay. Shoot." He stepped back and motioned them to come inside.

Norma Sue led the way inside, barreling past him to stand beside the kitchen counter. Esther Mae and Adela followed. They were a work in contradictions as they passed him one by one. Norma Sue in her jeans and button-down shirt, topped off with her white Stetson, Esther Mae in her grape slacks and orange shirt that fought hard with her red hair. And then refined Adela, petite and fragile in her pale pink blouse and cream slacks. She gave him a lovely smile as she entered.

"We are so glad we caught you before you started your day," she said, patting his arm. "We know how busy you are."

He gave a wary smile, feeling oddly nervous with

them looking like they were on official business. Matchmaking business, he presumed.

"We've come to ask you a favor." Norma Sue crossed her arms, looking like she dared him to say no. Luke knew she was like a steamroller when she got going, and he wondered if he was about to get mowed down.

"You know I'll do my best to help y'all any way I can." It was true. He loved and respected these ladies—despite being a bit scared of them. What were they up to?

"We think you should ask Montana to work for you," Esther Mae proposed, looking as if she'd just told him he'd won a million dollars.

He laughed because he'd already thought of the same thing. "You do? And what makes you think that?"

"We overheard Jess telling Sam that the business was growing and that you had been thinking about hiring some bookkeeping help."

He had been thinking that. He'd even thought about offering it to Montana last night, but then he'd gone and opened his big mouth and told her he loved her.

If he wanted to scare her off, he'd chosen exactly the right thing to say.

She'd almost run the seventy miles home from Ranger that night.

Offering the job to her might have put the last nail in his coffin, so he'd kept his mouth shut on the way home. "I've thought about it," he admitted to the ladies. "But I'm not so sure she would accept it. She—" He halted, the temptation to tell them he loved her churned inside of him.

"Why'd she get mad at you?" Norma Sue asked, studying him like a hawk.

Luke pulled at his collar. "I, ah—"

"You told her you loved her!" Ester Mae yelped. "Is that it?"

His mouth fell open. Instantly, three sets of eyes flew wide.

"Well, I'll be," Norma Sue hooted, slapping him on the back. "I'm impressed with you, Luke. You've got gumption."

"I didn't say—"

Adela smiled. "You don't have to explain. We're on your side."

Looking at their smiling faces, he caved. "I'm afraid I may have done more harm than good. She's not too happy about all of this. I'm afraid offering her a job might do more harm than good. She might not take it."

Esther Mae harrumphed. "Are you kidding? She'll accept. She wants to rodeo and this is right up her alley."

"Not to mention she'd get to be near you in the bargain," Norma Sue added, her plump cheeks shining, she was grinning so big.

Luke stared at the ladies. He needed any and all the help he could get. He'd planned on offering her the job because it would be perfect for her and help him out, too, both in the business and personally, since it would give him an excuse to see her.

Adela had said little as Esther Mae and Norma Sue rattled on about all the positives of the situation. Their excited chattering was neverending. Miss Adela was watching him with her wise blue eyes, so sure and steady that he felt certain that this was the move to make. She didn't have to say anything, just be there, giving him that look.

"I'll ask her," he said at last.

Norma Sue slapped him on the back again, so hard this time that if he hadn't been leaning against the breakfast bar, he'd have been knocked back a step or two. "There you go!" she boomed. "Now you're talking. I told them you were too smart a man to miss this opportunity."

"I'm so excited." Esther Mae clasped her hands together as if in prayer. "This is perfect."

"I'll head over there in a few minutes and go ahead and get it done."

"We'll pray for it to all work out." Adela laid her hand back on his forearm and squeezed reassuringly. "I'm feeling very good about this."

"Me, too," Esther Mae gushed, her cheeks pink with excitement. Norma Sue nodded, her eyes glinting with the thrill of a new match being made.

Luke wasn't so sure. He was beginning to think they might be holding out hope for a situation that just might not have the solution they wanted it to have. After Montana's reaction the other night, he kept thinking she was like a skittish colt with open pastures beckoning. But he wasn't a quitter. Not when the prize was right in front of him.

And that meant he had a job to offer the woman he wanted to spend the rest of his life with.

He wanted Montana. For now and for always.

Chapter Twenty

"A job?"

Montana was still shook up about Luke telling her he loved her, and now he was offering her a job? "No, I don't think that would be a very good idea." She'd been checking out the trailer she was going to use to haul Murdock to a rodeo in Stephenville, Texas, that weekend. She'd been startled when Luke had stopped by and dropped this new bombshell of a job on her.

"I know you need help paying for your expenses. And I got to thinking that I need some help with the business. It's growing, and I need professional help with my record keeping and paperwork. Montana, I'm offering you my heart, but since you're not ready for that—" he grinned sheepishly "—then I'm offering you a job instead. Yes, that'll mean you'll be near me and I get to make you fall madly in love with me somewhere along the way. But in the meantime you'll get to support your dream."

Montana tried hard to concentrate on the job part of his pronouncement, and keep her heart out of it. It wasn't helping that he looked nervous. Luke Holden wasn't the nervous type, yet he was right now. And sweet…and dear.

"It would be a win-win for us both," he continued when she didn't say anything.

How could she? Goodness, she loved looking into his eyes. Oh, how she could look at him forever…

No! Stop—she had rodeos to win and roads to travel and dreams to live.…

"Tell me more," she forced out. "Though I'm not sure it's good to even think about. I'm afraid you might get hurt in the end—"

He crinkled his forehead. "You let me worry about myself. I'm trying to take care of you."

Montana had a problem. She wanted to throw her arms around him and live happily ever after. She wanted to let him take care of her as he'd said. But that was part of her problem…she needed to do this on her own.

"Luke, I don't want someone to take care of everything," she said more aggressively than she'd meant to. She could tell her tone caught him off guard, but he recovered quickly.

"I didn't mean it literally," Luke said. "I'm not your father. I'm not planning on taking over your life."

"I hate this," Montana groaned, walking down the side of the horse trailer as she tried to fight the sudden flood of anger that surged forward. "I have too much to accomplish, and too much stuff going on inside my head. It hasn't been easy to let things go. I can't set this anger at my father aside. It's there, underlining everything I do."

Luke came up beside her. He looked straight ahead, staring out across the pasture where a group of cattle grazed between two rambling oaks.

"Montana, I hear the bitterness in you. You need to talk about this with your dad and try to resolve it."

"I *can't*. Why is that? Why can't I let go? Why can't I feel joy, reaching for my dreams?" *Or falling in love,* she wanted to add but didn't. She thought, from the shadow of sadness she saw darken Luke's eyes, that he hadn't missed the omission. "Why can't I move on?"

He nudged her shoulder with his own. "I think you're too full of resentment to feel real joy. You have to let it go. That's what I had to do."

She closed her eyes, trying for peace. None came.

"Forgiveness is a tough thing when you don't want to let it go. But it's something you have to do for yourself. And it's something that you have to work at sometimes."

Forgiveness. There it was, she thought with resolve. She'd been pushing it farther and farther back into the shadows, trying to get past it.

She was so angry at her dad that she really didn't want to let the anger go and forgive him. And yet, there was a part of her that did. A part of her that was still his little girl who wanted his love and affection. His approval.

She raised fingers to her temple. Her head was pounding and she felt hot. "I can't do it, Luke."

He turned and dipped his chin, giving her a very frank appraisal. "You can do anything you set your mind to. You're Montana Brown and you're fearless.

I've seen you ride." He gave her a devastating smile, his expression so sure.

She couldn't help smiling back, though it was small. "I don't feel fearless. I feel like I can't trust anyone anymore," she whispered.

"You can trust me, Montana. I know your dad let you down. But you can't let his behavior, his choices, affect your life anymore. You have to choose your own path."

"Like you've done?"

He nodded. "I'll admit that I've let my dad's prediction that I'd never amount to anything, that I'd be worthless, drive me all of my life. But I've tried to balance that with God's direction."

"You couldn't be worthless if you tried your hardest. You are worth something wonderful. God didn't make worthless people…they make themselves."

His eyes widened. "See, you do know a thing or two. Exactly. People pick and choose their character and the things that define them. My dad's lack of parenting and love affect my character only as far as I will allow it. When my brothers and I found ourselves basically on our own, I realized I had to make a difference for myself and for them. I think that's what made my dad despise me so much."

His words cut through her. How could a dad want his son to be worthless? How hard it must have been for Luke. "You are a true survivor, Luke. I respect you so much. But…" she took a deep breath, knowing suddenly that she had to understand about his mother, "…I need to ask you something."

"Anything."

Taking a few strides, she walked to the front of the trailer. There was a flatbed truck parked there, and she sat down on it. Her knees felt weak suddenly. Looking up at Luke, she knew she needed the answers. Needed to understand about his mother more than anything else.

Luke sat beside her.

"I'm serious, Montana, you can trust me. What do you need to know?" He took her hand in his and squeezed it. A million butterflies went crazy in her stomach. The air went light, even though they were sitting in the wide-open breeze.

You love him...

It's impossible not to love him.

Especially when he's squeezing your hand and looking deep into your eyes like now.

Montana closed her eyes and tried to still the voice inside her head. But when she closed her eyes, all she saw was Luke's smiling face.

Luke took Montana's hand and squeezed gently. He wanted to help her move forward. If she could, then maybe they could see where they stood. Montana had grabbed hold of him from the first day, and he hadn't been able to get her off his mind. He couldn't remember if it'd been Sam or App or Stanley who had said it for certain, but he remembered the warning, that one day he wouldn't be able to walk away.

That day had come.

"Montana, I need you to understand that my dad chose his path. He's the one who picked up a bottle. That sounds harsh, but it's true. I have a lot of resentment in me over that. My mom chose to leave, and for the longest time, I had resentment for that, too. But I had little brothers counting on me. And even though I was young, I could still work some and make sure they had food. We didn't always have electricity when I was younger, but we had bread and peanut butter."

Montana's fingers tightened around his and her eyes glistened. She turned her hand so that she was clutching his. "I hate the picture that paints. I hate that you lived through that."

Looking at her, he was more certain than anything that he loved her. The knowledge sent a thrill of anticipation racing through him. And an even stronger drive to help her past the pain that held her locked in its grip. "I won't kid you, Montana, I hated my dad for the longest time, and I wanted to hate my mother. But Clint's dad, Mac Matlock, helped me realize that we don't get to choose our parents. And sometimes a person doesn't get to choose the decisions that a spouse makes. Spouses can choose to leave for whatever reasons and there isn't anything the other person or the kids can do about it." He paused, remembering how painful it had been learning that lesson. He didn't wish it on anyone.

He gave her an encouraging smile. "Mac taught me what a person can control. What a man is supposed to be. He taught me that a man's character is the only real thing he can control. He did it through demonstration, in being there for his son and making his ranch a success by being honest and having his word mean something. And he did it with a Bible in his hand. He told me I could choose who I wanted to be, and not let circumstance dictate it for me."

Montana smiled. "You chose to forgive."

"Not as quickly as it seems to you now. Believe me, the Bible is filled with verses about forgiveness, but back then I was like you. I was so angry that I couldn't let myself give it up. Even though I knew that's what God would have me do, I couldn't just do it. But then I understood that I could be like my dad or I could be like Mac. That's when I chose. That's when it turned easy."

"That's why you were so patient with Erica, despite all the rude things she did to you. And that's why you forgave your mother, though she abandoned you."

"Because I chose to. I want to be the kind of man God wants me to be. I don't always make it, but I strive for that. I still have lingering bouts of anger toward my dad. He never regretted what he did to us. That's the difference between him and my mom. She regrets it every day of her life and still does. That's why she won't move here and live on the ranch. She's embarrassed and can't forgive herself."

Luke stood and wrapped Montana up in his arms. She felt so good there with her heart pounding against his. "Let it go, Montana. Make your life your own. Give it to God and then let Him guide you." *And let me love you.*

"Luke, I have a lot to figure out, and my life is about to get more complicated when I hit the rodeo circuit. I'll be gone most of the summer if I'm winning. If I'm going to make the championships, I have to be in the top twenty moneymakers. That means I have to ride everything I can, and as many big money purses as I can make it to. And even then I might not make it."

He placed his hands on his hips, looking unfazed by her ramblings. "Montana, you just ride. You and me, we'll take it one day at a time."

His words were like music to her ears. Montana had to get out of there. "I need to head in." She started walking away as fast as she could. She thought about running, but something had her swinging back around. "Thanks for everything," she said, breathless. There was so much to get done and so little time. She had to hit the road. She had to leave all of this behind and she had to win.

"Hey," he called. "I planned to tell you I'm going to meet Colt between here and the Oklahoma border tomorrow. I had planned to support you and watch you ride, but he needs me to bring him some of his gear. He's not going to have time to swing by and pick it up before heading to Reno."

Again the cowboy knew how to get to her. "You don't need to come see me. I'm fine, and Colt needs you. How's he doing?"

"He's worn slap out, but he's been winning, and that's what he wants. You know how that is."

She smiled. "Yup. At least I hope to. Hauling from rodeo to rodeo was hard, but state-to-state running for the big money was killer. A friend and I did it during the summer of my senior year before getting out of high school. I loved it, but still remember the endless road passing under our wheels. Thankfully, I didn't have to do the driving back then. This is going be different."

"I hate the idea of you on the road by yourself—"

Luke stopped himself. He didn't like it one bit, but that wasn't his call and he knew it. "Sorry." He longed to hug her and assure her that all would be fine. But she didn't need to be crowded any more than he'd already done. "Get some rest. You're going to need it," was all he would let himself say.

"Thanks," she answered, turned and walked away.

He wanted to believe everything was going to turn out fine. Talk about trusting God…he had to do it. But as he watched her go, something just didn't feel right.

If she was winning, then that meant she was going to be on the road, not here in Mule Hollow. Not here, where he could woo her.

Chapter Twenty-One

Montana maneuvered her trailer into a parking spot at the back of the lot. She was here. It had been a pretty good drive from Mule Hollow to Stephenville. Hopping from the cab, she jogged to the back of the trailer, anxious to get Murdock unloaded so she could head up to the announcer's box to check out the order of events and see where they had her in the lineup. She knew the barrels would be toward the end of the rodeo, most likely right before the bull competition.

"Hey, big fella," she said, as she led Murdock from the trailer. He pawed the ground as soon as he was outside. This felt great. A group of young cowgirls walking by were laughing and having a great time. Their excited voices rang out as they went. It reminded her of when she'd competed during high school. Back in the days when she was determined to be the best barrel racer there had ever been.

The thought made her smile as she headed toward the announcer's box. She had been so young back then. She wondered what Luke was doing. Her mind had drifted to him at random moments throughout her drive. He was never far from her thoughts. Several times she even pulled her cell phone out to call him. But she didn't.

In Mule Hollow, she wouldn't be able to reach him with her cell phone, but now she knew they were only a call away from each other.

She wondered if he'd thought about calling her.

Happy with the next-to-last spot on the list, she left the building, heading back toward Murdock and nearly jumped out of her boots when her phone rang. It hadn't rung the entire time that she'd been in Mule Hollow. The service was so bad in the tiny town that she'd even stopped carrying it. She'd only attached it to her belt because she'd been traveling.

"Hello," she said without glancing at the caller ID.

"Montana, this is your father."

She froze. She didn't know what to do. A slow internal vibration seemed to start deep inside of her as the anger and betrayal she'd been suppressing coiled more tightly.

"Hi." Amazingly, her voice didn't shake. There was no emotion at all. Her fingers tightened in conjunction with her insides, despite the emotional onslaught. It was hard calling him Daddy when she was so sick at heart. Her stomach rolled at the sound of his voice, though a part of her longed for all of what had transpired to go away. Longed for things to be back to normal.

Her mother was moving forward. Strange that she'd seemed better able to handle her father's betrayal than Montana was.

"Montana, when are you coming back home and taking your responsibility to this company seriously? I understand you took a few weeks off to come to terms with what's happened. But it's time for you to get back to work. People are depending on you."

There was no remorse or apology. There was only family responsibility—*her* family responsibility. None of his. She gritted her teeth and held back the high boil of her temper, counting to three—no way could she have made it to ten!

"Dad, I'm not coming back." It felt good, as the words came out sure and true.

"Montana..."

"Dad, I chose accounting for you and I can't do it any longer."

"Montana, you are taking what has happened between your mother and me far too personally. You are using it as an excuse to relinquish your responsibilities."

"No, Dad, I'm not. It's just time for me to do what *I* want."

Silence filled the space between them. In her mind's eye, she could see her father's lips flatten out in displeasure. She'd never liked seeing that look on his face. She'd always tried to make him smile, even at the expense of not doing what she wanted. It hit her, looking back, how selfish her father was.

"It's time for you to grow up, Montana. I've built this firm for you to take over someday. It's time for you to come back here and act responsible in front of the employees. I've been patient. Your mother and I are moving on. It's time for you to understand that. It's time for you to put this cowgirl nonsense out of your mind and come back here and tend to your responsibilities. And I mean now." Then the line went dead. Her father had made his demands and then hung up on her.

Montana just stood there in disbelief, holding the phone to her ear. Closing her eyes, she tried to calm down. She wished Luke was near so she could talk to him. Wished she could feel his reassuring embrace.

After all that her dad had done…after all the pain he'd inflicted on his family, he had called her dream nonsense? Told her she was being selfish?

Her dreams weren't nonsense. They weren't worthless.

"You okay?" a cowboy asked as he was passing by. "You look like you're going to pass out."

Montana gave him a tight smile. "I'm fine. Thanks."

He grinned. "Nerves will do that to you sometimes. Take a few breaths before you get out there, and you'll be fine."

Montana smiled and watched the pleasant cowboy head inside. Missing Luke all the more, she turned and headed back to get Murdock ready.

You have to forgive your dad, Montana. For your own good. Luke's words came back to her as she went. Her dad, so selfish and self-centered…and she was supposed to forgive him?

Let go of the bitterness. Choose who you want to be.

Montana stopped cold in her tracks. She was standing on the sidewalk before the parking lot, and it hit her—she didn't want to be angry anymore.

She didn't want her life to be dictated by her father or the anger she felt toward him.

She wanted to be the woman God had intended her to be. She wanted to let it go and be free of the heavy weight she'd been carrying around on her shoulders. It was unbelievable!

She needed to talk to Luke. She dialed his number, noticing a cowboy moving toward her from the direction where her truck was parked. He moved with a familiar gait. His hat shadowed his face, his dark hair curled from beneath it, and she knew… "Luke!" she called, beginning to walk toward the cowboy. She knew it was him. "Luke!" she exclaimed, knowing him anywhere. Her heart knew him, too, and lunged against her chest.

Realizing he might not see her for the cars splattered across the parking lot, she started running. Dashing off the sidewalk, she emerged from behind a trailer into the open. She waved as she ran, so excited to see him. "Luke—"

She never saw the truck blasting from around the corner of the building…until she heard the squeal of its brakes…

"Montana, can you hear me?" Luke couldn't think straight as he knelt beside her. She'd been looking at him when the truck came plowing around the corner. It stopped before it ran over her, but there had been contact. Montana was thumped hard by the truck, and sent flying to the pavement.

"Man, I'm sorry! I didn't see her."

Luke looked up at the young cowboy who'd jumped from the truck and was about to pass out with worry.

Montana started to sit up, but Luke held her down.

"Stay down," he commanded, as she looked straight at him.

"What are you doing here?" she asked.

"I came to see you ride, and you almost killed yourself in front of me?"

"Do I need to call the paramedics?" the cowboy asked, hopping from one boot to the other. "She's bleeding. See her arm—oh, man, oh, man it's bleeding. And she hit her head on the truck before she fell."

"No, I can get u—"

"Please call them," Luke cut her off, looking at her scraped hands and the tear in her jeans. This was worse than the time she fell off of Murdock. And she'd hit her head on the hood when she buckled forward. Luke was glad her eyes seemed clear. He didn't think the hit had been that hard, but they weren't taking any chances. "You stay put," he said when Montana tried to sit up again.

"I'm fine. I'll be ready to ride here in just a little while. I need to sit up and talk to you. I'm so glad you're here."

That sent a thrill racing through him. "You were hit by a truck, Montana, so don't move."

She gave him a dazzling smile as she looked up at him. "Okay, whatever you say."

Her easy agreement had him worrying about a concussion. He didn't see any lump forming on her forehead, so maybe she'd hit it harder than he thought.

"Does your head hurt?" he asked, leaning closer, to see if there was an injury of some kind that he was missing.

"Nope. I love you, Luke."

Her words froze him. He knelt beside her and he couldn't move. "You said you loved me? Just how many of me do you see?" he asked, figuring she'd had something knocked loose.

A slow smile spread over her face. "I see one of you, but I think you're worth twenty."

The crowd that had formed around them oohed over that statement, and he had to chuckle. "Okay, where's Montana Brown?" he asked, as the rodeo paramedics drove up in their ambulance and hopped out.

For the next twenty minutes Montana entertained the crowd and the paramedics. He was surprised when they bandaged up a few cuts and let her go.

"You'll probably be pretty sore tomorrow," one of them said, "but it's a wonder nothing was broken." They drove them over to her trailer and Luke helped her out. Then she waved to the paramedics as they drove off.

"Whew, I'm glad that's over," she said, winking at him.

Unable to hold back any longer, he pulled her carefully into his arms. "Montana, you scared me senseless."

She laid her head on his chest. "Sorry. I got a little reckless when I saw you. But you were supposed to be with Colt." She hugged him hard.

He pushed a loose strand of hair behind her ear and kissed her forehead. Thankful she was okay.

"I'm so glad you came. But what about Colt?"

Her words meant more to him than she could know. "He ended up being delayed a day, so I was only a couple of hours away from you—easy choice, I came to see you. I got here early and thought I'd surprise you. Little did I know you were going to throw yourself in front of a moving truck."

She chuckled despite the seriousness of the accident. He was sure the laugh was a release of tension more than anything.

A patient Murdock watched them with an expectant expression. The horse was ready to compete, just like Montana was. They were going to do well; he felt it.

"Luke," she said, not moving her head from his chest. "I told you I loved you earlier."

He stilled, trying to be nonchalant about it. "Yeah, I know. That's why I knew you'd had a hard lick."

She leaned back and held his gaze. "Not such a hard lick. I knew exactly what I was saying. That's what I was coming to tell you when I got hit."

"I think I need to sit down."

She gave a light chuckle as he reached for the door handle and pulled the back door open. Immediately, he sank to the seat, hanging on to her as he did. If he had his way, he wasn't ever letting her go. Not after what she'd just said.

"I love you, Montana, with all my heart. But what's happened? Why this sudden change of attitude?"

"My dad called and demanded that I come back to the firm because of my family obligations. He called my dreams nonsense and he took no responsibility for his actions. I was so angry, and then it hit me. I could hear you and God both telling me to let it go. I realized I didn't want all that anger hanging on me like weights. I wanted to feel free and happy. I wanted to know that I was in control of my life where my attitude and character are concerned. And above all, I knew God was in control. So I let it go, I let it all go. And I felt great. Then I wanted to see you so bad. I needed to share it with you, and then there you were! It was like a dream. I just couldn't believe you showed up. I still can't believe it."

He grinned at the joy in her words. "I'm so glad you're letting this anger go. One day, maybe you'll be able to mend fences with your dad. Letting the anger go and forgiving him is a way to open the door for that to happen. I'm proud of you. I knew you could do it."

She smiled. "I like that. I could get used to making you proud of me."

He laughed, feeling great. Then he sobered. "Do you think you could ever get used to living the rest of your life with me—you know, with the whole package, marriage, babies and a few National Rodeo Championships?"

She snuggled in close, hugging him tightly. "I would love it. But we'd have to have a plan."

"It can be done," he said, unable to believe he was hearing her right.

They grinned at each other, basking in the moment. He gently tugged on her braid. "I don't think that would be a problem at all," he said, and then he did what he'd been waiting to do—he lowered his lips to hers.

Montana kissed him, then sighed against his lips. "Life is good, isn't it, Luke?"

"It gets better by the moment. I love you, Montana Brown."

"And that is exactly what I've been needing to hear."

"I hope so, because you're going to be hearing it a lot."

"Bring it on, cowboy." She laughed. Murdock pawed the earth and snorted. "Okay, it's time to roll." She looked from Murdock to Luke. "You with me?"

Luke's heart was pounding with love and expectation of the future that lay ahead. "I'm with you, now and forever, cowgirl of mine."

Montana grinned. "Now *that's* what I like to hear!"

* * * * *

THE RANCHER'S
ANSWERED PRAYER

Arlene James

For Kay Hensley Strickland,
who has never lost her sweetness
and knows the true meanings of family and friendship.
DAR

For I know the thoughts that I think toward you,
saith the Lord, thoughts of peace, and not of evil,
to give you an expected end.
—*Jeremiah* 29:11

Chapter One

"Maybe Uncle Dodd didn't specifically mention the house in the will because he considered it unlivable."

Wyatt Smith glanced at his brother Jacob and back to the old house in front of them. Jake had only said out loud what everyone else was thinking. Barely a speck of white paint clung to the old two-story ranch house. Its once green scalloped shingles had faded to a military gray. The front door hung slightly askew, broken glass and all, and the porch showed gaping holes where floorboards ought to be. Obviously, Uncle Dodd hadn't spent any money on upkeep in his final years, so why had he sold off all the cattle, and what had he done with the proceeds?

"We'll make do," Wyatt stated flatly, ignoring the anxious hammering of his heart.

He and his brothers could camp out, if necessary, until they got Loco Man Ranch whipped into shape, but Frankie, Jake's three-year-old son and Wyatt's nephew, needed a safe, comfortable place to live. There had to be three or four habitable rooms in this big old house. Besides, it was too late to change their minds now.

They'd sold three businesses and two houses in Houston to make this move and raise the funds necessary to restock the ranch. Two thousand acres in south central Oklahoma could support a lot of cattle, and Wyatt was determined to bring the ranch back to profitability without selling off any acreage. Sink or swim, the Smith brothers were now officially residents of Loco Man Ranch on the very outskirts of War Bonnet, Oklahoma.

He'd never dreamed that the old house would be in such a sorry state, however. This was where he and his brothers had spent many a happy summer, playing cowboy and riding horseback every day. They'd stopped coming for the summer, one by one, after high school, but they'd each made time to see Dodd at least yearly until circumstances had kept them in Houston, occupied with the deaths of their dad and Jake's wife, as well as fully taking over the family's businesses. But they were ranchers now and, like three generations of Smith men before them, their hopes lay in the land beneath their feet. God willing, they were going to put Loco Man back on the map. And put the past behind them.

At least it wasn't too hot yet. The weather in mid-April was plenty warm but not uncomfortably so.

"Let's see what we're up against," Ryder said, striding forward.

At twenty-five, Ryder stood three inches over six feet, just like his older brothers. Thirty-five-year-old Wyatt prided himself on keeping in shape, but his build was blocky, while Ryder naturally carried his hefty two hundred pounds in his powerful arms, shoulders and chest. All three brothers had dark hair and brown eyes, but Ryder's hair was straight and black, whereas Wyatt's was curly and coffee brown. Jake's slimmer build and wavy hair gave him a more polished air, especially in a military uniform, so naturally he had been the first—and thus far the only one—of the brothers to marry. Wyatt suspected that he still grieved the death of his wife, Jolene, deeply.

Handing his son to Wyatt, Jake carefully followed in Ryder's path to minimize the possibility of falling through a weak spot in the porch floor. Wyatt waited, with Frankie in his arms, at a safe distance. The existing floorboards proved solid enough. The door, however, presented a challenge.

Jake elbowed Ryder out of the way and reached through the broken glass inset, saying, "My arm's skinnier than yours."

Gingerly fumbling for several moments, he frowned, but then something clicked and the outside edge of the door dropped slightly. Jake carefully extracted his arm from the jagged hole and stepped aside so Ryder could pull the door open. Wyatt followed his brothers inside.

Red-orange sand had blown into the entry through the broken glass, dulling the dark hardwood of the foyer floor and staircase. Framed photographs covered the foyer walls, all dulled by a thick layer of dust. Many of them, Wyatt saw at a glance, were poorly framed school pictures of him and his brothers, but others showed a sturdy girl with long, chestnut brown hair and heavy eyebrows, as well as a baby photo of a wrinkled newborn in a pale blue onesie. Everything else looked the same, dusty but familiar.

Antique furniture still stood around the cold fireplace in the parlor, dimmed by time and dirt. The dining-room wallpaper looked faded, and fragile gossamer webs coated the splotchy brass light fixture above the rickety dining table. Wyatt hoped the comfortable, roomy den and Dodd's ranch office were in better shape, but the important rooms right now were the kitchen and downstairs bath.

Despite the fact that he and his brothers had run through these rooms like wild boys summer after summer, Wyatt felt as if they were trespassing. A lack of human habitation seemed to have reduced the gracious old house to a shabby pile, and made Wyatt abruptly doubt his plan. Then Ryder pushed through a swinging door into the kitchen, and suddenly Wyatt saw home.

The appliances, cabinets and countertops were hopelessly outdated, and most of the paint had worn off the familiar old rectangular table. Thankfully, however, the room appeared as habitable now as it had the last time Wyatt sat in one of those old ladder-back chairs.

While Ryder checked the water, Jake took Frankie into the bathroom, and Wyatt tried the burner on the big, white stove. Pipes banged as water started flowing. Wyatt struck a match to ignite a tiny flame.

"Looks like we're low on propane."

"Pilot light on the hot water heater must be out," Ryder said, holding his hand beneath the gushing spigot.

"We can heat water on the stove until we can see to it," Wyatt determined.

Jake returned, Frankie following and hitching up

his baggy jeans. "Storage room is full of junk, but everything seems in working order in the bathroom."

That was good news because unless Uncle Dodd had updated the plumbing, which seemed unlikely, the only shower in the house was in that downstairs bathroom.

"Check the bedrooms," Wyatt said to Ryder, who strode off at a swift clip for the staircase. "Jake, think you can find a broom?"

Before Jake could even begin to look, the sound of a vehicle arriving turned them both toward the back door.

"Company already?" Jake asked, swinging Frankie up into his arms.

"Folks around War Bonnet are friendly," Wyatt commented, "but this is ridiculous." Through the glass inset in the back door, he saw a small, white sedan pull up next to the back stoop. He walked over and threw the deadbolt, relieved that the door swung open easily.

As Wyatt watched, a curvy brunette of average height slid from behind the sedan's steering wheel. Dressed in a simple gray skirt with a bright pink, sleeveless blouse, she presented a polished, feminine picture. Her short, stylishly rumpled, cinnamon hair framed a perfectly oval face with enormous, copper-colored eyes. Though she seemed oddly familiar, Wyatt couldn't place her. Maybe she was one of the town kids who the brothers had sometimes played with. Whoever she was, she was lovely.

If this is the War Bonnet welcoming committee, he thought, *things are looking up already.*

Then she parked her hands on her hips, tossed her cinnamon brown head and demanded, "What are you doing in my house?"

* * *

"*Your* house?"

After the week she'd had, Tina was in no mood to explain herself, especially not to some big lunk who probably thought he was God's gift to women. That's what all the good-looking ones thought, that women should fall at their big feet in stunned silence and stay that way. Well, she'd had enough of biting her tongue and hoping, praying, to be treated fairly. She'd come home—the only place she'd ever thought of as home, anyway—and here was where she intended to stay. Even if the house did look as if might fall down in a stiff breeze.

She reached into the car and grabbed her handbag. "That's right. *My* house." She lifted her chin at the big man in the doorway. "Who are you and why are you here?"

"I'm Wyatt Smith."

Oh, no. One of the Houston nephews. She should've expected this. Another man crowded into the doorway behind the first, a young boy in his arms. Both had the dark Smith hair and eyes. Wyatt slung a thumb at him. "This is my brother Jake and his son, Frankie."

Wyatt *and* Jacoby. Well, that was two of the brothers. "I suppose Ryder is also here."

Wyatt frowned. "Who *are* you?" he asked, as if he ought to know her, though they'd never met.

"I'm Tina Walker Kemp."

If the name meant anything to him, he didn't show it. He folded his arms across an impressively wide chest.

"What makes you think this house is yours, Tina Walker Kemp?"

"I don't *think* it," she said, placing one foot on the sagging bottom step. "I *know* it. My stepdaddy left me this house."

"Your stepdaddy," Wyatt repeated, his tone skeptical.

"Dodd Smith."

"Whoa!" Wyatt exclaimed. "Uncle Dodd left *us* this place."

She shook her head. "That's not what the will says."

"That's exactly what it says," Wyatt countered firmly. "And I have the will to prove it."

Tina lifted her eyebrows. "So do I."

Just then her six-year-old son, Tyler, yelled, "Mo-om, I gotta go!"

Tamping down her impatience, Tina turned back to the car and opened the door for him. They'd just driven four hours without stopping, after all, and she'd let him have that extra juice box. Besides, if the house was safe for Jake Smith's son, it must be safe for hers. She signaled for Tyler to join her, and he hopped down out of his seat, having already released his safety belt.

When Tyler reached her side, she automatically lifted a hand to smooth down the spike of reddish-blond hair that always managed to stand up. He automatically dodged her, jerking his head out of reach. The Smith brothers exchanged glances, and Jake stepped back, gesturing at Tyler.

"Come on in."

Tyler followed without bothering to look to his mother for permission. Sighing inwardly, Tina followed her son up the steps. Tyler squeezed past Wyatt, who didn't bother to move out of the way. Instead, Wyatt just stood there, challenging her with every ounce of his considerable weight. Mimicking his stance, Tina stopped on the narrow stoop, folded her arms, met his gaze squarely and purred, "Excuse me."

His shadowed jaw worked side to side as he ground his teeth, but then he stepped back and let her pass. She walked into the kitchen, both dismayed and comforted by its condition. Fortunately, she had learned long ago to keep her opinions to herself, so she made no comment. Just in case the Smith nephews thought she might be unfamiliar with the place, however, she pointed to the back hallway and addressed her son.

"Right down there, honey."

Tyler trotted off, flipping a curious wave to the youngest Smith, who hugged his father's neck with one arm and copied Tyler's gesture with the other.

"Potty," the boy said just as Tyler disappeared from sight.

"Frankie's what? Three now?" Tina asked Jake.

Nodding, Jake narrowed his eyes suspiciously before stooping to set the boy on his feet. "That's right."

The boy darted away from his father and into the arms of his uncle. Wyatt scooped him up with practiced ease. Jacoby, meanwhile, frowned at Tina.

"You sure seem to know a lot about us."

"I ought to. Daddy Dodd talked about you constantly."

"Unca Wyatt," Frankie asked, pointing a timid finger at Tina, "who's that?"

"Couldn't tell you," Wyatt replied dourly.

Tina sighed. "I told you. My name is Tina Walker Kemp. Dodd Smith was my stepfather. He left me this house and—"

"You are confused," Wyatt interrupted. "Uncle Dodd left this place to us, all two thousand acres of it."

"I'm *not* confused," Tina insisted. "Daddy Dodd sent me a paper which states clearly that the house and mineral rights to Loco Man Ranch are *mine*."

"That doesn't make any sense!" Jake erupted.

"In Oklahoma," Wyatt said, his voice low and growling, "mineral rights are separate from property rights. But nothing was ever said to me about the house *not* being part of our bequest."

Jake threw up his hands. "That's just swell."

Ignoring him, Wyatt demanded of Tina, "And just when did *Daddy Dodd* send you that paper leaving you his house and mineral rights?"

Ignoring the lump of fear that had risen in her throat—if Daddy Dodd had written a later will without telling her—Tina calmly answered, "Over two years ago, right after my divorce."

Wyatt scowled, but whether it was due to the time-line, the fact that she was divorced or the paper in her possession, Tina couldn't say. Not that it mattered. She had come home, and she had no intention of leaving. She couldn't. She had no other safe place to go.

"Now, why would Dodd leave you the house and mineral rights?" Jake wanted to know.

"Because he knew I love it here," Tina replied, sweeping aside a stray hair on her forehead. "I didn't want to leave when he and my mom split up, and I came to visit as often as I could."

Wyatt's dark eyes held hers. "You were how old when they split?"

"Almost sixteen."

"And that was how long ago?" Jake demanded. Grimacing, he added, "Sorry, you just don't look old enough to be the only stepdaughter I ever knew Uncle Dodd to have."

"Well, I am old enough," she retorted firmly. "I'm twenty-nine."

"So, thirteen years ago," Wyatt muttered. Suddenly, his eyes widened. "Wait a minute…you're Walker."

Tina couldn't help chuckling. "That's right. He called me Walker because my mother called me Tiny instead of Tina, and I had some issues with that nickname. He was the only person in the world to call me by my last name."

Wyatt finally put it together. "Your mother was Gina Walker."

"Correct." Though technically it was Gina Schultz Walker Haldon Smith Murray Becker. Gina hadn't believed in dropping the surnames of her husbands; she'd just added to them.

"That's you in the photos in the foyer," Wyatt deduced.

Tina grimaced. She'd been a tubby teenager, self-conscious about her shape, and her overbearing mother had called her Tiny in a futile effort to get Tina to slim down. When she looked in the mirror now, Tina still saw an overweight woman, but at least she knew how to dress for her figure these days.

"I think one of Tyler's baby pictures is hanging there, too," she said in a half-hearted attempt to change the subject. "At least that's where Dodd said he was going to hang it last time we were here."

"And when was that exactly?" Wyatt asked, sounding tired suddenly.

"Tyler was maybe eight months old, so about five-and-a-half years ago. Maybe a month or two longer. I think it was June." She thought a moment. "Yes, it was June. I was hoping to stay through the Fourth of July, but..."

She flashed back to the sound of the telephone ringing in the middle of the night. Her husband, Layne, had raged that she'd abandoned him when he'd needed her most and demanded that she return home. She'd stupidly gathered up her sleeping baby and hit the road, only to find that the emergency he'd referred to was nothing more than a lost commission. As his wife, accepting blame for everything that went wrong in his life had been her primary role, but at the time she'd still believed that if she was just patient and long-suffering enough, Layne would magically morph into the steady, loving husband and father she'd imagined he would be when she'd married him.

Pushing aside the unwanted memories, Tina cleared her throat. "Things were in better shape the last time I was here."

Wyatt shook his head grimly. "Wait'll we check the roof and plumbing, not to mention the electricity."

Fear tightened into a lump in Tina's stomach. The electricity had been downright scary the last time she was here, so she had no doubt that the wiring needed upgrading, but she refused to be daunted. "Doesn't matter. I'll set things to right." Somehow.

"You sound awfully sure of that," he said, "even though I stand here with a will that leaves me and my brothers everything."

She gave him her steeliest glare. "Oh, I *am* sure. One man has already taken me for everything I owned, and I'll never let that happen again."

Chapter Two

Well, this is a fine mess.

Wyatt looked at the two papers in his hands, but no matter how long he stared, nothing changed. Both were dated identically and drawn up by the same attorney, Rex Billings. Sighing, Wyatt dropped the papers to the table in the Billings' ranch house kitchen and rubbed a hand across his brow. What had Uncle Dodd been thinking? And how could the lawyer let him do this? Wyatt's stomach roiled.

Dodd had mentioned Walker over the years, even though his marriage to her mother hadn't lasted long, but Tina Walker hadn't meant anything to Wyatt, so he'd tuned out the old man whenever he'd started waxing eloquent about the girl. Obviously, he should have paid better attention.

That was in the past, however, and Wyatt had known the only way to settle the current dilemma was to talk to the attorney who had apparently drawn up these ridiculous papers. Using his cell phone, he'd called the number on the will and reached one Callie Billings, the wife of attorney and rancher Rex Billings. Now he and Tina Kemp sat in their warm, homey kitchen sipping coffee and ignoring each other. Callie, as she'd insisted they call her, was a pretty little blonde with a baby boy and a daughter about Frankie's age playing quietly on the floor. Callie moved about the kitchen with her son perched on her hip, pouring coffee and removing cookies from the oven with one hand.

"Rex should be here any minute," she said, shifting the baby to the other hip. The front door opened, and Callie smiled brightly.

They heard two thumps, followed by silence. A few seconds later, the swinging door between the dining room and kitchen opened, and a tall, dusty cowboy padded into the space on his stocking feet. The little girl on the floor jumped up and ran to greet him, throwing her arms around his thighs.

"Hello, darlin'." While Callie went to him, baby and all, he explained the situation. "My boots were filthy so I yanked them off. Now I need to wash my hands." Holding his hands away from them, he kissed the baby, then his wife.

Wyatt couldn't help but feel envious. He'd expected to be married and settled into family life by now himself, but somehow it just hadn't happened. Billings hurried to the sink to wash his hands. Finally, he turned back to the table.

"You must be Wyatt Smith."

Wyatt stood and put out his hand. "That's right. Thank you for seeing us on such short notice."

Shaking hands with Wyatt, Billings glanced at Tina and nodded. He looked to his wife then. "Honey, I've been dreaming about your coffee and cookies. Set me up." He sat down at the table. His daughter crawled up into his lap.

"Daddy, can I hab cookies?"

"*Have* cookies. What does Mama say?"

"Ask you."

"Then you can have *one* cookie."

"Yay!"

Callie had the cookie wrapped in a napkin by the time Billings set the girl on her feet.

"Sit on your blanket and eat," Callie instructed gently, as she poured another cup of coffee.

"We were sure sorry to hear about Dodd's passing," Billings began as Callie set the coffee in front of him.

"Thank you," Wyatt and Tina said at the same time.

Wyatt frowned at her. She spoke as if she were Dodd's next of kin. Then again, Dodd had spoken fondly of her over the years, though if he'd told his nephews nearly as much about her as he had apparently told her about them, they hadn't been paying attention.

"I was sorry that Dodd left instructions not to have a service," Billings went on, lifting his coffee cup. "It would have been well attended. He was much liked around War Bonnet."

"I appreciate you saying so," Wyatt told the other man, cutting a glance at Tina, who nodded and pressed her lips together as Callie placed a platter of cookies and three small plates in front of them.

"Now," Billings said, "how can I help you?"

"There seems to be some confusion about my uncle's will," Wyatt explained, passing the papers to Billings.

Rex swallowed some coffee and glanced over the

papers across the rim of his cup before stacking them on the table at his elbow. "No confusion. Dodd was very certain about what he wanted and how he wanted to do it."

"I don't understand."

Rex shrugged and reached for a cookie. "Your uncle wanted Ms. Kemp to have the house and the mineral rights. You and your brothers get everything else."

"I told you," Tina crowed triumphantly. She reached a hand across the table toward Rex. "I'm Tina Walker Kemp, by the way."

"Not Mrs. Smith, then."

Both Wyatt and Tina reacted at the same time. "No!"

Billings shot a glance at Wyatt before shaking Tina's hand. Then he released her and placed some cookies onto plates for her and Wyatt. "Eat up."

Tina nibbled, but after one bite of cookie, the world as a whole seemed a lot more palatable to Wyatt.

"Mmm. You should market these," Wyatt told Callie Billings, shaking a cookie at her.

"Don't even joke about it," Rex protested. "She has enough to do with me, these kids, my dad and helping her own father run his businesses."

"If you're looking to sell Loco Man," Callie said to Wyatt, "Rex and my dad might be interested in buying. You may know my father. Stuart Westhaven."

"The banker?"

"Among other things."

"Beware an ambitious businesswoman," Rex put in, shaking his head. "Always looking to expand." He reached out and pulled Callie close to him, kissing her soundly.

Envy knocked around inside Wyatt's chest again. Unbidden, his gaze stole to Tina Walker Kemp, who stared morosely at her empty plate as if wishing for the return of her cookie or perhaps another. Frowning at himself, Wyatt focused his mind on the subject at hand.

"We're not interested in selling," he stated firmly, though once his brothers heard that Tina's claim was real, they might have other ideas. Blanking his face, he asked, "You wouldn't know where we might rent a place to stay, would you? There's four of us, including my nephew, Frankie."

Rex shook his head. "Not offhand."

Wyatt grimaced before he could stop himself. "Something affordable to buy, then. Preferably on the east side of town."

"Lyons might have something for sale."

"Dix told me they sold that house they remodeled," Callie put in. "Saw him and Fawn at the grocery store."

"Well, there's a realtor in town. He'll know," Rex said casually. "I think your uncle was expecting y'all to share, though."

"Share!" Tina yelped, glaring at Wyatt as if he'd suggested the idea.

"Everyone knows the old house needs some work," Callie pointed out. She looked to Wyatt then, adding, "Even if you and your brothers aren't up to that, you could pay rent so Ms. Kemp could afford to hire Lyons and Son." She smiled at Tina. "They do excellent work, by the way."

Rent. Wyatt ground his teeth. His business plan didn't allow for rent, let alone buying a house for himself and his family. He especially did not like the idea of paying rent to live in what was rightly Smith property, but what was the option? Staying in the bunkhouse?

"What about the outbuildings?"

"They're yours," Rex told him. "Dodd was very intentional about it. The house and the mineral rights go to Ms. Kemp. Everything else goes to you and your brothers. Technically, you own the ground that the house sits on."

Well, that tipped the equation in his favor. Wyatt smiled cunningly at Tina Walker Kemp. "Maybe we can work something out."

She folded her arms mulishly, but Wyatt saw the worry in her big bronze eyes. Suddenly, he wanted to reassure her, promise not to pull the ground out from under her and her son. Literally. But the interested gazes of Rex and Callie Billings squelched the impulse.

Besides, whatever Uncle Dodd's foolish intentions had been, Wyatt meant to make a home on Loco Man Ranch for himself, his brothers and his nephew—Tina Kemp or no Tina Kemp.

Something told him that she would take nothing less than her due.

So be it.

Well, wasn't that just like a man?

Tina had never met a man who could keep his word. In the end, even Daddy Dodd had disappointed her. What did he think he was doing, leaving every square inch of the land to the Smith brothers and only the house that sat upon it to her? All right, the house *and* the mineral rights, for whatever that was worth.

At this point, she was afraid to hope. Where had hope ever gotten her? As the thought slid through her mind, she quickly followed it with a prayer.

Sorry, Lord. I'm just confused. And frightened. Lord, please, there must be some way to make this work, some way I can keep Tyler with me.

She'd snorted with derision when her ex-husband, Layne, had informed her that he intended to sue for custody of their son. Then his attorney had contacted her, and suddenly the threat had become all too real. Dodd had died only days before. In her grief and panic, she'd gone searching for the copy of the will he'd sent her. At the time, it had seemed as if Dodd had reached down from Heaven and handed her the answer to her problems. She could leave a job that demanded too much of her time and go home to Oklahoma with her son.

She hadn't given a thought to the land, only to the house. In the back of her mind, she'd sort of assumed that the ranch would go on as it always had, with Dodd's longtime foreman, Delgado, at the helm and reporting to the nephews. She'd never expected them to leave the big city of Houston, Texas, for the tiny town of War Bonnet, Oklahoma. She certainly hadn't expected them to take over *her* house.

She'd decided that she would open a bed-and-breakfast. With the nearest motel room at least 40 miles away, Dodd had often put up folks visiting War Bonnet. That neighborliness was one of the things that her mother, Gina, had disliked so much about small-town life.

Tina smiled wanly at Callie, wishing they had more

in common. Perhaps they soon would. Callie obviously placed making a home for her family at the top of her list, but she was also a businesswoman. The fact that Callie and her husband so clearly adored each other was the big difference between her and Tina. Well, that and the fact that Callie's house wasn't falling down around her.

Tina wondered if cashing in her small 401(k) to finance this had been wise, but what choice had she had?

Wyatt pushed back his chair and rose to his feet, stretching his hand across the table to Rex. The two men shook as if they were longtime friends.

"We would be most grateful," Wyatt was saying. "It's been a long time since I was on a horse, and I've never bought a cow in my life."

"We're just about through tagging and cutting the calves," Billings said, hooking his thumbs in the front pockets of his dusty jeans. "Give me another a few days, and we'll get at solving your livestock problem."

Callie chuckled. "Be warned. Rex especially loves to shop for horses."

"No one's more surprised by that than I am," Rex told her, hooking an arm about her waist and pulling her close again.

She laughed and said to Wyatt, "My husband has more in common with you than you know, Mr. Smith. He left Tulsa and a stellar law practice to come back here and help out when his father was ill. Then he found that the city no longer had any appeal."

It was obvious to anyone with eyes what had kept Rex in War Bonnet. Tina wanted to be happy for the couple, but to her shame she found that she could only be envious.

Had Layne ever looked at her like that? She highly doubted it. Why hadn't she been sensible enough to realize that the only thing about her that had attracted him was her attraction to him?

She had promised herself that she wouldn't follow in her mother's footsteps, flitting from husband to husband as if she were a bee darting from flower to flower. Yet, she had been the bee and Layne the flower in their relationship.

She wouldn't make that mistake again.

Thankfully, she had her son, and he was all she needed. She hadn't been enough for her own mother, and Tina was determined that her son would never feel that cold realization. Her father, whom she'd seen only a few times in her life, was little more than a name to her.

Tina wondered guiltily if she should relent and allow Layne to have custody of Tyler, but then she recalled her ex snarling at her that he would take everything she valued if she dared divorced him. He'd managed it, too, with everything and everyone but their son.

Dazedly, she felt a hand on her elbow. She didn't remember coming to her feet, but suddenly she realized that their meeting had ended. Wyatt now seemed determined to escort her from the premises. To cover her confusion and dismay, Tina subtly tugged free of him, smiled at their hostess and nodded at Rex before turning toward the door.

"Thank you for your time," she murmured.

Wyatt held open the door, saying something about

paying Rex for the consultation. Thankfully, Rex insisted that no payment was necessary. Relieved, she tried not to look at Wyatt's big, broad hand as she walked through the door. They moved through the dining and living rooms and into the foyer, Rex following in his stocking feet. Wyatt opened the front door for her. She pushed wide the screen and crossed the porch, stepping down onto the beaten dirt path that ran through the post oaks to the bronze-colored, double-cab pickup truck parked on the side of the red dirt road.

That truck was more luxurious than any vehicle Tina had ever ridden in. An electronic *beep* signaled that Wyatt had released the locks. Tina yanked open the door and stepped up onto the running board that automatically slid out from beneath the truck. She buckled her safety belt and waited for Wyatt to get in on the driver's side.

He started the engine and turned on the air conditioning. Then he spoke. "Looks like we're stuck with each other."

Stuck. That about summed up her life. She'd been stuck with her mother and then four subsequent stepfathers. No doubt Gina would have added another name to her long list if she hadn't tripped on the trailing hem of her dressing gown and fallen down a flight of stairs, breaking her lovely neck in the process. That's what had prompted Tina to accept Layne's marriage proposal, only to find herself stuck with a handsome chameleon who'd ultimately cheat on her.

She'd left Layne and met with a lawyer the next day. Layne had never again allowed her back into the house. With no choice but to find immediate employment, she'd found herself stuck in the job of secretary to a demanding real estate developer who expected her to toil the same endless hours that he worked.

Now here she was, stuck with the Smith brothers.

"Oh, Lord, why?" she prayed, not realizing that she'd spoken aloud until Wyatt sighed.

"When He answers, be sure to let me know."

Chapter Three

He didn't answer. God never seemed to answer her prayers.

She'd prayed that her mother's marriage to Dodd Smith would last. As easygoing and affable as he was hardworking, Dodd had been Tina's friend as much as her stepfather. After only nine months, however, Gina had declared herself bored beyond bearing and ended the marriage.

None of her prayers for her own marriage had been fulfilled, either, with one exception. Her son.

Now Layne wanted to take him, too.

For Tyler, she had left Kansas City and come here. For Tyler, she would put up with the Smith brothers and do everything in her power to make this move work.

"I'll trade you housing for help fixing up the house," she proposed, glancing from brother to brother.

She had taken a seat at the table in the dusty kitchen. The brothers had positioned themselves around the room. Wyatt leaned against the sink, his arms folded. Jake stood at the edge of the hallway as if listening to his son playing with hers in the laundry room, where the boys were taking turns rolling small cars into the corner of the sadly sloping floor. Ryder had hopped up to sit on the counter between the sink and the stove. Ryder Smith was only a few years her junior, but he had a sweetness about him that made him seem younger.

"I don't mind helping out," he said.

Wyatt shot him a glare. Ryder shrugged. "And once the house is fixed up, what then?" Wyatt wanted to know.

Tina lifted her chin. "You'll need to find other accommodations. I plan to turn this house into a bed-and-breakfast."

Jake snorted, and Wyatt rolled his eyes. Ryder, however, lifted his head in surprise and blurted, "Well, that makes sense. Uncle Dodd used to take in folks who came to visit family and friends in War Bonnet."

Tina could have kissed him. She noticed Wyatt again glared at Ryder. She knew instinctively that Wyatt was the brother she had to convince.

"We have a ranch to get going," he stated flatly. "We don't have time to remodel an old house."

"And we're going to live where while we're getting the ranch going?" Jake wanted to know.

"We can convert the bunkhouse into our living quarters." Wyatt turned his glare on Tina. "The outbuildings belong to us."

"I never said otherwise."

"Okay," Jake interjected, leaning a shoulder against the wall. "So, where do we live while we're converting the bunkhouse? It hasn't been used in decades, so I doubt there's even plumbing."

"Besides, why does it take all three of us to work the ranch when we don't even have any cattle?" Ryder wanted to know.

"We'll have cattle soon," Wyatt insisted, shifting his feet. "Rex Billings is going to help us find the livestock we need, including horses."

"You and Delgado can handle that, can't you?" Jake asked. "Meanwhile, I can work on the bunkhouse and Ryder can start putting this place to rights."

"What do a mechanic and a fight—" He broke off midword and scrubbed a hand over his face, heavily shadowed now with a day's growth of beard. "What do you and Ryder know about construction?"

"We know as much about carpentry as we do about ranching," Ryder put in softly. "I don't say we can do everything that's needed, but we can do a lot."

"Actually," Jake said, "we know *more* about construction than ranching. You forget that I remodeled my own house while Jolene was deployed and that Ryder worked in construction before…"

Tina glanced between the brothers, first at Ryder's bowed head, then at Wyatt, who studied his youngest brother with undisguised concern, and back at Jake. She saw sadness in all of them, deep, heavy sadness. But why? Some time ago, Dodd had mentioned that Jake's wife had died, but Tina sensed something else going on here.

Wyatt shook his head, then he looked at her and nodded. "Fine. Ryder will work for you while Jake takes care of the bunkhouse and I get the ranch started."

She doubted she would get a better offer. Still… She made a final demand.

"And you agree to deed me the land that the house sits on."

Wyatt's dark gaze held hers for several long, tense moments. "We'll see. I might just buy you out."

Surprised by the suggestion, Tina again glanced around the room. Apparently, Jake and Ryder were equally surprised.

"What makes you think I'll agree to that?"

He shrugged. "Maybe you don't have the money to renovate this old house."

He was right, but she'd learned a few things over the years, and she did have some connections to draw on. She knew where to find the very best bargains on building supplies and could call in a few favors.

"I'll manage," she told him.

"What about meals?" Jake wanted to know.

"I can cook," Tina drawled, "if that's what you're asking."

Jake looked pointedly at Wyatt, who seemed to require a moment to tamp down his irritation before saying, "We'll buy the groceries if you'll cook the meals."

"Done."

He waved a hand. "I suggest we figure out who gets what bedroom and settle in."

Jake pushed away from the wall. "Frankie and I can share."

"Actually," Ryder said, "we may all have to share. Some of the rooms are empty of furniture. Two are uninhabitable. The window is missing in one of the rooms, and either the roof leaks or something's chewed through the ceiling in another."

Dismayed, Tina gasped. All eyes turned her way.

"What do you mean the window is missing?"

"I mean that it's gone." Ryder spread his hands, palms up. "Including the casing."

"And something chewed through the ceiling?"

"Well, there are tiny teeth marks around the opening."

Wyatt let loose a long, gusty sigh. "Okay. Get up to the attic and see what you can find. But watch yourself. The last thing we need is for anyone to get hurt. Jake, you and Ms. Kemp look at the other rooms and decide who goes where. I'll start unloading our gear."

"Call me Tina," she corrected. If they were going to be living in the same house, it seemed only right to be on a first-name basis.

Wyatt inclined his head, laying a hand to his chest. "You can call me Wyatt."

Jake lifted his hand. "It's Jacoby, but everyone calls me Jake."

Tina knew this, but she simply nodded.

"And I'm Ryder," the younger brother said, smiling.

"Dodd told me all about the three of you," Tina said, smiling in return.

"That's more than we can say for you," Wyatt muttered, moving toward the door.

Ignoring him, Tina pushed back her chair and stood. With so much to do and so much at stake, she couldn't afford to worry about anything else. Time to get to work.

She and Jake spoke to the boys, warning them to stay in the house out of harm's way while the adults arranged their living quarters. Frankie nodded compliantly, but as usual Tyler argued.

"Why can't we go outside?"

"Because we haven't had a chance to look around yet," Tina told him. "It's too dangerous until we know the outbuildings are all clear of vermin and the porch is roped off."

"Aw, I ain't scared of no vermin," Tyler sneered.

"You should be," Jake said. "Rats, squirrels, raccoons and skunks often carry rabies."

"What's rabies?"

"A very serious illness," Jake explained.

"I don't care," Tyler grumbled mulishly.

"I hope you don't mind shots then, because rabies will keep you in the hospital for lots of shots," Jake informed him.

Tyler frowned, considering this. Finally, he said, "I better make sure Frankie 'n' me don't get rabies."

"I'd appreciate that," Jake replied gravely, but Tina saw by the twinkle in his dark eyes that he was amused.

"Call out if you need us," Tina instructed. "We'll just be upstairs."

Tyler nodded and went back to rolling the toy car, accompanied by the sound effects of a revving engine and screeching tires. Tina followed Jake from the room, aware that he silently chuckled, his shoulders shaking with mirth.

"Boys," he commented softly when she fell into step beside him. "I think they're all born with a certain amount of stubborn pride."

Tina sighed. "I think Tyler got more than his fair share."

"Oh, I wouldn't worry about him. He's played well and been very patient with Frankie today."

She smiled her thanks for that and wondered why it was so much easier to like Jake than his older brother. The same seemed to be true of Ryder. A pity that Wyatt was the better looking one.

Most attractive, least likeable. Thankfully.

The last thing she needed was any sort of romantic entanglement. She had long since vowed that she would not follow her much-married mother's path. The only thing on her mind now would be creating a safe, stable home for her son. She'd do whatever she had to do to make that happen. Then Layne and his lawyer could take a hike.

Resolved, she accompanied Jake upstairs to see what Herculean tasks awaited her.

"The last thing we need is possums in the house," Wyatt muttered, staring at Ryder, who was covered in dust from his head to his shoes. He had cobwebs in his black hair, which he attempted to brush out with his fingers.

They'd all crowded into the upstairs hallway to hear what Ryder had found in the attic. This day just kept getting worse and worse, in Wyatt's estimation. First they found the house in sorry condition. Then they'd learned that Tina Kemp actually owned the thing. Now they were obligated to help her fix it up, critters included.

"Could be worse," Ryder reported. "I found evidence of bats."

Tina surprised Wyatt by letting out a frightened *eep*. She hugged herself and asked, "Will they come back?"

"Hope not. I've blocked every entry point to the attic

that I could find, including the hole in the ceiling. I'll cover up the empty window, and tomorrow I'll fix the ceiling, but the roof will need to be addressed before long because I also saw evidence of leaks up there."

Tina muttered something under her breath, but Wyatt chose to ignore it.

"Good work," he said to Ryder. "You and I can take the room with twin beds. Jake and Frankie can share one of the full beds." He turned to Tina. "That just leaves you and Tyler."

"We'll share my old room for now. There's only a twin bed, but I can make up a pallet on the floor."

Wyatt had brought up her many suitcases, so he now carried them to the room with the pink gingham wallpaper, making two trips. Some of the bags had to stay out in the hall.

"I can't vouch for the bedding," he told her, as she began positioning suitcases around the room and opening them.

"I brought my own."

"Thank God," he said. "All we brought are sleeping bags, and I doubt Jake would want to share one with Frankie even for a single night. Kid's a mini tornado in his sleep, all flailing arms and legs." He chuckled, thinking of the nights he'd spent with Frankie when both Jake and Jolene had been deployed. If not for the overwhelming relief of having his brother return safely from the war zone, Wyatt might have been jealous of his brother for taking Frankie home with him. Then Jolene had been killed in a training exercise just weeks after returning home, and Wyatt's envy had turned to grief.

Tina looked at Wyatt, her expression solemn. "Are you the kind of man who normally thanks God?" she asked.

Wyatt blinked and nodded. "I am." To his surprise, her coppery gaze softened a bit before she turned away, a pair of worn jeans and a faded red tank top in her hands.

"Good to know. Now if you'll excuse me, I'd like to change. Then we can strip the beds and haul the mattresses outside to beat the dust out of them."

Why hadn't he thought of that? "Of course." He backed out of the room and caught Jake by the elbow as he was heading downstairs, informing him of their latest chore.

While he and Jake manhandled the mattresses down to the porch to whack the dust out of them, Tina wiped down and swept out all seven rooms upstairs. Thankfully, she found additional bedsheets in the linen closet at the end of the hall. After tumbling them in the dryer to remove dust and anything else that might have found its way into the folds, she made up the beds. In the end, the sleeping bags weren't needed, so Wyatt had her use those to make a comfortable pallet for Tyler.

Unfortunately, the dryer repeatedly threw the breaker in the outdated junction box in the laundry room. Worse, more than one outlet sparked noticeably when they tried to use it. So, after the sheets were refreshed, they turned off the electricity. Considering the poor wiring, a portable generator—if they could even find one—didn't seem wise.

"Guess I'd better put an electrician at the top of my

list," Tina said tiredly as the waning sun threw shadows across the room.

"Looks like it," Wyatt agreed. "We can manage with flashlights for a while. Tomorrow I'll order some propane and see about changing the utilities into—"

"*My* name," Tina said flatly, dropping down onto the chair.

Wyatt sighed but remained silent.

"For the record," she went on, looking as weary as Wyatt felt, "I intend to divide two of the bedrooms upstairs into bathrooms. That will leave five bedrooms, though I intend to turn one of those into a sitting room that can be shared by the back two bedrooms. Just so you know."

"That leaves just four bedrooms for six people."

"Eventually, Tyler and I will sleep downstairs."

"In what? The den?"

"The den can be divided," she pointed out. "It's an enormous room. And there's the junk room."

Man, he hated this added complication. He and his brothers already had enough to deal with. They didn't need all this confusion, what with rooms being divided all over the house.

Lord, show me how to get through this, he silently prayed. *Don't let me say and do things I'll regret. We need the ranch to work for us.*

"Is there any food?" Tina asked, running a hand through her thick, spiky hair. "If so, I'll start supper as soon as the water is heated."

She had two huge pots of water on the stove for the boys' baths, but the adults would have to make do with cold showers tonight.

"I'm afraid there's not much here," Wyatt informed her. She looked too tired to cook, anyway, but he didn't say so. "Jake offered to head into town to pick up burgers for supper, if that's all right with you."

"Works for me. I'll hit the grocery store tomorrow and buy some food."

Wyatt's stomach applauded that plan. He just hoped she could actually cook. If not, they'd be back to living on canned goods, cereal and the limited fare from the town's single eatery. Wyatt had fond memories of the old diner, but he wouldn't want to eat there three times a day.

"You didn't seem to bring much in the way of housekeeping supplies," Ryder commented, rubbing his dark head with a thin towel.

She shook her head, her short chestnut hair flopping over her eyes. Pushing aside the glossy strands, she said, "Didn't have much to bring, but surely Dodd left enough pots and pans to see us fed."

"I wouldn't count on it, but we should have everything you need," Wyatt told her, heading toward the bathroom. "In fact, I don't know where we're going to put all the furniture."

"You're moving in furniture?" Tina squawked in obvious surprise.

Actually, they had enough furniture for two households, but he kept that information to himself for the moment.

"Don't get in a huff," he said, coming to a halt. "The moving company will store our things until the bunkhouse is ready. You'll have plenty of room for your furniture." That came off as surly, which was not his intention. Before he could soften his remarks, however, she wearily lifted the back of her forearm to her brow.

Sighing, she muttered, "I don't have any furniture. This is it for us."

Wyatt frowned. "What? Not even a TV?"

She shook her head again. "Nearly everything was rented, and what wasn't, I sold."

Suddenly, Wyatt felt guilty because he'd silently grumbled that she'd brought more suitcases than he and his family together.

"Besides," she said, keeping her gaze averted, "I didn't have room for anything else."

That was the truth. The car had been stuffed. He'd assumed that the bulk of her goods would follow, but now he remembered something she'd said earlier.

One man has already taken me for everything I owned, and I'll never let that happen again.

Apparently, she'd left her marriage with very little. Wyatt had been under the impression that belongings were divided equitably during a divorce. Maybe she and her husband hadn't acquired much, but she and her ex should have had at least four or five years to acquire a few furnishings.

Had her ex sent her and her son into the world without the necessities? Wyatt frowned at the thought. Not that it was any of his business. Besides, he disliked the curiosity that her situation aroused in him. In fact, he disliked her, though he couldn't honestly say why.

This situation wasn't her fault, after all. When it came right down to it, what she did with this house was no business of his. The house and everything in it belonged to her. But what on earth had Dodd been thinking when he'd created this mess?

Wyatt hurriedly showered and dressed. He decided not to shave, despite his scruffy appearance. Staying clean-shaven was a near impossibility with his heavy beard, and he wasn't eager to attempt a smooth shave with cold water. Plus, with daylight fading, he needed to leave time for the others to clean up.

Tina was next and dressed in fresh jeans and a baggy T-shirt. With her hair wet and her subtle makeup scrubbed away, she could have passed for sixteen. For the first time, her hair looked as dark as her gracefully arched brows.

She had the most amazing skin he'd ever seen. Her big, almond-shaped eyes were a bright shade of light brown, somewhere between amber and copper. Wyatt had to work at not staring.

Relieved when she went back into the bathroom to scrub the tub, he got Frankie ready for his bath. Then he helped Ryder carry in the hot water and fill the tub. After adding cool water to achieve the perfect temperature, Tina bathed the boys together and dressed them in pajamas.

With his dad gone to get dinner, Frankie crawled up into Wyatt's lap at the old kitchen table while Tina scrubbed the table top. The odd domesticity of the situation felt both peculiar and satisfying at the same time.

He hadn't shared a house with a woman in the nearly twenty years since his mother, Frances, had died, leaving him a fifteen-year-old with younger brothers, aged ten and five, to care for. Their father had been devastated after the auto accident that had taken his wife.

Once he'd recovered from his own injuries, Albert Smith had buried himself in work and grief. The job of raising his younger brothers had chiefly fallen to Wyatt. Long before a heart attack had taken their father, almost six years ago now, Wyatt had assumed the role of family patriarch.

Jake's wife, Jolene, had been the only significant female influence to enter the Smith realm in all the years since Frances's death. As a soldier, Jolene had been as much warrior as woman in Wyatt's estimation, so in many ways, she'd felt like one of the guys.

He couldn't think of Tina Kemp that way.

It would be best then, Wyatt told himself, if he didn't think of Tina at all.

As he entertained Frankie, Wyatt surreptitiously watched as Tina ruffled her damp hair with a towel. Women with short hair didn't usually appeal to him, but Tina couldn't have appeared more feminine.

The woman wasn't just lovely—she was a beauty, which meant that this living arrangement was going to be a real trial.

Chapter Four

Jake finally returned home with supper, and Tina set out everything and got the boys situated at the table. Tall for his age, Tyler required no help reaching his food. Frankie, however, needed a lift. She found a small plastic tub sturdy enough to serve as a booster seat.

According to his brothers, Jake was famous for his hot showers, so no one was surprised that he came out shivering in his jeans and white T-shirt. Wyatt and Ryder laughed at him, bantering about bathing conditions in Afghanistan and the average military barracks. Tina was not surprised to learn that Jake was former military. Something in his manner marked him as a soldier; yet, Wyatt remained the undisputed head of this family.

Once they were all seated, Wyatt bowed his head. Tina froze in the act of unfolding the paper wrappings on her burger. She caught Tyler's glance and put her hands together to show him that they were going to pray, something she'd let slide recently. Frankie obviously had been through this routine many times. Folding his chubby hands, he bowed his little head along with his father and uncles.

Wyatt glanced up at her. "Uh, would you like to say grace?"

Tina took the opportunity to prompt her son. "Tyler, maybe you'd like to pray over our meal tonight."

Grimacing, Tyler bowed his head and intoned the familiar words. "God is great. God is good. Thank You, Lord, for this food. And maybe we can go back home soon. Amen."

"We are home, son," Tina corrected softly.

That unenthusiastic prayer stuck in Tina's head as she ate her meal and the Smith brothers talked over the next day's plans. With the house a wreck and the cattle gone, she couldn't help wondering why they were even here. She thought about explaining her own situation and appealing to the brothers' compassion in the hope that they would simply return to Texas. In truth, however, she needed their help. Actually, if not for Wyatt, she'd be quite happy with the situation.

What was it about him, she wondered, that disturbed her so?

It didn't matter. She couldn't see any option other than to follow through with her plan. Maybe Wyatt would be too busy with the ranch to waste time making her life difficult.

Vain hope, that. He was a man, wasn't he?

On the other hand, despite the fiasco of the wills, Daddy Dodd had been a caring, stalwart friend when she'd most needed one. Maybe his nephews were more like him than first impressions had indicated.

Strange, but that thought brought neither hope nor

relief. She could only pray that Wyatt would be so dili-
gent about getting the ranch into shape that he stayed
out of her business. Too weary to worry about it, she
and Tyler retreated to their room as soon as it was dark.
She slept surprisingly well, waking far later than usual
to find Ryder frying eggs and bacon that Jake had jour-
neyed back into town to purchase. Thankfully, Wyatt
had already departed on ranch business, according to
Ryder, who had no idea when Wyatt would return.
Tina silently thanked God for that small blessing, and
sat down with pencil and paper to discuss with Ryder
what repairs were most urgently needed.

Wyatt shook the dusky hand of the man he had ever
only known as Delgado. Relief bolstered his hope.
They'd agreed to meet at the diner in War Bonnet,
where both had enjoyed a decent breakfast and excellent coffee, while ignoring the obvious interest of the
locals. They'd quickly come to terms about Delgado's
continued employment.

"I'm very glad to get you back at Loco Man," Wyatt
said as he pushed through the glass door to the sidewalk.

"I am glad again to work for a Smith," Delgado replied.

The smiling vaquero's once dark hair had turned to
a dull salt-and-pepper shade that would soon be more
salt than pepper, but he'd maintained his lean, ropy
strength.

"Do you have time to drive around the ranch with
me?" Wyatt asked. "Rex Billings has offered to take

me to a sale barn in Tulsa to purchase horses in a few weeks, so we can't ride."

"Yeah, *sí*," Delgado said with a grin. "We take my old truck. No reason to batter yours. No one better with horseflesh than a Billings, but we had ATVs in the barn, unless Dodd sold those, too."

"There are two," Wyatt confirmed, falling into step beside the ranch foreman, "but they don't seem to run."

"They pro'ly just need gas and spark plugs," Delgado surmised.

"I'll have Jake look at them. He's our mechanic. Meanwhile, your truck will do fine."

This wouldn't be his first time riding with Delgado behind the wheel. Crazy as it seemed, he'd once taken the passenger seat as Delgado had raced his battered old truck across a bumpy pasture while Uncle Dodd had roped a particularly troublesome stud from the truck bed. That was not a feat Wyatt intended to repeat, but because of it he had no qualms about letting Delgado take the wheel.

"Meet me at the house," Wyatt instructed, "and we'll go from there."

"Yeah, *sí*."

Wyatt chuckled at the familiar double assent. As a young boy, he'd assumed that *ya-sí* was the Spanish word for *yes*. Only later had he realized that Delgado frequently spoke in a combination of English and Spanish.

A few hours later, neither of them could manage a smile. As he brought the dusty old pickup truck to a stop beside the house, Delgado's expression registered as much confusion as Wyatt's. Dimly, Wyatt noted that in the intervening hours Ryder had repaired the floor of the porch, rehung the front door and replaced the broken glass pane. Wyatt's immediate concern, however, was the puzzling condition of the ranch.

They'd driven past fenced acreages sown in what appeared to be a variety of grasses. Those large plots, some of them thirty and forty acres, didn't even have gates to let cattle in to graze. Some were irrigated with portable, aboveground systems powered by rackety old windmills. Some were not.

"Was Dodd experimenting?" Wyatt mused. "Could he have been trying to figure out which grass was most hardy and would best support cattle?"

Delgado shrugged and shook his head. "He never say. When the worms got the cattle, some had to be put down. The rest we treat and sell. Then he start dragging in old windmills and drilling wells. 'Times change,' he say. And he start the grass, many kinds. He hire that Pryor kid to do it, the one with the farming equipment. And we build fence roun' the grass."

"Fences without gates," Wyatt murmured. "It doesn't make sense."

"Some say he lost his mind," Delgado reported bluntly, "that he was loco like his great-grandfather, but I think no."

The legend was that Wyatt's great-great-grandfather had illegally paid others during the land rush to stake claims to the vast acreage that eventually became the Smith ranch. Then, when authorities called him on the scheme, he'd pretended not to understand the problem, no matter how it was explained to him, leading others to label him loco or insane. Wyatt somehow doubted that a reputation for insanity would have swayed the authorities, even back then, to simply allow Great-Great-Grandpa Smith to keep his ill-gotten gains. Nevertheless, he'd named the ranch Loco Man, with an apparent tongue-in-cheek reference to the rumors.

"I just wish I knew what Dodd was thinking," Wyatt admitted on a sigh.

"So, we run cattle at Loco Man again, yeah, *si*?" Delgado asked.

"We are most definitely going to run cattle at Loco Man again," Wyatt confirmed, "but there's a lot to be done before we can stock up. I think I'll talk to this Pryor fellow to see if he knows what Dodd was up to."

"Rex Billings, he'll tell you how to find Pryor. He marry Billings' sister."

So, Pryor was Rex's brother-in-law. That was welcome news.

After Delgado left, Wyatt walked into the main house to find Tina scrubbing a huge cast-iron skillet. She blew a strand of hair out of her eyes and jerked her head at the old ice chest on the floor.

"If you're hungry, I made some sandwiches. There's fruit on the table and chips in the pantry."

"Sounds good. Thanks."

"The cooler has iced tea, too. I didn't sweeten it, but there's a sugar bowl next to the fruit bowl."

Wyatt didn't offer an opinion on that. Every real Texan knew that tea had to be sweetened while it was hot. He guessed they did things differently where Tina was from. After tasting the tea, though, he decided he could tolerate it unsweetened, as it was surprisingly mellow. He sat at the table and ate his lunch, pondering Dodd's actions and trying not to watch Tina as she vigorously scoured the heavy pan. Finally, she rinsed the skillet and transferred it to a flame on the stove, which flared considerably higher than the day before.

"Guess the propane delivery came," Wyatt said between bites of his ham sandwich.

She dried her hands with a towel, glancing at him. "It did."

"How bad was it?" he asked.

She pulled a folded piece of paper from the hip pocket of her jeans and showed it to him. He lifted his eyebrows and made an executive decision.

"We'll split the bill with you."

Tina blinked at that. "You will?"

"Seems to me we ought to be sharing all the utilities. And paying for groceries. At least so long as we're sharing the house."

"I'm not going to argue with that."

He bit his tongue to keep from blurting out how much that surprised him. Somehow he'd expected her to argue about every little thing, even when it worked to her advantage. Finishing his sandwich, he plucked an orange from the bowl on the table and sat back in his chair to peel it.

"Where are the boys?"

"Giving Ryder headaches, I imagine," she replied. "He was supposed to put Frankie down for a nap before patching the ceiling in that one bedroom. I told Tyler not to tag along with them, but Ryder said he didn't mind. Since Tyler and I are going to start his home-schooling tomorrow, I let it go."

Wyatt nodded, unconcerned but puzzled. Ryder was

good with Frankie. He didn't see why Ryder couldn't handle Tyler, too. On the other hand, he didn't understand why Tina didn't give the War Bonnet elementary school a chance. She had more than enough to do without adding homeschooling to the ever-growing list.

"I've always understood that the school here in War Bonnet is above average, with small classes, dedicated teachers and a solid curriculum. There was a time my folks thought about moving up here so my brothers and I could attend this school. If Dad's business hadn't taken off so well, I think they might've done it."

After his mom's death, his dad had almost sent him and his brothers here to live with Dodd. Wyatt would have welcomed that, but even at fifteen he'd understood that sending them away would have meant the end of Al Smith. Their dad had needed them as much as they'd needed him, so Wyatt had argued against the plan and promised to take on more responsibility than a fifteen-year-old ever should.

He wasn't certain that it had made any real difference in the end. It seemed to him that all Albert had ever done was go through the motions until he'd just given up. Sort of like Tina was doing right now. She pretended great interest in the condition of the worn wooden countertops, scrubbing them with a rag, though they already looked cleaner than Wyatt had ever seen them.

"Semester's already half-through," she said, industriously rubbing away with that limp rag.

"What difference does that make? At least Tyler would have a chance to make friends his own age."

"I know what's best for my own son," she snapped, whirling around to confront him.

Wyatt held up his hands in surrender. "I just wondered, that's all."

"Well, don't," she muttered, turning back to her task. At the last moment, she gave it up, tossing the rag into the sink.

Changing the subject, Wyatt asked, "Did Dodd say anything to you about planting grass?"

"Grass?" she echoed uncertainly. "Not that I recall. Why?"

Wyatt explained about the fenced fields of grass and the windmills. She shook her head.

"That doesn't make a bit of sense."

"Doesn't seem to, but Dodd usually knew what he was about."

She parked her hands on the edge of the counter behind her. "Like leaving you the land and me the house that sits on it?" she drawled sarcastically.

Maybe the old man had been losing it, after all. Wyatt pushed back his chair. "Think I'll head over to the Billings place and see if anyone there has a clue."

"Supper at six," Tina told Wyatt, as he made for the door, "and it's flashlights again tonight. Electrician can't come until tomorrow."

"At least there's hot water," he pointed out, pushing through the screen door, giving Tina one last surreptitious look before walking outside.

Why couldn't he seem to stop staring at the woman? He saw women every day who he barely noticed. Now the prickliest one he'd ever encountered, the one who'd messed up all his carefully designed plans, had him gawking like a teenage boy.

Lord, whatever You're doing here, he prayed silently as he strode for his truck, *I wish You'd let me in on it.*

God brought nothing to mind, however, as Wyatt drove toward Straight Arrow Ranch, so he supposed he'd just have to muddle through as best he could.

He caught Rex finishing up his lunch. His father, Wes, was there, along with the very fellow Wyatt most wanted to see.

Dean Pryor was a tall, muscular, fair-haired man with a ready smile. Wyatt could see why Delgado had referred to him as a boy. He had a sense of relaxed fun about him that was usually associated with carefree children. Still, no one could doubt Pryor's maturity or resist the sparkle of his blue eyes. Wyatt imagined that he was just the sort to charm every woman he met. He happily answered Wyatt's every question.

Unfortunately, Dean didn't have any idea why Dodd had hired him to sow grasses on the property, five varieties in all, especially as every site had been covered with natural grass already standing tall. The selections of sites and grasses had been well planned, however. Dodd had made sure that those varieties that most needed water had water available. The more drought-resistant varieties had gone in where no immediate water source was located.

"I thought he might be cooperating with a government test," Pryor reported, "but when I suggested that, he just about doubled over laughing."

"Did he explain why he fenced the grass fields?"

Pryor spread his broad, capable hands. "I didn't know he had."

No one else around the table seemed to have any answers for him.

"Boys, we better get back at it," Wes interjected before taking a final slug of his coffee. "I've got a list a mile long of things to get done before the wedding."

Wyatt glanced at Dean, though he definitely recalled Delgado saying that Pryor had already married Rex's sister. As if he knew what Wyatt was thinking, Dean grinned.

"Don't look at me. I'm married and got two kids already."

Everyone laughed. Wes raised his hand, saying, "I'm the groom. Y'all think you're so funny."

"Dad roped and tied the local doc," Rex chortled.

"Don't let Alice hear you say that," Callie scolded. "She'll rope, tie and sedate you."

"I'll be all for it by the time we get these calves cut," Rex declared, pushing up to his feet.

Dean, too, rose. "I might as well get back to playing cowboy before my wife comes looking for a babysitter."

"You picked a good day. It's Wednesday. We'll have to knock off early for prayer meeting tonight," said Wes.

"Stark might be able to pitch in," Rex suggested. "Why don't I give him a call?"

"Stark Burns is the busiest man I know," Wes said, shaking his head. "Even if that daughter of mine has slowed him down a notch or two."

"Wait," Wyatt interjected, pointing at Dean. "I thought he was married to your daughter."

"I've got two daughters," Wes said with a big grin. "Three, counting Callie here."

She went on tiptoe to kiss her father-in-law's cheek.

"If you need a hand, maybe I can help out," Wyatt volunteered.

"You know anything about cutting calves?" Rex asked.

"Not really," Wyatt admitted, "but I ought to, and I'm a fast learner."

"Can you ride and rope?" Wes asked.

"That I can do, but I might be a bit rusty."

"You're hired," Rex decreed. "We've got a bumper crop of bull calves this year, and the sooner we make 'em steers, the sooner they'll fatten up for market."

"I can call our ranch foreman, Delgado, to come over if you like."

"Now, why didn't we think of Delgado?" Rex asked.

The men all headed for the door, Wes joking, "I'm getting married soon. I've got enough on my mind. Why didn't *you* think of Delgado? You're the brains of the operation."

"Y'all heard him, boys," Rex bantered. "I am the official head of the Billings brain trust. Just remember that."

They were stomping into boots and reaching for hats in the foyer when Wyatt pulled out his cell phone to call Delgado. While he waited for the other man to answer, Rex glanced at the hat pegs on the wall, asking, "Where's your hat? You're gonna need it."

"Oh, I don't have one," Wyatt admitted, breaking off when Delgado finally answered. Wyatt explained the situation and heard the delight in his foreman's voice as he agreed to hurry over to the Billings ranch. "He's on his way," Wyatt announced, sliding the small phone back into his pocket. He looked up to find Wes and Rex standing with piles of battered cowboy hats in their hands.

"Let's try this one," Wes said, passing a stained, cream-colored hat to Wyatt.

After a moment, Wyatt realized he was meant to try on the hat. Unfortunately, it wobbled atop his head like a crown.

"Too small," Rex announced, plucking the hat off and pushing it into the bottom of his stack. "Maybe the straw." He plunked it onto Wyatt's head. Wyatt pushed it up out of his eyes.

"Too big," Wes decided. "Let's go with the old silver belly."

Tired and more than a bit floppy, the once handsome hat nestled down onto Wyatt's head as if made just for him.

"That's the one," Rex announced.

"It'll keep the sun from baking you, at least," Wes said, "but the satin lining's not exactly cool."

"Good thing it's not full summer yet," Dean put in, grinning as he pulled a baseball cap from his hip pocket and slung it onto his head.

"How come you get away with that?" Wyatt asked, only half teasing.

"Aw, I only wear cowboy hats to impress my wife," Dean said, "and that thing you're wearing would surely *not* do it."

They all walked out laughing, but Wyatt couldn't help thinking that a cowboy hat, even an old droopy one, surely made a man stand just a little prouder. As he strode along in the company of these men, Wyatt felt a surprising twinge of guilt at not calling to explain the situation to Tina. Then again, he decided, he hadn't promised to help repair the house. He was doing exactly what they'd agreed he'd do.

For some reason, he thought of her scrubbing that old skillet with such vigor. Then he pictured Callie Billings moving around her comfortable kitchen, and a pang of something like regret or disappointment struck him midchest. Ridiculous.

Tina Kemp was nothing like Rex's sweet wife. Her snappishness contrasted sharply with Callie's gentle admonitions. He suspected that Tina's silly ideas for opening a bed-and-breakfast in the Loco Man Ranch house were bound to end in failure, no matter how much he and his brothers tried to help, but maybe that was all part of God's plan. They'd have the house in good shape when she finally agreed to sell it to them. He'd have to ask Rex what a fair price might be. Later.

Or not.

Chapter Five

Wyatt dragged in to the house dusty and sweaty around five thirty that evening.

"I have never been so tired in my entire life."

Tina could believe it. He looked as if he'd been put through a meat grinder. She'd had a trying day herself. She'd climbed the stairs so many times today that her legs ached, but—between the shopping, cleaning and cooking—she'd managed to fix up Tyler's room and move her own things into the room with the missing window, which Ryder had temporarily boarded over. He'd carried in a bed from the bunkhouse for her, and she was already looking forward to sleep, so when Wyatt announced that he and his brothers were going to prayer meeting with the Billings family, she could only stare at him for several moments.

"Seriously?"

He nodded. "Don't know about you, but I've got plenty to be praying about."

"So do I," she admitted, "but I'll have to do my

praying here. I just don't have the energy to dress and go to church tonight."

"Your choice," Wyatt said lightly, glancing over the papers she'd left on the kitchen table. "What's this?"

"Utility transfer."

"I told you I'd take care of that," he reminded her, an edge to his voice.

"Yes, well, I had to drive into Ardmore to find everything Ryder needs, so I swung by the electric company. Turns out we don't have to worry about water and trash. We've got our own wells and have to haul our own trash."

"I think we can get trash pickup from the Town of War Bonnet if we want it."

"That would be great," she said. "I'm sure not up for hauling off my own trash."

"I'll check it out." Frowning at the papers, he said, "That's a big deposit for out here."

"Yeah, well, in Kansas City I rented an apartment with utilities included, so I don't have much of a record with the utility company." What records she did have, Layne's name was on the account as well as hers. She prayed they would not inform him for some reason. He was bound to find her eventually, but she hoped to be well established by then, with a presentable home for Tyler.

"I've got a lengthy track record with utility companies," Wyatt was saying. "I'll get over there and see if I can have this reduced."

"Don't bother," she snapped. "We can't even use the electricity. Besides, it's not your house."

He tossed his hands in the air. "I thought we agreed earlier today to split the utilities."

"Fine," she grumbled, knowing she was being unreasonable. The amount of the deposit, on top of the propane bill, had truly shocked her, and she was already fighting every moment of every day not to lose faith. Still, she didn't know why she had to take it out on him. Sucking in a deep breath, she calmed herself. "Having the account in both our names is the best thing. Thank you."

"No problem," he muttered. Then he added, "I'm hitting the shower."

"Water's hot," she told him, "but Ryder says the hot water heater will have to be replaced soon. The bottom is almost rusted out of this one."

Wyatt stared at her for a long moment before simply nodding and walking off.

Jake came in the door, sniffing. "Smells good. What's for supper?"

"Spaghetti with meat sauce."

Pipes squealed and banged, followed by the sound of water gushing.

"That Wyatt in there?"

"Yes."

"He tell you about prayer meeting?"

"I won't be going," she stated firmly. "Not tonight."

"Okay. Been a tough day, I take it."

She lifted the pot lid on the sauce. "You could say that, yeah."

"I'll wash my hands and set the table," he volunteered.

Shooting him a smile, she felt her mood lift ever so

slightly. Now, why didn't Wyatt's offers of help give her the same boost? Instead, everything he did irritated her in ways she couldn't even explain.

She opened cans of green beans, the salad she would have preferred being out of the question until they had refrigeration. So much seemed out of the question just now, even basic things like electricity. She wanted to sit down and have a good cry, but instead she turned back to the stove.

When Jake finished placing the plates, napkins and flatware, he went for glasses and filled them with ice from the ice chest before sitting the plastic jug of tea on the table.

"Hope Wyatt didn't insult your tea," Jake said conversationally. "He drinks what we call syrup tea, equal parts tea and sugar."

"The sugar's right there," Tina pointed out, waving a hand. "He can have all he wants."

Jake's eyes went wide. "You can't properly sweeten tea at the table. The sugar has to go in while the tea is boiling hot so it can dissolve as the tea steeps."

Tina waved an empty green-bean can at him. "Who says?"

"Texas." He chuckled at the expression on her face.

"For your information, Mr. Smith, at lunch your brother drank a full glass of my tea without a speck of sugar in it."

Jake feigned exaggerated shock, thumping himself in the chest. "My brother? Are you sure? He must be sweet on you if he drank your tea without sugar." Truly stunned by the mere suggestion that Wyatt might be sweet on her, Tina gaped at Jake. Stopping his teasing, Jake straightened. "It was just a joke."

"It wasn't funny."

Tina and Jake looked around to find Wyatt standing there wearing a clean white undershirt, his feet bare beneath the hems of his clean blue jeans.

"What smells so good?" Wyatt asked. Coming toward the table.

Tina whirled back to the stove.

Behind her, Jake said heartily, "Spaghetti. With meat sauce. And, uh, green beans, I think."

Walking a wide path around Wyatt and the table, Tina went into the foyer. At the foot of the staircase, she called loudly, "Supper!"

Tyler came running down the stairs. Ryder followed with Frankie perched on his shoulders. Tina saw at once that Frankie had managed to cover himself in the plaster Ryder had been using to mend the ceiling and cracks in the walls. She reached for the boy as Ryder stepped down onto the floor beside her. Frankie came into her arms easily, but he was so heavy that she nearly dropped him. Letting him slide down onto his feet, she dusted her hands and stepped back. Tyler seemed to have fared somewhat better, to her surprise. Still, his hands were covered with the stuff.

"Maybe I ought to hose you boys down before I put you in the tub." She glanced at Ryder, who wiped his dirty hands on his dirty shirt. Obviously, if he was going to prayer meeting with his brothers, he was going to have to clean up first. "Wash your hands and eat. Then, Ryder, you'd better clean up. I understand prayer meeting is on the agenda."

"Yeah?" He looked down at his hands and shrugged. "Okay."

"You clean up in the kitchen," she suggested. "I'll take the boys into the bathroom."

Nodding, Ryder went off to do as he was told. Not for the first time, Tina mused that he was a big, sweet-natured overgrown boy, whereas Wyatt... Wyatt Smith might be overbearing and assume he was in charge of the world, but he had no *boy* in him. He was all man.

By comparison, her ex, Layne, was urbane, polished, charming...selfish, spiteful to the point of brutality, deceptive. That was one thing she could say for Wyatt; he wasn't deceptive. When she got right down to it, the trait that so irked her about him was his arrogance.

She shepherded Tyler and Frankie down the hall to the bathroom. Once she had them as presentable as possible, Tina sent the boys to the kitchen. And she followed soon after.

Frankie sat atop the plastic tub again, while Tyler knelt on his chair seat.

"Sit on your bottom, son," she admonished gently as she went to put the finishing touches on the meal and carry it all to the table. He grumbled but complied. As she sat a steaming bowl of green beans in front of him, however, Tyler began to whine.

"I don't want that. I want spaghetti."

"We have spaghetti, but we need vegetables, too. Besides, you like green beans."

"Don't tell me what I like!" he shouted.

Tina recoiled at the familiar reprimand. It was something his father had said, often and hatefully. She'd put a dish on the table that Layne had previously praised only to find that he suddenly hated it. When she'd reminded him that he'd liked it before, he'd always snapped back just as Tyler had.

Momentarily stunned, Tina felt caught in the old quandary: Fight back or ignore it? From the corner of her eye, she caught Wyatt and Jake exchanging troubled glances. Her face heated, but she reminded herself that her six-year-old son was not his hateful father and she was the grown-up in this situation. As calmly as she could, she spooned green beans onto Tyler's plate and proceeded to do the same with the spaghetti.

"Eat," she ordered quietly.

Tyler frowned, but then he picked up his fork and dug into the spaghetti. Everyone else began filling their plates. Then they bowed their heads and Wyatt spoke the prayer.

"Father God, we thank You first for Your Son and then for all the many other blessings You've showered upon us. I thank You especially for new friends, this meal and the hands that prepared it. Amen."

Tina sent him a limp smile in acknowledgment for mentioning her—however obliquely—in his prayer, but she couldn't look him in the eye. She remembered the words that she'd thrown at him earlier.

I know what's best for my own son.

But did she really?

The meal rejuvenated Wyatt somewhat, but he still dragged along the edge of utter exhaustion. Yet he was eager to go to church. He wanted the comfort and assurance of prayer. Plus, he wanted to further his acquaintance with the Billings family and get to know the rest of his neighbors. He could learn a lot from Wes and Rex, and he couldn't have asked for more friendly company today. Besides, prayer meeting had to be better than sitting here in the dark house with Tina and her disrespectful son.

Wyatt was so used to correcting his brothers and nephew that he'd almost given Tyler a scolding when the boy had mouthed off at his mother. He had to give her points for remaining calm, though she obviously teetered on the edge of exhaustion herself. Still, if she didn't get control of that boy soon, she never would.

Wyatt didn't kid himself that his advice on the subject would be welcome, however. She'd made herself plain on the matter earlier.

I know what's best for my own son.

Wyatt kept his opinions to himself and concentrated on the food in front of him. It was simple but plentiful and tasty enough, especially considering that she was working without conveniences…like electricity. If she didn't get that fixed tomorrow, he'd see to it himself, though she was likely to tear a strip off his hide for it.

Having eaten his fill, he sat back and lifted the glass of tea that he hadn't yet touched.

"That was good. Thank you."

"You're welcome. I'll sweeten the next batch of tea while it's hot."

Wyatt glanced at her before taking a healthy swig of the tea. He let the cold tea slide down his throat before saying conversationally, "Actually, I like this. It's not at all bitter. What brand do you use?"

After a somewhat shocked silence, Tina named her preferred brand.

Ryder, who had demolished two plates of food to Wyatt's one, chugged his tea and reached for the plastic pitcher for a refill. "Wyatt's tea is like battery acid," he remarked easily. "Can't drink it without sugar."

"Hey!" Wyatt objected, much to Jake's amusement, though he couldn't deny the truth. "I never claimed to be a domestic whiz."

"You sure worry and fuss like someone's mother, though."

Wyatt rolled his eyes. "Just because I didn't want you to fight—" Too late, he broke off, grimacing and tilting his head in apology to Ryder.

Tina flashed a glance around the table. "I wouldn't want Tyler to join the military, either," she said, assuming the most obvious interpretation of Wyatt's comment. Then her eyes widened, and she addressed herself to Jake. "That is, unless he truly wanted a military career. It is a noble profession. I just wouldn't want him in harm's way."

Jake smiled warmly and ran his fingertip around the rim of his tea glass. "I didn't exactly give our mother hen over here the opportunity to talk me out of enlisting."

"You didn't," Wyatt accused, relieved to have the conversation channeled in this direction. He looked at Tina, lifted an eyebrow and said, "He joined the day after his eighteenth birthday. Reported for basic training within weeks of graduating high school."

"One of the best decisions I ever made. Served over ten years."

"But then you got out before you reached retirement age," Tina prodded gently.

Jake looked down, licking his lips. "I took a hardship release when my wife passed away."

Tina grimaced. "I'm so sorry. I didn't realize."

Jake shrugged. "She was military, too. You have to expect it when you marry a soldier. Training exercise."

Tina pulled in a deep breath. "I'm very sorry for your loss."

"She was doing what she loved," Jake said softly. "That's what I try to remember."

Tina merely offered him a small smile.

Again, irritation swamped Wyatt. He didn't like the feeling, and he didn't even want to know why. He couldn't be jealous of his own brother. Could he? Certainly not over Tina. He didn't even like her. Except... he wasn't sure anymore what it was about her that he disliked so much. He cleared his throat.

"I don't want to be late for prayer meeting."

Ryder finished his second glass of tea and plunked the tumbler onto the table. "I need to clean up."

"Well, don't take all night," Jake called after him. "I've still got to get Frankie cleaned up."

"Why don't you let Frankie stay here with Tyler and me?" Tina suggested, smiling at Jake again.

That smile rankled Wyatt. The two of them seemed to be getting along like a house on fire. She could barely be civil to Wyatt, but she was all smiles for Jake. The thought made Wyatt cringe. Oh, yeah. A good night for prayer meeting.

"I don't want you to have to bathe him tonight," Jake

was saying, waving a hand at Frankie. "He's filthy, and you're tired."

"I've got to bathe Tyler anyway."

"I can wash myself," Tyler objected loudly.

Tina smiled stiffly at Jake. "There. Tyler can wash himself, so I'm free to take care of Frankie."

Tyler opened his mouth, but Wyatt cut him off, fed up with mouthy kids and this Tina-Jake thing. "I guess y'all want to turn in early since you start Tyler's classes tomorrow."

"What classes?" Tyler demanded, frowning.

"Schoolwork," Tina replied lightly. "We don't want you to fall behind in your studies."

"They have a good school here in town," Jake pointed out.

"I told her that."

"I made a thorough check before I agreed to this move," Jake went on.

Suddenly, Tyler gripped the edge of the table in front of him and shouted, "I want to go to my old school! I want to go home!"

Visibly blanching, Tina tried to placate him. "Son, we are home. And tonight you can sleep in your own room. It has all your toys and books in it and the same blanket and pillows. Your stuffed fox is there, and—"

Tyler leapt to his feet, bawling at her. "It's not my room! That's stupid! *You're* stupid!"

"Whoa," Wyatt said, at the very end of his patience, but Tyler was already running down the hallway.

Obviously embarrassed, Tina quickly rose to follow her son, but first she apologized for him. "I'm sorry for that. He's unsettled and confused and..." Her explanation dwindled away.

"He called you stupid," Wyatt pointed out. "You can't let him get away with that."

Her chin came up but not her gaze. "He's just repeating what he heard his father say so often."

Wyatt's stomach churned. No wonder she was prickly. He softened his tone. "All the more reason to put a stop to it. People shouldn't speak to each other that way. Males especially shouldn't speak that way to females. He has to learn that."

She nodded and turned away, softly saying, "I'll clean this up later."

"We'll handle this," Wyatt told her. "You go talk to your boy."

"I'll take Frankie into the shower with me," Jake decided aloud, "and get him ready for bed."

"Thank you," she replied in a choked voice. Then she followed Tyler from the room.

When she was gone, Jake pointed a finger at Frankie. "I don't ever want to hear you say anything so disrespectful to any adult." Big-eyed, Frankie nodded, and Jake immediately softened. "I know you won't. Hopefully, in time, Tyler will learn not to misbehave like that, too."

"Hopefully," Wyatt muttered, but with a father who called his mother names in front of him, the kid already had a strike against him. Wyatt felt a new empathy for both Tina and Tyler.

Oh, yeah. Tonight was a really good night for prayer meeting.

Chapter Six

Apparently, showing up for prayer meeting at the Countryside Church was tantamount to announcing to the community at large that the Smith brothers were in residence. The first to mention it was the electrician recommended by the Billings family, who stopped by the next day.

"Everyone's excited to have y'all at Loco Man Ranch," the thin, fortyish man said to Tina. "Wouldn't be the same without a Smith here, and now there's five or six of you."

"Three," Tina corrected. "That is, four: Wyatt, Jake, Ryder and little Frankie."

"Oh, you're not a member of the family?"

"Uh, not exactly." She didn't want to go into details, so she said simply, "Dodd was my stepfather."

That raised his shaggy eyebrows, so she quickly turned the conversation to business. After describing the problems, she wasn't surprised to hear that the entire house would need rewiring, and while the price of the project was not as much as she'd feared, she still broached the subject of providing the materials herself. The electrical contractor proved amenable, so she took out her cell phone and turned it on. She had been careful to keep it off for fear that Layne would try to track her through it, but she needed to call the wholesaler.

Thankfully, the conversation was brief. It took the electrician longer to write out a detailed list than it did for the wholesaler to agree to provide the materials at wholesale.

After some finagling, the electrical contractor left to get the supplies, promising Tina they would have power in at least part of the house by nightfall.

As soon as the electrician departed, guests began arriving. A battered pickup arrived, containing three women, one of them a mere teenager who couldn't have graduated high school even a year earlier. They brought with them a cake in a foil pan.

"Mrs. Smith?"

"I'm Tina Kemp, Dodd's stepdaughter. There is no Mrs. Smith."

"Well, that's good news," declared one of the women, a willowy blonde with sharp features and entirely too much makeup.

Tina was shocked into silence as the elder of the women introduced herself as Sharon Umber. Sharon introduced her daughters, Peggy and Olive.

"We met the Smith brothers at church last night," Peggy gushed.

"And of course we want to welcome them to War Bonnet," said her mother. "Uh, I mean, we want to welcome all of you." With that, she pushed the pan at Tina. "Chocolate cake."

"Thank you," Tina managed to say, inviting them to sit at the kitchen table with a wave of her hand.

While she filled glasses with iced tea, Peggy asked, "Are the Smith brothers here?"

"Jake's around here somewhere," Tina said. "Ryder's upstairs working. I'm not sure where Wyatt is, but he's on ranch business, I'm sure."

"And you're what? The housekeeper here?" Mrs. Umber wanted to know.

"I'm the homeowner," Tina stated flatly. "Dodd left the ranch to his nephews and the house to me. They're only staying here temporarily."

Sharon Umber looked confused, but then she glanced around the old-fashioned, bare-bones kitchen and remarked, "I imagine someone will be building a new house soon, then."

"Well, it won't be me," Tina said. "I like this house, and I intend to refurbish it."

"There's sure nothing around here to rent," Mrs. Umber said. "I hear Lyons is building apartments, though."

"A rancher doesn't want to live in an apartment." Her youngest daughter scoffed. "Especially if he's got a wife."

"Better and better!" declared Peggy, giggling.

Tina almost choked on her polite laughter. No doubt Sharon and her daughters were calculating which of the brothers was most likely to build that new house and just how likely he needed a wife. Tyler and Frankie ran into the room just then, asking for a snack.

Tina cleared her throat. "How does chocolate cake sound?"

The boys bounced up and down, yelling, "Yay!"

Tina parked them at the table, introducing each to the Umbers, and went for paper plates and the milk carton. She was still dishing out cake when another vehicle arrived, with two women this time: Mrs. Carla Landis and her friend Marti Jewel, a single woman in her thirties. They brought cookies. Tina made room at the table and went for more glasses. When the third car showed up, the Umbers finally excused themselves.

Meri Billings Burns and her sister, Ann Billings Pryor, brought flour, sugar, canned vegetables and homemade jams, which would come in very handy. Moreover, they were there to see Tina rather than check out the trio of bachelor brothers. Meri showed photos of her baby girl. Ann, too, had a daughter, a toddler, as well as a son in first grade.

"We'll have to get Donovan and these boys together soon," Ann said, smiling at Frankie and Tyler.

"That would be wonderful," Tina said. "Tyler could use a friend closer to his age."

"We'll make it happen," Ann promised. "And I'll have Donovan look for Tyler at school. I hope we can expect to see you both on Sunday as it's Easter."

"Easter," Tina echoed uncertainly. She'd forgotten all about it. She'd always made a big deal of Easter with Tyler, and this year she hadn't even thought of it.

"Yes, we'll be at Easter services," she promised, returning to the table, "but Tyler won't be attending public school."

"Why ever not?" Carla Landis wanted to know. "My sister and brother-in-law both teach there. It's an excellent school."

"I—I just think Tyler is…safer at home for now."

Carla and her friend Marti immediately said they had to leave. Fearing she had offended them, Tina thanked them for coming as she walked them to the door. Turning back to the Billings sisters, she sighed.

"I didn't handle that very well."

"Oh, don't worry about Carla," Meri said. "She's thin skinned, but she gets over it quickly."

"I hope you'll reconsider sending Tyler to public school, though," Ann added.

Tina shook her head. "I can't. I just…can't."

The sisters smiled and changed the subject. Tina again promised that she and Tyler would be in church on Sunday. The women made approving sounds before getting to their feet.

"I need to start Stark's lunch," Meri said.

"And we really should rescue Callie," Ann put in. "She's got her kids and ours today."

"Thank you so much for coming by," Tina said, ushering them to the door, "and please give Callie my best."

The sisters took their leave. Sighing with mingled relief and pleasure—Meri and Ann were two women she felt she could truly be friends with—Tina turned back to the table, only to spy Ryder standing there with his arms folded.

"You hiding from someone, Tina?"

"What? Don't be silly." Flustered, she forced herself to walk calmly across the room to begin clearing the table. "Why would you ask such a thing?"

He looked at her for a long moment; then he dropped his hands to his waist. "Takes one to know one, I guess," he muttered, turning away.

She wanted to call him back, ask what he meant by that, but she didn't dare. A woman who couldn't bear questions couldn't ask them, either. She just couldn't chance that one of the brothers would decide she was unfairly keeping her son from Layne and notify him.

Recalling what Meri had said about making her husband's lunch, Tina started building sandwiches. Wrapping them, she stowed them in the cooler before slicing an apple and rinsing the slices in pineapple juice to keep them from browning. She'd serve the remaining juice to the boys with their supper. All the while, she pondered her situation.

Could she really operate this decrepit house as a B and B? She looked at the old refrigerator. It wasn't nearly large enough, but until it was running again, she dared not open any of the jars that the Billings sisters had brought with them or even stock the larder sufficiently.

For the sake of her son, she would somehow make this work. She knew in her heart of hearts that Layne would destroy the child out of sheer maliciousness if he ever gained full custody. He'd turn Tyler into a hateful, belligerent younger version of himself just to hurt her.

So, yes, she would hide, and she would homeschool, and she would spend every penny she had to keep Tyler from his father.

And she would pray.

For all the good that seemed to do.

"You sure you're not letting your own situation color your judgment?" Wyatt asked softly, dropping down next to his brother on the porch step two evenings later.

Ryder shook his head, his gaze focused on his hands. Apparently, he'd deliberated quite a while before telling Wyatt what he'd overheard.

Ryder and Tina had made real progress over the past few days. The place was clean and organized. The porch was sound and the ceiling patched. Wallpaper had been stripped away in the dining room and new drapes hung. Nearly the whole house had been rewired, so they had lights, refrigeration and hot water out of the faucet. Wyatt was looking forward to a little TV tonight, but he'd returned from visiting area cattle breeders to find Ryder hanging around outside, waiting for him.

"If she's not hiding, why won't she let that boy go to school?" Ryder wanted to know. "And why does she keep her phone turned off? The electrician complained about it, said he normally calls his clients if he needs something while he's working, but with her, he has to stop what he's doing and go in search of her because she keeps her phone off."

Wyatt frowned. "Maybe she just doesn't want to run down the battery. When you asked her, she denied that she was hiding. Right?"

"Yeah," Ryder admitted. "Sort of. I'd have let it go after that if not for what the electrician told me. And there's something else."

"What's that?"

"Tyler asked me to call his dad and tell him where they are."

Wyatt grimaced. "Man, I do not want to get in the middle of that."

"I understand," Ryder said, "but if she's hiding Tyler from his father…"

Wyatt shook his head. "We don't know that. But I'll talk to her after supper, see what I can find out."

Ryder nodded. "I hate to be the one to bring this up, considering my own situation."

"You're hiding from the press, not a legal situation."

"Still, if anybody knows there are good reasons to hide, I do."

Sighing, Wyatt clapped his baby brother on the shoulder. Would he ever recover from the tragedy? Accidentally killing his sparring partner in practice had nearly broken Ryder.

Then Uncle Dodd had died and left them the ranch. The solution had fallen straight into Wyatt's lap, and he was still convinced that it was the right move, despite the complication of Tina.

So far, Wyatt had dealt with her by having as little to do with her as possible. That didn't keep him from thinking about her, though. Her beauty seemed to blossom more fully every day, particularly as he came to see a softer side to her. She was more vulnerable than she wanted anyone to know, especially when it came to her son, which meant that Wyatt couldn't put off this conversation.

After a supper that included an excellent meatloaf, he made sure that Jake got the boys ready for bed while he helped Tina clean the kitchen. He meant to take her into the den for a private conversation, but no sooner had she folded the last dish towel than she pushed open the screen door and walked down the steps out into the night. Wyatt followed, closing the back door behind him.

She turned, arms crossed, when she heard the door close, then she turned away again. "I could never get enough of the stars. They're always so bright out here. Dodd and I used to sit on the front porch steps and gaze up at the night sky while Mom watched one of her silly shows. Having the old TV working again made me think of those nights. People in the city don't even realize how many stars there are."

"That's true," Wyatt said. "The night sky in Houston is a murky gray with a few dim twinkles." He waited, sliding his hands into the pockets of his jeans, but she didn't say anything else, so he took the bull by the horns. "Tina, we need to talk."

She glanced over her shoulder, her eyes gleaming in the moonlight. "What about?"

"Are you hiding from someone or something?"

Looking away, she hugged herself a little tighter. "Ryder asked me that earlier, and I can't imagine why either of you would think such a thing."

Wyatt noticed that she hadn't exactly denied the accusation. "Would you tell me if you were?"

"That would be foolish, wouldn't it?"

Disappointed, Wyatt bowed his head, sending up a quick prayer for the right words. "It's starting to look like you're hiding Tyler from his father."

Gasping, she whirled around. "Why would you say such a thing?"

He heard the tremor in her voice and sighed. "Tina, if he has custody of Tyler—"

"I have custody of Tyler," she interrupted hotly. "Full custody granted by a court," she added. "But Layne is threatening to sue for custody. His lawyers advised me b-before I left Kansas."

Wyatt rubbed his hands over his face, suddenly quite tired. "I see. So, this is your way of avoiding a custody battle you fear you'll lose."

Tina rushed forward into the rectangle of light thrown onto the ground from the window in the door behind and above Wyatt. He caught his breath. She was the most amazingly beautiful woman he'd ever seen, but he couldn't let that sway him. He had to know the truth.

"You don't understand," she said. "Layne's parents have money, lots of it. They've never been particularly interested in being grandparents…or parents, so far as I can tell, but their usual way of dealing with Layne is to simply give him what he wants. Art school in Paris. A lavish wedding. A house. Cars."

"So, he basically has unlimited funds to fight you in court."

"Yes."

"Why didn't he do it at the time of the divorce then?"

"Tyler was too small, too much trouble, I imagine. He and Layne simply weren't that close, but as Tyler has gotten older, Layne's tried to influence him. He pushes Tyler to pick sides between us, and he courts him with expensive gifts and entertainment. He tells Tyler lies about our marriage, and he knows I won't tell him the truth because it's not good for Tyler to know that I caught Layne cheating on me."

Wyatt could hardly imagine such a thing. Why would a man cheat on a woman like Tina? Wyatt rubbed the nape of his neck.

"I'm sorry you had to go through that, but I have to ask if you're allowed to take Tyler out of state without his dad's permission."

"Yes. But that won't keep Layne from filing for custody. He claims that I can't provide adequately for Tyler and that I don't spend enough time with him. He's even tried to say that I've alienated Tyler's affections, though it's Layne who's tried to do that. I never criticize him to Tyler, because it's not good for Tyler to hear awful things about his dad." She shoved her fingers into her hair, adding, "He'll eventually figure it out on his own, anyway. Unless Layne warps him, which he would do just to spite me." She flailed her arms in a gesture of exasperation.

Wyatt tucked his hands back into the pockets of his jeans to keep from reaching out and pulling her into his embrace.

"Like you said, Tyler will eventually figure it out."

"If he has the chance," she qualified. "I'd hoped this move would bring us closer together. I don't intend to keep him away from his father. I just want a chance to build a closer relationship with him myself."

"The B and B is a way for you to spend more time with him, isn't it?" Wyatt realized suddenly.

She nodded. "I'd hoped he'd love it here as much as I do," she said in a small voice. "I think eventually he will. If he spends enough time here."

"Makes sense," Wyatt admitted, though he was far from comfortable with the situation.

"What scares me most—" she went on in a voice barely above a whisper "—is to what lengths Layne would go to hurt me through Tyler. I—I really believe he's too lazy and self-involved to actually..." She blinked back tears. "To *physically* hurt Tyler."

Chilled by the prospect, Wyatt hurried to reassure her. "Surely not. He'd have to be psychotic to actually harm his own son."

"Right." She tried a smile, but it was wan and fleeting. "It's just that... I'm not sure Layne is truly capable of loving anyone other than himself, Tyler included."

Rocked, Wyatt said, "We'll certainly pray that those fears are unfounded, and in the meantime you're both safe here."

"Yes," she said, sounding as if she was trying to convince herself. "This is the safest place for us."

"Well, thanks for telling me what's going on."

She nodded. "I—I was afraid to before. Afraid you'd insist on telling Layne where we are."

"No, I won't do that. Not at this point. But you should know that Tyler has asked Ryder to call his dad."

Shaking her head, she clapped a hand over her mouth. Several seconds ticked by before she dropped her hand and whispered, "Thank you."

"You don't have to thank me," he told her.

"Actually," she said, "you've been pretty good about everything. You and your brothers."

Wyatt grimaced, knowing he hadn't been very nice in the beginning. "It was the shock at first," he admitted. "And, well, I can't let anything interfere with our plans."

"I understand."

"You don't, really," he said, bowing his head. What could he do except tell her then? "It's Ryder." He explained the situation, how Ryder had accidentally killed a young man while practicing for a cage fight. "It almost destroyed him, and he still carries a huge burden of guilt, though he and the trainer were both cleared, even of the negligence charge. That didn't keep the press from hounding them mercilessly, though. I had to get him out of Houston."

"Oh, no," she said. "That's heartbreaking. Ryder's so patient and gentle with the kids. I can't imagine him as a fighter."

"Mixed martial arts was a fitness thing with him. But he has skills, and people noticed. Before I knew it, he'd signed a contract to compete in the MMA circuit. He won his first two matches. Then Bryan died in a freak accident... I thought we were going to have to bury Ryder, too."

"I'm so sorry."

"I'd appreciate it if you wouldn't say anything to him."

"I won't."

"We'll make this work for everyone," Wyatt promised. "Listen, do you mind if I speak to Tyler? I'd like him to know that he can come to me or my brothers with any questions or problems."

She pondered that, then nodded. "If you need me, I'll be sitting on the front porch."

He smiled and turned toward the steps, silently praying for wisdom, discernment and the strength to avoid the temptation of Tina's beauty.

The last thing either of them needed at this point was another complication.

No matter how lovely that complication might be.

Chapter Seven

Wyatt tapped on Tyler's bedroom door before opening it. The boy lay atop his narrow bed, a book in his hands.

"What's that?" Wyatt asked lightly. "Bedtime story?"

Tyler nodded and turned a page, letting Wyatt know that this interruption was unwelcome. Wyatt let him know that he wasn't going away by coming fully into the room.

"Has your mom read that to you?" Wyatt asked, but Tyler shook his head.

"I read it myself."

"Not many six-year-olds can read books all by themselves."

Tyler dropped a finger onto the page and read aloud, "Look at the baby bird. It has no…no…feats…feats her."

"Feathers," Wyatt corrected. "It has no feathers. That's very good, Ty."

The boy frowned over the top of his book. "That's not my name."

Wyatt smiled. "It's a nickname, a shortened version of your whole name. You know, Frankie is a nickname, too. I suppose someday he'll outgrow Frankie and we'll start calling him Frank, but his real name is Francis."

Tyler dropped his book onto his lap. "What kind of name is that? I didn't hear that name before."

"Francis is one of those names that can be used for a girl or a boy, depending on how it's spelled. Frankie is named after my mom, his grandmother."

Tyler sat up in the bed. "I wouldn't want to be named after no girl."

Wyatt shrugged. "It's our way of honoring our mom. She was great, and we loved her."

"I'd hate to be named after my mom."

Chuckling, Wyatt said, "Yeah, that wouldn't work too well. There's no boy equivalent of Tina. What's her middle name?"

"Lynette."

"Guess she could have named you Tyler Lynn."

He shook his head. "I'm Tyler Walker Kemp."

"Walker is your mom's maiden name, so you are named after her."

Tyler's mouth dropped open. Obviously, he'd never made the connection. "I don't want to be named after her! She's stupid!"

Shocked, Wyatt had to work to keep his cool. "Your mother is not stupid."

"She is! My dad says so."

White-hot anger flashed through Wyatt, but he tamped it down. "Real men don't call women stupid, Tyler."

"Even if they are?" the boy shot back.

"Your mother is an extremely intelligent woman," Wyatt stated, "and I don't ever want to hear you say she's stupid again. She's brilliant and obviously talented. Just look at what she's done with this room."

Tyler glanced around, clearly puzzled. Three of the walls had been painted a rich, deep blue. The fourth had been painted a restful green to match his bedspread, which was covered with colorful race cars. On the green wall, she'd hung an old mirror, the simple frame of which she'd painted yellow to match the chest of drawers beneath it. On either side of the mirror, she'd hung yellow-and-white checked flags. Car posters had been placed strategically around the room, on the yellow closet door, at the head of the yellow-painted bed, on the ceiling above it and over a short set of yellow shelves filled with books and toys. All in all, she'd done an amazing job with nothing more than a couple of cans of paint.

"What's more, yours is the only room in the house that's finished," Wyatt went on. "She put you first. She always puts you first."

Frowning, Tyler picked at his bedspread. "If she's so smart, how come she was such a bad wife my dad had to divorce her?"

Wyatt had to think about how to answer that. He couldn't break Tina's confidence about how her marriage had ended, but he couldn't let Tyler go on believing the divorce was Tina's fault. Walking over to the bed, he sat on the end and fixed Tyler with a blunt look.

"It takes two people to make a marriage work, Tyler, and it takes two people to destroy one."

"He wouldn't of cheated on her with that other woman if she'd been a better wife," Tyler shot back.

Wyatt felt his jaw drop. "Your father told you about that?"

Tyler nodded. Wyatt couldn't tell if he was confused or ashamed. Maybe both.

"He had no business telling you that," Wyatt stated evenly. "Do you even know what *cheating* means?"

Sullenly, Tyler shrugged. Somewhat relieved, Wyatt chose his next words carefully.

"Your mom could have told you about your dad's cheating, but she didn't want to make him look bad. She wants you to love and respect your father. Whatever he says, their divorce was not your mother's fault, certainly not hers alone. Someday you'll understand that. Meanwhile, I hope you're big enough, smart enough and brave enough to trust that your parents' divorce has nothing to do with you. They both love you. You need to leave it at that. And so does your father."

"He says he's gonna run her out of money and take me to live with him," Tyler revealed, sounding worried. "And then I won't see her no more."

Obviously, Tina had been right about everything. To tell his young son about his cheating and blame Tina for it was the act of a selfish, egotistical individual. Obviously, Layne Kemp wasn't fit to be a father, but Wyatt wouldn't say so to the boy.

"Your mother will never let that happen," Wyatt assured Tyler. "You're the most important person in the world to her. She made this move to Oklahoma so she can spend more time with you and give you a great life. You need to stop giving her a hard time about it.

And when you see your father again, I hope you'll let him know that you want to spend time with both him and your mother. You do, don't you?"

"Yes," Tyler whispered.

"Good," Wyatt said, standing up, then leaning over to help ease Tyler down onto his pillow. "I'm glad to hear that. And if you ever need to talk about stuff, Ty, you can always come to me. Or my brothers. Okay?"

"Okay, Wyatt," Tyler said.

Wyatt ruffled the boy's reddish blond hair, pleased to get a grin out of him. Then he tucked the covers around him and said good-night before slipping from the room. Unfortunately, now he had to tell Tina what Tyler had revealed.

Hearing the door open at her back, Tina inwardly sighed. She'd been arguing with herself about the wisdom of letting Wyatt talk to her son in private. On one hand, Wyatt had a right to check her story, which he was no doubt doing. On the other, she could never be sure anymore how Tyler would react. She had no secrets now, so she didn't worry that he would expose her, but she could only hope that he wouldn't make an enemy of Wyatt.

Wyatt walked across the porch and sat down on the top step beside her. The night breeze swirled his scent around her, an earthy smell, part grass, part wood and part male. Her heart skipped a beat. She closed her eyes, focusing on thoughts of her son.

"Did you find out what you needed to know?"

"We established that I can call him Ty from now on." That surprised her, and she looked around, eyebrows raised. "The rest of us have nicknames. Everyone but you."

She relaxed. "Unless you count Mom as a nickname."

"There is that," Wyatt agreed with a smile, but then he sobered. "I'm afraid you're right about everything you said about your ex. He told Tyler that he cheated on you."

She gasped. "He *told* Tyler?"

Wyatt took her hand in his, nodding. "But he told Tyler it was your fault for being such a bad wife."

"Oh, that's so like Layne!" she exploded bitterly. "He doesn't care that he's burdened his son with information that he's too young to understand. All he cares about is vindicating himself and hurting me."

No wonder Tyler was acting out. He had to be so confused and angry. She'd tried to protect him from the truth of his father's infidelity, and all along Layne had been feeding him a warped version of what had happened. Her poor boy. Suddenly, it was all too much. She burst into tears.

Long, strong arms came around her from the side. "Please don't cry."

"I'm s-sorry," she stuttered, scrubbing at the tears.

"No apology necessary," he crooned, brushing back her bangs. "You didn't tell your son things he shouldn't know, and you've read your ex correctly. Take comfort in that. Ty says he's filed for custody in an effort to bankrupt you, so now we can plan accordingly."

We. Even as she told herself how foolish it would be to take Wyatt literally, that one tiny word comforted her. She gulped down the remainder of her tears.

"I thought he was my white knight," she went on. "He asked me to marry him the day after my mother's funeral. I felt rescued and grateful. I thought he loved me."

"I'm sure he did," Wyatt said softly, "as much as he was able."

"He isn't able. It wasn't long before I realized that I'd married the male equivalent of my mother." She straightened, breaking contact with him. "Layne refused to split anything, and because his parents' names were on the deed to the house, he didn't have to let me back inside, so all I had was what I left with. Thankfully, I never added him to my car title, or I wouldn't even have transportation."

"Layne didn't even provide for his son?"

"He agreed to child support, but he hid most of his income. By the time he finally signed the papers, all I wanted was to be free of him. And custody of my son."

"Sounds like you had your priorities right."

"Doesn't matter. I always vowed I'd never get divorced. I don't want to be like my mother. She was married five times."

"Whoa. That had to be tough for you."

"It was. She couldn't be alone but she couldn't be in love, either. Until my marriage busted up, I never realized how hard being alone could be."

"You'll find the right man."

"No," Tina said, "I won't. I haven't dated since the divorce. And I don't intend to."

He seemed surprised. "Don't you ever want to marry again?"

She shook her head. "How could I be sure it wouldn't turn out like the first time?"

"You have to trust yourself. You have to believe you won't make the same mistake twice."

"But I can't believe that," she countered. "My mother is proof that you can make the same mistake repeatedly."

"You can, but you don't have to, especially if you pray about the matter."

She rolled her eyes. "Do you think I haven't prayed about this? For so long I believed that no self-respecting man would want me. When Layne showed interest, I thanked God. But I was just fooling myself."

"How could you possibly believe that no man would want you?"

She lifted her shoulders, muttering, "My mother was very beautiful."

"So are you."

She stared at him skeptically. Suddenly, everything changed. Her heartbeat stuttered to a stop. She held her breath, watching as he fought the urge to kiss her. Part of her hoped he would, if only to prove that she was desirable, lovable; part of her wanted to bolt, in case that kiss proved to her just how truly vulnerable she was. She didn't move so much as an eyelash.

After a long moment rife with tension, he leaned back slightly and shifted his gaze. Unexpected disappointment crashed through Tina, but she had lots of experience in keeping a placid, enigmatic expression.

"Listen," he said, "don't worry. I'll talk to Jake and Ryder, make sure they understand the situation. They don't need all the details, but I promise they'll agree with me. You and Ty are safe here."

Tina stared up at the night sky. "I can't tell you how much I appreciate your understanding."

"I'm just glad you told me," he said softly. "I wouldn't have wanted to unintentionally put you or Tyler at risk."

He pushed up to his feet then. Keeping her seat, she looked up at him. Oh, how she wished he was not so disturbingly attractive. That coupled with his kindness and his strength made him very nearly irresistible. It was the last thing she needed right now.

She hadn't counted on wanting Wyatt Smith's support, his understanding, his advice, his faith. Him.

Maybe she was more like her mother than she even knew. All the more reason to focus entirely on her son.

After Wyatt left, she went upstairs to check on Tyler. He was sound asleep, so she kissed his forehead and tiptoed from the room.

The next morning, she greeted him with great good cheer. "Happy Easter!"

Nothing was said of his discussion with Wyatt the night before. Tyler seemed pleasant enough initially, but the situation quickly deteriorated into all-out rebellion.

He didn't like the clothes she'd laid out for him to wear to church. He didn't like his breakfast, though any other day he'd have begged for cold cereal. He didn't like the idea of going into a Bible class of strangers, even if they were his own age. And he really, really did not want to ride to church with Tina.

"I want to ride with Frankie!" Tyler insisted for the umpteenth time, refusing to get into her car.

Tina dug deep within for patience. "We don't have time for this."

"Tell you what," Jake said, coming through the back door and setting Frankie onto his feet. "We'll get you a second safety seat for Wyatt's truck. That way we won't have to take the time to move the seat. That's what we've done for Frankie. When we get the extra safety seat for Wyatt's truck, you can ride with Frankie. But for today, you ride with your mom. Deal?"

In reply, Tyler folded his arms and tucked his chin stubbornly.

"No? Sorry. I don't think you have any other options this morning."

"You're not the boss of me!" Tyler bawled at Jake.

Tina felt her face flood with color and immediately took her son by the arm, bending close to whisper, "Stop this. Right now."

She felt Wyatt step up beside her. "You may not like what Jake has to say, Ty, but I am the boss of the whole Loco Man Ranch, so you *will* listen to me." He didn't shout, but he didn't leave any wiggle room, either. "It's time we laid down some rules. One, the children on the Loco Man will not speak to adults with disrespect. That goes for your mom, Jake, me, Ryder, Delgado and any other adult who comes on the place. It means no shouting, ugly names or insults. And no stomping feet. Got it?"

For a long moment Tyler did not respond, but then he nodded sullenly. Tina sent an apologetic glance at Wyatt, who continued speaking.

"Second, it's fine for you to ask for what you want. You can even argue for it. But shouting is out. If you can't make your point without shouting, then you don't have a good point to make. The moment you start shouting, you've lost the argument. Understand?"

Tyler's chin trembled, and he started to cry, wailing brokenly, "I wanna go home."

Tina slid her arm across his shoulders. "Sweetie, I keep telling you that we are home. I know you don't like the house much right now, but in time we'll have it all fixed up. You'll see. Besides, our old apartment has been rented to someone else by now." That made him turn his face into her body and sob all the harder. "Oh, Tyler," she crooned, "if you just give Loco Man Ranch a chance, I know you'll come to like it here. And listen, we're going to color eggs and hunt for them later."

As she spoke, Frankie walked over to Tyler and patted him. "S'okay."

Tyler shrugged off his hand. "You like it here 'cause you got your dad."

Tina traded concerned looks with Wyatt, who said, "You'll see your dad before long."

"I don't never see him," Tyler grumbled.

"You know that's not true," Tina countered.

"Not as much as I want."

She couldn't argue with that. Even in Kansas City, Layne hadn't taken full advantage of the many opportunities to see his son, and when he had, Tyler had come home even unhappier than before. Frankie patted Tyler again, pointing to Wyatt with his free hand.

"Unca Wyatt be your daddy," he said, as if offering Tyler a prized toy.

Tina's jaw dropped, and when she looked at Wyatt, his hung agape, too. Ryder and Jake laughed behind their hands.

Her face burning hot, Tina ignored Frankie's gesture and tried to reassure her son. "You'll see your dad as soon as the B and B is operational. If not before. I promise."

To her surprise, Tyler started drying his eyes.

"We'd better go. Don't want to be late on Easter Sunday," Wyatt muttered, heading toward his truck. Jake took Frankie by the hand, drawing him along with him as he followed Wyatt, Ryder falling into step beside them. He and Ryder still chuckled and whispered together.

Tina quickly turned to open the back door of her car for Tyler. He climbed up into his seat without argument, and she smiled her appreciation as she buckled his belt.

All the while, she couldn't help thinking that Wyatt would be an excellent father, far better for her son than Layne. But then, so would all the Smith brothers. Not that she would ever consider marrying any of them.

Still, she remembered the way Wyatt had looked at her the night before. She couldn't suppress feelings and emotions that she hadn't felt in years.

Chapter Eight

"We could make a morning of it," Ann Pryor said, smiling at Tina as they stood in the foyer of the church after the service. Wyatt listened with unabashed interest. "Bring Tyler and Frankie," Ann went on. "You and I can get to know each other better, and the boys can play. Dean's grandmother will want to make lunch for us, I'm sure."

Tina frowned even as Tyler practically danced on air. He had gone from petulant to delighted in the ninety minutes or so that he'd spent in children's church. "Yeah, Mom. Donovan said he don't got school tomorrow."

"Teacher workday," Ann confirmed. "Dean's going to be over at your place, so we might as well get together at mine."

Wyatt jumped in to explain. "I've contracted Dean to spray the pastures for the worms that cost Dodd his last herd. It's got to be done before the horses and cattle can be purchased."

Tina nodded. "It's just that I have so much work to do at the house."

Wyatt knew Tina well enough by now to recognize the concern that she wore like sackcloth. She worried that Tyler wouldn't behave properly, but Wyatt felt he would be happier with a new friend, especially one like Donovan Pryor.

Wyatt sidled up to Tina, softly encouraging her to agree. "Ty needs a friend his own age." Donovan was a year older, but he was closer in age to Tyler than Frankie.

"I'm sure Frankie would enjoy a morning of play," Jake put in heartily, "provided you're sure he won't be any trouble to include."

Dean hoisted up a flame-haired little girl into his arms, her ruffled skirts fluffing. "Maybe Frankie can entertain Glory," he said hopefully. "Otherwise, Donovan will be toting her everywhere."

"He's a very protective big brother," Ann said with a chuckle. "We had to conspire to keep him away from Glory to get her walking. It will do him good to have some time with a new friend."

"Every anchor to War Bonnet and Loco Man Ranch is a good thing for Tyler," Wyatt whispered.

"What about your lunch?" Tina hedged. "Who'll cook for you guys?"

"We can fend for ourselves once in a while."

"And if you're interested in gardening, Grandma Billie will be only too willing to show you her vegetable patch," Ann prodded. "That way, if you simply must work, you can pull weeds."

Tina laughed, but Wyatt caught the note of tension

in the sound. He placed an encouraging hand on her shoulder. Finally, she gave in.

"How can I turn down such a gracious invitation? Thank you."

Ann smiled brightly. "We'll expect y'all around nine tomorrow morning. All right?"

"Sounds fine," Wyatt confirmed before Tina could change her mind.

The adults said their farewells, and Wyatt slid his hand to the small of Tina's back, urging her toward the church's exit. In truth, Wyatt didn't know if Ty could put aside his resentment and confusion long enough to mind his manners and enjoy the playdate, but he believed wholeheartedly that Ty needed this friendship, and Wyatt expected that the Pryors were more than capable of handling one unhappy little boy if the need arose. Moreover, he felt that Tina could benefit from the relationship, too. He didn't know Ann Pryor very well, but his dealings with the Billings family had shown him that they were solid, caring, generous people. Tina could use a friend like Ann.

What Tina apparently didn't need was him. He walked her to her car and helped Ty into his safety seat. She got into the car and drove away without a single word for him. She'd looked so pretty in her flowered Easter dress. Sighing, he turned toward his truck, only to find his brothers looking at him with lopsided grins on their faces.

"What?" he demanded. "Donovan will be a good influence on Ty."

"You would know," Ryder said. "You and Donovan have that protective big brother thing in common."

Wyatt made a face. So he *liked* being the big brother. Nothing wrong with that.

"Make fun if you want to, but we all know that Tyler needs a friend his own age."

"Uh-huh," Jake said. "That isn't all he needs."

Irked, Wyatt shot back, "It's not that she doesn't try to discipline him. She's doing the best she can in difficult circumstances."

Jake just grinned and turned for the truck.

"He means that, from all you say, Tyler needs a real dad," Ryder explained. "And even Frankie can see who the likeliest candidate for that job is."

Recalling the moment when Frankie had offered Unca Wyatt as Tyler's daddy, Wyatt felt heat burn its way up his neck. Wyatt snatched Frankie from his father's side and lifted the boy into his safety seat. He couldn't help thinking that, for all practical purposes, Frankie had three fathers, all of them fully capable of seeing to his needs. It didn't seem fair that Tyler didn't have even one.

Jake clapped a hand on Wyatt's shoulder. "What Ryder's trying to say is that it takes a good big brother to know one."

"Look, it's about time you thought about someone other than the three of us," Ryder told Wyatt. "Maybe it's time to think about what you want and need."

"So, you think I need a prickly woman soured on marriage and a brat?"

"I think you need—"

"And deserve," Jake interjected.

"—a woman who loves you. And a family of your own."

"*You're* my family," Wyatt said, his voice gravelly with emotion. "You two plus Frankie." Besides, Tina had made it perfectly clear that she couldn't—wouldn't—love him or any man.

"Of course we're your family," Ryder said, "but we're big boys now. You don't have to look after us anymore."

"And you've proved with Frankie that you're a great substitute father," Jake added. "Besides, we didn't stop being family when I married Jolene, did we?"

Wyatt shook his head. "No, Jolene just added to the family, and so did Frankie. I'm not sure it would be the same with Tina and Tyler, though."

"But you want to find out," Jake prodded.

Wyatt shook his head again. "I don't know. I'm not sure she even likes me. In fact, I think she likes you and Ryder better."

Jake laughed. "She's not attracted to either of us. We don't threaten her single existence."

"We see how she looks at you," Ryder teased, "and how you look at her. Go for it, man. What have you got to lose?"

His heart, for one thing. And the odds were certainly against him with Tina. Still, the worst that could happen is that he'd get shot down. It wasn't as if she'd take away anything he already had, anything more than the ranch house and the mineral rights, anyway. He found that he didn't so much mind losing those things now. And his ego could take it if she wasn't interested. He'd just have to keep his heart safely locked away until he knew which way this thing would go.

"We want you to be happy," Jake said.

"And to stop worrying about us," Ryder added urgently.

Too moved to speak, Wyatt slapped each of them lightly on the cheek and got into the truck. Maybe it was time he started thinking about his own future. Jake and Frankie were getting on with life after losing Jolene. Ryder was far removed from the anger and pain of what had happened in Houston. Loco Man Ranch would soon be a real operation again.

Tina said she didn't want a man in her life, but she'd tolerated his interference with Tyler and let him convince her to accept Ann Pryor's invitation. That had to mean that she at least trusted him.

Didn't it?

He supposed he could ask God to guide him and see what happened.

What happened didn't give him much hope. Despite his attempts to engage her in friendly conversation, Tina kept her distance, barely looking at him as she went about her business. Still, he couldn't seem to leave her alone. After a Sunday dinner of baked ham and all the fixings, Tina and the kids dyed eggs. Jake and Ryder went out to hide them while Tina took the boys into the den.

Wyatt wandered in to see what they were watching on Dodd's old TV. The ancient antenna outside received only two stations, but Wyatt had arranged for cable and internet, which would be installed in the next day or two. Meanwhile, Tina had set up a DVD player and several videos appropriate for children. The one currently playing was an animated superhero film. While the boys watched the ridiculously small television screen, Tina sat to one side, reading a book. Wyatt stood there for several minutes, waiting to see if Tina would acknowledge him. He knew perfectly well that she realized he was there, but she neither looked up nor spoke.

Finally, he said, "We have a flat-screen TV that we can hang on the wall there."

"That'll be nice," Tina murmured without looking up from her book.

"Might have some furniture you want to use in here, too. We won't need it all in the bunkhouse."

She turned a page. "Better wait and see what you need first."

Deflated, he left the room. So much for her interest in him.

He watched from the sidelines as the boys hunted for Easter eggs. Then, feeling restless, he went out to the barn and fired up one of the ATVs that Jake had gotten running. After driving around the ranch for a couple of hours, he felt better, but he was still puzzled by all those fenced parcels of grass. He decided to search Dodd's office for any related papers, but the search proved fruitless.

He did, however, find a safety deposit box key. Leaving the key where he found it, Wyatt decided to go down to the bank in town sometime soon to see if the key fit a box there.

When he walked into the kitchen a few minutes later, he found Tina building thick ham sandwiches. He went to the cabinet to get out plates.

"I thought we'd use paper plates tonight," she said without stopping what she was doing. "Less cleanup."

He closed the cabinet door. "Okay. Want to unlock your car, then? I'll transfer Frankie's safety seat from my truck to your car before it gets dark. That way it'll be in place when you're ready to leave for the Pryors' farm tomorrow."

She sent him a look from the corner of her eye as she walked to the small, decorative table next to the back door. Taking her keys from her handbag, she pointed them outside and remotely unlocked her car doors. Then she returned to the sandwiches.

Wyatt removed Frankie's seat from his truck and carried it around to the passenger-side door of the back seat of Tina's little sedan. She came out then to open the vehicle door for him and clear away several items of Tyler's. Wyatt installed the seat, while Tina stood there with her arms folded. He didn't know what was eating her, but he wanted to.

"Dean and Ann Pryor are excellent people," he told her, just for something to say. "All the Billings family are."

"I know that."

"I met Donovan the day I went to talk to Dean about the spraying," Wyatt went on. "I was impressed by the boy's behavior."

"Meaning you think Tyler will benefit from Donovan's example."

Wyatt faced her. "I do think Donovan will be a good influence."

Tina huffed out a sigh. "I never know anymore whether to be offended by your high-handedness or grateful for your concern."

He flattened his lips, choosing his words carefully.

"You can think I'm high-handed if you want, but I meant what I said to Tyler this morning. I won't put up with his disrespect for you or any other adult around here. I can't. Frankie looks up to Tyler."

She lifted her chin, holding his gaze. Then, without another word, she flounced off, heading back into the house.

Wyatt shook his head, but something told him that she wasn't as upset as she wanted either of them to believe. He hit the lock and closed the car door, wondering if he ought to ask Rex about interstate custody petitions. Maybe it would be high-handed of him, but he couldn't see how it would hurt to know the facts, especially when all he wanted to do was help.

Setting aside her tea glass, Tina laughed heartily. She hadn't laughed so much in…she couldn't remember when. Ann's tales of Donovan and his dog, Digger, had kept everyone in stitches for a good hour.

Ann's sister, Meri Burns, had been there when Tina had arrived. They had discussed the upcoming wedding of Ann and Meri's father, and Tina had found herself volunteering to contribute to the effort. Afterward, the women had toured Billie's vegetable patch, which was less a patch and more like a small farm, since it covered at least an acre. Tina had learned plenty to help her with the much smaller garden that she planned to plant on Loco Man Ranch next year. Then Meri had left to put her little one down for a nap and make her husband's lunch. Dean's grandmother, Billie, who lived with Ann and Dean, was considerably younger than Tina had expected. She'd prepared an excellent lunch and offered to teach Tina how to can and freeze her eventual harvest.

Billie and Ann were obviously close. Tina envied them, and she had to admit that Donovan was a good influence on Tyler. Donovan's manners were impeccable, and Tyler eagerly followed his example in an apparent effort to ingratiate himself with the older boy.

The two boys had been playing outside for some time, while Frankie and Glory entertained themselves in the living room. Donovan ran in just then, followed by Tyler, and came to his mother's side, standing quietly until she smiled at him in acknowledgment.

"Can Tyler and me play in my room?"

"Why don't you bring some toys down to the living room, so the younger kids don't feel left out?"

Donovan agreed easily. "Okay. Come on, Ty."

To Tina's surprise and delight, Tyler looked to her and asked, "Is it okay if I help Donovan get his toys?"

"Why, of course you can," Tina replied. "Just be sure that you help pick up the toys after you're through playing with them."

"I promise!" Tyler vowed, rushing off after his friend.

Soon, he and Donovan were racing toy cars around a track while Frankie and little Glory played with a busy center. Frankie pushed the same buttons over and over, and Glory giggled every time. Digger lay at Donovan's side patiently watching the play. From her seat at the dining table, Tina could see that Tyler occasionally reached over and stroked the dog.

She wondered if Wyatt would object if she got a dog for Tyler, then she scolded herself. The house belonged to her. She could get a dog if she wanted one. Thinking of Wyatt made her check the time.

She gasped. "I had no idea it was getting so late."

"Oh, do you have to go so soon?" Ann protested. "We've had such a good time."

"I need to get supper in the oven," Tina said regretfully.

"That reminds me. I need to pull a casserole out of the freezer," Billie Pryor proclaimed. "Where is my head today?" She rose from her chair.

"Where it always is," Ann countered affectionately. "Wrapped around taking care of this family."

"You have the kids to look after and the business," Billie said, heading for the kitchen.

"The business?" Tina queried, smiling at Ann.

"Our custom farming business," Ann answered. "I just handle the books and scheduling. Dean does nearly all the tilling, planting and harvesting in this county, along with a lot of other things. Because equipment is absurdly expensive, local farmers are happy to pay Dean to do the work. They don't have to borrow money for equipment, and we're showing profit. We've also put in our own crops for the past two years now, which means my husband works much too hard."

"Honey, that man wouldn't know any other way to work," Billie said as she returned. "Besides, it takes a hardworking man to make it out here."

"True," Ann agreed. "Dean wouldn't be happy with any other life, though, and I wouldn't be happy if he wasn't happy. Meri does pretty much the same thing for Stark that I do for Dean."

"That's the way it is out here," Billie said. "Takes

everyone pitching in to make this life work. It's a good life, though."

Nodding, Ann smiled. Tina couldn't help thinking of Wyatt and his brothers. While Layne had complained about having to return phone calls, preferred to sleep late and painted only when conditions were exactly right, the Smith brothers got up early every morning and went to work happily with no complaints. None of them ever seemed to lack for work, either. While she kept Ryder busy in the house, Jake had completely reconfigured the bunkhouse, and Wyatt had gone from research to repairing the barn and corrals and purchasing tack and equipment. Just today he'd gone out to buy a cattle hauler, after discovering that Dodd's old trailer had rusted clear through. Now that they had cable and internet service—the technician had arrived as Tina and the children were leaving this morning—Wyatt would be setting up books and accounts on his computer next.

Thinking of all that Wyatt and his brothers were doing, Tina got to her feet. "I really have to go, but I've so enjoyed myself."

"We're very glad you came."

"So am I." She got to her feet and went into the living room, Ann following, just in time to hear Donovan say, "That stinks. My first mom didn't want me, but it's okay. Dad wants me lots, and Ann's my real mom, anyhow."

Momentarily stunned by the topic the two boys were discussing, Tina whipped a glance at Ann, who simply smiled and whispered, "It's true. Dean would've married her, but she just handed over the baby and apparently never looked back." Obviously, the subject wasn't a secret in the Pryor household.

"My mommy in Heaven," Frankie said matter-of-factly. "Maybe she come back."

"That won't happen," Tyler informed Frankie bluntly. "No one comes back from Heaven."

"Nor would we want them to," Tina interrupted, fearing Frankie's reaction. "Heaven is a wonderful place, and everyone there is very happy."

Frankie frowned, then yawned.

"Someone seems ready for a nap," Ann remarked with a chuckle.

Tina crouched before Frankie. "Would you like to go home and take a nap now?"

He nodded, rubbed his eyes and reached for her. She gathered him up, standing with him on her hip. Like all the Smith males, he was large and his weight nearly staggered her, but she remembered happily how it had felt when Tyler had reached for her, begging to be held. Looking down, she saw the envy on Tyler's face and felt a jolt of joy. He remembered those times, too. If only his father would stop trying to poison him against her, they could have a lovely relationship. Still, she knew the days of him wanting to be held were behind them.

She knew she would never have that particular experience again.

Unless she remarried and had more children of her own.

But she was already blessed with one son. She wouldn't ask for more.

Smiling, she set Frankie on his feet and addressed Tyler. "Help Donovan clean up, sweetie, so we can go."

"Aw, Mo-om," Tyler whined, but he started helping Donovan break apart the racetrack and stow the pieces in a plastic tub.

Ann added the busy center to the tub and picked up Glory, saying, "Thank you, Tyler. Donovan will take the toys upstairs."

To Tina's surprise, Donovan got up and hugged both her and Frankie. "Bye, Mizz Kemp."

"Goodbye, Donovan."

Not to be outdone, Tyler leaped up and ran over to give Ann a quick hug. "Bye, Mizz Pryor."

"Goodbye, Tyler, and thank you for coming."

"Thank you for having us," Tina replied.

Tyler looked at Donovan. "Maybe you can come to my house tomorrow."

"Not tomorrow," Ann said, "but soon."

Dissatisfied with that, Tyler began to whine again. "But when? Why not?"

"Donovan has school tomorrow," Tina quickly pointed out, "but we'll set up another playdate soon."

Tyler bowed his head in obvious disgust, but he didn't protest further.

As she drove back to Loco Man Ranch, Tina thought about all that had happened. Wyatt had been right on every count. Ann and her family were wonderful people. Tina was grateful to have made friends with her and her sister, and she was thrilled that Tyler wanted to emulate Donovan's behavior. She'd never met a better behaved, more loving, well-adjusted child than Donovan.

Looking into the rearview mirror, Tina said to her

son, "You made me proud today, Tyler. You behaved very well. And I promise you'll get to see Donovan again as soon as possible."

Smiling slightly, he nodded and turned his head to gaze out the window.

Yes, Wyatt had been right. Again. Tina was coming to realize that he usually was.

She couldn't help wishing that she had met Wyatt first. If it had been him instead of Layne...

She shook her head.

Why wish for the impossible?

It was enough that she and Tyler had Wyatt and his brothers in their lives now.

Chapter Nine

As soon as Tina brought her car to a stop at the ranch, Frankie sat up straight and looked around. He spied Wyatt walking toward the house from the barn and pointed. "Unca Wyatt! Unca Wyatt, get me."

Chuckling, Tina got out and walked around to let the boy out of his safety harness while Tyler unclipped his own belt and opened his own car door. Waving to Wyatt, she called out to him. "I think Frankie wants you to put him to bed for a nap."

Wyatt lengthened his stride and was standing next to her by the time Frankie crawled down from his seat. Tyler came around to join them.

"Did you guys have fun?" Wyatt asked.

"It was a blast!" Tyler exclaimed.

Frankie just nodded and lifted both arms in a silent plea for Wyatt to hold him. Wyatt easily swung the boy up against his chest.

"Unca Wyatt," Frankie asked solemnly, "my mama come back from Heaven?"

Wyatt curled a finger under the boy's chin. "Who told you your mama would come back from Heaven?"

Cringing inwardly, Tina shook her head. "I'm afraid Tyler told him that his mother would *not* come back from Heaven."

"I didn't mean to," Tyler whined plaintively.

Tina sent him a look before turning her attention back to Wyatt. "I don't know how they got on the subject. Donovan said that his first mother didn't want him but that it was okay, because his dad does want him and Ann is his real mother. That's when Frankie said his mother might come back from Heaven, and Tyler told him that wouldn't happen."

Apparently unruffled, Wyatt looked to Tyler. "Well, these things happen. Kids talk. We expect Frankie to have questions from time to time." He smoothed Frankie's curly hair. "Frankie, do you remember your mother?"

Frankie pondered a moment, his finger stealing into his mouth, then he laid his head on Wyatt's shoulder. Wyatt and Tina exchanged glances. Clearly, the boy had no firm images of his mother, but perhaps he remembered the warmth of her arms or the sound of her voice. Apparently, he missed her more than anyone had realized.

Wyatt patted him and said, "Let's go talk to your dad. He usually has a photo of your mom on him."

Wyatt carried Frankie toward the bunkhouse. Tina shoved the car door closed, grabbed Tyler by the hand and hurried to catch up with them.

"Do you mind if we tag along? Tyler caused this, after all, and he needs to make an apology."

Wyatt glanced at Tyler. "I don't think Jake will mind you two being there."

She fell in beside them, taking two steps to every one of Wyatt's, Tyler trailing at the end of her arm. Wyatt slowed down to accommodate her and Tyler, so that they walked side by side. For some reason that small gallantry moved her. She tried to remember if Layne had ever made such adjustments for them, but she mostly just remembered trailing along behind him with Tyler in a stroller. It had seemed perfectly natural at the time. Now it seemed telling.

They reached the bunkhouse. Jake had added a pair of steps and a sizable front deck. Someone had arranged a pair of rusty, old metal lawn chairs to one side of the door. Wyatt pulled open the new screen door and stepped inside.

Jake stood atop a ladder in the small front room, connecting a ceiling vent to a wide, flexible insulated hose. The living area couldn't have been more than ten feet square, much too small for five people and a ladder, let alone for three big men to relax in comfortably. She knew from supper conversation that Jake had made a space for a small two-burner stove and three or four running feet of cabinet and countertop in a nook just around the corner. The brothers had discussed how to fit a sink into the small space. She hadn't given much thought to the size of the old bunkhouse, but she was beginning to realize that with a kitchenette, bathroom and three bedrooms, the place was going to be cramped at best.

"You about got that central air hooked up?" Wyatt asked.

"Yeah, but I won't turn it on until I get the ceiling in," Jake said, still looking up. "No point in cooling the rafters."

"When you're done there," Wyatt said, "Frankie wants to talk to you."

Jake glanced down then back up at the clamp he was tightening. "This should do it." He dropped a small screwdriver into the pocket of his leather tool belt and began backing down the ladder, speaking to his son as he did so. "Did you have fun at the Pryors'?"

Frankie nodded and looked to his uncle, who said, "Let's have a seat on the porch."

He carried the boy back outside and sat down in one of the old lawn chairs with Frankie on his lap. The old metal chair creaked ominously but held their combined weight. Tina took a spot on the corner of the porch. Tyler stood next to Wyatt's chair, patting Frankie on the shoulder.

Heavy gray clouds gathered in the east, but it would be some time before the rain reached them. Meanwhile, the air felt unusually still and thick.

"It seems that Frankie has been thinking his mom might come back from Heaven to visit us one day," Wyatt said as Jake took the chair beside him.

Jake glanced at Wyatt and Tina before pulling Frankie onto his lap. "We'll see your mama again someday, son, but in Heaven, not here on earth."

"She don't come back?" Frankie asked.

"No, son. She won't come back, but we'll all go there, not all at the same time, but one by one until we're all together again. I don't think she'd want us to come too soon, though, because when we go there, we won't come back here until we all come with Jesus."

"With Jesus," Frankie parroted.

"That's right," Wyatt said. "Mommy's with Jesus, and we'll all be with Him someday, too."

"I wan' see her," Frankie said, holding out his hand.

"I think he'd like to see a picture of her," Wyatt explained.

Jake took out his wallet and pulled a photo from behind a plastic window. He passed the small photo to Frankie. "That's you and your mama the day we brought you home from the hospital."

Frankie studied the photo and touched it with a damp finger. "She smilin'."

"She was very happy that day," Jake told him. "She's happy now, too. She loves you very much, but she's happy with Jesus in Heaven."

"Okay," Frankie said, hooking an arm around his father's neck and laying his head on Jake's chest, the photo still clutched in his grubby little hand.

Jake hugged the boy. "We'll put a framed picture of her in our room," he said to Frankie, "so we can see her every morning and every night. What do you think of that?"

"Okay," Frankie said again. He yawned widely.

"Looks like you need a nap, little man," Jake said. "Want to take a nap in here with me? I've got a sleeping bag you can use."

Frankie nodded, yawning again.

Jake tapped him on the end of his nose. "I think you were so excited about going over to Donovan's today that you didn't sleep much last night."

Frankie just closed his eyes and sighed. Tyler went over and patted Frankie's shoulder again. Jake looked at Wyatt and Tina.

"I hope he behaved himself today," he said to Tina, and she nodded.

"Oh, yes." She smiled at Tyler, pleased that he seemed to realize he'd blundered and wanted to comfort Frankie as best he could. "They both did." Tyler stood a little straighter.

"You put him down for a nap. We'll talk later," Wyatt told Jake softly. Nodding, Jake got to his feet and carried his son into the bunkhouse to the room they would soon share on a permanent basis.

Tina felt a pang of guilt at the idea. It wasn't right. Tyler had his own room; Frankie ought to have one of his own, not to mention Jake. She bit her lip, pondering the situation. All along, the Smith brothers had been helpful and cooperative. No doubt, from their point of view, they'd gotten a raw deal when Dodd had left the house to her, but they'd adapted and been pleasant about it.

They were the kind of men she wanted her son to emulate: hardworking, caring, responsible and church-going. Layne's idea of attending church was putting in an appearance at Easter or Christmas. If he couldn't manage to get out of it.

But how did she broach what she was thinking now? How did she ask three unmarried men to live with her and her son?

Especially when she couldn't seem to stop thinking about one of them in particular?

Tina slid off the porch and stood up. Tyler jumped

down next to her. Wyatt walked down the two steps and took her by the elbow, pointing her toward the house. Tyler rushed to walk on his other side, and Wyatt laid a hand on his back.

"We're sorry this happened," Tina said.

Wyatt looked down at Tyler. "There was no malicious intent, and I doubt this is the last time Frankie will have questions about his mom."

"You and Jake are both so good with Frankie," Tina said. "Ryder, too. I noticed that from the very beginning."

"We all love that boy. Ryder and I cared for him when Jake and Jolene were both deployed."

"I didn't know they could do that," Tina said. "Deploy both parents at the same time."

"It was a four month mission for Jolene, and she got a promotion out of it. Then she died stateside in a training accident a few weeks after her return. I thank God we were there for Jake and Frankie during that awful time."

"So do I," she told him, "but it's more than just being family. You genuinely like having Frankie around."

"Why wouldn't we?"

"Lots of men don't like having kids around."

Wyatt chuckled. "That's just laziness. Or selfishness. Maybe both."

"Yes, I see that. I just wish more fathers were like the three of you." She sighed. "Children follow the examples set for them." Sometimes Tyler came home from Layne's saying the most awful things. He'd been sent home from school once for repeating something Layne had said in front of him.

"If parents don't teach kids acceptable behavior," Wyatt said, "life will. Someone somewhere will take exception to unacceptable words and actions."

"I'm just glad that the Smith brothers set a good example."

"We try to. Thank you for noticing."

She turned to look at him. "How could I not?" Glancing at the bunkhouse, she made a decision. "I was thinking, Wyatt, that it might be best if you all stayed in the house with us. The bunkhouse is too small for the four of you."

He stepped back, seeming genuinely shocked. "What are you suggesting, Tina? That we stop work on the bunkhouse now?"

Shaking her head, she said, "We could always rent out the bunkhouse, as a sort of annex to the main house."

"There's only seven bedrooms in the house and you're splitting some of them into bathrooms."

"I know, but we could fix up the attic, too. That would give us two bedrooms in the house to rent plus the bunkhouse."

He stroked his chin. "I don't know. The bathroom in the bunkhouse is super tiny. Jake took the space out of it for the kitchen."

"We could split the corner bedroom into two private baths, one for each of the remaining bedrooms, and use the current bathroom to enlarge the kitchen. The footprint would have to be changed a bit, but it could be done. Couldn't it?"

"That way everyone gets his or her own bedroom,

and you'll have four rooms to rent—two in the house, two in the bunkhouse."

"I think it's the best solution all around."

"Maybe Ryder and I should take the bunkhouse, let Frankie and Jake take rooms in the main house."

"Or maybe Jake and Frankie would like to have their own place in the bunkhouse," Tina suggested casually. "We can work this out any number of ways."

Smiling down at her, Wyatt nodded his approval. "I'll talk it over with Jake and Ryder, and let you know."

Tina turned toward the house again and felt Wyatt's hand settle in the small of her back. Together, they casually strolled toward the door.

Feeling that she'd done the right thing, Tina had never enjoyed a simple walk more.

Tyler's presence made it difficult for Wyatt to tell Tina what he'd learned from Rex that day about interstate custody fights. He noticed that when Tina suggested Tyler fetch his crayons and a coloring book and keep her company while she started supper, the boy readily agreed. He noticed, too, how pleased Tina was by Tyler's instant agreement. Things seemed to be improving there. Taking advantage of the moment, Wyatt stepped close to Tina.

"Can we talk later? After Tyler goes to bed?"

She blinked at that, but nodded. "Sure. What about?"

"I'd rather not get into it now." He didn't want to include Tyler in what should be an adult conversation, and if she was going to fuss and fume about Wyatt's high-handedness, he'd rather she did it in private. "Besides, I need to get on the computer."

"Okay."

"By the way, I've arranged for the moving truck to arrive in a couple weeks. We've cleaned out a suitable space in the barn to store what we can't use right now."

"All right."

He smiled and said, "You know, we've got two refrigerators, and neither of them are going to fit in the bunkhouse."

Looking at the ancient little fridge at the end of the cabinet, she retorted dryly, "I guess we'll just have to find a place for them." They both laughed.

Tyler returned then, a heap of coloring books under one arm and a shoebox-sized tin of crayons in the other. Wyatt took himself off to Dodd's office and got busy. Listening idly to Tina and Tyler in the kitchen, Wyatt set up his laptop. He'd previously cleared away the stacks of papers littering the old desk, using a pair of boxes as filing drawers.

Dodd hadn't been much for filing. He'd left a box labeled Tax that contained receipts and such, and another filled with unopened bank statements, which Wyatt had been gradually working through. Nothing in either box told Wyatt anything about Dodd's intention with the fenced acres of sowed grass, but they did tell another story.

Dodd's financial situation had been alarmingly precarious. He'd had less than a thousand dollars in the ranch account. He'd used his Social Security to pay the utilities and buy groceries. He could've hung on for another year, at least, and then he could have sold acreage to pay taxes. No one would have blamed him.

Wyatt could only imagine that Dodd had been experimenting with varieties of grass that wouldn't host worms, in the hope of somehow being able to restock. Maybe the veterinarian, Stark Burns, knew something about that. Wyatt had made an appointment for Stark to inspect the range after Dean finished the spraying. He would ask Stark what he knew then.

Meanwhile, Rex had told Wyatt where to download software to help track everything from expenses to well-animal treatments and veterinary visits. Rex had talked a lot about ranch-fed beef, too. He made a good case for raising one's own fodder rather than buying manufactured feeds or using feed lots. For Loco Man, those were decisions for the coming year, not this one.

Tina showed up in the open doorway to say that supper was ready. He lost no time in closing out the program he'd set up and heading for the kitchen, where he found Tyler setting plates on the table. Frankie followed him, placing forks next to each plate. Jake reached over them to set glasses of tea on the table.

"You've got a couple of good helpers here," Wyatt told Tina, winking at the boys. Ty beamed at him. "I'm not sure about the tall one, though."

"He stinks," Frankie stated matter-of-factly, and everyone but Jake laughed.

"All right, all right. I'll go clean up," Jake grumbled, scowling despite the mirth glinting in his eyes.

"Wait," Tina said, waving Jake and everyone else to the table. "All of you. You're fine, and I won't be happy if you let this meal get cold."

Jake eagerly pulled out a chair. Ryder came in and went to wash up in the bathroom. Wyatt pulled out a chair for Tina, then went to wash up at the kitchen sink. Tina sat so Jake would. He lifted Frankie onto his boosted seat and pulled the chair close to the table.

They enjoyed a fine meal. Afterward, Wyatt and Ryder helped Tina clean up the dishes while Jake got the boys ready for bed. Then the boys played in Tyler's room with Ryder and Jake tried out the new cable TV. Wyatt caught Tina's eye and nodded toward the front of the house. The two of them slipped out onto the porch.

"What did you want to talk about?" she asked as soon as he pulled the door closed behind them.

Wyatt took a deep breath. "Now, don't bite my head off, but I spoke to Rex about what's involved in a custody battle like yours."

To his relief, Tina merely nodded. "And?"

"And it could be a very expensive proposition for both parties."

Tina wandered across the porch to sit on the steps. The days were getting longer, and it wasn't dark enough for more than a bit of moon and a few stars to show through the gloaming. Wyatt walked over and sat down next to her.

"I know that's not what you want to hear."

She shook her head, studying her fingernails. "I told you before. Layne is heir to a large family fortune. He can do as he pleases."

"And you've got just what you're investing in this place," Wyatt surmised gently.

"That's about it."

He balanced his forearms against his thighs, hands linked. "I'm sorry, Tina."

"Not your fault."

"I'll help any way I can."

A wan smile quirked her pretty lips, but she didn't look at him. "Thanks, but I don't know what you could do."

"I can pray, at least."

In a strained voice, she said, "I hope your prayers have more power than mine." Suddenly, she wiped tears from her eyes. "I can't tell you how many times I've prayed for God's intervention, only to be disappointed."

Reaching for her hand, he stayed silent, letting her talk.

"Every time my mother married, I prayed it would be the last time. That my new stepfather would want me as a daughter as much as he wanted her as a wife, but that never happened with anyone but Dodd, and she left him. She just couldn't stay interested in any one man. She had five husbands. Five."

"You don't need serial marriages to make you happy," Wyatt said softly. "Just one. The right one."

"Maybe. But I obviously got her judgment genes. Look who I picked."

"You must've been young when you married him."

"Twenty-one. Just barely."

"It's easy to be swept off your feet that young."

"I was in my junior year of college, but I really hadn't dated much." She shrugged. "I didn't want to make a mistake, but when this handsome, successful artist who'd lectured in one of my classes asked me out, I thought he was the answer to my prayers. A few months later, my mother died. I—I had no one and nowhere to go. I hadn't seen my father since I was ten. When Layne asked me to marry him, I—I thought God was telling me he was the one."

"Why are you so certain He wasn't?" Wyatt asked. "What's best for us isn't something we can easily decide for ourselves. We have to trust that God knows best."

"You think Layne was best for me?" she asked incredulously.

"Maybe at the time. Without him, you wouldn't have had Tyler."

"That's true," she admitted.

"Without a doubt, you had to be what was best for Layne," Wyatt said evenly.

She cocked her head, looking at him with intense interest. "What do you mean by that?"

"You were Layne's chance to be the man he should be. It's not your fault he didn't take advantage of the opportunity. It's your fault if you don't take advantage of the opportunities God gives you."

Wyatt could tell by the look on her face that she had never considered such a possibility.

Gradually, her features softened, her big, coppery eyes filling with sadness for what might have been.

She squeezed Wyatt's hand, warming his heart with that simple gesture.

"Thank you."

He knew then that he wanted more from Tina than simple friendship or a business partnership. He didn't know why he hadn't seen it from the beginning, but that didn't matter now. She did.

Without a clue as to how it had happened, he knew that she mattered now.

Very much.

Chapter Ten

For a long moment, Wyatt couldn't seem to break eye contact with Tina. He had completely misjudged her in the beginning. She wasn't selfish and entitled. Her prickliness was a result of her hesitancy to trust, and who could blame her, given what she'd been through? They had both lost their mothers at a young age, but he'd had fifteen years of calm, loving, wise support to prepare him for the loss. Tina had had only disappointment and instability. Yet, as a mother herself, she was a calm, loving, wise support for her son and doing her best to give him the stability that she had lacked.

It saddened Wyatt to realize that everyone she'd ever trusted had betrayed her in some way, even Dodd to a degree. What had that old man been thinking to leave her his house while seeing to it that his nephews owned the very ground it sat on? Given her situation, she must have been horrified. Yet, she had cooperated in every possible way, even if unhappily at first. She had to be as puzzled by Dodd's actions as Wyatt and his brothers.

Dodd had always had a funny way of reasoning, but

he usually had figured out what was needed. Wyatt couldn't for the life of him understand what the old man had been trying to accomplish with this will situation. Had he simply wanted to remember Tina in some way? Had he expected Wyatt and his brothers to buy her out? Or was something else going on here?

An odd thought struck him. Had Dodd been matchmaking? He'd rambled on and on about Walker, but Wyatt hadn't paid much attention. In his mind, Walker had been a mere acquaintance of Dodd's, not someone Dodd had loved. Eventually, she'd become just another name associated with the ranch, like Delgado. Wyatt hadn't given her much more thought than that. Now he wondered if Dodd had hoped that one of his nephews would realize what a special lady this beautiful woman truly was.

She suddenly laughed gently, rolling her eyes.

"What? What's so funny?"

"I was just thinking of Frankie offering you to Tyler as a substitute father. Out of the mouths of babes, right?" She shook her head. "If only it were that easy. If only I could say, 'We'll take this one instead.' It would be so simple if there was a father store. 'This one comes with good sense, authority and genuine concern. This one is a good provider, a hard worker, kind.' Wonder if I could get a money-back guarantee?"

"Maybe you could upgrade every time a new version came out, like cell phones," Wyatt teased, but she shook her head, her eyes suddenly wide.

"Uh, no. That was my mother's approach."

Wyatt spread his hands, trying to get the conversation back on track and away from the source of her fears. "I was actually pleased that Frankie came up with that. He was pretty attached to me when Jake came home. I think it hurt Jake a lot. Maybe it was just losing Jolene, but there were times when Frankie reached for me instead of his father, and Jake's pain was tangible. I felt like I was walking a tightrope, trying to comfort and care for Frankie and subtly shift his dependence to Jake at the same time."

"While you love them both."

"Of course. That's the bottom line, isn't it? There are no perfect dad stores, no perfect uncles, either. There's just love to cover all the inadequacies."

"I loved Layne," she whispered. "It wasn't enough."

"It takes two to keep that kind of love alive, two people willing to work and forgive and make each other a priority. My folks used to say that they were a single unit and they had to work to keep their connection healthy and whole. Then together they put God first and their children second. As individuals, they put themselves at the bottom of the list. It's an imperfect analogy, but they made it work. Their relationship was so solid that my dad was never the same after he lost her, but he wouldn't have had it any other way. He loved her without end, and I know she loved him the same way."

"That's beautiful," Tina said, her eyes shining.

"*You're* beautiful," Wyatt heard himself say to her.

She blinked those big, glittering eyes at him. He wanted to kiss her. Obeying the impulse, he lifted his hand to the back of her head. He felt the sleek, clean strands of her short hair and the warmth of her skin beneath as he captured her mouth with his.

She stiffened for an instant, and then she melted into his arms.

Mine, he thought. *This is what it's all about.*

Excitement flooded his veins, bolstered by a soaring hope. That kiss became something precious and momentous. His future seemed to be taking shape before his mind's eye. Then suddenly Tina shoved against him, and before he knew what was happening, she stood halfway across the porch.

"No!" she exclaimed, trembling. "No. I—I won't go from man to man. I'm not..."

Not her mother. She didn't have to say it.

Wyatt rose to his feet, twisting around to face her. He kept his movements slow and easy, his tone gentle and even. "Tina. Sweetheart. You're not—" the next instant, he was talking to air "—anything like her." The door closed between them before the words were hardly out of his mouth.

He ran his hands over his face. Well, he couldn't have blown that any worse with dynamite.

"You want to come out to the bunkhouse and see what we've done with the furniture you sent there?"

Wyatt stood just outside Ryder's bedroom door in the upstairs hallway, his expression guarded. Shaking her head, Tina turned her attention back to the bed she was making up. The Smith goods had arrived and been dispersed as she had designated. The old fridge had gone to the bunkhouse. Two new stainless steel versions replaced it: one in the kitchen, the other in the laundry room. With electricity and new appliances, they were starting to live in the twenty-first century once again.

While something of a mishmash, all the furniture was of good quality and comfortable, and just having the things in the house made the whole place feel more like home. She had reluctantly let go of the rickety antiques and filled the parlor with comfy, over-stuffed leather couches. The boys were thrilled with the huge flat-screen television now hanging on the wall, especially with the cable working. Plus, they had real beds and fresh linens for all the bedrooms, not to mention dressers for storage and even a lovely cheval glass that had belonged to Frances Smith. Tina had set aside Dodd's old kitchen table to use as a desk and replaced it with Wyatt's long, rectangular wrought-iron one. She loved its terracotta tile top, which had fired her imagination for remodeling the kitchen. Jake's warm oak dining set, with its spacious buffet, now occupied the dining room, though the inexpensive drapes she'd hung in there no longer felt appropriate.

In so many ways, the old house had come to life. Tyler certainly seemed better satisfied. Still, she had more important things to do just now than worry about furniture placement.

"I'll worry about that later. Just be sure you don't damage anything with the painting and finish work. When I'm done here, I need to start calling contractors. Ryder can't go much further until the roof is repaired, and we have rain in the forecast again. I need to bring in a professional ASAP. There's the plumbing and bathroom fixtures to be installed, too." She stopped smoothing and tucking the sheets and straightened, lifting the back of her hand to her forehead, her mind whirling. "I won't know how much money I'll have for decorating until the essential work is done, so there's no point in worrying about the bunkhouse now."

Behind her, she heard Wyatt's feet shift on the hard-wood floor. That reminded her she needed the floors refinished, too. So much to do. Yet, she knew she was mainly looking for ways to avoid Wyatt.

All they'd done for nearly two weeks now was avoid each other. Ever since that kiss on the front porch. The one she couldn't seem to forget. Giving the sheet one more tug, she placed her other hand on her hip. Avoidance was surprisingly hard work, especially when she wasn't sleeping well.

Lately, no matter how hard she worked during the daytime, she tossed and turned at night. Maybe if she didn't dream during her brief moments of sleep, she'd have more energy. That kiss wouldn't leave her mind, though. She remembered all too well the rise of joy in her heart, the warmth of his embrace.

She dreamed of that kiss. She dreamed of his strong arms cradling her against him as if she was the most precious thing in his world. Then suddenly Wyatt would turn into Layne; Layne's arms holding her, Layne's expensive cologne overwhelming her. In her dreams, she could not get away. She struggled frantically, only to wake twisted in the bed covers, her chest heaving in panic. Alone was better than trapped with a selfish, abusive, hateful man.

Deep down, she knew that Wyatt was nothing like Layne, but she couldn't seem to convince herself that he wouldn't eventually act just as hatefully as Layne.

Shaking her head, she pushed away memories of her ex, the dream and the kiss.

With one last glance around the room, she headed for the door, relieved that Wyatt had disappeared. She hurried along the hallway to the stairs. In her haste, she almost tripped on the steps. Remembering how her mother had fallen, she slowed down. Moving over to the table that she'd claimed for her desk, she opened her laptop to get online.

Moments later, she perused a list of available contractors in the area, jotting down phone numbers and making notes. Lyons and Son was the only local option. They'd already been recommended to her, but she made a few other calls first.

A couple of the contractors couldn't give her an estimate for more than a month. Others did not handle roofing or plumbing or floor refinishing but offered to give her numbers for subcontractors they used, some from as far away as Oklahoma City and Wichita Falls, Texas. One fellow drove down from Duncan that afternoon. Lyons admitted they were busy, but because she was local, they promised someone would stop by in the early evening.

Both men listened attentively to her needs and plans. They promised detailed estimates the next day. Both had impeccable references, and their approaches were similar. Tina felt inclined to go with Dixon Lyons, the son in Lyons and Son, simply because he was local, but she couldn't afford to make a mistake, and she knew that if she asked any of the lifelong locals, they'd recommend Lyons. As newcomers, Wyatt and his brothers might be more unbiased, but she didn't want to ask

Wyatt. She had enough trouble just sitting at the dinner table with him. On the other hand, excluding him from any conversation on the subject would be even more awkward than ignoring him.

Ann had encouraged her to attend prayer meetings on Wednesday nights, and suddenly that felt like a good idea tonight. God didn't seem to pay much attention to her one-on-one, but maybe He'd hear her better in church. Maybe He'd pay more attention if hers wasn't the only voice calling out to him. Maybe, in this instance, God would give her obvious direction and guidance.

The Smith brothers routinely attended prayer meetings, but Tina had thus far resisted the midweek service. She'd started to wonder if she wasn't being somewhat petty. Was she staying away because God hadn't answered her prayers the way she wanted? What did that say about her faith?

What's best for us isn't something we can easily decide for ourselves. We have to trust that God knows best.

She wanted to believe that she trusted God to do what was best for her, but Wyatt's comments had made her wonder if she wasn't substituting her judgment for God's. Previously, she'd told herself that she hadn't attended prayer meeting because she didn't want to spend more time than necessary in Wyatt's company. But wasn't that just another way of saying God had put her in the wrong position? Or had she put herself there by ignoring God's will?

She needed reassurance that God was listening and had a purpose for all that was happening in her life.

Staying home and keeping so busy that she had no time to think would not provide such reassurance. Something had to give. Still, she dithered on making the decision until after supper that evening.

As usual, Wyatt and his brothers had knocked off work early enough to change before the meal. Jake even got Frankie cleaned up and dressed. Usually the boys put on their pajamas after their baths, but after that first Wednesday here, Jake had made a point of taking Frankie with him to church. It was only an hour, as he pointed out, so it didn't delay the boy's bedtime. Tina had refused Jake's offer to bathe Tyler along with Frankie. If she decided to go to prayer meeting, she could bathe Tyler afterward. Meanwhile, she wouldn't have to decide just yet whether to put Tyler into his pajamas or street clothes.

She mulled the decision all during the meal preparations, gradually becoming aware of a deep need for spiritual solace, and she knew that she was fighting the urge to attend the service simply because Wyatt would be involved. She couldn't face staying home while the others went to church, however. Not again. She had to go. She just had to attend prayer meeting tonight.

The instant the decision was made, she felt overwhelming relief. She placed a bowl of corn on the table and announced, "I think Tyler and I will attend prayer meeting tonight. Ann's been inviting me, and I know Tyler would like to see Donovan again."

Jake, Ryder and Tyler all made approving statements, but Wyatt said nothing. When she dared to glance over at him, however, she found him staring at her with a gentle smile on his face and warmth in his eyes. Delight mixed with panic welled up in her, and she quickly averted her gaze. But she wouldn't change her mind. He reached for the corn, and she pulled out a heavy wrought-iron chair to take her place at the long table.

The meal progressed in near silence, with everyone concentrating on cleaning their plates and getting out of the house on time. Afterward, everyone pitched in to make the cleanup go rapidly. Then Tina grabbed up her handbag and led the way out the back door. She knew she'd dressed better than usual today because she'd intended to go to church all along. Wondering how often she lied to herself, she reached back to encourage Tyler to hurry. That was when her son threw a monkey wrench into the works again.

"I wanna ride with the guys!"

Tina looked down at him with exasperation. His behavior had improved significantly of late, but he still demanded his way from time to time. Usually, she could negotiate a compromise without too much trouble, but time was short just then. She prepared to lay down the law and suffer the consequences, but before she could speak, Wyatt did.

"I can move his seat to my truck. Jake can drive, and I'll ride with you. If that's okay."

Tina desperately wanted to refuse, but Tyler deserved some reward for his recent behavior. And if she were truthful, she longed for the ease she'd had with Wyatt before that kiss. They didn't have to talk about personal matters.

Tyler waited hopefully for her decision.

"Up to you," Wyatt murmured.

She told herself that she and Wyatt could discuss the contractors. Abruptly, she realized that she trusted Wyatt's opinion and advice above all others. And why shouldn't she, after witnessing the way he was going about getting Loco Man Ranch back into production?

She addressed her son. "All right. Wyatt will bring your car seat."

Pressing the tiny remote control in her hand, she unlocked the car and moved to the driver's door while Wyatt slipped around her to access Tyler's safety seat. He had plenty of experience installing such seats because of Frankie, so he made quick work of the change and soon returned to sit down in the front passenger seat.

She didn't give him a chance to say anything before she brought up the subject she'd convinced herself should be the focus of their conversation. "I can't make up my mind which contractor to use."

"Oh?"

She started the car and began backing around to follow Jake in Wyatt's truck. "They both seem entirely capable, and I haven't seen the estimates yet, but one of them is local and the other is out of Duncan."

Wyatt considered the matter as she drove. "The estimates will tell you a lot. If one is much lower than the other, you have to wonder if someone's bumping up his price or if the other is intentionally underestimating."

"Either could be disastrous."

"Exactly. If they're close, you have to consider which one you feel you can best work with."

She shot him an inquisitive glance. "And how am I

to do that? I don't know either of them well enough to make that sort of judgment."

"You may know more about them than you realize. For instance, did either show bias in any way? Some contractors can be dismissive or even disdainful of women."

She shook her head, keeping her gaze trained out the front windshield. "Both were completely respectful."

"Glad to hear it. Well, then, did either question your instructions or plans?"

She thought over her conversations with both men. "No, not really. Each one made suggestions and comments. They each pointed out the same concerns, so obviously I should take those seriously."

"Sounds wise. Did either act as if you might not be able to understand their reasoning? Was either reluctant to explain his conclusions?"

"Actually, one of them was all too willing to explain every little detail, but when I told him that details could be left for later, he just smiled, nodded and shut up."

Wyatt chuckled. "Smart fellow. He understands that you're the boss."

"Oh. I guess so."

"Sounds like either one would do nicely," Wyatt said. "All things being equal, I'd go with the local guy. It never hurts to create goodwill in the town where you live."

"I thought that, too. I just don't want to discount the other man because he doesn't live in War Bonnet."

Wyatt gave her a curious look, one she couldn't quite discern. "I applaud your fairness. But something has to tip the balance."

"True."

"Is the local contractor by any chance Lyons and Son?"

"Yes. Why do you ask?"

"I've heard only good things about them."

"Me, too."

"I haven't met Lyons or his son, but Dixon, I think his name is, was pointed out to me in the diner not too long ago, him and his wife. They had a baby with them, too little to walk yet, but Delgado said she was his sister. Apparently, they're raising her as their own."

"That speaks well for them," Tina remarked.

"I thought so. Unless Lyons does something unexpected with the estimate, I'd say that's the way to go."

She smiled. "I agree. Thanks for your input."

"My pleasure."

They drove in silence for a minute or two before Wyatt said, "Actually, I want to talk to you about something."

Oh, man, here it comes, she thought grimly. *He's going to bring up the kiss.*

Hoping to stop him, she spoke. "Can this wait until—"

At the same time, he said, "I've discussed it with my brothers, and—"

Mortified, Tina squawked, "What? You discussed it with your brothers?"

He stared at her, clearly puzzled, until she turned her gaze back out the windshield.

"We're willing to help pay for the renovation."

Shocked, Tina lurched forward in her seat. As the implications of his statement fully sank in, her jaw dropped. Several heartbeats later, she managed to speak. "Y-You're willing to help pay for the renovations?"

He made a show of relaxing, one elbow propped against the passenger window. "Seems only fair if we're going to be living in the house."

Trying for a calm response, she meant to say, "Good," but it came out as a cough.

"That's still the plan, isn't it?"

"I…yes. Sure. B-But would we split the profits of the B and B then?"

"I don't see why," Wyatt said, his tone contemplative. "You'll be handling that on your own. And you won't be sharing in the profits from the ranch. But if you'd rather we just paid rent, we can negotiate that."

That didn't seem fair, especially if she was going to be renting out the bunkhouse, which belonged to them. She shook her head. "No, I…this is just getting more complicated than I'd planned."

"Doesn't have to be. We can talk it over with Rex if you want, draw up some paperwork about how we want to structure things."

"We could do that," she decided, trying to tamp down her elation in order to picture how it all might work.

"I've been thinking," Wyatt said next, enthusiasm entering his voice. "The house needs central air. And you and Ty shouldn't have to share that clunky old bathroom downstairs. You should have private bathrooms like the rest of us. Then we could incorporate the old bath into the laundry room, make it a real workable space. And you could use the storage room for an office. I've poked around in there and haven't found anything worth keeping. Of course, you could always share office space with me."

She hadn't even thought of the storage room, but sharing an office with Wyatt? "Uh. I don't know. That's a lot to think about."

"Well, mull it over. You can decide later." Clearly, the decisions were hers to make.

She couldn't help smiling. For the first time, she felt that it could actually happen. Her dream of providing lodging for War Bonnet visitors and a stable home for her son might actually be feasible.

It had been so long since she'd felt optimism that she almost didn't recognize the feeling, but her mood had lifted significantly by the time she parked the sedan in front of Countryside Church.

If God wasn't listening to her, He must certainly be listening to Wyatt Smith.

Either way, she couldn't be anything but deeply grateful. To both of them. God and Wyatt.

Chapter Eleven

Pleased that Tina had asked and thanked him for his advice, Wyatt finally relaxed. He'd expected for her to lash out at him for that kiss, but she was obviously as eager to forget about it as he was. Too bad he couldn't figure out how to do that.

Kissing her had been a horrible mistake. One that he'd enjoyed immensely and would repeat again if given the opportunity. He did not expect such an opportunity ever to materialize, not even when she placidly filed into the pew with him and his brothers and took a seat between him and Ryder.

Small sheets of paper were passed around so people could write down their prayer requests, with or without a signature. A typewritten list of ongoing requests was also provided. Wyatt jotted down his request and signed it:

Wisdom to discern God's will in domestic and business matters.
Wyatt Smith

Tina scribbled something onto her sheet. It lay in

her lap for several moments while she looked over the typewritten list. Curiosity got the better of him, so Wyatt surreptitiously glanced at what she'd written, smiling because it so closely mirrored his own request:

Important home and business decisions.

He noticed that she didn't sign her name, but after a moment, she retrieved the pen from its holder once more and added another line:

Favor in family court.

So, she expected the custody issue to wind up in court. He hoped—prayed—she was wrong. Rex had outlined a number of instances in which she could easily lose custody. Wyatt hadn't seen the point in detailing them for her, but he'd been praying about the matter ever since his discussion with the friendly rancher and lawyer. Thankful that she would request corporate prayer on the matter, even anonymously, Wyatt smiled to himself.

The congregation, which numbered about half of those who attended on the average Sunday, stood to sing a hymn. Then the pastor read aloud Philippians 4:6.

"Be careful for nothing; but in every thing by prayer and supplication with thanksgiving let your requests be made known unto God."

He went on to explain that the verse meant have no grievous care for anything; do not be anxious or worried. Instead, those with concerns should take their cares and worries to God and be thankful for what they'd already received.

One of the elders read the prayer requests aloud. As usual, Ryder had submitted an unsigned request for the family of Bryan Averett, the young man who had died while practicing with Ryder back in Houston. Some folks jotted down each request. Some took occasional notes. Others, like Wyatt, committed the requests to memory or merely let them sink in. They were instructed that those who wished to speak their prayers could do so as they felt led. Others could pray in silence. They bowed their heads. A few moments of silence ensued before, one by one, various voices put their petitions and those of others into words.

A few prayed with eloquence. More were simple and direct in their praise, gratitude and requests. Several mumbled and bumbled their way through. Wyatt knew very well that it was all the same to God. He refrained from speaking aloud simply because he wanted to address both Ryder's and Tina's unsigned requests in detail. He added requests that Tyler would find peace and joy in his situation and that Layne Kemp would drop his custody suit and stop trying to alienate Tyler from his mother. Wyatt also prayed that Ryder would let go of his guilt and put Bryan's death behind him.

Wyatt and his brothers had attended prayer meeting only sporadically back in Houston—until the tragic death of Bryan. Wyatt had found real peace and comfort in prayer meeting after that, but he could only hope it was the same for his brother. Prayer meetings always seemed brief to Wyatt, but especially so tonight with Tina sitting at his side, looking as pretty and sweet as any woman could in a simple top and jeans. Just knowing that she was there next to him lifted his spirits.

Scary thought. Especially if he was the only one feeling such things.

Pushing away unwelcome thoughts, he smiled and shook hands with all those around him as he made his way out of the sanctuary, Tina at his side, his brothers trailing them. When they reached the foyer, Tina and Jake went to retrieve the boys from their respective groups. Tina returned with Ann Pryor and her son, as well as Tyler. Donovan's beaming smile made Ty's mulish scowl all the more obvious.

"I'm sorry, but I just can't manage it tomorrow," Tina was saying. "Perhaps in—"

"I never have any fun!" Tyler erupted.

"You know that's not true," Tina corrected calmly. "You and Frankie have been having a great time together. I know you want to play with Donovan, and I'm happy for you to do that, but I cannot take you to Donovan's tomorrow."

"You're mean, and I hate you!" Tyler bawled, tearing off toward the door.

Tina sighed. "I'm so sorry, Ann. He's overtired and…" Her words faded away.

Wyatt stepped in. He couldn't help himself. "We appreciate the invitation, and we'll make sure the boys get together again soon."

"And that Tyler is rested and better behaved," Tina added.

Grateful that she didn't appear ready to take him to task for overstepping his bounds, Wyatt blindly reached for her hand and found it, giving it a comforting squeeze. To his everlasting delight, she held on even after he relaxed his fingers.

"Think nothing of it," Ann was saying. "We look forward to hearing from you."

Wyatt smiled, slipped his hand free and lifted it to the small of Tina's back. Together they walked calmly across the foyer and out the door, which hadn't fully closed when Wyatt softly spoke.

"Do you mind if I have another word with Ty?"

"He listens to you a lot better than he does me these days," she answered wryly.

"He's confused by all the changes. Any boy would be," Wyatt said softly as they moved toward the car. Jake already stood beside the truck with Frankie and Tyler, keys in hand.

"That's what I keep telling myself."

He patted her back consolingly, and she sent him a wan smile.

Wyatt asked Jake to move Tyler's safety seat back to Tina's car. Ty folded his arms and stuck out his bottom lip, pouting angrily, but he didn't argue with Wyatt, who stared at the boy in silence while Jake worked and Ryder quietly buckled Frankie into his seat in Wyatt's truck. After securing Tyler's seat, Jake offered the truck keys to Wyatt, but Wyatt shook his head.

"I'm riding with Tina and Tyler."

Nodding, Jake shot Tyler a sympathetic glance. Wyatt took the boy by the arm and walked him around the car. Rather than wait for him to climb up into his seat, Wyatt lifted him into it. Then he got into the back with Tyler. Wyatt caught a glimpse of Tina biting her lip as she slid behind the steering wheel. Without a word, she started the engine and headed home. Tyler started to cry before they got out of the parking lot.

"Sorry, dude. That's not going to work," Wyatt said evenly. "We've already had this discussion. You are not allowed to speak to your mother with such rudeness and disrespect. Everything she does, she does for you, and everyone knows how hard she works. No Christian man would ever dare speak to his mother the way you did just now, not in private and certainly not in public. Do you realize that Mrs. Pryor thinks you're a brat now? Donovan would never be so disrespectful to his mother. If he did, his father would put an immediate stop to it."

"He would?" Tyler queried, tears dripping off his chin.

"Trust me. I know Dean Pryor, and he's a very nice guy, a great dad who loves his kids, and he would never put up with Donovan back talking his mom."

Tyler's brow furrowed as he thought about that. Wyatt hoped that the boy was comparing Dean's parenting with his own father's, but how sophisticated Tyler's reasoning powers were no one could say. Wyatt's hopes rose when Tyler bowed his head and apologized to his mother without prompting.

"I'm sorry, Mom."

"Thank you, honey," Tina said softly. Wyatt suspected that she was crying, too, but he resisted the urge to reach forward and clasp her shoulder. Instead, he kept his focus on Ty.

"Here's the thing," he said firmly. "If you'd just been patient and polite, I would have offered to take you to Donovan's tomorrow, but I will not reward your rude behavior, so you'll just have to miss this playdate."

Stunned, Tyler reacted with anger. Obviously, being so close to getting the playdate and missing out on it anyway infuriated him. "You're not my dad! You can't tell me what to do!"

Wyatt locked eyes with Tina in the rearview mirror. "I may not be your father, but I am the boss on Loco Man Ranch, and that gives me certain authority. I make the rules." He dropped his gaze to Tyler again. "Do we understand each other?"

Tyler nodded. Wyatt could almost see the wheels turning in his little head as he tried to reconcile this new reality with what he'd known up to this point, but Wyatt couldn't let himself soften. Yet.

"You'll have to earn that next playdate, Ty."

"What does that mean?" Tyler practically wailed, dashing away tears.

"If you behave yourself, treat your mother with respect, speak politely and do as you're told, then we'll set up the playdate. The better behaved you are, the sooner it will happen. Got it?"

"That starts right now," Tina told the boy. "And there's just one way to reply, son."

Tyler flattened his lips, but after a moment he muttered, "Yes, ma'am."

Wyatt smiled to himself when she said, "There are two adults in this car."

Tyler slid a look at Wyatt from the corner of his eye, straightened his shoulders and said, "Yes, sir."

Wyatt patted him on the knee. "You might be surprised how much more often you get your way when you go about it respectfully. Pleasant behavior yields better results. I guarantee it."

Tyler nodded mutely. Wyatt let it rest there. All in all, he was very pleased with how it had gone. He wondered if Tina realized that the two of them had operated as a unit in this. They'd presented Tyler with a united front, and while he might not like it, he had to respect it. They'd given him no other choice.

When they reached the house, Tina went around and opened the back door for Tyler, who didn't make a move until she did so. Wyatt got out on his side and waited while Tina instructed Tyler to go in and get ready for his bath. Then she turned to Wyatt, a soft smile on her face. He had to shove his hands into the pockets of his jeans to keep from reaching for her.

"Thank you," she said quietly. "I know he's not your responsibility, but he looks up to you and your brothers. He has behaved better lately."

"I've noticed. All the more reason to hold firm. Look, I hope you don't think I'm overstepping or that I'm criticizing you. I see that you're doing your best with him and everything else, but it's obvious he needs masculine guidance."

She ducked her head. "I know I've let him get away with behavior that I shouldn't." She looked up then, admitting, "I've just been so afraid that he'd choose his father over me, given the chance."

"I can understand that," Wyatt told her, "but I've learned that kids always respect the better parent and instinctively feel safer when adults maintain control and expect proper behavior. It takes time and effort to make children behave and conform to standards. Kids may not like it, but deep down they realize that parents who don't do the hard work of parenting just don't care as they should."

"In my case," Tina mused, tilting her pretty head,

"I put my own emotional needs ahead of my son's. I've been so afraid he won't love me as much as he loves his father that I haven't been the disciplinarian that Tyler needs me to be. Thank you for helping me see that."

Wyatt shook his head. "I care about Ty. We all do, and we see that you fear for your son's future. That's perfectly natural."

"It is," she agreed, "but it's more than that, and you know it. Tyler and I both change *now*. So. Again. Thank you."

"I just want what's best for you and Tyler. I want that above all else." With a shock, Wyatt realized how deeply he meant those words. When had Tina and Tyler Kemp become more important to him than even his brothers or the ranch?

Tina smiled and stepped close, her gaze moving over his face. Then she went up on tiptoe and kissed his cheek just at the corner of his lips. He held his breath as she turned and went into the house. Only then did he remove his hands from his pockets and suck in a deep breath. And all the while he smiled.

Tyler behaved well the next couple of days, but Tina thanked God when Ann called to invite everyone to a picnic that weekend. She couldn't accept for the Smith family, and she didn't want to undercut Wyatt's authority in Tyler's eyes by accepting for Tyler and herself until she'd discussed the matter with Wyatt. She felt a deep gratitude and comfort in partnering with Wyatt on this. He was so much like Dodd in so many ways. She wondered if he knew that.

When she relayed the invitation to Wyatt, she made

sure to do so in front of everyone else, so they could all have their say. That meant broaching the subject on Friday at lunch.

Wyatt looked to Jake first, who shrugged and nodded. At the same time, Ryder said, "We've all been working hard. A picnic would be a nice break."

Wyatt caught Tina's gaze and held it for several seconds. Smiling as she dished out the meal, she glanced at Tyler before speaking. "The boys have certainly been on their best behavior."

Wyatt smiled at Tyler. "So I've noticed." Tyler brightened and sat up a little straighter. "Ask Ann what we can contribute and what time they want to meet tomorrow."

Tyler almost shot out of his seat in delight when Tina revealed that Dean wanted to meet early so he could take the boys fishing at War Bonnet Lake.

"I think I can find a tackle box and a couple of fishing poles somewhere around here," Wyatt said.

"I hab fishies in *my* room," Frankie insisted. Everyone laughed.

"We're not talking about goldfish, son," Jake told him. "The kind of fish you find in a lake is the kind you eat."

"Fish sticks!" Frankie crowed happily.

They all laughed again, though Tyler looked uncertain.

"Obviously, I should make fish for supper more often," Tina quipped.

"You wouldn't hear any of us complain," Wyatt told her. "We're from the Gulf Coast, remember?"

"You don't complain anyway," Tina replied softly. Wyatt just smiled.

He smiled again the next morning when Tina walked into the kitchen in a sundress. The soft, sleeveless black-and-white-checked dress with a full skirt and a skinny red belt fell to midcalf. Combined with red flip-flops and a broad-brimmed white straw hat, the dress felt pretty and summery.

Sadly, it wasn't quite warm enough to swim in such a large body of water yet. Only Ryder wore shorts. Jake wore a baseball cap with his T-shirt, jeans and boots, but Wyatt stood there in a natural straw cowboy hat. His brothers had teased him about his new wardrobe, but he took Tina's breath away in his pale yellow T-shirt, dark jeans and brown boots. He had shaved, but already the dark shadow of his heavy beard skimmed his jaws, chin and upper lip.

She plopped her white hat onto her head and dipped a knee in a mock curtsy. His smile widened.

"I didn't know a picnic could look that good."

She wrinkled her nose. "It's not too much?"

"Uh-uh." He lifted his gaze to hers. "Perfect."

She wanted to throw herself into his arms, and that very impulse made her step back and break eye contact.

Tyler moved between them then, politely asking, "Is it okay if I ride with the guys again? Please."

"Works for me," Wyatt said, looking to Tina.

She knew that he was asking if he could ride with her again, and she couldn't keep a smile off her face. "I have no problem with it."

Wyatt handed his keys to Jake, and picked up the small cooler containing the strawberry shortcake and lemonade that were the Loco Man Ranch's contribution to the picnic. Tina reached for the old, faded quilt that she had left folded atop the kitchen table, and they all followed Wyatt outside, where he secured the cooler on the back floorboard of Tina's car. She dropped the quilt on top of the cooler while Wyatt moved Tyler's safety seat to his truck. As he buckled the safety seat into place, he muttered, "We really need to get another one of these."

"And a vehicle big enough for all of us," Ryder chimed in, folding his arms.

"Yeah? What would that be?"

"Minivan. Or an SUV with three rows of seats," Ryder supplied.

"And who would drive it?"

"Tina. Or Jake. In fact, I'll buy Jake's truck myself if he wants to go the SUV route."

"Something to think about," Jake said, lifting Frankie into his car seat.

Wyatt looked at Tina, but she kept her expression bland and noncommittal. In truth, she'd felt a little thrill of delight when Ryder had suggested that they needed a vehicle big enough to carry everyone. In a strange way, they'd become a family. Almost.

The Pryors arrived just then. Dean rolled down the window of an SUV exactly as Ryder had described. Wyatt and Tina looked at each other and grinned.

"Y'all want to ride with us?" Dean asked, meaning her and Wyatt. Not even a full-sized SUV could accommodate six adults and four children in safety seats.

Tina waved toward her car. "Our cooler's already loaded."

"We'll follow you," Wyatt said.

Nodding, Dean rolled up the window and swung his vehicle around in a wide U-turn. Wyatt waved at Jake, who slid behind the wheel of Wyatt's truck as Ryder climbed onto the passenger seat. Then Wyatt lifted a hand, gesturing for Tina to get into her car. She thought about it for a few seconds while Jake started the truck and backed around to follow Dean. Reaching into one of the deep pockets of her dress, she pulled out her keys and pressed them into Wyatt's hand.

"Why don't you drive?"

He tilted his head, smiling. "Okay."

She dropped down onto the passenger seat with a deep sigh. The car was warm from the morning sun, but the air felt just right. The relaxation started now.

Wyatt had to slide back the driver's seat and hand her his hat before he could even get in. Dean and Jake were already turning onto the two-lane highway when he started the car. Tina rolled down her window, leaving the air conditioner off, and Wyatt followed suit. He caught up with the others soon enough. When they turned off onto a tree-lined dirt road, the temperature immediately dropped several degrees, but the vehicles in front of them kicked up so much dust that they had to roll up the windows and turn on the air. The red-orange dirt of south central Oklahoma coated all three vehicles by the time Dean brought their little convoy to a halt in a small park beside the lake.

It was a perfect spot with recently mown, fresh green grass and spreading shade trees. A concrete picnic table flanked by benches stood next to a small grill fixed in place atop a metal pole set into the ground.

Jake and Ryder let the kids out and started unloading lawn chairs and fishing gear from the bed of Wyatt's truck, while Ann and Dean pulled boxes and coolers from the back of their vehicle. Ann wore jeans and sandals with a pretty ruffled blouse, making Tina feel that she had overdressed.

Plucking at her skirt, she told herself it was too late to worry about that now. To her surprise, Wyatt reached over and covered her hand with his. When she looked at him, he shook his head.

"Don't ever worry about how you look. Every time I think you can't possibly get any more beautiful, you prove me wrong."

In that moment, she knew she was falling in love with him.

It wasn't part of her plan. It could only complicate matters. But how could she not fall in love with such a man?

How could any woman not fall in love with a man like Wyatt Smith?

Chapter Twelve

"Can I go fishing now? Pleeease."

Tyler twisted his fingers together anxiously. Impressed that he hadn't just run off after Dean and Donovan, Tina smiled.

"Of course you may."

"A well-behaved boy is entitled to have some fun, I think," Wyatt said, winking at him.

"Just be sure to do everything Dean tells you to do."

"I will!" Tyler vowed, grinning broadly as he ran off toward the lakeshore.

With baby Glory on her hip, Ann wandered by the blanket where Tina and Wyatt sat. "Don't worry about him. I'm going to take this one down to see what all the excitement is about."

"Should I go with you?" Tina asked, slipping on her skimpy shoes.

"No, no. Just sit and relax."

"Can I do anything while you're gone?"

Ann waved that away. "Plenty of time to lay out

lunch when we get back." She leaned forward slightly, repeating her previous advice, "Relax."

Tina smiled. As Ann turned away, however, Wyatt unfolded his long legs and got to his feet. "How about a walk? There's a path over there beneath the trees. Want to see where it goes?"

Nodding, Tina pulled her feet up beneath her. Wyatt reached down a hand. Leaving her hat on the quilt, she caught his hand and let him pull her to her feet. He kept her hand in his as they strolled the narrow pathway. Tina clasped his hand loosely. For some time, they walked in silence, listening to the others chatter in the distance, before Wyatt chuckled.

"I'll be surprised if there's a fish on this side of the lake, considering how much noise they're making."

"I'd just as soon not have to clean any fish myself," Tina replied dryly, and he grinned at her. She got lost for a moment in his dark gaze. More to cover her reaction to him than anything else, she dredged up more words. "Thank you for recognizing Tyler's good behavior."

He squeezed her hand. "Good behavior should be recognized. But maybe I was more interested in walking out with his pretty mama alone than his behavior."

A little frightened by the thrill that his compliments gave her, she scoffed. "Flattery isn't necessary."

"It's not flattery." He sounded a little offended. "It's fact."

"Oh, please."

"Don't you realize how lovely you are?"

Shaking her head, she answered with determined candor. "I'm well aware that I'm overweight."

He stopped dead in his tracks, tugging her around to face him. "Overweight? Where'd you get that idiotic idea?"

Blinking, Tina wished she hadn't brought up the subject. She shook her head, but Wyatt pulled her closer, the dark slashes of his eyebrows drawing together.

"I'm serious. I want to know where you got the ridiculous idea that you're overweight."

Shrugging, Tina told him, "My mother for one. Layne for another."

"Your mother and your husband told you that you weigh too much? That's insane."

Something inside Tina opened, lightened. She felt her bottom lip begin to tremble but refused to allow herself to shed a tear. She'd already cried rivers over this issue.

Clearing her throat, she said, "My mother was tall and slender. I—I couldn't measure up to her ideal. She was telling me that I was too heavy by the time I was ten. That's why I so resented the nickname Tiny." She looked down, adding, "Layne said I was fine until I got pregnant. Then he started saying I was too round. After Tyler was born, Layne complained that I was too curvy."

"Too curvy," Wyatt echoed, rolling his eyes. "Curvy is not overweight. Your curves are perfect. I have no idea what you looked like at ten, but you're certainly not overweight now. How can you look in a mirror and not see perfection?"

Tina couldn't quite accept that, but hearing him say it exhilarated her. Wyatt was very much a man's man, and so handsome that he made female hearts flutter. No one's compliment could have affected her more. Yes, he could be very commanding, but he was also caring, dependable, hardworking and considerate. She'd come to realize how much he carried on his broad shoulders, and no one could deny his fairness and generosity, least of all her.

Stepping close, she confessed, "I misjudged you badly in the beginning, Wyatt, and I'm sorry for that. You're really very—" *wonderful, adorable, wildly attractive*, but she settled on "—sweet." He grimaced slightly, as if that wasn't what he'd hoped to hear, so she stepped closer still and went up on her tiptoes to kiss his cheek. Embarrassed by the impulse, she turned back to the path, only to find herself pulled around once more by the hand that Wyatt still clasped.

His gaze capturing hers, he stepped into her, his free hand slipping about her waist. Then he simply dipped his head and kissed her. Tina felt small and delicate and treasured. Without even realizing what she was doing, she lifted her arms about his neck. Everything about the kiss felt genuine and cherished.

This was real. This was true. This was what she'd wanted, needed, what she'd been searching for without even realizing it. How could she have settled for Layne's shallow courtship? Hadn't she learned anything from her mother?

Her mother.

She had become her mother, going from man to man.

Appalled, Tina yanked away, stumbling backward. Wyatt stood there with his arms open, confusion all over his face. "Sweetheart, what's wrong?"

"I—I'm not my mother," she blurted. "I'm not marrying every man who shows interest in me!"

Wyatt's expression clouded, hardened, his arms slowly sinking to his sides. "Who said anything about marriage? I was only—"

Stung, she declared, "Well, I'm certainly not the kind of woman to settle for anything less!"

"I never implied that you were!"

"Isn't that what the mauling was all about?"

"The mauling." He scrubbed his face with his hand. "You are a beautiful woman. I like you. I more than like you. Of course I want to kiss you. That's not *mauling*. And you started it!"

"I did not! I only…" But she had started it. When she'd kissed his cheek, she'd hoped he would do exactly what he'd done. Swallowing the excuse on the tip of her tongue, she raised her chin.

A rustling in the brush at the edge of the tree line caught their attention. Tina turned her head to see Tyler running toward them, a fish dangling at the end of a short length of line.

"Mom! Mom! Look! I got a fish!"

He'd obviously heard their raised voices and crashed through the brush in his excitement to show off his catch. Wyatt was the first to react. Smiling, he examined the fish still dangling from the hook.

"That's a nice catfish you've got there."

"Look at its long whiskers," Tyler said proudly.

Tina's smile felt stiff, but she kept it in place. "Good job, son."

"You'd best get that into the keeper," Wyatt counseled.

"Yeah," Tyler agreed authoritatively. "Mr. Pryor's got a bucket of water special for it."

"Let's go find it," Wyatt suggested, patting the boy's shoulder.

They turned back down the path, leaving Tina to follow. The walk back to the picnic spot took far less time than their earlier stroll away from it, but with every step, Tina's mood sank.

She'd made a fool of herself. Again. What was wrong with her? Was there nothing she couldn't ruin?

Wyatt couldn't believe how foolishly he'd behaved. He relived that kiss and the following argument multiple times over the following days, castigating himself for leaping forward when Tina obviously wasn't ready. He doubted that she ever would be ready, and frustration ate at him, so much so that he couldn't seem to concentrate on any task for longer than a few minutes at a time. Not even the drive to and from a Tulsa-area sale barn and painstakingly culling half a dozen horses from the animals on sale there had kept his mind off her. Rex had asked him more than once what was eating him, but Wyatt had blamed his lack of attention on Dodd's mysterious grass plots.

At the moment, Wyatt was supposed to be helping unload the horses. He'd dropped Rex at the Straight Arrow Ranch and come home to meet Delgado, who had plowed and raked the ground inside the corral next to the barn during Wyatt's absence. Dodd had built the corral of welded metal pipe years ago and it was still sound, so Wyatt and Delgado had merely painted it after readying the stalls in the barn for the horses.

Now Delgado was preparing to back the cattle hauler into the corral, and Wyatt was supposed to guide him. Instead, he was staring at Tina, who stood with Frankie and Ty, an arm around each of them, as they clung to the corral railings.

He kept thinking about the wedding invitation that Rex had hand delivered that morning. The moment Rex had mentioned his father's upcoming wedding, Wyatt had thought of Tina.

I'm not marrying every man who shows interest in me!

Cut to the quick, he'd lashed out with a crack about no one mentioning marriage. The truth was that he had begun thinking along those very lines. What else could they have between them, after all, if not marriage?

I'm certainly not the kind of woman to settle for anything less!

He knew that, of course, and the implication that *he* would settle for anything less than marriage had wounded and infuriated him. He'd long ago determined not to even date any woman with whom he could not at least ponder marriage. Consequently, he hadn't dated anyone in quite a while.

Maybe that was the problem. He and Tina hadn't been on an actual date. Sadly, he didn't see that happening now. Oh, why had he kissed her again? But he knew the answer to that.

He'd kissed her because he'd wanted to.

He still did.

His burgeoning feelings for her had taken over every part of his life. His prayers revolved around her and Ty. Her needs and schedule took precedence over his. He was even making business decisions based on emotion rather than sound financial planning. He had forked over money to refurbish the house when he should be concentrating on building up the ranch. The reality was that he'd bent over backward to please her, and what had it gotten him? Nothing but heartache.

After the picnic, he'd told himself that he was going to ignore her, but it wasn't possible to completely ignore someone living in the same house, especially when she had to be consulted about so much. Wedding invitations, for instance. He'd told Rex that he'd have to check with the family before accepting for anyone but himself, and to Wyatt's mind, Tina was part of his family.

Delgado beeped the horn on the truck to get Wyatt's attention. Snapping to, Wyatt waved his hand, signaling Delgado to continue backing the trailer toward the open corral gate. Once the trailer edged into the corral itself, Wyatt gave Delgado the signal to stop. Delgado killed the engine and came around to help Wyatt pull out the ramp and open the trailer gate. One of the horses, a silver gray roan that Wyatt fancied for himself, had gotten loose from his headstall and turned around inside the trailer, but the big bay gelding backed down the ramp as if he'd been trained to it before trotting around the corral.

While the roan helped himself to a drink of water, Wyatt and Delgado freed and brought out the other four horses, starting with a handsome red dun with a white blaze and then two more bays, one of them an unusual mouse brown with the requisite black mane, tail and stockings. Just a little darker than a buckskin,

the mouse lacked the dorsal stripe that marked buck-
skins. The final animal was a beautiful copper perlino
mare. A very pale gold with a coppery mane and tail,
the mare wasn't a small horse, but something about her
seemed dainty and feminine. Wyatt had imagined Tina
on that horse from the moment he'd first seen it. The
perlino was an affectionate thing and nuzzled Wyatt's
chest as if looking for pockets that might hide treats.
The boys seemed taken with her.

"Ooh, pretty horsie," Frankie crooned, holding out
his hand. The mare ambled over and sniffed his fingers, making him giggle.

"What's his name?" Tyler wanted to know.

"*She* doesn't have one that I know of. The big gray-
ish one is called Blue Moon, and the red one over
there—" he pointed at the dun "—answers to Handy."
The dun picked up his beautiful red-brown head, ears
perking. "But none of the others have names yet." He
pointed to the light brown bay. "I think we should call
that one Mouse because he's a mouse brown."

The boys laughed at that and started debating names
for the other bays. They decided on King and Lucky—
not very original names, but acceptable. When it came
to the mare, however, they were way off base with
names such as Whitey and Fizzle. Wyatt pointed out
that the horse was pale blonde rather than white and
that Fizzle was somewhat derogatory. He suggested
Blondie, but Tina nixed that.

"Pearl," she stated firmly. "Just look at her. What
other name could you give her?"

"Pearl it is," Wyatt decreed abruptly. Then he silently rebuked himself for catering to the woman's

every whim. Yet, he knew that he'd do that and more to get back into her good graces. The problem was he didn't think that possible.

Stark Burns arrived, as previously arranged, to look over the new mounts. A brother-in-law of Rex's, the busy veterinarian had been a great help to Wyatt. Stark had recommended that Wyatt buy Loco Man's starter herd from a single source, then augment with a good bull and sale-barn cows as needed. After much research, Wyatt had purchased one hundred head of Black Angus heifers and calves from a rancher in the northwest part of the state. Delivery would be made in a few weeks.

Parking his truck next to the corral fence, Stark eased his tall, lean body from the cab. He fit his sweat-stained straw hat to his head while shaking out his long legs in great ground-eating strides. It occurred to Wyatt that he was about to lose his best opportunity to speak to Tina about the wedding, so he quickly plucked up his courage and got to it.

"By the way, Rex gave me an invitation to his father's wedding next week. I thought I should talk to… everyone…before I accepted."

She met his gaze for the first time in days. "Ann and Meredith invited me a while ago. I've already agreed to contribute to the wedding feast and decided what to wear."

Of course. Just because he thought of her as family didn't mean she thought of him the same way.

"I see. Well, I'll discuss it with my brothers then."

Nodding, she turned to look at the tall, dark veterinarian. Wyatt made the introductions. Tina couldn't have been more gracious.

"I've so enjoyed getting to know your wife. Can I offer you a cold drink, Dr. Burns?"

"My wife's friends don't call me Doctor," he replied with a smile. "It's Stark. And yes, ma'am, you surely can. I'd roll in the dirt for a drink of cold water."

"We can't have that," Tina said with a chuckle. "And you can forget the ma'am. I'm just Tina."

"Thank you, Tina."

As if an afterthought, she turned her head slightly and asked, "Wyatt? Would you like a drink, too?"

"That would be great. But please include Delgado."

"I'll send out three bottles of cold water," she said, starting for the house. "Come on, boys."

Wyatt helped Frankie to the ground while Tyler hesitated, his gaze locked on the horses milling in the corral. "Go on," Wyatt encouraged lightly. "You can stay and watch after you bring out the water."

Ty shot him a smile and jumped backward, sending up puffs of reddish dust. The boy ran to catch up with Tina and Frankie.

"Frosty," Stark said matter-of-factly.

"What?"

Stark hung his forearms on the top rung of the fence. "The lovely Tina Kemp. According to my wife, you are in hot pursuit, but I detected a chilly breeze in your direction just now. So, what's the deal with you two?"

Wyatt stalled, refitting his hat to his head. He was somewhat shocked that anyone outside the family had put him and Tina together as a couple. Sighing, he wasn't sure how to answer. In the end, however, he gave the other man the truth.

"She's got some issues about her past."

"Ah. Who doesn't?" Stark slipped off his sunglasses and looked Wyatt straight in the eye. "You're looking at the king of baggage right here."

"Oh?"

Stark nodded. "I was married before, you know. My wife and daughter died in a car crash. I felt...responsible, I guess. Because I survived."

"Man, I'm sorry to hear that."

"Took years for me to get past it. If you can get past such a thing. Actually, I didn't move past it at all until Meri showed up. Then it was just a matter of time." Grinning, he slipped his shades back into place and shook his head. "She and Ann say it's just a matter of time for the two of you."

Wyatt looked at the horses. "I'm not sure it's that simple."

"But you wish it was," Stark stated bluntly.

Wyatt made no comment, just dropped his gaze to the ground.

"I'll say a prayer for y'all," Stark said, pushing away from the fence. "If it's meant to be, it'll come right."

Wyatt could only hope, muttering, "Thanks."

"I'll get my gear, and we'll look over these horses. Good-looking animals."

"I'll get the paperwork out of the truck cab," Wyatt answered, turning in that direction. "I've got vaccination records and all that." But his mind wasn't on the horses. All he could think about was Tina.

Together, they could really build something here. If she could trust him enough to give him her heart.

He was very much afraid that she already owned his. Whether she even wanted it was another matter entirely.

Chapter Thirteen

On the morning of the wedding, Tina dressed with care. The Billings family in general seemed a relaxed, informal bunch, but weddings were important events. She should know; she'd attended enough of them.

Her mother had insisted on traditional weddings with all her husbands except Dodd. Gina had later cited their elopement, rather than her own addiction to the trappings of romance, for the failure of the marriage.

Tina herself would have been happy with a small, informal affair when she'd married Layne, but his parents had insisted on a huge, expensive wedding that had left Tina feeling like a performer in a play rather than a happy bride. Looking back now, she knew that the wedding should have served as a warning about the life she would live with Layne. Everything was more image than reality with him.

She silently prayed that Wes Billings and his bride would have more success building a life together than either she or her mother had ever enjoyed. Wes and Alice were an older couple, and both had been married before and widowed. The idea that they would marry again at this point in their lives puzzled Tina, but she liked Ann Billings Pryor and Meredith Billings Burns, and she wanted to cement her friendships with the sisters, so she'd allowed herself to be drawn into the preparations. Now that the day of the wedding had arrived, however, Tina wished heartily that she could just stay home.

Knowing that she couldn't be that rude, she checked the fit of her bright coral knee-length sheath once more. The snug dress didn't exactly hide her curves, but she felt that the sleeves distracted the eyes enough that she could get away with the fit. Ending at her elbows with a double row of wide ruffles, the sleeves brought a chic accent to an otherwise very simple outfit. Foregoing stockings, she stepped into matching heels before slipping the hooks of coral-and-turquoise drop earrings into the tiny holes in her earlobes. Finally, she fluffed her hair to add fullness, then left the room to help Tyler dress.

Before she reached the door of her son's bedroom, another door farther along the hallway opened and Wyatt stepped out, tugging at his cuffs. He wore a somewhat longer-than-normal black jacket over dark navy jeans and a bright white shirt, as well as a high-crowned black straw cowboy hat.

Dumbstruck, Tina stopped, taking in the handsome man before her. She'd never seen a better looking man. He exuded such masculinity that she felt a quivering of something elementally feminine in her chest. Just as she stared at him, he blatantly looked her over before lifting off his hat and strolling forward. She couldn't make her feet move for the life of her.

As he passed her, he murmured, "Gonna put the bride to shame today."

Smiling at the compliment, Tina stayed as she was until she heard his footsteps on the stairs. Then and only then could she move toward her son's door.

He was playing on the bed when she opened the door, but he immediately hopped to the floor. With Wyatt's image still fresh in her mind, she went to his closet and pulled out Tyler's newest jeans, along with the navy blue jacket of his only suit and a white polo shirt with a soft collar.

"Put these on please." While he changed clothes, she pulled out his best sneakers and a pair of clean socks. Ann had told her that many children would attend the wedding reception and that they'd be given the run of the place.

As she helped him pull on his socks, Tyler smiled and said, "You look pretty, Mom."

"Why, thank you."

As soon as he was dressed, they went downstairs together. The men waited in the kitchen. They were all dressed similarly to Wyatt. Jake even wore a pale straw cowboy hat, but he'd put Frankie in jeans and a striped T-shirt with white sneakers.

"You're a handsome lot," Tina announced, her gaze straying automatically to Wyatt.

"Just trying to look worthy of you," he replied smoothly.

"Don't think we're quite up to snuff," Jake said, smiling.

"You look real good," Ryder added.

Smiling, Tina bowed her head in acknowledgment. "Thank you. Would you load those two big pans of scalloped potatoes into my car? You can use dish towels as potholders."

Ryder and Jake swiped the folded towels from the counter and picked up the pans.

"Mom," Tyler began, "I want to—"

"Ride with the guys," she finished for him, not nearly as upset by the prospect of riding with Wyatt as she should have been.

She fought a spurt of disappointment when Wyatt suggested, "Why don't we fix it so Frankie can ride with you and your mom instead?" Meeting Tina's surprised gaze with his own bland one, he added, "We'll carry the potatoes in our car."

"They need to go to the house, not the church," Tina pointed out, trying not to sound snarky.

"We'll take them to the house and meet you at the church, then."

She nodded, trying to feel relieved, but she just couldn't find the emotion. What she felt instead was keen regret.

The wedding was short and sweet, with Wes Billings and Dr. Alice Shorter vowing that theirs would be a marriage founded on Christian principles.

"Til death do us part," Wes intoned the traditional wedding vow. He then winked at the pastor and quipped, "Considering how long it took me to run her to ground, I'm not about to untie her now."

Everyone laughed, including the bride, whose butter yellow suit complemented the bright yellow roses that she carried and wore in her upswept blond hair.

Tina had made a point of not sitting with Wyatt and his brothers. Murmuring that it wouldn't be wise to let the boys sit together, she'd shepherded Tyler to a narrow space at the end of a pew several rows closer to the front of the church. Using a combination of wisteria and yellow roses, a flowery bower had been created over the happy couple.

After the ceremony, the beaming newlyweds entered a luxury auto and led their guests back to the Straight Arrow Ranch, where a number of neighbors and friends busily laid out a sumptuous buffet to go with the steaks beginning to sizzle on several portable grills. Music poured out into the yard via four outdoor speakers, as children darted about in frenzied play.

Stripped of his wedding finery, which had been replaced with a T-shirt and shorts, Donovan met Tina's car with a big grin plastered on his face. Tina had Tyler leave his suit coat in the car, then kept the boys with her until Jake arrived to grant permission for Frankie to join in the fun. The Smith brothers showed up in their shirtsleeves and were quickly surrounded by chattering neighbors, most of them women. Tina went into the house and found Ann, asking what she could do to help, but Ann shook her head.

"No, no. Not in that dress. I love it, by the way."

"Thanks, but just give me an apron."

"None left. Go and enjoy yourself. Better yet, fill plates for our boys and see if you can get them to eat. If we let it go too long, they'll wear themselves out and be asleep before we can feed them. I'll get you some plates."

Tina went out to round up the boys, her heels sinking into the dusty red dirt. Eventually, she took them off and picked her way barefoot out to where the children ran around in a game of chase. Donovan readily agreed to accompany her back to the house. Tina could tell that Tyler wanted to argue, but he fell in line with Donovan. Frankie was already looking exhausted and ready for a nap, so he didn't balk when she took his hand to lead him inside. After dropping her shoes in a corner, she found disposable plates stacked on the dining table and quickly filled them for the boys, whom she sat on the floor around the living room coffee table.

Jake came in to make sure that Frankie was okay. Seeing that the boys had plates in front of them, he stayed to feed Frankie. The excitement of the day could easily distract even a hungry, sleepy child, so getting Frankie to eat required patience. Wyatt entered the room a few minutes after Jake, talking with Stark, who carried a sizable cardboard box.

Stooping, Stark set the box on the floor, and everyone in the room immediately began oohing and aahing at the trio of fluffy black-and-tan puppies tumbling over themselves.

Tyler gasped and watched enviously as Wyatt reached into the box and examined the puppies one by one. Finally, he held up one with a white face, black eyes and ears and what would soon be a ruff of tan fur. Its body splotched with black and tan, the pup showed white front feet and a curly black tail tipped in white. Wyatt looked the dog in the face then turned it for the boys to examine. It was Tina to whom he addressed himself, however.

"What do you think? Should we keep him?"

Smiling, Tina nodded. Tyler whooped and reached for the pup. Wyatt carefully placed the animal in Tyler's hands. Tyler hugged the puppy to his chest, grinning at Frankie. "We got a dog, Frankie."

Sleepy-eyed, Frankie pointed to the pup. "Pretty."

"What are we going to name him?" Wyatt asked, using a finger to unfurl the tail.

"Curly?" Jake suggested.

"Puppy," Frankie said.

"He won't be a puppy when he grows up," Tyler pointed out. "I think we should call him Tippy."

"Maybe Tipper?" Wyatt suggested.

"Yeah, Tipper!"

The other puppies were quickly parceled out to other guests, Stark explaining that they'd come from a client of the veterinary clinic. As best he could determine, they were a mix of border collie, Pomeranian and coonhound. They'd already received their puppy shots and been weaned from the mother, so they were ready for homes.

Frankie petted the newly dubbed Tipper for several minutes before crawling into his father's lap. Sitting cross-legged on the floor, Jake cradled the boy, whose eyelids drooped lower and lower, despite the cacophony of many voices and music. Donovan eagerly gave Tyler advice on raising the new pup before carrying his emptied plate into the kitchen. Tyler clutched the pup as if he'd never let it go.

Dean came in and took a seat on the couch next to

Wyatt. Donovan returned and sat on the floor between his father's feet, his arms around Dean's legs. Dean stroked the boy's head as he talked with Wyatt about how to train the puppy.

Tyler stood next to Tina, taking it all in, but she saw the desperate envy in his eyes as he gazed at Frankie and Donovan with their fathers and then adoringly at Wyatt. Aching for him, she slipped an arm around his shoulders. Suddenly, he moved away from her. She looked around, catching Wyatt's gesture. Apparently, he had noticed Tyler's envious gaze and beckoned the boy with a simple wave of his hand. Tears glazed Tina's eyes as Wyatt casually pulled Tyler and the puppy onto his lap and looped his arms around them. Smiling and stroking the puppy, Tyler laid his head back on Wyatt's shoulder and listened avidly to Dean's instructions.

At one point, Ty asked, "Will he get to sleep on my pillow with me?"

"When he's housebroken," Dean answered.

"What's that?"

"When he's trained to go outside to use the bathroom," Wyatt explained. "We'll want him trained to work cattle, too. Dogs can be a great help on a ranch."

Tyler hung on every word, but Tina knew it wasn't so much the talk that enthralled him as the puppy and the loving male attention. He was truly one of the guys at that moment, treasured by a man whom he respected.

Tina had to turn away to keep from making a fool of herself. She bumped into Meredith Burns, who insisted that she eat.

"You haven't touched a bite," Meri said, tugging her into a corner, a plate of food in one hand. "Now, you sit right here and eat." She pushed the plate into Tina's hands and pulled over another chair. "I'm not moving an inch until you do." She dropped down onto the chair, smiled and folded her hands.

Laughing, Tina ate and enjoyed a chat with Meredith, even with her mind on Wyatt and her son. She somehow managed to remember the recipe for the scalloped potatoes, which Meredith jotted down on a paper napkin. Then Callie appeared, saying that it was time for the wedding cake. Tina volunteered to help serve.

The cake was actually several cakes of different flavors. Callie had prepared a pretty little two-layer cake for the bridal couple to cut, as tradition dictated. Decorated with yellow roses, it made a lovely display, but Wes and Alice ate the small top layer, and Callie boxed the other one. It would be saved in the freezer for their first anniversary. The guests, meanwhile, were served other cakes prepared and decorated for the occasion by helpful neighbors and friends. Alice made sure to have a photo taken of every cake.

Wyatt showed up at Tina's cake station with an excited Tyler. Knowing her son, Tina immediately cut a piece of chocolate cake for him. Wyatt chose German chocolate.

"Doesn't get better than chocolate, coconut and pecans."

Tyler went off to eat his cake with Donovan at the coffee table, but Wyatt claimed a chair, and began to eat right there at the table while Tina cut cake for others. After finishing, he pitched his trash into the container behind her. Only then did he look at her and ask, "What's your favorite cake?"

"Oh, wow. How to choose? We have everything from carrot cake to lemon and strawberry. But I think the most unusual flavor is a ginger cake with apples in it. I'm saving a piece of that to have with a cup of coffee."

"Mmm, coffee," Wyatt said, glancing around. "Where is it?"

"In the kitchen."

Rising, he headed in that direction. The next thing she knew, she had a steaming cup sitting next to her elbow and Meri was there to relieve her.

"Go. Go," she insisted, all but pushing Tina from behind the small table.

"Don't forget your cake," Wyatt said.

Tina took the plate of cake in one hand and the disposable coffee cup in the other. Wyatt steered her to a spot on the couch. Just as she sat down, Donovan popped up from the floor.

"Dad, will you play soccer with us?"

Dean smiled and hauled himself up off the couch. Tyler looked expectantly at Wyatt, who still stood to one side. Wyatt gave the boy a crooked smile and nodded.

"Leave Tipper in the box, then let's go work off that cake."

Grinning broadly, Tyler placed the puppy on the blanket in the box. "I'll be back to get you soon, boy." Straightening, he grabbed Wyatt's hand, and the pair followed Donovan and his dad out the door.

Ann abruptly dropped down onto the sofa next to Tina, saying, "Those two seem to be getting along well."

Tina reached for her coffee cup. "It's surprising, really. Wyatt's a lot more strict with him than Layne or I. But I'm working on it."

Ann patted her knee. "It's worth the effort. Kids know when you care enough to stand your ground. I had to learn that with Donovan."

Shocked, Tina blurted, "Donovan is a prince."

Ann smiled. "Yes, he is, but he's also a child, and no child is perfect. Once Donovan ran off in the middle of the night with Stark's niece. They were spending the night here, but Meri upset them." She waved a hand negligently. "She and Stark broke up that day, and she was a mess. Anyway, the kids decided to come to our house. Across the pasture. Without telling anyone."

Tina gasped. The Straight Arrow Ranch was almost as big as the Loco Man. "What happened?"

"Meri and Stark found them the next morning. At first, we were too relieved to think of punishing Donovan, especially as Stark and Meri came back from the search with a new understanding between them."

"Wow."

"Crisis has a way of clarifying things, you know. Anyway, we quickly realized that there had to be consequences. The problem was deciding what those consequences would be. I tried to push the decision off on Dean, but he didn't let me get away with that. We decided together, and we enforced the punishment together. And I've been Donovan's 'real' mom ever since."

"Was he not accepting of you before?"

"Oh, he was. He desperately wanted a mom and, being a redhead himself, he figured my red hair made me a prime candidate. But now he knows that I'll do what's best for him no matter what. Just like his dad."

"Dean's a great father," Tina mused.

Ann nodded. "He is. I think Wyatt would be just like him. He's obviously fond of Tyler, and you say his expectations are high."

"Wyatt took care of Frankie while his parents were both deployed," Tina divulged quietly.

"No kidding? A single guy like him? I'm impressed."

"I'm sure Ryder helped out," Tina said. "They all take a hand with Frankie now."

"If you let that get out, you'll have to hire guards to keep the women away," Ann joked.

Long after Ann returned to her duties as a hostess, Tina mulled over that last comment. She was surprised that Wyatt hadn't already married. No doubt he'd had his choice of women back in Houston. He certainly did here. And she was the idiot who kept pushing him away. She winced, recalling her reaction the day of the picnic. Could she be any greater a fool? Wyatt Smith was a rare man. As Dodd's nephew, he'd have to be, but she kept overreacting to his kisses.

How did she tell him that no man's kisses had ever affected her the way his did?

How did she make up for past assumptions and behavior?

A simple apology couldn't begin to mend what she'd broken. But maybe… Just maybe, if God was willing and she could find the courage, she and Wyatt could find a way to get past her stupidity.

Chapter Fourteen

Smiling to himself, Wyatt watched Tina dust off her feet before stepping into her heels. She'd been barefoot all day. Those heels did amazing things for her legs, but the juxtaposition of that gorgeous dress and the informality of delicate bare feet enchanted him.

He wanted to kiss her while she stood against him in those heels.

He wanted to kiss her while she stood barefoot.

While she chatted with her friends.

While she shepherded the boys.

He wanted to kiss her. Period.

More than that, he wanted her to wish for the future they could have together.

Feeling Tyler slump against him, Wyatt looked down. The boy had utterly exhausted himself. All day he had sought Wyatt's attention and approval, and Wyatt knew perfectly well why. The other kids had dads to watch over them and occasionally join in the play. The way Tyler avidly watched their interactions told Wyatt that he'd never experienced that kind of relationship with his own absent father.

Wyatt wondered if Layne might somehow be encouraged to develop that kind of relationship with his son, and if so, how.

Practically asleep on his feet, Tyler swayed. Even the puppy enthusiastically licking his face couldn't keep his eyelids from sinking.

Reaching down, Wyatt swung both the boy and the puppy into his arms. Tyler laid his head on Wyatt's shoulder, cradling the puppy against Wyatt's chest. Frankie, who had enjoyed a short nap that afternoon and now rode comfortably in Jake's arms, stretched out a hand and patted the dog, giggling when it licked his fingers.

"It's been a long day," Tina observed. "They're both exhausted."

"Let's get them home," Wyatt said.

He and Jake carried the boys to Tina's car and tucked them into their safety seats, while Ryder went in search of the truck. The puppy traveled in Ty's arms. Wyatt suspected they'd have a hard time getting the dog away from him, so he didn't try.

After following Tina's car home, Wyatt sent Ryder to the barn to find a suitable box to use as a crate for the pup. It wasn't yet full night, but both boys had fallen asleep.

Wyatt passed the puppy to Tina, then pulled Ty from his car seat and carried him into the house. After penning the dog up in the laundry room, Tina ran upstairs to change while Jake and Wyatt got the boys ready for their baths. She returned wearing soft knit pajamas and a long robe belted tightly at the waist. Wyatt smiled at her bare feet and left her to shampoo Tyler's hair while he made a bed for the dog with an old blanket and the box Ryder had found.

Jake carried Frankie into the kitchen wrapped in a towel. Ryder helped him dress the boy for bed, and Jake carried him upstairs to bed. When Tina herded a sleepy, cranky Tyler into the room, his footsteps dragging, Wyatt hoisted the boy into his arms.

"Come on, dude. Bedtime."

"My puppy," he whined.

Wyatt nodded at the box on the floor. "Mom will bring him along."

Tyler smiled all the way up the stairs, but he refused to lay down until the dog arrived in its box. Tina placed the box near the head of the bed, and Ty obediently stretched out. The moment his head hit the pillow, he closed his eyes and pretended to fall asleep. When Tina attempted to pull up the covers, the boy grunted a complaint and kicked the covers out of her hands without ever opening his eyes. She looked at Wyatt, a droll smile curving her pretty lips. They both knew that Tyler wasn't really asleep and that he wanted Wyatt to tuck him in but didn't know how to ask.

Thinking of Frankie, who had two uncles, in addition to his father, to love him, Wyatt moved between Tina and the bed. He pulled up the covers and carefully tucked them around Tyler. Then, on impulse, he bent and kissed the boy's temple, just as he'd have done with Frankie. Tyler gave himself away with a smile, but he didn't open his eyes. Tina adjusted the light in the room and followed Wyatt into the hallway.

"What a great day," Tina said softly, pulling the door closed behind her.

"Those Billings know how to throw a wedding, don't they?"

She nodded. "Thank you for spending time with Tyler today, and for the puppy. I've never seen him so happy."

"He's a good kid. He just wants what everyone else around him has."

"He's a *better* kid, thanks to you. I wish…" She shook her head.

Wyatt couldn't stop himself. He reached out and pulled her to him. Soft and feminine, she huddled against him, her arms folded up against her sides, hands pressed to his chest. After silently praying for the right words, he spoke.

"You know, sweetheart, the Billings have it right. Wes joked about it today, but the truth is that true marriage leaves no room for divorce."

She said nothing for a moment, her cheek pressed to his collarbone, her head tucked neatly beneath his chin. Then she pulled in a breath and asked, "But what if you make a mistake?"

"Then you trust God to help you fix it. My folks always said that you both have to believe. Then you put the other first, and together you honor God. If you do that, divorce never needs to be an option."

"But it takes two people to make that work," she argued softly.

"That's right," he agreed. "The key is to choose someone who will work at marriage as hard as you do.

It requires a level of trust that too many people simply ignore before they leap into a relationship."

She sighed and pulled away, lifting her lovely amber gaze to his. Her voice shook as she said, "The thing is, I guess I trust you more than I trust me."

Smiling, Wyatt cradled her cheek with his hand. "Then trust me when I tell you that you're not your mother."

She seemed to mull that thought for a moment. Then she simply walked to her bedroom door. There she paused and hesitantly smiled at him. Then she closed the door.

In that moment, he made up his mind that he was going to give this thing between them his best shot. His very best shot.

When Wyatt woke in the morning, his first thought was of Tina.

How could he help her?

How could he show her how much he cared for her?

He made it his mission to find out over the next few days, observing all that she did and making mental notes. It rained for a couple of days straight, which made it convenient for him to entertain Frankie and Tyler one afternoon so she could watch a favorite program on TV uninterrupted. They played with the puppy, who was quickly learning what was expected of him.

When the opportunity arose, Wyatt sat down with Tina to go over her plans for the house, and consulted with his brothers and Dixon Lyons.

He drove into Ardmore and bought rocking chairs

for the front porch, and every evening after the boys were in bed, he sat next to her, rocking gently as she watched the stars or spoke quietly of her past and her hopes for the future.

He made sure that he was available to watch Ty and Frankie while Tina and Ann drove into Ardmore to have their hair done one day. Afterward, he complimented Tina.

"Looking fabulous. But then you always do."

She looked even better wearing a soft smile and a blush on her cheeks.

When he came down the stairs on Thursday morning of that next week, she was at the stove, dressed in jeans and a neatly fitted cotton blouse. She glanced over her shoulder, smiling.

"Coffee's ready."

"Great. I'll help myself after I set the table."

She turned around, watching him as he went to the cupboard. "You don't have to do that."

"I know. But it's better than sitting at the table watching you work. Not that I don't like to watch you."

She ducked her head, the corners of her mouth quirking as she fought against a smile. Turning back to the stove, she poked at bacon sizzling in the skillet on the burner.

"I've been thinking," Wyatt said, pulling down plates from the shelf in front of him. "I'd say it's time to paint the outside of the house. Wouldn't you?"

For a few seconds, she said nothing. Then she tentatively began to speak. "Lyons will do it, but they can't get to it for some weeks yet. I've been thinking of starting it myself, now that the rotted siding and trim have been repaired. Shouldn't be any big deal to roll on some paint. Can't be that different from what I've been doing inside."

Wyatt carried the plates to the table and set them down before speaking. "I really don't want to see you up on a ladder wielding a paint roller. You pick out the paint. I'll get the house painted."

"The cattle are coming today. You don't have time—"

"I have as much time as you do. At least I'm not homeschooling the cows."

"We'll be done for the summer soon."

"Good. I'm thinking it's time Tyler learned to ride."

Tina turned just as Tyler let out an eager whoop of delight, nearly dropping Tipper in the process. Wyatt hadn't intended to speak in front of the boy, but he hadn't seen Ty enter the room. Frankie came running a moment later, followed by Jake and Ryder.

"I get to ride a horse?" Ty asked excitedly.

"Soon," Wyatt hedged, looking to Tina. "Provided your mom agrees." Tyler's arms were wrapped around Wyatt's waist before he finished speaking, the puppy on the floor at his feet.

"Every boy who lives on a ranch learns to ride horses," Tina said, bending to sweep up the pup and place it in its box. "Every girl, too, for that matter."

"So you ride, do you?" Wyatt asked, grinning.

"Of course. But it's been a while."

"I ride horse, Daddy?" Frankie asked Jake.

Lifting the boy onto his booster seat, Jake smiled. "Sure. Someday."

Happy, Frankie kicked his feet, shifting side to side on the chair. Tina smiled and nodded at Tyler.

"Let's wash our hands. Then you can get the silver-ware from the drawer."

Tyler released Wyatt and ran to obey. Wyatt shared an approving look with Tina.

"About painting the house," Wyatt pressed gently.

Ryder spoke up. "Jake and I are going to do it. We can rent a sprayer."

Tina beamed as Wyatt said, "I'll buy the paint, then."

Her eyes glistening, Tina spread a soft smile around the room. "I don't know how to thank you all."

"Maybe you can work on the kitchen next," Wyatt told her, glancing at the tired countertops and flooring.

Turning back to the stove, Tina said, "I really hate to give up this old stove. It has so many ovens and burn-ers. They don't all work, though."

"Maybe we can recondition it," Wyatt suggested, stepping up close behind her.

"Th-that would be wonderful," she said brightly, but everyone heard the grateful tears in her voice.

How had he ever thought her cold and prickly?

"Shouldn't be too much of an issue," Jake put in. "I'll look at it after breakfast."

Tina bent her head, obviously overcome, and Wyatt quietly slipped his arms around her from the back. She kept turning bacon in the skillet, muttering that he was going to get burned if he wasn't careful.

"I don't mind," he whispered into her ear. He had to bite his tongue to keep from speaking. Now was not the time to tell her that he loved her.

Sniffing, she asked loudly, "How do you want your eggs, boys? Scrambled? Over easy? Sunny-side up?"

"Scramble!" Frankie yelled, and everyone chuckled.

"Scrambled it is." She turned off the burner and moved to one side, reaching for the carton of eggs on the counter. Wyatt tucked his thumbs into the waistband of his jeans, watching as she took a bowl from the cabinet over her head and began cracking eggs into it.

A throat cleared behind him. He'd forgotten that he had an audience, but he didn't have a problem with that. No secrets here. Pivoting on one heel, he raised a loosely closed fist and tapped his chest, just in case either of his brothers didn't understand how things stood with him where Tina was concerned. Jake lifted an eyebrow and gave him a thumbs-up. Ryder just grinned and headed to the coffeepot.

It was Tyler's stare that most moved Wyatt, however. He'd been pretty tough on the boy, but no one could mistake the hungry, hopeful look on Tyler's small face. Winking at him, Wyatt went to the refrigerator for milk.

Now, if only Tina could return his feelings... It had to be more than gratitude, more than simple partnership.

He went into his day with that silent prayer.

Two eighteen-wheelers loaded with cattle arrived a couple of hours later. Surprisingly, Ty showed up in the barnyard, widely skirting the two idling tractor-trailer rigs.

"Your mom know you're out here?"

His eager gaze locking on the two saddled horses standing in the corral, he nodded. "Yes, sir. I finished my lessons already and took Tipper out."

"Good job. Go stand over by the corral fence and

stay there until the rigs pull into the pasture." As he spoke, Delgado swung open the wide metal gate for the trucks. The ranch had numerous passages protected by cattle guards set into the ground, but none of them were wide enough to accommodate big rigs. Only the main gate behind the house was wide enough for that.

Keeping one eye on the cattle haulers and the other on Ty, Wyatt made a decision. While Delgado waved the trucks through the gate, Wyatt asked Ty if he wanted to ride out with them.

"Yes, sir! Please."

"We'll ask your mom. But don't say anything in front of Frankie. I can't put you both on my horse."

Eyes wide, Tyler nodded. They went into the house and found Tina studying paint colors on the computer. She glanced up as they entered the room.

"Is it okay if Tyler rides out with Delgado and me? He'll ride with me on my horse."

"Don't tell Frankie," Ty whispered, lifting a finger to his lips.

Tina pursed her lips against a grin and nodded. "Okay. But you need a baseball cap. Go to your room and get one. Quietly."

"Yes, ma'am." Ty slipped out to do as told.

"He deserves this," Wyatt said, smiling. "I'll take good care of him."

"I know."

"I'll take care of you both," he promised gravely, "if you'll let me."

The corners of her lovely lips curled upward even as her gaze dropped. "I know."

He stood there for a moment, debating with himself. The word *patience* whispered through his mind. Tugging on the brim of his hat, he turned. Walking out of that room without kissing her took more willpower than anything he'd ever done, but Tyler slammed into him before he got two steps away.

The boy righted himself and slapped the cap onto his head. "Ready!" He called to his mom, "Tell Frankie to take care of Tipper for me!"

Wyatt could see a second dog in their future, as Tyler had firmly claimed Tipper as his own. Eventually, Frankie would want the same. Well, it was a big ranch.

Wyatt and Tyler hurried out of the house and crossed to the corral, where Delgado waited on horseback. Wyatt threw Tyler up into the saddle and mounted the big blue roan behind him. They exited the corral through a gate that opened onto the pasture and cantered around to haze and count the cattle that poured from the trailers. With every head accounted for, Wyatt signed off on the transport. Delgado rode back to open the gate for the rigs again, while Wyatt and Tyler drove the herd away from the opening.

When they came to the first of the fenced grass sections, Wyatt climbed down and took a pair of wire cutters from his saddlebag. Dodd had taught his nephews to carry certain supplies with them, especially those needed to repair fencing.

"Might as well start figuring out which of these grass fields is best for our cattle. Right?"

"Right," Ty agreed, as if he actually knew what Wyatt meant.

Explaining as he went along, Wyatt cut the wire mesh fencing and rolled it back to secure it so the cattle couldn't get caught up. A few head of cattle milled around outside the fence when Wyatt and Tyler rode away, heading back to the house.

What they found there shocked Wyatt. The cattle haulers were gone, but a pair of flatbed trucks and a strange sort of combine had replaced them. Both Delgado and Tina stood in the yard talking with a khaki-clad man holding a clipboard. Wyatt rode into the corral, tied up the horse and lifted Ty from the saddle before walking out into the barnyard. Tina pointed in his direction, and the man turned to meet him, hand outstretched.

"Mr. Smith, sorry to hear about your uncle. I'm Carter Bishop with Guaranteed Sod, Inc." He reached beneath some papers and pulled out a slip. "The check's made out to Loco Man Ranch, so we shouldn't have to rewrite it."

"The check?" Wyatt echoed in confusion, taking the slip of paper. His eyes nearly fell out of his head when he looked at the amount, but he tamped down his excitement. "I don't understand."

"We contracted with your uncle for sod, and we're here to cut now. Unless the crop's unsatisfactory. Our last inspection showed no problems, and he submitted the correct spraying schedule, so—"

"Sod!" Wyatt exclaimed, flapping the check. "Grass sod! Of course!" He shoved the check at Tina. "Sweetheart, look! This is what Dodd was doing."

She took the check, her eyes popping out at the amount. "Oh, my."

"The sod!" Wyatt exclaimed again. "I cut the fence!"

Turning, he ran for his horse, Tyler on his heels and crying, "I can help!"

Wyatt didn't argue. He just threw Ty into the saddle and leapt up behind him. They were tearing across the pasture at breakneck speed in seconds. Only one heifer was grazing on the bright green grass when they arrived. Leaving the horse outside the fenced field, Wyatt bailed off and ran, yelling at Tyler to stand in the gap of the fence.

"Just lift your arms and yell if the cows come close."

Tyler stood in the center of the opening and raised both arms. The heifer spooked and ran in the wrong direction at first. Wyatt turned the critter and drove it back toward the opening, praying that the cow hadn't wreaked too much damage. He yelled at Ty to get back. The boy scrambled aside as the heifer charged through the opening then he resumed his post.

"Good work, cowboy."

Ty beamed.

Turning to survey the field with new eyes, Wyatt could only laugh. Sod. Why hadn't he seen it sooner? He caught Ty, lifted him under the arms and whirled him around, crowing, "God bless Uncle Dodd!"

They quickly repaired the fence with supplies from Wyatt's saddlebags, mounted up and galloped back to the house. Meeting Delgado and the sod cutters on the way, they stopped for a quick discussion. Delgado knew as much about the grass fields as Wyatt did, so he took on the role of supervisor for Loco Man Ranch.

"Uh, just one thing," Carter Bishop said, hanging out the open window of his truck. "Dodd told us he'd have room for my crew to spend the night."

"No problem," Wyatt told him happily. "Bunkhouse will be ready for you."

"We should be out of your hair by tomorrow afternoon," Bishop said.

"Take as long as you need," Wyatt told him, grinning so broadly that his cheeks hurt.

Bishop waved a casual salute and pulled back into the cab. The sod cutter's truck was trundling along behind the other machinery when Wyatt spurred the roan toward the house.

After they reached the corral this time, Wyatt swung down from the saddle and reached for Ty with a smile. To his surprise, the boy wrapped both arms around Wyatt's neck and held on for a long time.

Hugging the boy close, Wyatt said, "Let this be a lesson to you, son. God has ways of fixing things, ways we can't even imagine. All this time I've been trying to figure out what Dodd was doing, and he was raising a cash crop. That's money in the bank, money none of us counted on."

"Cool."

"Very cool." He set the smiling boy on his feet and started unsaddling the horse. "Want to give me a hand with this?"

"Sure."

"Okay. Stay in this area right here." He carefully swung an arm, indicating the safe space, just as Dodd had taught him. Working together they led the horse into the barn and stripped away the tack. "We'll brush him down. Always remember that when working around a horse, you need to keep one hand on him as much as possible. That way he won't get startled and kick you."

"I'll remember," Tyler promised with a nod of his chin. After a moment, he sighed with satisfaction. "It's a good day."

Wyatt chuckled. "A very good day."

Together they groomed the horse, put out extra feed and walked to the house.

Hand in hand.

Chapter Fifteen

Tina waited for Wyatt and Tyler at the kitchen table. She popped up as soon as they came through the door.

"Everything okay?"

"Everything's great. Can you believe this?"

She shook her head, looking at the check in the center of the table.

"God fixed it," Tyler announced gaily. "He's got ways."

Tina laughed. "Yes, I suppose He does."

Wyatt couldn't help himself. He hugged her. "Everything's going to be fine now, sweetheart. I know it."

She looked up, lifting a hand to his face. "It feels that way at the moment."

He almost kissed her right there in front of Ty. Thankfully, Jake and Ryder showed up with Frankie just then. Wyatt explained the whole situation. Ryder plopped down in a chair and picked up the check, astonishment all over his face, while Jake clapped his hands and laughed.

"Guess this move was the right thing, after all," Ryder said.

Jake clapped him on the shoulder. "God's got it all in hand, little bro. He's got it all in hand."

Ryder smiled up at him. Wyatt stood with his arm around Tina's shoulders, appreciating the scene before him. It had been a long while since he'd seen his family this happy. He didn't think he'd ever felt such delight himself, but he knew it wasn't just that check in Ryder's hand. It had much more to do with the woman at his side, those gathered at the table and this place.

Home.

They were truly home now, all of them.

A thought suddenly occurred to him, and he quickly turned to Tina. "I forgot to tell you. The sod-cutting crew will be staying the night. Is there anything we need to do to get the bunkhouse ready?"

"The beds need sheets. That's all. But what about supper? Do they have their own groceries? Are they planning to go into town? If so, they can't work too late."

Wyatt hadn't even thought of that. "What do you suggest?"

Shrugging, she bit her lip. After a moment, she said, "Tacos. I have lots of ground beef in the freezer, and they're easy to fix for a crowd. I can run into War Bonnet for the rest of the ingredients."

"Sounds good."

Nodding, she hurried to the freezer and began extracting packages of meat.

"Sounds like a party to me," Jake said, grinning.

"Birthday party!" Frankie yelled.

When they stopped laughing, Jake explained, "It's not a birthday party. It's a blessing party."

"Bessing party!" Frankie cried, making everyone laugh again.

"A party means treats," Tina said, moving toward the small table near the door where she kept her handbag and keys.

"Treats!" Frankie shouted, jumping up and down.

She paused to look at Wyatt and Tyler. "Will you be okay here?"

"We're good," Wyatt told her, parking his hands at his waist. He looked down to find that Tyler had mimicked his stance.

"Good," the boy echoed with a nod of his head.

"Yes, you are," Tina said, lifting her gaze to Wyatt's.

"We'll make the beds in the bunkhouse while you're gone," he told her.

"Are you sure?"

"Sweetheart," Wyatt said, "we've been making our own beds for years. Go on. Do what you need to do."

Smiling, she turned for the door. "I'll be back soon."

The instant the door closed behind her, his brothers began teasing him. "Yeah, *sweetheart*, we're old hands at making beds."

"And if we weren't, Wyatt would make us learn."

"Yes, I would," Wyatt admitted with a broad, unrepentant smile.

That and more. So much more. Whatever it took.

The evening turned into a real celebration, especially after Carter Bishop pronounced the sod excellent and urged Wyatt to sign another contract.

They discussed the details around the table in the dining room, and Tina was surprised to learn that only about a half inch of soil was taken with the harvested grass. The root tips and other detritus left behind helped recondition the soil for new planting. Bishop stated that his company had been harvesting and selling sod produced on the same property for as long as forty years. Considering that it paid over five thousand dollars an acre, with Guaranteed Sod doing the cutting, it was a very profitable business. Given the acreage of Loco Man and the preparations already done by Dodd, it seemed like a no-brainer to Tina. But then, it wasn't any of her business. Until Wyatt made it her business.

He reached across the table and covered her hand with his. "What do you think, sweetheart? You should have a say in this. Loco Man Ranch is your home, too."

Sweetheart. That endearment was getting to be a habit with him, one Tina wished didn't thrill her every time she heard it. That thrill consumed her to the point that she almost didn't hear Jake and Ryder agreeing with Wyatt.

"We've had our say in the house," Ryder pointed out. "Only fair you should have a say in the ranch."

"You're a part of this, even if it's not formal," Jake put in. Grinning at Wyatt, he added, "Yet."

Squeezing her hand, Wyatt asked, "So, what do you think?"

"I think you'd be foolish not to do it."

He sat back in his chair, freeing her from his clasp. Tina quickly tucked her hand into her lap, telling herself that she was reading too much into the situation.

Tapping the edge of the table with two fingers,

Wyatt said, "It's unanimous then." He smiled at the guest sitting next to him. "You've got yourself a deal, Carter." The two men shook hands on it.

"When your uncle first came to us with this idea, we weren't too sure," Carter admitted, "but he convinced us to sign the contract, and he obviously did his research and picked perfect spots to plant. Given the size of the Oklahoma City market, we couldn't be happier."

"Contract," Wyatt repeated, stroking his chin. "I haven't found a contract anywhere." He snapped his fingers. "I forgot about the safety deposit box. It must be there. I'll check first thing in the morning."

One of the Guaranteed Sod flatbeds had already left. Much of its haul would be on the ground before the second truck left the next afternoon. Because it had rained recently, the sod was perfect for cutting, but Carter warned Wyatt that certain sections, which would be harvested in another month or so, would need a good wetting before he returned with the cutters. Wyatt promised to see to it.

The four extra men at the table ate heartily and complimented Tina on the meal, but the German chocolate cake she'd thrown together with the help of a boxed mix got raves, especially from Wyatt, who ate two pieces. Later, after the sod-cutting crew left for the bunkhouse, he helped her put Tyler to bed, praising the boy for his help.

"You stood in the gap for me today. You're going to make a fine cowboy and an excellent ranch hand."

"Then I can get boots like Donovan's," Ty said happily. Tina traded knowing glances with Wyatt. Not too long ago, Tyler would simply have demanded boots. Now he hinted.

Wyatt pretended to consider. "Hmm. You know, we probably ought to get you a hat, too." Reaching out, he ruffled Tyler's hair.

Tyler beamed so broadly that Tina had to look away to keep from laughing. Her son was flourishing under the influence of Wyatt and his brothers, much as she had done with Daddy Dodd.

She suddenly missed the old man keenly. She should've known that he would look after all their best interests.

As Tyler hugged her good-night, Tina realized that if he ever had to leave here now, it would be the same for him as it had been for her. He'd forever feel that he'd lost his true home and family. He'd forever miss the comfort, caring and wisdom. They hadn't heard a word from Layne since their arrival in War Bonnet, but the threat of a custody battle hovered on the horizon like an angry cloud, and Tina couldn't help worrying about it. As of yet, she had no independent means of support, and Layne would undoubtedly exploit that.

God fixed it. He's got ways.

She closed her eyes and said a quick, silent prayer. *Thank You, Lord. Thank You for everything that's happening here. Please fix the rest of it, for my son's sake. And mine. If that means Wyatt and I together... give me courage to accept Your will, whatever it is.*

Tyler lay back on his pillow, and Tina and Wyatt gently tucked the covers around him. Wyatt kissed the boy's temple, and Tyler settled in with a happy sigh, reaching down to pet Tipper in his box and closing his eyes. Tina had little doubt that she'd find Tipper on the pillow with Tyler the next morning, but she didn't mind. After adjusting the light, she and Wyatt left the room and walked down the hallway to the top of the stairs, where he stopped and pulled her into his arms.

"What a day, huh?"

"The best. I'm so happy for you and your brothers."

"For all of us. We can really do up the kitchen now. And I was thinking this evening that the formal dining room could use a more finished look. You've done a good job in there, but I heard something about shutters instead of curtains."

She remembered that conversation. She'd been talking to Rob and Jake as they'd moved the dining-room furniture into place. She hadn't realized that Wyatt had been listening. If she'd known at the time, she'd have been angry at Wyatt's eavesdropping. Now just the fact that he remembered her preference for shutters over curtains touched her deeply. He was a supremely caring man.

Nevertheless, she shook her head. "They'd have to be specially made to fit the windows. I'm not going to spend your money that way."

"Why not?"

"It's not fair, Wyatt. What if we have a falling out and—"

He gave her a quick squeeze. "We're going to fall out, Tina. Not too often, I hope. But it's going to happen. Again." He chuckled. "That doesn't mean anyone has to leave. Let's just settle this right now." He spread his hands against her back "Whenever we butt heads around here, we cool down, and we work it out. Deal?"

What she felt for him spilled over then, swelling up in her heart and flooding every cell of her body. She tipped back her head. "Deal."

She hoped—prayed—that he'd kiss her again. But that wasn't all she wanted. She wanted to know that he felt the same way she did. She wanted to hear him say it. She wanted him to ask her to make this all formal. To her shock, she wanted him to ask her to marry him.

It seemed, for once, that she was on a roll here. Life was good, and she could almost believe that it was going to get better. With Wyatt. Because of Wyatt.

She stood expectantly, as his gaze roamed her face. But then the only kiss he bestowed was to the center of her forehead. Tina tried not to let her disappointment show as he released her and started down the stairs.

That was when she began to pray that both God and Wyatt would ignore her previous protestations and give her the one thing for which she'd vowed never to ask. She wanted to marry again. She wanted to be the wife of Wyatt Smith. It was time to let go of the past, both her mother's and her own.

The next day, Wyatt drove into War Bonnet to the bank, where he was shown the safety deposit box that Dodd had rented. He watched as the bank manager opened the box and left the room. Pulling out the drawer inside, Wyatt carried it to the table in the center of the small vault and lifted the hinged lid. He found copies of the wills on top, followed by a couple of hundred dollars in cash, three slotted folders filled with silver coins and two piles of stapled papers. The first group of papers was the contract with Guaranteed Sod, Inc. The other made him gasp in surprise.

Standing at the waist-high table, he scanned the pile of documents. Then he rolled up the papers and tucked them under his arm. He left the wills and the money in the box and returned the drawer to its slot, closing the lock face and removing the key, which he tucked into a pocket. Then he hurried home, laughing and praising God for His generosity.

When he got to the ranch, he had to look for Tina. He found her in the bunkhouse making beds and generally cleaning up after the sod cutters. He tossed the papers onto the bed, saying, "I take back every unkind thought I've ever had about Uncle Dodd. The man was a genius."

Turning, Tina smiled at him. "You found the contract."

"Oh, sweetheart, that's not all I found." He reached around her and picked up one of the stapled stacks. "Take a look at this."

She gingerly accepted the papers and began to scan them. "Dodd sold the mineral rights."

"To raise money for the sod, I think. But he didn't sell the mineral rights. Those belong to you. He sold the right to exploration and drilling. Look here." He folded back several sheets and pointed.

"They start drilling in June!"

"That means they've done the survey and they're pretty sure they've got oil and natural gas on Loco Man." Tina blinked at him. "It's got to be out there." He flung out an arm. "It's two thousand acres of Oklahoma, one of the richest oil and gas fields in the world!"

"Royalties," she whispered, clearly stunned. "It's going to pay royalties."

He cupped her face in his hands. "You're going to have ample income, you and Tyler. You don't have to worry anymore."

"God fixed it," she whispered.

"He's fixed it all," Wyatt confirmed, grinning broadly.

"Almost," she said, her eyes glazing with a faraway look. "All that's left is Layne and the custody suit." She crushed the papers to her chest and squeezed her eyes shut, tears leaking from their corners.

Wyatt knew that, even as she silently rejoiced, she'd give every cent of Dodd's gift, everything that she owned, to keep her son safe with her. He wrapped his arms around her and kissed her forehead.

"God's got this," he told her. "God has it all in hand. I know it."

She rested her head in the hollow of his shoulder. "I believe. I do. I believe with all my heart."

Exactly one week later, God put that belief to the test.

It had been a lovely week, despite a sudden and un-expected tornado warning that had everyone on the place crowding into the cobwebbed cellar out back of the house. Tina had clasped Wyatt's hand as he'd held a trembling Tyler on his lap and prayed for the storm to dissipate without injury to anyone. After that, Frankie had started playing with the flashlight, elicit-ing laughter with the funny faces that he'd made. Tyler had gotten in on the act. By the time the thin wail of the tornado siren in town had signaled the all clear, Tipper was happily chasing the flashlight beam and the boys were reluctant to leave the cellar. Now, remembering how they'd frolicked across the yard, making faces at one another, Tina smiled out the open window above the kitchen sink.

The outside temperatures continued to rise, so they would soon have to close the house for the summer and turn on the new air-conditioning unit. Tina found herself reluctant to do so, but she recalled how hot Oklahoma summers could be. No matter the daytime temperatures, she hoped that she and Wyatt would continue to sit out on the porch in the evenings. Often, they failed even to speak, but just sitting there with him brought her a delightful peace.

So much had happened since she'd come back. She could hear the boys laughing upstairs. As she washed the breakfast dishes that morning, her thoughts wandered from the coming summer and the boys to the dishwasher Wyatt had ordered and the shutters that Dixon Lyons was building, not only for the dining room but the parlor, as well. Lyons and Son would begin the attic and den remodel on Monday. So much for which to be thankful.

Closing her eyes, she mentally repeated the same personal prayer she'd been praying the past week.

Father God, how I thank You for all You've done. Give me wisdom, and make Your will clear to me. If Wyatt is Your will for me, help him see my love and teach us how to grow a strong, permanent relationship. If that's not what You want for us, give me the strength to let go of that dream. To Your glory and in the holy name of Your Son. Amen.

When she opened her eyes again, she saw, through the window screen, a car turn into the yard. She didn't have to look twice to know who had arrived. Horrified, she recognized Layne's flashy red convertible all too well.

At first, she froze. Ryder and Jake were outside painting the house, however, and the instant Layne got out of the car, Layne addressed them. Pushing back the sides of his trendy sport coat, he splayed his hands across his ribcage just above his waist and looked up at them through the lenses of his expensive sunglasses, his blond hair gleaming in the morning sunlight.

"This the Loco Man Ranch?"

"That's right," Ryder answered.

"Is there a woman named Tina Kemp here? She might be using some other name. She's about this tall." He held up a hand at about shoulder height. "Short brown hair and brown eyes. There's a boy with her."

Frightened, Tina dimly became aware of two things simultaneously: the boys were playing in Tyler's room upstairs and the Smith brothers were coming down the ladders. Panicked, even her breathing suddenly hurt. She felt as if her world had just crashed around her.

Then she heard Jake ask, "Who wants to know?"

Her gaze sharpening, she watched Layne's slow, smug smile. "Her husband."

Instantly enraged, Tina slung water from her hands and flew to the door. Yanking it open, she pushed through the screen door and stepped out onto the narrow stoop, parking her hands at her waist.

"My *ex*-husband," she stated, loudly and clearly. "What are you doing here, Layne?"

Not that she had to ask. She knew perfectly well why he'd come. What she didn't know was what he hoped to accomplish. Taking a deep breath, she sent up a silent prayer.

I believe. You've got Your ways, Lord, and You can fix anything. I believe.

From the corner of her eye, Tina noticed that Ryder took out his cell phone and turned away, but her own focus targeted Layne like a laser.

"Thought you could take my kid and hide, did you?" He slid a glance around the place, his nose wrinkling. "I thought even you had better taste than this, though."

Tina let the insult roll off her as she had countless others, feeling a calmness settle over her.

"We're happy here, Layne. This is where we're staying."

He chuckled, scuffing the toe of his Italian leather shoe in the dirt. "You can stay. I couldn't care less what you do. But my son goes with me."

Panic flashed over her again, but she widened her stance, refusing to show it. That was when she heard Wyatt.

Striding from the barn, he raised his voice, saying, "You'd better be armed with a custody order from the State of Oklahoma, then. Otherwise, Ty's not going anywhere."

Layne whirled to face Wyatt. "Who the—"

"Wyatt Smith."

"And just why should I care who you are?" Layne sneered.

Ryder stepped closer. At six feet three inches, Ryder stood just as tall as his brothers, but he was heavier due to the bulk of his muscles. Anyone could tell just by looking at him that he was amazingly strong. Not once had Ryder wielded that strength in a threatening manner, however. Until now.

Frowning, Layne turned to Tina once more. "Just what's going on here?"

"None of your business."

"Who are these men?"

"We're the Smith brothers," Wyatt answered. "This is our ranch."

Layne goggled at Tina. "And you're living here with one of them? Or *all* of them?"

Before she could respond, Wyatt chuckled dryly. "Oh, that's rich. You were caught cheating, and you dare to throw accusations on *her*? Guess that corresponds with all the lies you've told your son about her."

Layne's expression hardened. "Where is my son? I want to see him."

"You'll see him," Wyatt countered easily, "but you're not leaving here with him unless you have a court order mandating that we turn him over to you, and I don't believe you do. Our attorney would have been notified of any court dates or decisions."

"'*Our* attorney?'" Layne parroted sneeringly.

Wyatt looked at Tina, smiling. "That's right. *Our* attorney. Tina is a valued business partner. And a complete lady."

"'A valued business partner?'" Layne mocked. "Only if you value stupidity. And a lady?" He raked a scathing gaze over Tina. She refused to react. "That's a laugh!"

Wyatt shook his head and looked at Tina again, his

gaze as warm as the sun shining down on them. "She's beautiful and compelling and bright, and one of the classiest women I've ever met."

"So, you're the one she's shacking up with," Layne crowed. "Well, you're welcome to her. Play house all you want. I couldn't care less. She's not worth the effort, though, I warn you."

Once that might have wounded Tina, but she watched Wyatt's hands curl into fists, and her heart swelled. She almost spoke out to ask him not to hurt Layne, for fear of losing Tyler's affection, but then Wyatt's hands relaxed. She should've known he would keep his cool.

"No one's 'shacking up' or 'playing house' here," Wyatt said calmly. "We all realize that Tina deserves nothing less than marriage and complete fidelity, both of which she could have in a heartbeat. Whenever she's ready to marry again. Given past experience, her reluctance is entirely understandable."

Layne lost every shred of his urbane, charming veneer then, demanding, "Get my kid out here. He'll tell you what a failure she is as a mother and wife. And he'll beg to leave with me. You'll see."

Suddenly, the screen door behind Tina creaked, slapping her in the shoulder as it was flung open. Tyler flew past her, down the steps and straight at his father. Tina's heart dropped—until she realized that Tyler's fists were flailing at Layne.

"Liar! You're a liar! She's not a bad mother! You're a bad father!"

"Whoa." Wyatt caught the boy by the collar, pulling him away from his stunned father. Shaking him gently, Wyatt admonished him in a soft tone. "Hey. That's uncalled for. He's your dad. Be respectful." He cupped Tyler's face in his big hands. "You know how to be respectful. You do it every day around here. With me and your mom, Ryder and Jake, even Frankie."

His face crumpling, Tyler threw himself into Wyatt's arms and sobbed out, "I'm sorry."

"I know." Wyatt patted his back. "But I'm not the one you owe an apology."

Sniffing, Tyler stepped back and turned to face Layne, muttering, "I'm sorry."

Wyatt patted the boy's shoulder approvingly, and Tyler turned a teary smile over his shoulder at him. Layne suddenly reached out, snatching Tyler by the forearm and pulling him toward his car. Tina gasped and started down the steps.

"Come on. Let's go."

"No!"

She halted as Tyler jerked free of Layne. Wyatt stepped up to make sure that Layne couldn't snatch the boy again, wrapping an arm across the boy's upper chest. As Tina let out a relieved breath, Layne resorted to wheedling.

"Don't you want to come with Dad? It's what we've talked about. We'll have fun, buddy. You'll see."

"I'm not going!"

"You don't want me to spend Father's Day all alone, do you?" Layne cajoled, bending to bring his face level with Tyler's.

"You don't have to spend Father's Day alone," Wyatt interjected, looking down at Tyler. "You're welcome to come back and spend Father's Day with your son.

At church and then here on the ranch. But you'll keep a civil tongue and you won't be taking him with you."

"You don't tell me when and where I can see my son," Layne snarled.

"No, but his mother does, and what she says goes."

"According to who?"

"Me. My brothers." Jake and Ryder nodded at that. "And our attorney. You see, he read the current custody agreement, which you did not contest when it was implemented. It states clearly that she has complete custody and your visitation with her son is based entirely on her wishes. Funny how your only objection at the time concerned child support, which—correct me if I'm wrong—you do not pay."

"She agreed to it," Layne pointed out sullenly.

"And you agreed to the custody arrangement," Wyatt retorted. "Wonder what changed your mind."

Tina knew perfectly well what had changed Layne's mind about the custody agreement: Tyler had finally gotten old enough for Layne to use him against her.

"I miss my son," Layne sniffed.

"So come see him," Tina said, looking at Tyler. "We'll work out a visitation schedule so you can see each other as often as you like."

"Oh, you'd love that," Layne snapped. "Having me at your beck and call."

"I'm willing to work with you, Layne. I always have been. We'll schedule visits at your convenience."

"*My* convenience? This isn't about my convenience. When I agreed to have him, you promised he would never inconvenience me, and it's been nothing but inconvenience since the first time he kicked in the womb!" Layne threw up his hands. "And it just got worse and worse after we brought him home from the hospital!"

Realizing belatedly how that sounded, Layne switched his gaze to Tyler, who looked as if he'd been struck. Tina doubted that her son even understood the full implications of what his father had just revealed, but Tyler was smart enough to comprehend instinctively that Layne hadn't really wanted him.

Pinching the bridge of his nose, Layne attempted to make reparations. "Hey. That was then, you know? This is now. We're buddies now. Right?"

"Frankie and Donovan are my buddies," Tyler whispered, mentally putting it all together. As the implications settled into place, he backed closer to Wyatt, stumbling slightly over Wyatt's big, booted feet.

Wyatt tightened his arms around the boy, crooning softly. "It's okay. Don't worry about any of this. It doesn't change anything." Tyler nodded solemnly. Then he suddenly whirled and threw his arms around Wyatt again.

Layne angrily rolled his eyes. "Oh, forget it. You're not worth the effort. Either of you. I'm done!" He stabbed a finger at Tina before waving his hands in a slashing motion. "I'm done with both of you."

"Layne," she began, knowing how that must hurt their son, but Layne had already whirled and yanked open the door of his car. "Wait," she entreated. "Let's talk." But the only sound was that of his car door slamming shut.

After that, he started up the engine, backed the car around in an angry scatter of gravel and dust, and drove away so fast that his tires squealed when he turned the corner onto the highway. As the red-orange dust settled around them, Tyler sobbed. Tina ran to him, wrapping her arms around him and Wyatt both.

"Don't cry, baby," Tina pleaded, going down on her haunches. "He didn't mean it. You'll see him again."

"He's just upset," Wyatt added. "He'll cool down. Tell you what. We'll write to him, invite him back again to visit. How would that be?"

Sniffing, Tyler rubbed at his eyes with both fists. Finally, he nodded, letting out a weak, "Okay."

"Give him time," Wyatt counseled. "He'll remember what a great boy you are and how much he misses you. He said that. Right? He said he misses you."

Tyler nodded again, his breath hitching repeatedly. "Yeah."

"There you go," Tina said encouragingly.

Suddenly, Tyler threw his arms around her neck. Both thrilled and brokenhearted, Tina hugged him. "I love you so much, son. I'm so proud of you."

"I love you, too, Mom," he said, bringing tears to her own eyes.

He pulled back as Wyatt said, "Someone needs to go check on Frankie."

"I will," Tyler declared, squaring his shoulders.

Jake moved forward then, offering his hand. "I'll go with you."

Tyler took Jake's hand, flashing a weak smile up at him, and the two moved toward the house. At the same time, Wyatt reached down and hooked his hands under Tina's arms, pulling her up and against him. She buried her face in the curve of his neck and let the tears flow, his arms tightening until she could barely breathe.

Tina didn't know where Ryder disappeared to, but when she lifted her head again, she and Wyatt were alone. Wiping her face with both hands, she calmed herself enough to say, "Thank you."

To her surprise, Wyatt spun away, bringing his hands to his hips and twisting with agitation. "I wanted to strangle him. I wanted to wrap my hands around his throat and throttle him. If he wasn't Tyler's father…"

Realizing how much self-control he'd just displayed, Tina's love doubled. She went to him and gently placed her hands on either side of his strong neck.

"You know," she said through a smile, "I would consider marrying again. If the right man asked me."

Wyatt's face went blank, his gaze searching hers. Then he let out a whoop, wrapped his arms around her waist and swung her in a circle. "Thank God. Thank God!"

Tina laughed, threading her arms around his neck. "Is that the proposal?"

He set her on her feet. "I love you. I want to marry you more than anything else in this world."

"I love you, too. I think I have almost from the beginning, but because I've never really felt it before, I didn't know."

Beaming, he asked, "Is that a yes?"

"It's a yes," she confirmed, laughing when he hugged her so hard her feet lifted off the ground. "But let's keep it between us for now. Tyler's had so much come at him today. I think he needs a little time to adjust."

Wyatt nodded, bringing his forehead to settle against hers. "Whatever you want. Just don't keep me waiting too long."

"I promise."

Standing there within the safe, loving confines of his arms, she knew that God had just answered her prayers.

God will fix it. He's got ways.

The third Sunday of June brought a blessed silence. No saws buzzing, hammers hammering or sanders screeching.

The work had gone quickly, and Tina could not complain about the quality. The old house felt solid and strong, with modern conveniences and upgrades. More and more Loco Man Ranch felt like home, but the reality far surpassed what she'd envisioned.

Wyatt, who had run upstairs to grab his forgotten Bible while the others loaded into the brand-spanking-new full-sized SUV now parked in the yard, came pounding down the stairs. He'd already had the concrete pad poured for the extended carport that would soon provide shelter for their vehicles. Tina had concentrated on planting flowerbeds and landscaping. Already green shoots were poking through the dirt. Soon flowers would blossom.

Smiling at the thought, she felt Wyatt's hand in the fold of her elbow. As he pulled her around to face him, her smile grew.

He stepped close and lowered his head to kiss her.

Leaning into him, Tina gave herself to the kiss. They'd stolen every moment alone they could these past couple of weeks, and her love for this man had only grown. She'd begun planning their wedding in her mind. She wanted a quiet church ceremony, perhaps in the evening. They'd show off the house at the reception afterward, nothing too ostentatious, just appetizers and cake—unless Wyatt preferred something else. She'd ask him. Later.

A scraping sound reached her ears, but she didn't immediately identify it. With the door hinges freshly oiled and the screen door on a hydraulic arm that automatically closed it to keep it from banging shut, she didn't even think about anyone joining them. Until Tyler let out a yell.

"Whoa!"

Breaking apart, both Tina and Wyatt stared at him, stunned. The grin on his face signaled his approval, but neither of them were prepared for what he did next.

Shoving open the screen door again, he shouted, "Guys! Mom and Wyatt got married! Like Mr. Wes and Dr. Alice."

"We're not married," Tina hastened to correct.

"Yet," Wyatt added, slipping an arm about her waist and pulling her to his side. He smiled down at her. "But soon. Right? That is, if you'll still have me."

Considering that Tyler was hopping up and down with excitement, she saw no reason to delay further. "I'd be a fool," she told him, "not to take what God has given me."

Wyatt was hugging her and laughing, her feet dangling off the floor, when Jake and Ryder pushed through the door.

"What's this?" Jake asked.

At the same time, Ryder said, "About time. You two haven't been fooling anyone, you know."

"Okay, okay. We're engaged. In fact—" Wyatt reached into his jacket pocket and brought out a diamond ring "—I've been prepared for this moment for some time."

Laughing with delight, Tina let him slip the ring onto her finger. "It's lovely."

"You're lovely," Wyatt said, kissing her quickly. "Now, about the wedding date, I am firmly against long engagements."

Tina's smile was so big it hurt her cheeks, but she couldn't tame it, not that she wanted to. "Now that you mention it, I've always wanted to be a June bride. If you're all right with a small wedding…"

"Ready, willing and able," he declared, folding her against him again. But then he released her. "Ty, what do you think? Will you mind having me for a stepdad?"

Tyler flew across the room, throwing himself against the pair of them. "Now I got a whole fam'ly. A dad and a cousin and uncles. Wait'll I tell Donovan!"

Wyatt picked him up and hugged him. Laughing and crying at the same time, Tina looked around her.

She was home at last, financially secure with a business still to launch and a man who loved her and her son, who was happier and safer than he'd ever been. She had good friends and more family than she'd dared hope for, and maybe eventually Tyler would have at least one sibling.

Even prayers she hadn't yet prayed were coming true.

She thought of Daddy Dodd and how God had set

this plan into motion long ago through him. What else could a woman be but thankful?

"Let's get to church," she said through her smile.

She had some praising to do.

And she couldn't wait to tell Ann and Meri her news.

Or to be Mrs. Wyatt Smith.

* * * * *

WE HOPE YOU ENJOYED
THIS BOOK FROM

LOVE INSPIRED
INSPIRATIONAL ROMANCE

Uplifting stories of faith, forgiveness and hope.

Fall in love with stories where faith helps
guide you through life's challenges, and discover
the promise of a new beginning.

6 NEW BOOKS AVAILABLE EVERY MONTH!

"Isaac, we have a visitor. This is Leah Porte. She's an *Englischer* friend of ours, staying with us a few months. Leah, this is Isaac Sommer."

For a moment Isaac was struck dumb by the newcomer. With her dark hair tamed back under a *kapp*, and her chocolate eyes, he barely noticed the ugly red scar bisecting her right cheek.

Leah stepped forward. "How do you do?"

"Fine, *danke*. Where do you come from?"

"California."

"Please, sit. Both of you." Edith Byler gestured toward the table.

Isaac found himself opposite Leah and gazed at her as the family gathered around the table. When all heads bowed in silence, he found himself praying he could get to know the visitor better.

At once, chatter broke out as the family reached for food.

"We hope you'll have a pleasant stay with us." Ivan Byler scooped corn onto his plate .

"I…I'm not familiar with your day-to-day life." The woman toyed with her fork. "I don't want to be seen as a freeloader."

"What is it you did before you came here?" Ivan asked.

"I was a television journalist," she replied. Isaac saw her touch her wounded cheek and glance toward him. "But after my…my car accident, I couldn't do my job anymore."

Journalist! What kind of God-sent coincidence was that? He smiled. "Maybe I should have you write some articles for my magazine."

"Magazine?"

Edith explained, "Isaac started a magazine for Plain people. He uses a computer to create it. The bishop gave him permission."

"An Amish man using a computer?"

"Many *Englischers* have misconceptions of how much technology the *Leit* allows," Ivan intervened. "You won't find computers in our homes, or cell phones. But while we try to live not *of* the world, we still live *in* the world, and sometimes technology is needed to keep our businesses running. So, some bishops have decided a little technology is allowed."

"What's the magazine about?" Leah asked.

"Whatever appeals to Plain people. Farming. Businesses. Land management."

"And you want *me* to write for it?" she asked. "I don't know anything about those topics."

"But that's what a journalist does, ain't so? Learn about new topics," Isaac replied. Her opposition made him more determined. "Besides, you're about to get a crash course while you stay here. Maybe you'll learn something."

"I already said I had no intention of being a freeloader."

He nodded. "*Gut.* Then prove it. You can write me an article about what you learn."

"Sure," she snapped. "How hard could it be?"

He grinned. "You'll find out soon enough."

Don't miss
The Amish Newcomer *by Patrice Lewis,*
available September 2020 wherever
Love Inspired books and ebooks are sold.

LoveInspired.com

LIEXP0820